D0708829

## Praise for the

# ROSEMARY ROGERS

"[A] perfect beach book."

"From the high roads of England to the French
countryside, this is a classic sexy, adventure romance…
Rogers continues to play on the timeless themes of the
genre, providing a wonderful, albeit nostalgic, read. You
can go home again."
—*RT Book Reviews* on *A Daring Passion* (4 stars)

"The queen of historical romance."
—*New York Times Book Review*

"Rogers' legion of readers will be delighted to find that
her latest historical romance features the same brand of
arrogant, bold, and sexy hero; stubborn, beautiful, and
unconventional heroine; and passionate plot that first
made this genre wildly popular in the early 1980s."
—*Booklist* on *Sapphire*

"Her novels are filled with adventure, excitement, and
always, wildly tempestuous romance."
—*Fort Worth Star-Telegram*

# ROSEMARY ROGERS

## SCOUNDREL'S HONOR

ROGERS

Recycling programs
for this product may
not exist in your area.

ISBN-13: 978-0-373-77456-2

SCOUNDREL'S HONOR

Copyright © 2010 by Rosemary Rogers

Thank you always, new readers and old.
—RR

# SCOUNDREL'S HONOR

# CHAPTER ONE

THE VILLAGE OF YABINSK in the Volga River Basin near Moscow was the typical cluster of low, sturdy homes scattered near a wooden church. On the distant hills the wealthier citizens built their redbrick mansions to overlook the lesser folk, while small fishing boats painted in cheerful colors lined the meandering river.

On the very edge of the village, a three-storied coaching inn with attached stables squatted next to the narrow road leading to Moscow to the south and St. Petersburg to the north. With a tile roof and recently painted shutters the building managed to appear respectable, if not prosperous. It was an image that was enhanced by the meticulously clean foyer and the small chambers upstairs that smelled of wood polish and dried flowers.

Behind the stables was a small wattle-and-daub cottage nearly hidden behind the stone wall that divided the property.

It was little more than a kitchen, a front parlor and two bedchambers in the attic, but it was sturdily built to keep out the worst of the Russian winters and filled with delicate birch and cedar furnishings that were more suitable for the palaces of St. Petersburg.

In truth, Fedor Duscha had been a master craftsman before his untimely death and in great demand by many of the finest noble families. The furniture was worth a tidy sum of rubles, but his daughter Emma Linley-Kirov would have starved before selling it off. It had been wrenching enough to convert her father's precious workshop into the coaching inn for a means to make money for her and her younger sister, Anya.

On this cool autumn day, however, she barely noted the scrolled settee set beneath the window of the parlor or the hutch that held her mother's English china.

Instead, she paced the threadbare carpet, her stomach knotted and her hands shaking as she smoothed them down her plain gown of brown kerseymere. At last she turned to meet the concerned gaze of Diana Stanford, who was currently seated on the settee.

Although nearly ten years older than Emma, the English nanny was her dearest friend. Emma's own mother had been raised in England and after her death there had been a comforting familiarity in Diana's companionship.

A traditional English rose, Diana possessed fair hair and blue eyes that lent her an air of deceptive fragility. Emma on the other hand had inherited her father's honey-brown hair, which she kept pulled into a knot at the nape of her neck, and a pair of hazel eyes that regarded the world with a grim determination that tended to intimidate any who hoped to take advantage of a woman forced to stand on her own.

A necessity for keeping her inn profitable and for raising her sixteen-year-old sister, but decidedly detrimental to her relationship with the local villagers. Most of her neighbors condemned the mere thought of a lady attempting to run her own business, let alone raise an impressionable girl. A proper, well-behaved female depended upon a man. Only an overly forward tart would dare to toss aside convention and remain independent.

The others found her a source of amusement, whispering behind her back and ensuring that she felt suitably unwelcome at the local gatherings.

Until today, she rarely allowed their opinions to trouble her.

"No, you must be mistaken," Diana said, breaking the tense silence. "Anya might be stubborn and occasionally impulsive—"

Emma snorted. "Occasionally?"

Diana smiled wryly. Emma's younger, far more beautiful sister was a volatile mixture of absurd fantasies and caprice.

"But she is not utterly bird-witted," her companion continued. "She would never leave her home with two strangers who have no family connection to her."

Emma reluctantly handed over the crumpled note she had found on Anya's empty bed when she had awakened that morning.

"She would if those two strangers happened to be wealthy noblemen who promised her a career upon the stages of Europe."

Diana read through the short missive, her brows drawing together.

"An actress?"

"You know how Anya has always dreamed of a glamorous life far away from Yabinsk."

"Fah. What young lady does not fill her head with such nonsense? Every girl in the village has dreamed of attracting the attention of a handsome prince who will carry her away." With a rustle of her pale peach gown, Diana slowly rose to her feet. "Yourself included, Emma Linley-Kirov."

Emma shrugged. Any dream of handsome princes and tender romance had died along with her mother.

"Yes, but most of us put aside such fancies with our dolls. Anya, however, refused to accept there were no such things as fairy tales." She wrapped her arms around her waist, shivering at the cold sense of dread that held her captive. "I blame myself, of course. After father's death I did not devote nearly enough attention to her."

"Good heavens, Emma, you have sacrificed everything to provide a home for your sister. You should take great pride in all you have accomplished."

"Ah, yes, my accomplishments," Emma said, her voice thick with bitterness as she glanced toward the nearby inn. "They are quite amazing."

"Yes, they are, my dear," Diana firmly said. "You were barely more than a babe when your poor mother died and you were forced to assume the duties of the household, not to mention caring for Anya. And then to lose your father." The older woman clicked her tongue. "Well, any other girl would have fled such burdens, or at least have depended upon the charity of others. But not you."

"No, I was determined to stand on my own, no matter what the cost."

"Which you have done with remarkable success."

Emma shook her head. Her friend was too loyal to mention the fact that Emma's accomplishments had barely provided the essentials for her sister. And that she had managed to ostracize them both from local society.

"At the cost of Anya."

"Absurd."

Emma breathed in deeply, inanely astonished by the familiar scents of wood smoke and freshly baked bread. Since she discovered Anya's disappearance, she had felt as if the world had become a strange nightmare.

"I convinced myself that I was teaching Anya the importance of being self-sufficient," she rasped. "Now I have to wonder if I was merely being selfish."

"Selfish?" Diana wrapped a comforting arm around Emma's shoulders. "You are the most generous and kindhearted young lady I have ever known."

Emma reluctantly forced herself to overcome the pained embarrassment that had held her silent since her father's death nearly four years before.

"No, Diana, I could have accepted Baron Kostya's offer."

"Offer?" The older woman dropped her arm and stepped back in shock. "He proposed?"

"Not marriage, although his arrangement did include having me in his bed." Emma grimaced, the memory of the night the baron had arrived on her doorstep with her favorite apricot-and-honey sponge cake seared into her mind. God almighty, she had been so stupidly naive. He had assured her that he was there to ease the burdens she was carrying and she had wildly imagined that he intended to invest in her coaching inn, or even to offer Anya a position as a maid at his mansion overlooking the village. It had never entered her mind that he would shame her with the demand that she become his mistress. Or his threat to make her life a misery if she did not accept. "No. He wished to offer me carte blanche and he was prepared to be remarkably generous."

"Good heavens." Diana pressed a hand to her impressive bosom. "That certainly explains his odd behavior. One day he was singing your high praises and the next—"

"He treated me as if I carried the plague," Emma finished, not needing to add that his cruel attitude had only encouraged the villagers to turn their backs on her.

"Why did you not tell me?" Diana breathed.

Emma plucked at the frayed hem of her sleeve, a familiar sickness rolling through the pit of her stomach.

She had been horrified by the baron's offer, but more than that, she had been deeply hurt.

Once her family had been highly respected in the area, and she could have chosen from a number of eager suitors. The very fact that the baron had felt free to offer such a shameful arrangement had revealed just how far she had fallen.

"It is hardly something I wished to discuss," she muttered. "I was desperate to avoid any further gossip."

Diana regarded her with sympathy. She better than anyone understood the sacrifices a woman on her own was forced to make.

"Well, I must admit that I would have counseled you to decline such a scandalous offer, but there is no denying that he is quite wealthy and I do not doubt his offer to have been generous."

"Generous enough to ensure I could have devoted myself to Anya rather than to keeping a roof over our head."

"Yes, I suppose so, but that is no assurance that Anya would not have had her head turned just as easily."

"We both know it would have been far less likely." Emma waved a hand to encompass the barren room. "Not only would she have possessed the small luxuries she has always desired, but I would have had the opportunity to look after her properly. She spent far too much time alone."

Without warning, Diana reached to grab her hand, her eyes dark with concern.

"Hear this, Emma. You are not to blame."

"But I am." Emma heaved a sigh. "I could not bear to sacrifice my virtue, and now Anya is paying for my foolish pride."

"If you must blame someone, then it should be those horrid strangers for taking advantage of a silly young girl. What sort of gentlemen would do such a thing?"

Emma's aching fear was replaced with a flare of pure fury.

When the two elegant travelers had first arrived at her coaching inn she had been delighted. They were not only swift to pay their bills, but they were lavish with their tips. She had already begun to imagine the small Christmas gifts she could purchase with the extra funds.

Now she would give everything she possessed if they had never come to Yabinsk.

"No true gentlemen."

Diana blinked. "You believe they were imposters?"

She gave a restless shake of her head. "I am not certain what I believe, but I know I must do something."

"What can you possibly do?"

That was the question, was it not?

When she first discovered Anya missing, she had been too shocked and bewildered to consider what should be done. She simply couldn't accept that her sister had truly allowed herself to be carried off by strangers.

Eventually, however, the fierce determination that had allowed her to survive any number of disasters had her thrusting aside her pained sense of guilt and considering how to rescue Anya.

"Patya overheard the men in the stables speaking of their return to St. Petersburg. At the time he thought nothing of it, but when I went to the stables to discover precisely when the gentlemen had snuck away, he conveyed their conversation."

Diana's grip on her fingers became positively painful as she regarded Emma with disbelief.

"You intend to follow them?"

"Of course."

"Emma, please do not be hasty," Diana pleaded. "You cannot possibly travel to St. Petersburg on your own."

"I will take Yelena with me," Emma assured her, referring to the aging maid who assisted at the coaching inn. "If we catch the stage this afternoon, we should be in St. Petersburg within two days."

"But—"

"I am quite determined, Diana, and you know it is a waste of effort to argue with me," Emma firmly interrupted the looming lecture.

The older woman pressed her lips together in disapproval. "Always assuming you manage to arrive in St. Petersburg unscathed, how do you propose to find Anya? St. Petersburg is not a quiet village where neighbors are well-known to one another. You could search for weeks and never cross her path."

Emma smiled wryly. She might be a provincial old maid, but she was not without a measure of common sense. She had known from the moment she'd made the decision to travel to St. Petersburg that she could not expect to stumble across Anya.

"I intend to request Herrick Gerhardt's assistance."

"Gerhardt? The emperor's advisor?"

"Yes. He is rumored to possess mysterious powers that allow him to be aware of all that occurs in the empire. There are those who refer to him as the 'Spider' for his ability to spin webs that capture even the most clever of traitors."

Diana stepped back, studying Emma as if she feared she'd taken leave of her senses.

"Whatever they may call him, Herrick Gerhardt is one of the most powerful gentlemen in Russia. You cannot just arrive on his doorstep."

"As a matter of fact, I can."

"Emma."

"Do not fret." Emma held up a slender hand. "He is related to my mother—a distant cousin I believe—and he sent a very kind letter after Father's death inviting me to call upon him if he could ever be of service to me."

Diana did not appear particularly reassured. "I do not approve of this dangerous scheme."

Emma did not particularly approve of it herself.

Unfortunately she had no choice.

"Anya is all I have left in this world," she said, her voice raw with suppressed emotion. "I will not fail her again."

BLESSING THE FULL MOON that washed the elegant study in silver light, Dimitri Tipova knelt beside the mahogany desk. He had finished his search through the papers and journals in the drawers, now his slender fingers ran over the carved panels in hope of discovering a hidden compartment.

What gentleman did not have secrets to hide?

And Pytor Burdzecki had more to hide than most.

Intent on his self-imposed task, Dimitri nearly missed the soft footfall just outside the door, and it was only his swift instincts that had him straightening and moving to stand casually near the bay window. Wisely, he had opened it before beginning his search; a successful thief always had a ready escape prepared.

The door to the study was slowly pressed inward and Dimitri cast a downward glance to ensure his black jacket and silver waistcoat were properly buttoned and as crisp as could be expected, considering they had recently been tossed on a bedroom floor. A searching gaze would no doubt detect his cravat was hastily tied and the raven hair pulled back in a queue was still rumpled from feminine fingers, but with luck the darkness of the room would conceal such imperfections.

And if not…well, he possessed the means to keep his presence in the St. Petersburg town house a secret.

Reaching into the inner pocket of his jacket, Dimitri closed his hand over the pearl handle of his small pistol, prepared to kill until a slender, obviously female shape stepped over the threshold.

"Pierre?" the woman called softly.

Dimitri swallowed an impatient sigh. He had hoped to slip away before Pytor Burdzecki's young bride, Lana, realized he was gone.

The pretty woman with auburn hair and wide blue eyes had been easy enough to seduce. He had only to pretend to be a visiting French diplomat who occasionally crossed her path at the opera, or at the Gostiny Dvor where she would shop with her maid. Within a handful of days she allowed him to escort her to the nearest coffee shop with giggles and inviting glances.

She had no reason to suspect that he was the infamous Beggar Czar, ruthless leader of the underworld, or that his interest in her was merely a means to enter this palatial home that was heavily guarded by trained soldiers.

Loosening his grip on the gun, he smoothly stepped toward her.

"*Ma belle,* I thought you were asleep."

She glanced about her husband's private study with a frown. "What are you doing?"

"Preparing to leave, I fear."

"Did you lose your way?"

With another step he was close enough to tenderly tuck a dark curl behind her ear. She was a vain, self-absorbed little creature, but she was harmless. Which was more than her husband could claim.

Or Dimitri, for that matter.

"I prefer to slip away unnoticed by the servants," he murmured, speaking the perfect French all Russian nobles favored. He was also fluent in Russian and English, and could comprehend several of the Germanic dialects. He was an excessively well-educated thief, thanks to his mother's insistence that his bastard of a father pay for his schooling. "I would not desire such a beautiful creature to be the source of ugly gossip."

"Oh." She batted her lashes, eager to accept his smooth lie. "Must you leave so soon?"

"Hardly soon. I risk being castrated by your husband if I linger any longer."

She pouted, grasping the lapels of his jacket as she pressed against him in unspoken encouragement.

"He never returns before dawn, if he even bothers to

return at all." She kissed the tip of his chin. "If we are fortunate, we could enjoy the entire day together."

Dimitri narrowed his whiskey-gold eyes. "I never depend upon luck, *ma belle*."

"But, when will we meet again?"

"Who can say when fate will be kind enough to cross our paths again?"

"Tonight—"

"We shall allow destiny to unfold," he interrupted, firmly removing her hands from his maltreated jacket and lifted them to his lips. "Return to the warmth of your bed. You shall find a small token of my esteem tucked beneath your pillow."

As expected, Lana was readily distracted. "A present?"

"*Oui*. I hope you will think of me whenever you wear them."

"Wear them?" Her blue eyes sparked in anticipation. "What are they? Gloves? Earrings?"

"Why do you not go and discover for yourself?" he urged, smiling wryly as she giggled and hastily skipped from the room.

Despite the fact she was wed to a sexual deviant more than twice her age, Lana was little more than a *jeune fille* in many ways. Nothing like the women in his world who were rarely allowed a childhood.

Listening to the sound of retreating footsteps, Dimitri slid through the open window and dropped into the garden below. He had not yet finished his search of the house, but Lana was certain to have attracted unwanted attention among the guards, and he could not risk being caught.

He landed with the ease of an avid sportsman, his hand reaching for his pistol even as he straightened. The instinct that had kept him alive more times than he could recall was prickling in warning.

"Come out," he growled softly.

A lean form draped in a heavily caped coat detached from the shadows of a marble fountain.

"I must admit to my own share of curiosity," an aggravatingly familiar voice taunted. "What did you leave beneath the pillows?"

Dimitri's lips tightened, realizing the open window had allowed this man to hear his entire conversation with Lana.

Of course, Herrick Gerhardt did not need to lurk beneath open windows to discover the information he desired, Dimitri ruefully conceded. Although he did not believe the advisor to Alexander Pavlovich possessed mystical powers as some did. He was, after all, intimately aware his methods were more mundane.

"A pair of diamond earrings," he grudgingly confessed.

Herrick arched a brow. A gentleman of Prussian descent, he possessed a gaunt countenance, a thick crop of silver hair and piercing brown eyes that held a cold, ruthless intelligence.

"A rather generous gift for a female you bedded for the sole purpose of searching her husband's study."

Dimitri shrugged. "Lana might be a shallow tart with the soul of a merchant, but she still deserves better than being bartered to a husband twice her age whose sexual perversions cause even me to shudder in disgust."

Herrick deliberately glanced toward the neoclassical palace looming behind Dimitri.

"No doubt most of society would consider her well compensated."

"Only because their lives are as cold and empty as the marble crypts that await their deaths."

"A philosopher, Tipova?" Herrick demanded.

"A simple criminal."

Herrick's chuckle floated on the chilly October breeze. "As if I would ever be foolish enough to underestimate you. What did you discover?"

Dimitri folded his arms over his chest, his expression guarded. Since he had come to the attention of Herrick Gerhardt and the Duke of Huntley several weeks before, he had reluctantly become Alexander Pavlovich's most secret weapon against the traitors who stirred discontent. One did not say no to the Emperor of Russia.

His presence in Pytor Burdzecki's home, however, was personal business he did not intend to share with anyone.

"Nothing that would be of interest to Alexander Pavlovich."

"You would be surprised at the emperor's vast interests," Herrick countered.

"The emperor or his most trusted advisor?"

"It is one and the same."

"Is that why you are here?" Dimitri demanded. "To discover what I might find among Burdzecki's papers?"

Herrick waved a dismissive hand. "Actually I am here to discover you."

Dimitri stilled, his eyes narrowing with suspicion.

"And how, I wonder, did you know I would be here?"

"You are not the only gentleman with the ability to gather information."

"Yes, but—" Dimitri bit off his words. "Never mind, I shall eventually uncover the traitor." He waved a hand toward the empty flower beds and the marble fountains that had already been covered in preparation for the brutal Russian winter. "If you wished to meet with me you had only to send a message. There was no need to creep about in damp gardens."

The smile faded from Herrick's face, his eyes hard with the ruthless resolve that lurked just below his charm.

"You do not promptly respond to my summons."

"I am not a toady of the empire."

"No, but you are a loyal citizen, I trust?"

Dimitri dropped his arms, his hands curling into fists. Despite his considerable power, he never allowed himself to forget that Herrick Gerhardt need only speak the word and Dimitri would disappear into the nearest dungeon.

"Are you threatening me, Gerhardt?"

The silver head dipped in apology. "Forgive me, Tipova. You have proven your devotion to Czar Alexander more than once."

"As if I had a choice," Dimitri grumbled. "What do you want of me?"

"On this occasion I believe we can be of mutual benefit to one another."

"I have no need of the royal coffers."

"My business with you is of a personal nature and I offer something far more intriguing than money." Stepping to the side, Herrick glanced toward the sleek black carriage that was waiting in the mews. "Will you join me?"

Dimitri paused, studying Herrick's impassive face. Then, with a sigh, he conceded defeat. The older man would not leave him in peace until he had his way.

"Why do I sense I am going to regret this?" he muttered.

# CHAPTER TWO

DIMITRI REMAINED SILENT as Herrick led him to the carriage and they settled into the soft leather seats. There was a small jerk as the driver urged the horses into motion, then they were traveling through the streets of St. Petersburg that were still crowded despite the late hour.

"Brandy?" Herrick inquired, pouring two glasses of the amber liquid and pressing one into Dimitri's willing hand.

Taking a cautious sip, Dimitri lifted his brows in surprise. There was no mistaking the smooth ease with which the liquid fire slid down his throat.

"You must be anxious for my assistance if you are willing to share from your private cellar," he said.

Herrick leaned back in his seat, his gaze hooded as he studied Dimitri.

"As I mentioned, I think our arrangement will be mutually beneficial."

Dimitri could not prevent a small flare of curiosity. Herrick Gerhardt had devoted his life to Alexander Pavlovich. What private business could he possibly have?

"I am willing to listen to this…arrangement."

"First I must bore you with a bit of family history." Herrick swallowed his brandy and refilled his glass. "As you perhaps know I was born in Prussia to a respectable, albeit poor family. I was fortunate enough to travel to St. Petersburg to finish my education when I was just seventeen and eventually to capture the attention of Alexander Pavlovich. My elder cousin, on the other hand, chose to seek his fortunes in England where he wed and produced several children."

"Fascinating."

"One of my cousin's daughters became a governess to a Russian family to teach the children English. She in turn wed a local furniture maker and had two daughters before she died."

Dimitri tapped his finger against his glass, his brows pulled together in a frown.

"I presume this tedious story has an end?"

"As I was saying, there were two daughters, Emma and Anya Linley-Kirov," Herrick continued, ignoring Dimitri's growing impatience. "After their father was tragically killed by a poacher, Emma transformed her father's workshop into a small coaching inn."

Dimitri's frown deepened. He adored women. All women. And it was well-known that any man who mistreated a female beneath his protection was a certain means to a brutal beating, if not death. Still, he could not deny he preferred to avoid those women with more spirit than sense.

In the end they not only brought misery to themselves, but those who cared for them.

"How very unconventional of her."

"It was quite admirable of her," Herrick corrected, easily sensing Dimitri's lack of approval. "Unfortunately her considerable courage did not protect her from the nefarious gentlemen who stayed at her coaching inn for several days."

"Nefarious?"

"When they left the inn they took Anya with them."

Dimitri stilled, his attention fully captured. "The sister?"

"Yes."

"How old is she?"

"She just turned sixteen."

Draining the last of his brandy, Dimitri carefully set aside the glass, silently considering the unexpected revelation at the same time he accepted that his personal investigations were not quite so secret as he believed them to be.

"And Emma Linley-Kirov is certain she was taken by the gentlemen?" he demanded.

"Quite certain. Anya left a note explaining she was to become a famous actress."

Dimitri was careful to keep his expression unreadable, even as his heart gave a jolt of recognition at the familiar ruse used by his father and his cohorts to lure young females from their homes.

"Did the note also mention the gentlemen were traveling to St. Petersburg?"

"A groom overheard the gentlemen discussing their return to the city."

"And the woman is certain she would recognize them if she were to see them again?"

"Yes."

Dimitri casually glanced out the window, not surprised to discover they had made a circuit of the Upper Nevsky and were nearly back to Pytor Burdzecki's palatial home. There was never a moment when he was not acutely aware of his surroundings.

"What made you believe that I would have interest in your tragic, though not uncommon, tale?"

"It has not escaped my notice that you keep a very close watch upon Count Nevskaya and his associates."

Dimitri absently studied the Anichkov Palace that had once housed Catherine's favorite lover, Prince Potyomkin, and had been recently refurbished by Giacomo Quarenghi to house the Imperial Cabinet. Unlike many, he preferred the classical colonnade to the earlier, more flamboyant style.

Not that Czar Alexander had requested his opinion.

Grudgingly he turned his attention back to his companion.

"As you have no doubt surmised, the count is my father."

A smile touched the older man's lips as his gaze deliberately studied the elegant lines of Dimitri's features, lingering on the aristocratic thrust of his nose and high, Slavic cheekbones.

"It is difficult to overlook the resemblance."

Dimitri's jaw hardened. He often used his considerable male beauty to his advantage, but he cursed the resemblance to the man who had brutally forced himself on a young, defenseless female.

"We share the same countenance, but make no mistake that is where the similarities end," he said, his voice colder than a Siberian winter.

Herrick dipped his head in acknowledgment. "That is difficult to overlook as well, which is why your constant surveillance of the count piqued my interest. It was obvious you were searching for particular information."

Dimitri was not pleased. He spied on others, they did not spy on him.

"You have an annoying habit of meddling in my private business."

"It is my duty to meddle in the business of others."

"You play a dangerous game, Gerhardt."

Herrick shrugged, unperturbed by the threat in Dimitri's soft voice.

"And you are intimately familiar with dangerous games, are you not, Tipova?" he asked. "The count would be most displeased to realize his bastard son suspects he is involved in illegal activities."

Dimitri briefly considered the pleasure of tossing the older man into the nearby Fontanka Canal, then disregarded the notion. As pleasant as it might be to see Herrick's impervious calm rattled, it was not worth the loss of his head.

Besides, there were more important matters to consider at the moment.

"What would you have of me?"

Herrick leaned forward, his dark eyes glittering in the moonlight.

"Meet with Emma Linley-Kirov. I truly believe the two of you are searching for the same answers."

"I knew I was going to regret this meeting."

PEERING OUT OF THE carriage window, Emma studied the pale stone building built with a columned portico in the center and two wings that spread along the canal. Although newly arrived in St. Petersburg, she would presume that the far side of the building was devoted to gentlemen lodgers. Why else would the small cluster of men be standing on the paved walk and keeping such a close watch on the passing traffic? On the other side was a more familiar coffee shop with several small tables and a back counter that held trays of tempting pastry that made Emma's mouth water even at a distance.

"There it is," she said, turning her head to meet her maid's sour expression.

Yelena had firmly disapproved of Emma's decision to meet with the Beggar Czar, Dimitri Tipova.

Of course, the elderly maid with a thatch of gray hair and slender body wrapped in a black cloak had disapproved of traveling to St. Petersburg, of accepting Herrick Gerhardt's surprisingly warm welcome, and even of being sheltered by Herrick's dear friend, Vanya Petrova in her beautiful mansion beside the Fontanka Canal.

Emma, on the other hand, was deeply grateful to the older man who had greeted her without a word of condemnation of her forward behavior and had promised he would do whatever possible to help her locate Anya.

"It does not appear to be a den of iniquity," Yelena at last muttered. "Are you certain this is the proper address?"

Emma wrinkled her nose. "Appearances are too often deceptive, as I have so painfully discovered. It is rather public, however."

"I should think it is public." Yelena folded her gnarled fingers in her lap, her lips pinched together. "You cannot meet with a strange gentleman in private without so much as a proper introduction."

Despite her raw nerves, Emma couldn't contain her sudden chuckle. "I am about to request the assistance of the most renowned criminal in all of Russia and your concern is our lack of a proper introduction?"

The older woman sniffed. "I have a great number of concerns."

Instantly contrite, Emma reached across the elegant carriage that Vanya had kindly insisted she use during her time in St. Petersburg, and patted her companion's hand. Yelena was one of the very few people who had stood by her through the years.

"Forgive me, Yelena. I fear my nerves are in tatters. I did not mean to snap."

Yelena's expression immediately softened. "The past week would try the patience of a saint."

Surely truer words had not been spoken, Emma acknowledged with a sigh. She did not wish to recall the grueling journey to St. Petersburg, or her sick trepidation as she had approached Herrick Gerhardt's beautiful home to beg for his assistance.

It was enough to concentrate on today's troubles.

Perhaps more than enough.

Pretending that her stomach was not cramped with fear, Emma managed a smile as the uniformed groom pulled open the carriage door.

"Remain here."

Yelena frowned. "Emma—"

"We have been through this," Emma interrupted. "The message was quite clear that I come alone. Besides, if I do not reappear then I shall need you to storm the fortress and rescue me."

The maid pressed a shaking hand to her bosom. "Dear Lord."

"I am merely teasing, Yelena. All will be well." Keeping the strained smile intact, Emma allowed herself to be assisted from the carriage and headed for the door of the coffee shop. "Please God, let all be well," she muttered beneath her breath.

Entering the coffee shop, she took the seat closest the window as the message had demanded. Thank goodness she had wrapped herself in a sturdy gown of dark gray that buttoned to her chin and brushed the wooden floor past her sensible leather boots. And that her honey hair was covered by a wool scarf her mother had knit. There was a roaring fire across the room, but so close to the door there was a distinct chill in the air.

Settling uncomfortably in the wooden chair, Emma cast a swift glance about the wide room, relieved that many of the tables were empty. There were two elegantly attired gentlemen playing chess by the fire, and a group of more roughly dressed men at a table that ran the length of the far wall, but she was quite alone in her corner.

Her appreciation for her solitude, however, began to wane as an hour passed, and then another. Where the devil was Dimitri Tipova? Had he invited her here just to see if she would risk her reputation by meeting with a notorious criminal? Was this a mere hoax at her expense? Or were

Beggar Czars so busy they found it impossible to keep their appointments?

Tapping an impatient finger on the table, Emma found her anxiety hardening to a simmering anger.

She was accustomed to being treated with disrespect. She was even accustomed to being ignored by others who thought themselves above her. But she could not afford to waste an entire day on some ridiculous game. If Dimitri Tipova did not wish to be of service then he should at least have the decency to send his regrets.

On the point of rising to her feet, Emma was caught off guard when a large man approached her table and settled in a chair at her side.

"Well, well. Such a tender little morsel," he husked, his face with its heavy jowls and beady blue eyes far too close. "I wonder if you taste as sweet as you look."

Emma tilted her chin, shifting away from the hulking body attired in a faded green coat and the heavy boots of a laborer.

"Please move along."

A cruel smiled curved his lips. "Perhaps I do not want to move along. Perhaps I intend to take you to the back room and sample your wares."

Emma should no doubt have been terrified, but at the moment her temper was fully aroused and in no mood to endure the man's rude behavior. Even if he was twice her size.

Grasping the cup of coffee she had bought in an effort to pass the time, she narrowed her gaze.

"Either you leave me in peace or I will pour this exceedingly hot coffee into your lap," she warned. "Perhaps that will teach you not to impose your vile presence on unfortunate maidens who might cross your path."

The intruder blinked, as if stupefied by her threat. "You…"

His lips had barely parted when another man joined them, this one far more slender, although the scar running down his cheek from his eyebrow to the edge of his mouth made him appear far more sinister. Her companion seemed to think so as well, as his face paled and sweat beaded his forehead.

"Semyon, return to the docks and make certain that the ship that arrived this morning is properly unloaded. You know how our employer dislikes unnecessary attention to our business."

"Yes…of course."

Stumbling to his feet, the man performed an awkward bow and headed for the door. Emma straightened from her seat as well, her temper not appeased.

She had been ignored for hours, and then rudely insulted by that brute. She had endured enough.

"Emma Linley-Kirov?" the man demanded.

"And you are?"

"Josef. I am here to escort you."

Her lips tightened. So, Dimitri Tipova could not be bothered to greet her in person.

"Escort me to where?" she demanded.

The servant waved an indifferent hand toward a door at the back of the room, clearly unimpressed with his current duties.

"Merely to the private rooms upstairs. There is no need to be afraid."

She squared her shoulders. "I am not afraid, I am furious. Do you know how long I have been waiting?"

A startled silence filled the entire room as Josef regarded her with astonishment.

"Dimitri Tipova is a very busy man," he said, his tone chiding. "You are fortunate he agreed to meet with you at all."

Emma sniffed, refusing to be intimidated. "Ah, yes, you

cannot imagine how honored I am to be graced with a few moments of the Beggar Czar's precious time."

With a muttered curse, the slender man headed toward the back of the room.

"This way."

Stiffly, Emma followed in his wake, acutely aware of the hard gazes trained in her direction. Josef pulled open the door and led her up a narrow flight of stairs, then reaching a landing, he motioned her toward a small room with a brocade sofa and two scrolled chairs set beside a marble fireplace.

"Wait here."

Not bothering to turn, Josef continued toward a door on the opposite side of the landing, shoving it open and stepping through. Ignoring good manners, Emma remained poised on the landing, blatantly attempting to overhear the low conversation between Josef and whoever was waiting in the room.

"She arrived?" A man that Emma presumed was Dimitri Tipova demanded, his dark voice sending an odd tingle down her spine.

"Regrettably," Josef muttered.

"Why regrettably?"

"The woman is sour enough to curdle milk."

"No doubt she is concerned for her sister."

"It is not concern that makes a woman into an overbearing shrew. She is the nasty sort who tosses out orders and expects them to be obeyed."

"Naturally." The gorgeous male voice held an edge of resignation. "I should have known Gerhardt would take pleasure in plaguing me with his old maid cousin. No doubt he is seated before a warm fire, relishing his peace while I am stuck with the harridan."

Emma winced, then gritted her teeth, pretending she

wasn't wounded by the familiar mockery. She had not traveled to St. Petersburg to charm the local thieves.

Stepping over the threshold, she had a brief impression of a small study with bookshelves lining the walls and a porcelain stove set between two leather wing chairs. Then a tall man lifted himself from behind a heavy walnut desk and her mind abruptly refused to function.

He was just so absurdly beautiful.

Her stunned gaze traced the bronze perfection of his features. The wide, intelligent brow. The slender nose and full, sensual lips. The slash of his prominent cheekbones. The chiseled brows that were the same raven-black as his long hair pulled into a tail at his nape.

It was his eyes, however, that stole her breath.

An astonishing gold that shimmered in wicked temptation, they were surely the eyes of the devil.

Or perhaps a fallen angel.

All Emma knew for certain was that he was a compelling combination of lethal power and male sensuality that would make any poor woman go weak in the knees.

An odd, heated excitement fluttered in the pit of her stomach as that golden gaze flared over her tiny form. An excitement that was swiftly replaced with hollow disappointment as his lush lips twisted with a familiar male disapproval.

What did she expect, she mocked her temporary insanity?

That Dimitri Tipova might be unconventional enough not to judge her bold manner? That a man forced to survive in a harsh world was capable of understanding the need for her to do the same?

Thrusting aside the inane thoughts, Emma conjured the icy composure that was her only protection.

"I may be an old maid, but I at least possess a few manners," she stated, her gaze never wavering from the unnerving golden eyes. "Something sadly lacking among you and your loathsome band of cutthroats."

DIMITRI SHOULD HAVE been amused.

The tiny female wrapped in layers of wool barely came to his chin and weighed less than his wolfhound. To have her burst into his room and chide him as if he were a naughty child rather than the most dangerous man in St. Petersburg was absurd.

It wasn't amusement he felt, however, as his gaze rested on the honey curls that peeked from her scarf to lie against the purity of her ivory skin and the steady hazel eyes that held unwavering strength.

There was something about her that challenged him at his most primitive level.

He wanted to loom over her until she dropped her bold gaze in silent defeat. He wanted to bluntly inform her that he was an unrepentant tyrant who expected immediate obedience from others.

He wanted to haul her against his body until the defiance faded from her beautiful eyes and her lush lips softened in invitation...

Thankfully unaware of the currents of prickling awareness that swirled through the air, Josef folded his arms over his chest.

"What did I say? Curdled milk," he muttered.

Dimitri never allowed his gaze to stray from Emma Linley-Kirov's stubborn expression.

"That will be all."

"Are you certain? There is nothing more dangerous than an angry female."

"Thank you, Josef, I believe you have done quite enough," Dimitri dryly assured his friend, waiting for his servant to leave the room before he rounded the desk and perched on the corner.

His lips twisted as her gaze skimmed down his tailored, cinnamon jacket that he had paired with a cream satin waistcoat. He had tied his crisp cravat in an Oriental knot and a diamond the size of a thimble winked in the perfect folds. Clearly the woman had expected him to be a savage rather than the sort of sophisticated gentleman who could appear comfortable in the finest home.

"There is a saying that listeners rarely hear good of themselves," he at last broke the silence.

An indefinable emotion flared through her eyes before she was jutting her chin in silent condemnation.

"I am indifferent to your opinion of me, sir—"

"Dimitri," he smoothly corrected.

"I beg your pardon?"

"I am no gentleman as you have so graciously implied. You will call me Dimitri."

Her lips tightened, whether in disapproval at the informality or at being given an order, it was impossible to determine.

"If you insist," she grudgingly conceded.

"I do."

"Can we please discuss my sister?" she snapped. "I have wasted enough of my day."

Dimitri narrowed his gaze, shoving from the desk and prowling toward the woman regarding him with an imperious scowl. A surge of male satisfaction raced through him as she instinctively backed away from his approaching form, even as his more civilized nature was shocked by his fierce reaction to the delicate slip of a woman.

What the hell was wrong with him?

Herding her until she was pressed flat against the bookcase, he reached to grasp the shelves on either side of her shoulders.

"Perhaps we should discuss the nature of our—" his

brooding gaze lowered to the tempting curve of her lips "—relationship, Emma."

Heat flared beneath her ivory skin, but her eyes shimmered with rebellion.

"There is no relationship, merely a set of unfortunate circumstances that have forced us to join our resources for the time being."

He pressed closer, caught by surprise when a raw awareness of her slender body seared through him. It was inconceivable. He enjoyed his women soft and vulnerable. The sort who depended upon him to offer support and protection. Not aging tartars who smelled of soap and starch.

"Then let me clarify the *joining of resources.*"

Her color deepened at the hint of huskiness in his voice. "What do you mean?"

"You desire my assistance, then you will have to follow my rules. Otherwise you can turn around and leave now."

A tense silence filled the room he had recently converted into his private office, then without warning, Emma was shoving him away and pacing toward the window that overlooked the street.

Dimitri couldn't deny a grudging respect for her courage. He knew only one other woman who would not have fainted or fled by now.

His mother.

The realization did nothing to ease his potent need to tame the prickly female. His mother's courage had put her in an early grave.

"Fine." Slowly turning, Emma regarded him with an unflinching gaze. "What are these precious rules?"

"The first is that I will not tolerate an ill-tempered termagant in my presence. If you cannot control your sharp tongue, then I will discover a means to tame it."

Her eyes widened. "Tame? If you think I will tolerate being beaten by—"

He was moving before he could halt the impulse, his hands holding her face steady as he lowered his head and covered her mouth in a soft, coaxing kiss. He had intended to teach her a lesson in controlling her shrewish tongue, but at the first taste of her honeyed innocence his passions stirred, his body hardening. His hands tightened on her face as he deepened the kiss.

Just for a moment she softened against him, her lips parting in a sweet surrender. Then, with a choked moan, she jerked back, her eyes blazing with a fury that did not entirely mask her startled desire.

"Why, you…"

Well versed in the ways of women, Dimitri easily caught the hand she lifted to slap his face, bringing her fingers to his mouth.

"The second rule is no striking your master," he could not resist taunting.

Flecks of gold smoldered in the hazel eyes. "Master?"

He kissed her slender fingers. "You are in desperate need of my assistance, which means that while you remain in St. Petersburg you are in my power."

"I will not be treated as if I am a serf."

"You will do precisely as I say and you will do so without complaint."

She jerked her hand from his grasp, marching toward the door with her chin high and her back stiff.

"This is absurd."

"If you walk out that door, Emma, I can assure you that you will never find your sister."

# CHAPTER THREE

EMMA HALTED AT THE soft threat.

Dimitri Tipova was not at all what she had expected. She had been prepared for a rough, ill-mannered oaf who used his fists, not his wits, to control the underworld. Certainly, she had never dreamed he would be a sophisticated, well-educated gentleman who was as beautiful as an angel and as wicked as Lucifer.

And that kiss…

No. She hastily thrust aside the feverish memory of her first kiss.

She was suitably rattled without the distracting thought of Dimitri's warm, seeking lips and the potent heat that speared through her body.

Slowly turning, she met his ruthless gaze. "You know where she is?"

"No, but—"

"Then I will find someone less offensive to help me."

He strolled forward, the scent of sandalwood and warm male skin teasing at her senses.

"There is no one in all of Russia who has devoted the time and resources that I have to uncovering the habits of those noblemen who prey on children." Halting directly before her, he cupped her chin, his gaze briefly dipping down to her mouth before returning to meet her wary gaze. "And more important, I have only to whisper in the requisite ears and there will be no one in St. Petersburg willing to lend you help."

"Herrick warned me that you had your share of

arrogance, but you cannot possibly believe you possess the power to influence every citizen in St. Petersburg."

"So naive," he mocked. "Tell me, Emma, how many merchants would be willing to speak with you once it became known that the goods they purchase from my warehouses were about to double in cost? And how many servants would agree to speak with you once they learn you are a suspected spy for Alexander Pavlovich in search of traitors to the crown? As for society..." His soft chuckle brushed over her cheek, causing her stomach to clench with a startling excitement. "Well, even presuming they would be willing to meet with a commoner, they would have you tossed in the nearest dungeon for daring to implicate a noble in such a wicked crime."

She clenched her hands, wanting desperately to walk away from the conceited beast and never look back. Unfortunately, she suspected his words were not empty boasts.

Could she truly risk the opportunity to find Anya just because this man threatened to drive her to madness?

"Why are you being so cruel?" she demanded.

"Not cruel—efficient," he corrected. "As you said, for the moment we have need of one another. I have no intention of spending the next days, perhaps weeks, being flayed by a shrill-tongued harpy. If you behave as a lady and do as I say, we shall rub along quite nicely."

"So I am expected to be a proper lady while you are at liberty to behave as an ill-mannered brute?"

"You are at least intelligent." A slow, wicked smile curved his lips. "Do we have a bargain?"

Emma sucked in a sharp breath, not for the first time wishing she had been born a man. How delightful it would be if she possessed the power to knock the arrogant toad onto his backside.

"Do I have a choice?" she gritted.

"Of course." He peered deep into her eyes, almost as

if willing her to obey his words. "You can return to your home where you belong."

"I will not leave St. Petersburg without my sister."

"Even if I give my word I will do my best to discover her whereabouts and return her to you?"

"And why would I trust the word of a—" Her insult was sharply interrupted as his head swooped down and he kissed her with a seeking demand that made her heart skip a beat. Dear...Lord. After the death of her father she had resigned herself to becoming an old maid. At the time she had regretted the loss of many things, most notably the lack of a companion who could share her joys and fears and the mundane events that were all a part of life. It had not occurred to her that she might rue the lack of a man's touch. Not until Dimitri had revealed just how potently addictive that touch could be. Arching back, she struggled to breathe. "Stop that."

He studied her from beneath his thick tangle of lashes. "I did warn you that I would tame your unruly tongue."

Emma grimly stiffened her spine, refusing to dwell on her tingling lips or the restless, achy sensation that gripped her body. Obviously she was coming down with a chill.

"I cannot believe that Herrick would request that I meet with you," she muttered. "Do you make a habit of attacking helpless females?"

"Helpless?" His sharp burst of laughter echoed through the room. "I have hired savage, fully-armed bandits who inspire less fear than having to face your expression of cold disapproval."

She turned her head to stare at the leather-bound books lining the shelves, determined to hide her reaction. What did he expect? Simpering and batting her lashes was not going to save Anya from disaster.

"You have already assaulted me, there is no need to mock me, as well."

With a surprisingly gentle touch he forced her face back to meet his searching gaze.

"It was a simple kiss, hardly an assault," he murmured, his arm wrapping around her waist. "You have been kissed before, have you not, Emma?"

"Release me."

"What an odd contradiction you are," he breathed, the golden gaze searing over her face with a disconcerting intensity. "You wrap yourself in fire and brimstone, but beneath that armor is a bewitching innocence."

Her heart fluttered and she abruptly shoved away from his disturbing touch.

"I came here to discuss my sister, not to indulge in foolish games."

For a tense moment she feared he might haul her back against his chest. And more important, she feared she might not protest.

Then, with a rueful shake of his head he waved a hand toward the wing chairs.

"Have a seat, and I will order tea."

She stubbornly remained standing in the center of the floor. "Do not pretend to be civilized on my account."

He leaned against the desk, the late afternoon sunlight slanting over his elegantly chiseled features.

"Most of my guests find my manners exquisitely polished and my hospitality without equal."

"Indeed?"

His lips twisted. "It is only you who seems to rouse my more barbaric nature."

"Do you intend to assist me or not?"

"Tell me of the gentlemen who you believe abducted your sister."

Unprepared for his abrupt question, it took Emma a moment to gather her scattered thoughts.

"They were obviously noblemen."

He arched a raven brow. "How can you be so certain? Even the most common criminal can mimic his betters with enough wealth and the proper training. I possess a number of employees who could attend a ball at the Winter Palace without stirring the least curiosity."

She grimaced. "It was not their fine clothing or their elegant speech that marked them as nobles."

"Then what?"

"It was their utter contempt for those they considered beneath them, and how they expected others to bow to their every whim."

He seemed surprised by her explanation. "You are very perceptive."

"Obviously not perceptive enough," she said, her voice edged with bitterness. "I should have suspected that such elegant gentlemen would never willingly remain at my modest coaching inn without some nefarious purpose."

"What explanation did they offer?"

She shrugged. "They claimed to be searching for a small estate to purchase that would be suitable for a hunting lodge."

Dimitri nodded, as if he'd expected a similar story. "What names did they use?"

"Baron Fedor Karnechev and his younger brother Sergei."

"And you would recognize them?"

A cold, dangerous smile curved her lips. When she found the men who had taken her sister, she intended to rip out their hearts with her bare hands.

"Without a doubt."

Amusement smoldered in the whiskey-gold eyes as Dimitri watched fury ripple over her face.

"Does your sister resemble you?"

"There are some similarities, but Anya's hair is lighter

in color and her eyes the shade of a summer sky." A wistful smile touched her lips. "She is quite beautiful."

"I was referring to her temperament, not her physical attributes."

Emma frowned in puzzlement. "What does her temperament matter?"

"Gerhardt divulged the fact that Anya went willingly with her captors, believing she was to become a famous actress." His gaze swept down her tiny form before returning to study the stubborn line of her jaw. "I find it difficult to imagine you ever allowing yourself to be so easily persuaded."

She shifted, feeling awkward beneath his relentless scrutiny. "She is very young and gullible."

"More likely she is vain and spoiled."

She jerked at the unexpected attack. "You know nothing of Anya."

"I know that a young lady with the least concern for her family does not abandon her home and allow herself to be carried off by the first gentleman to turn her head with a bit of flattery."

The very fact he was right did nothing to ease her flare of anger. In truth, she was horrified that Anya had been so easily led astray, but she did not blame her younger sister. No. Any blame should be laid directly at her own feet.

"I have endured enough." Blinking back hot tears of shame, Emma once again headed for the door. "I do not understand why you agreed to meet with me, but it is obvious you have no interest in helping me."

She had managed to reach the hallway when a pair of warm, ruthlessly strong arms wrapped around her waist and tugged her back into the room. Bending his head, Dimitri spoke directly into her ear.

"You truly must learn to control that temper of yours, *milaya*."

FOR A CRAZED MOMENT, Dimitri savored the sensation of her feminine body pressed against his arousal. Then with a curse at his deranged reaction to an ill-tempered spinster, he quickly released his tight grip, not at all surprised when she spun around to stab him with a furious glare.

"Are you going to rescue my sister or not?"

If he possessed a shred of sense Dimitri knew he should have allowed the woman to stomp away. Herrick Gerhardt could not expect him to force himself on an aggravating woman who was too foolish to appreciate his assistance. Instead, he met her glare with a ruthless smile.

"First we must discover the identity of the gentlemen who abducted her."

Her glare remained, but she gave a grudging nod. "I can describe them if you wish."

"There is a more practical means. You will accompany me this evening."

"Accompany you where?"

"I own a number of gambling establishments that cater to the aristocrats of St. Petersburg. If the gentlemen who visited your inn are truly noblemen and they have returned to the city, then they will eventually make an appearance at one of my clubs."

Her mouth fell open. "You intend to escort me to a gambling club?"

Thoroughly enjoying her shock, Dimitri shrugged. "I intend to escort you to several gambling clubs."

"You must be jesting."

"Tell me, Emma, when you came to St. Petersburg did you expect to discover your sister being kept hostage in a church?" he taunted. "Or perhaps awaiting you in the throne room of the Winter Palace?"

The ready color crawled beneath her cheeks. "Of course not."

"Then why the maidenly outrage?"

There was a tiny pause before she was jutting her chin in a stubborn angle, her magnificent hazel eyes hardening with determination.

"I was merely caught off guard."

With a silent curse, Dimitri spun away, disturbed by Emma's combination of vulnerability and determination.

"If you wish to capture the dregs of society you must hunt them in the gutters," he said, his voice unnaturally harsh. "Are you prepared to do what is necessary?"

"Yes."

"We shall see." Sucking in a deep breath he turned back to meet her guarded gaze. "Where are you staying?"

"Vanya Petrova was kind enough to offer her hospitality."

Dimitri nodded, already having suspected that Herrick would turn to his dear friend to provide Emma a home.

"Then I will collect you at nine this evening."

"Very well." With a stiff nod, the woman headed for the door.

"Emma," he called softly.

She froze, her hands clenching before she forced herself to turn and meet his brooding gaze.

"Yes?"

"Staid spinsters do not visit gambling clubs. If you wish to avoid unwanted attention you might consider a gown that does not smother you in wool."

Her eyes flashed with the sort of fury that made Dimitri relieved that there was no knife at hand.

"I am not the one who needs to fear being smothered."

EMMA PEERED OUT THE window of the carriage, allowing her maid's incessant lecture on what happens to females who spend an entire afternoon in the company of known criminals to flow past her. She did not need to be reminded she had been a fool to meet with Dimitri Tipova. Or that she was an even greater fool to have agreed to his outrageous suggestion that she allow him to escort her to his gambling clubs.

For goodness' sake, if she were recognized she would never overcome the scandal.

Whatever the dangers she fully intended to travel from one den of iniquity to another until she located the men who had abducted her sister. There was no point in dwelling on the insanity of her behavior.

Instead, she studied the overwhelming beauty of the city around her.

Over the past two days she had been too occupied with her troubles to truly notice its magnificence. Now she allowed herself to appreciate the stunning palaces that lined the narrow canals.

How odd to realize that such glory could rise from such brutality.

Her lips twisted as she recalled her history lessons. The cold-hearted Ivan and his private army, the *oprichniki,* who had terrorized the boyars until the Tatars attacked Moscow. Ivan had ordered any number of bloodbaths to maintain his ruthless rule until he had tumbled into utter madness and he was at last murdered by his own heir.

As much a monster as Ivan had been, however, the period of chaos that followed his death had proven the need for a strong leader to rule the vast empire. It had been the desperate Cossacks and outspoken *Streltsi,* and even a group of more prosperous peasants, that had demanded the *zemsky sobor* be called to name a new czar.

Eventually, Peter had come to the throne, his life already scarred by being forced to witness his closest family butchered when he was just ten years of age. Not that his years of being condemned to the remote hunting lodge on the Yauza River had been wasted. Indeed, they had offered him a rare opportunity for self-education.

Left to entertain himself, he studied with the local craftsmen to acquire skills in everything from blacksmithing to carpentry. He also gathered devoted friends who assisted him in mock battles and discovering the best means of drilling an infantry. Long before acquiring an army he had practiced besieging a scale-sized fortress and could calculate the ranges for his artillery.

Perhaps most important, he developed an obsessive fascination with sailing.

With remarkable foresight he had realized the future of his country depended upon opening itself to the world, and with a cruel efficiency he conquered a path to the Baltic Sea and then set about building a city that would rival Versailles.

There was a clatter of hooves as the carriage crossed the Fontanka River over the Semyonovsky Bridge and Emma realized they were nearing Vanya's home.

Tugging the scarf more tightly around her neck, she was prepared as the carriage halted in front of the imposing mansion with its columned balcony and massive jade lions that guarded the double doors. Leaving the carriage she climbed the steps and entered the marble foyer.

There was an awkward moment as the uniformed servants scurried about her, attempting to perform small services before Emma waved them away. She would never become accustomed to having others wait on her.

Hovering uncertainly by a rosewood table that held a delicate Chinese vase, Emma was relieved by the sudden appearance of a strikingly beautiful woman with silver hair and a tall, curvaceous form attired in a morning dress of lavender silk.

"At last. I was becoming quite concerned," Vanya murmured, a hint of worry in her pale blue eyes.

"I am sorry." Emma removed her scarf and tossed it aside. "The impossible man kept me waiting for near two hours. As if he were royalty rather than a common criminal."

Taking Emma's hand, Vanya led her up a curved staircase. "I should never consider Dimitri Tipova common," she said with a small sigh. "He is sinfully handsome, is he not?"

A dangerous sensation fluttered in the pit of her stomach. "I suppose he is handsome enough, although that does not compensate for his utter lack of civility. He is the rudest man I have ever encountered."

Vanya allowed a mysterious smile to curve her lips as she led Emma into a private salon with emerald wall panels and gilt cornices. The furniture was a dark mahogany with gold velvet cushions and the wooden floor covered by an Oriental rug. The overall atmosphere was one of rich sensuality.

A perfect setting for Vanya.

"Odd." Vanya settled on the sofa and pulled Emma down next to her. "I have always thought him to be surprisingly gracious."

"You are well acquainted?"

Leaning forward, Vanya poured two cups of tea from the tray left on the low table, adding a generous amount of milk and sugar before handing a cup to Emma and leaning back into the cushions.

"He performed a great service for a dear friend of mine," she explained, sipping her hot tea. "I consider myself in his debt."

Emma hastily tempered her words, far too polite to insult a man her hostess held in high esteem.

"No doubt it is my fault." She took a reviving sip of tea, hoping it would help the lies tumble from her lips. "He did mention that I stir his more primitive nature."

"Did he?" Vanya's smile widened. "How very intriguing."

Intriguing? Emma found it utterly vexing. As if she were to blame for his irritating lack of manners.

"Let us hope our time together is of short duration."

"Did he agree to assist you in your search for poor Anya?"

"Yes."

"Thank goodness." The older woman reached to pat Emma's arm. "Whatever your opinion of Dimitri there is no gentleman more suited to helping you."

Emma battled the urge to roll her eyes. "So he has told me."

Vanya's smile faded, her fingers gently squeezing Emma's arm.

"Emma, do you prefer that I find another to lend you assistance?"

Her lips parted with a cowardly urge to agree to Vanya's suggestion. Dimitri Tipova was arrogant and provoking and...

Dangerously attractive.

Then, she hastily swallowed the ridiculous words. If both Herrick and Vanya considered Dimitri Tipova the most suitable man to help her rescue Anya, then she would be inexcusably selfish to turn him away just because she... what? Feared him?

"No, of course not," she said, her tone brisk. "Indeed, I need your help to prepare for the evening."

"You have made plans?"

"I am to accompany Dimitri Tipova to several of his gambling establishments in the hopes I will recognize the gentlemen who lured Anya to St. Petersburg."

If she was shocked by Emma's revelation, then Vanya hid it well. Indeed, she nodded as if it were perfectly reasonable for a young, innocent maiden to allow herself to be escorted by a renowned criminal to his wicked clubs.

"Ah."

"I shall need a means to disguise myself," she firmly insisted. "I cannot risk being recognized. Who can say what the odious creatures will do to Anya if they realize I have followed them?"

"Do not fear, my dear." A gleam that Emma did not entirely trust sparkled in Vanya's blue eyes. "I shall ensure that not even your sister will recognize you."

## CHAPTER FOUR

THE SUNKEN ROSE GARDEN was thankfully wrapped in shadows as Dimitri strolled past the Italian sculptures and marble fountains. Despite his connections among the most elite members of the Russian court, he was still a bastard. Which meant he entered the fine homes by the servants' entrance.

He was moving toward the narrow door at the back of the garden when his instincts prickled and he turned to discover a statuesque woman stepping into the garden from the French windows.

"Dimitri."

Hiding a smile at Vanya Petrova's imperious tone, Dimitri followed the flagstone path to halt before the older woman and perform a deep bow.

Vanya was one of the few aristocrats he truly admired.

"Vanya, as beautiful as ever," he murmured. "I trust Richard Monroe appreciates just how fortunate he is to have captured your fair hand?"

A warm smile curved her lips at the mention of the Englishman who had been her devoted suitor for the past twenty years. Much to the surprise of St. Petersburg, Vanya had at last agreed to Monroe's proposal.

"I presume he does." She touched the large strand of pearls that encircled her neck. "The wedding is less than a month away and he has not yet bolted."

"If I were not a dedicated bachelor I would attempt to steal you away."

Vanya allowed her gaze to roam over his jacket in a pale blue-and-silver waistcoat that he had matched with black knee breeches. She smiled, almost as if she suspected he had taken particular pains with his attire.

"Every gentleman is a dedicated bachelor until he encounters the perfect woman."

He clicked his tongue. "I did not expect such a predictable response from such a delightfully unconventional lady."

"I intend to be even more predictable when I warn you that I am depending upon you to protect my young and decidedly innocent guest."

"You have no need to fear. I promise that Emma Linley-Kirov will not leave my side."

Vanya narrowed her eyes. "That does not entirely relieve my unease."

Dimitri frowned, pretending that he had not spent an inordinate amount of time dwelling on his encounter with the bothersome female.

"For all my sins I am no debaucher of the innocent. Especially not when that innocence is wrapped in such a prickly package."

"Do not allow her indomitable spirit to deceive you. Emma has taken on responsibilities that would have broken a lesser woman," Vanya chastised. "Underneath all her pretense of courage, however, she is a young maiden who is terrified for her sister."

His expression hardened. He was unaccustomed to being lectured as if he were a school lad. Not even the most cutthroat villain dared to question him.

"I will attempt to keep that in mind."

There was the sound of footsteps and they both turned to watch Emma step from the house.

"Ah, here she is," Vanya murmured.

Briefly caught in the candlelight from the house, Emma's

honey curls tumbled freely about her shoulders, but Vanya had cleverly hidden the young maiden's face with a charming hat made of gold feathers and a diamond-encrusted veil that ended just above Emma's lush lips. It added a hint of provocative mystery that would stir a man to investigate more. With the same masterful touch, Vanya had wrapped Emma's slender body in a long cape of black velvet trimmed with matching gold feathers.

There was not a soul who would recognize her.

"Well done, Vanya," he murmured. "I knew I could depend upon you to be rid of the nasty wool."

The older woman chuckled, as if she harbored a secret. "You have no notion. Good luck, my dear."

Moving toward the house, Vanya paused to kiss Emma on the cheek before disappearing through the French doors. Dimitri traced her footsteps, halting at Emma's side to offer an arm.

"Shall we go?"

She hesitated, and Dimitri sensed her silent battle to overcome her fear. Then, with that courage he knew beyond a shadow of a doubt was destined to lead her into trouble, she laid her hand on his arm and allowed herself to be led to the carriage Dimitri had left next to the mews.

Assisting her into the vehicle, Dimitri placed the heated bricks at her feet before settling at her side and tugging the rug over both of them. The night air was crisp enough to be uncomfortable.

He waited until the driver had set the matching black horses into a brisk trot before he reached into a drawer built beneath the leather bench and retrieved a silver flask and two small crystal glasses.

Pouring them both a measure of the potent spirits, he pressed one of the glasses into Emma's unwilling fingers and lifted his own glass in a toast.

"*Za vas.*"

She cautiously sipped the expensive liquor, predictably choking as the fiery liquid slid down her throat.

"Good Lord. What is it?"

"Cognac." Dimitri took a far more appreciative sip, savoring the nutty flavor of the well-aged spirit. "It will help keep you warm."

She frowned, but she took another sip, perhaps hoping to ease her nerves.

"Is it a great distance to your club?" she demanded.

"No, it is quite close." Dimitri refilled her glass, studying her brittle expression. She appeared ready to bolt. Clearly a distraction was in order. "Is this your first visit to St. Petersburg?"

"This is the first occasion I have ever left our tiny village." A rueful smile touched her lips, her hazel eyes shrouded in mystery behind the gossamer veil. "I suppose that makes me impossibly provincial?"

"I refuse to be baited, Emma Linley-Kirov. Do you wish me to point out the more historical buildings we will pass on our journey?"

"I…" She paused, then offered a small dip of her head. "Yes, I would be very interested, thank you."

Scooting closer to her, Dimitri glanced out the window as the carriage turned onto the Nevsky Prospekt.

Within moments the stunning Our Lady of Kazan Cathedral came into view. The domed church was an impressive sight with its sweeping colonnade that framed a small garden complete with a fountain.

"Perhaps you know Emperor Paul intended the structure to imitate Saint Peter's Basilica in Rome despite the church officials' outrage at having a replica of a Catholic church."

As he had hoped, Emma's tension eased as she pressed her nose to the window, obviously eager to enjoy the spectacular view.

"My father told me that Alexander Pavlovich had commanded the church become a memorial to the defeat of Napoleon."

"Yes," Dimitri agreed dryly. The emperor had been quite eager to ensure that his victory over the Corsican monster was suitably commemorated throughout the city. "The great Mikhail Kutuzov is laid to rest in the cathedral and the keys from several European cities and fortresses were placed in the sacristy in honor of Russia's victory."

The carriage rattled onward and Dimitri pointed out the Stroganov Palace with its massive entrance arch supported by two Corinthian columns. Like much of St. Petersburg it had been designed by Rastrelli. Turning eastward they passed the Admiralty and headed toward the Palace Square. It was, of course, the crowning jewel of the city with its lavish facade painted a pale green and trimmed in white. Massive statues lined the roof and at one end an onion dome dominated the skyline. Next to the palace were the Hermitage houses that held Catherine's vast collection of paintings as well as the theater built for Catherine by Giacomo Quarenghi.

Dimitri hid his smile as Emma pointed toward the passing buildings, asking endless questions and unabashedly enjoying the short tour. It had become fashionable to pretend a jaded indifference to the world, and he could not deny it was refreshing to be in the company of a woman willing to reveal her emotions.

Her eyes widened in fascination as she spotted the Peter and Paul Fortress on the northern bank of the Neva, she sighed at the beauty of the summer gardens, and shivered at the forbidding Mikhailovsky Castle, a fortress built by an insane Emperor Paul where he was later to be murdered.

It was almost a disappointment when they crossed the bridge leading to the lower Nevsky and turned onto a narrow street lined with unpretentious elegant buildings.

Emma turned to him in surprise. "Why are we slowing?"

"I prefer not to leap from a moving carriage unless absolutely necessary," he informed her dryly.

She sucked in a sharp breath, her gaze taking in the building painted a brilliant yellow with a wide entrance that was guarded by two servants. Although it was early, there was already a steady line of opulently clad gentlemen climbing the stairs and producing their gilt-edged cards that marked them as members.

"This is your club?"

Ridiculously, Dimitri discovered himself offended by her shock. "Did you expect a hovel in a dark alley?"

She drained the last of her cognac before setting aside the empty glass.

"I have never given much thought to gambling establishments. Now I realize they must be quite profitable."

He shoved open the door, assisting her onto the paved walk. "Sin is not without its reward."

"Spoken by an unrepentant sinner."

"Of course," he agreed.

As the bastard of a nobleman he had received a fine education, but was forbidden to take his place among society. At the same time, he was too cultured to be accepted among the peasants. With no true place in the world, he had turned his ruthless willpower to creating an empire of his own making.

Leading Emma up the stairs, he nodded toward his guards and entered the large octagonal vestibule that was tastefully decorated with a black-and-white-tiled floor reflected in the silver-framed mirrors that lined the walls.

At their entrance a tall servant with a regal bearing approached to offer a deep bow.

"Vladimir will take your wrap," Dimitri informed his silent companion, his brows lifting as she clutched the velvet cloak with a white-knuckled grip. Did the chit fear his servant intended to make off with her clothing? "I promise you it will be returned."

"Very well."

Her chin lifted as she tugged off the cloak with a swift motion and handed it to the waiting servant. In a heartbeat, the crowd came to a captivated halt as all eyes turned toward Emma.

It was not that her gown was particularly shocking. Indeed, it was a deceptively simple sheath cut to reveal her shoulders and gathered beneath the gentle swell of her bosom. It was more the shimmer of the gold satin that molded to her slender body. And the tiny diamonds that glittered along the low-cut line of her bodice that drew attention to the perfection of her ivory skin.

Combined with the satin tumble of honey hair and the promise of her sensuous lips, it was enough to make every male in the club crave to have her in his bed.

Including Dimitri.

Muttering a startled curse, he grasped her upper arm and hauled her through a nearby alcove, tugging her down the short hall until he could thrust her into the privacy of his office. It was a plain room, with cream walls and parquet floor. The desk set near the fireplace was a pale cedar that matched the rest of the furnishing and the draperies were a soft shade of rose.

Slamming shut the door, he turned to glare at his companion in the muted light of the fireplace.

"What the devil are you wearing?"

With a sharp tug, she freed her arm from his grasp. "You were the one to insist I dress in an appropriate fashion."

Clearly, he had been out of his mind, he acknowledged, searing a hungry gaze over the delectable curve of her breasts.

"Appropriate, not designed to create a riot."

"It is no more revealing than those gowns worn by the finest ladies in St. Petersburg," she protested.

"Then why did Prince Matvey nearly knock himself senseless by walking straight into a wall? And why did one of my most trusted servants drop an entire tray of champagne?" he growled.

"You are being ridiculous. I witnessed women wearing far more daring gowns before you so rudely hauled me away."

A voice of reason whispered that he was overreacting, but Dimitri was in no mood to listen. Not when his entire body burned with the need to haul her to the nearest bed.

"Perhaps more daring," he husked, "but none so enticing."

She nervously licked her lips, the unwitting gesture making Dimitri groan in frustration.

"First you complain my gown is too prudish and now you complain it is too revealing. Are you never satisfied?"

Unable to resist temptation, he stepped close enough to trail his fingers along the elegant line of her shoulders. His body stirred, hardened; responding to her with a near painful intensity.

It wasn't uncommon for him to desire a woman.

He was a healthy male with all the normal appetites.

But this biting ache combined with a fierce possessiveness was utterly unfamiliar.

And equally unwelcome.

"Ironically I was quite satisfied until my peaceful existence was disrupted by an intimidating spinster who is far too fond of her independence."

She shivered as his fingers traced the plunging line of her bodice.

"Dimitri."

He stepped closer, breathing in the tantalizing scent of warm woman and clean soap.

"I never knew such skin truly existed," he rasped. "It is as soft and perfect as fresh cream."

"We are supposed to be searching for the gentlemen who took Anya."

"In a moment." Wrapping one arm around her waist, he carefully lifted the veil, his gaze sweeping over her pale, beautiful features. "First I must taste you."

"No—" Her protest fell on deaf ears as he captured her lips in a branding kiss. He wanted to wrap her in his arms until she melted with soft compliance. He wanted to mark her with his touch, his scent, his desire. He wanted to ensure that every man who caught sight of this woman understood that she belonged to him. Only him. "As sweet as honeyed almonds," he muttered, his tongue teasing her lips until they slowly parted in invitation. "Yes, *moya dusha*, open for me."

She groaned, her hands clutching at his shoulders as if she struggled to keep herself upright.

"The cognac..." she muttered.

He gripped her hips, pressing her against the blatant evidence of his arousal.

"It is not the cognac that is causing your head to spin and your heart to race."

She arched back to stab him with an angry frown, but Dimitri did not miss her small shiver of awareness.

"You believe yourself to be irresistible?"

"It is the hunger that burns between us that is irresistible," he corrected, his voice hard. He had made his fortune on catering to other's weaknesses. He had never dreamed he might himself become a victim. "I always thought this sort of craving a myth. Now I do not know whether to have you locked in my dungeon or hauled off to Siberia."

She licked her lips, and Dimitri swallowed a groan as his cock hardened with tormenting anticipation.

"Do not say such things," she breathlessly commanded.

"Even if they are the truth?"

An unmistakable fear darkened her hazel eyes as she lifted her hands and pressed them against his chest.

"I may be attired as a tart, but I assure you I am a lady," she gritted.

His lips twisted. "I am painfully aware you are a lady, Emma Linley-Kirov, and for the moment you are under my protection."

"Then release me."

His gaze lowered to her honeyed lips that could drive a saint to sin.

"Is that what you desire?"

"You must."

"Damn." Pushing away from the delectable heat, Dimitri shoved his hands through his hair and struggled to regain command of his rebellious body. "You should never have come to St. Petersburg."

AT ANY OTHER TIME, Emma might have been dazzled by her surroundings.

Who knew that a den of iniquity would be a sprawling honeycomb of ivory-and-gold rooms with crimson carpets and marble columns that soared up to the vaulted ceiling painted with Greek gods playing among the clouds? Or that the massive chandeliers would cast a blazing light over the elegant gentlemen who weaved their way among the card tables and flirted with the women dressed in low-cut gowns?

She had assumed the place would be dark and cheap with furtive men hunched over their cards, or tossing dice in the corner.

Which only proved she truly was naive as Dimitri claimed.

Dimitri…

She covertly glanced at the man walking at her side, a dangerous excitement fluttering in the pit of her stomach. Even elegantly attired, there was no disguising the ruthless predator that lurked just beneath Dimitri's polished exterior.

Not that his dark beauty and experienced touch was an excuse for the manner in which she had melted beneath his kiss. Or the prickling awareness that continued to torment her. She was supposed to be a sensible female of advanced years, not a giddy maiden who dreamed of being rescued from her life of drudgery by a handsome prince.

After all, she was quite reconciled to being a spinster, and even if Dimitri were a prince rather than the Beggar Czar, he was not interested in making her his princess. Just like Baron Kostya, Dimitri considered her worthy of a quick tumble, but nothing more.

She felt an odd pain knife through her heart, but before she could consider the cause, a tall, silver-haired gentleman in a burgundy jacket and gold-striped waistcoat that did nothing to flatter his rotund figure deliberately stepped in their path.

"Tipova," he said, his beady eyes skimming over the veil that once again hid Emma's face before latching on to the swell of her bosom. "As always you have managed to create a sensation."

Dimitri wrapped an arm around her shoulders, shielding her from the rude leer.

"I fear I cannot take the credit on this occasion, Prince Matvey."

"Do you intend to introduce me to your companion?"

"Actually she is visiting from Moscow and prefers to keep her privacy." His smile was one of sheer male possession. "Is that not so, *moya dusha?*"

She huddled in the protection of Dimitri's arm. "Yes."

"Ah." The prince licked his fat lips. "A mystery."

"Have you seen Count Fedor?" Dimitri demanded.

"Tarvek?" The prince glanced around the crowded room. "Not this evening, although I encountered him at the Winter Palace last eve."

"Then he returned from his journey?"

"Yes, I believe he returned with Sergei last Sunday. Do you have a particular need to speak with him?"

Emma sucked in a sharp breath, her suspicious gaze studying Dimitri's cold expression.

"I am a businessman at heart and I make a habit of knowing where to locate those who are in debt to me," Dimitri drawled.

"Yes, of course." The prince blanched and tugged at his elaborately tied cravat, as if it were too tight. "If you will excuse me?"

Dimitri smiled. "Certainly."

Waiting until the prince had vanished among the crowd, Emma struggled to put a measure of space between them.

"You told me that you did not know who had taken Anya—"

"Shh." He lowered his head to speak directly in her ear. "I had a suspicion when you said their names. It seemed a strange coincidence that the men arrived at your inn claiming to be brothers and possessing the names Fedor and Sergei, but I cannot be certain since they at least had the sense to alter their title. It would be dangerous to leap to conclusions."

She stilled, ruefully accepting the truth of his words. "Very well."

Pulling back, he regarded her with an unreadable expression. "We will take a turn through the dining room to ensure we have not overlooked our prey and then take our leave."

"How many clubs are we to visit this evening?"

A muscle clenched in his jaw as he steered her toward an arched doorway.

"One has been more than ample."

"I do not understand."

"My nerves are quite shattered," he drawled, the golden eyes blazing with an indefinable emotion as he glanced down at her puzzled expression. "I intend to return you to the protection of Vanya."

"But—"

He placed a silencing finger against her lips. "Do not play with fire, Emma, unless you wish to be burned."

## CHAPTER FIVE

THE MANSION THAT COUNT Fedor Tarvek shared with his younger brother Sergei was not the finest in St. Petersburg. Situated on the banks of the Neva, it had once been a grand structure with an ornate frieze carved over the front entrance and tall windows that overlooked the formal gardens. Unfortunately, time and neglect had stolen the original charm, and there was no hiding the growing shabbiness of the estate.

Slipping silently through the cavernous rooms, a portion of Dimitri deplored the rotting floorboards and the mold marring the once handsome furnishings even as he appreciated the lack of servants. He preferred to invade another's privacy without interruption.

Intent on his search through the upper bedchambers, he nearly missed the slender man who silently approached the house through the kitchen garden.

With a lift of his brows, Dimitri hurried down the stairs.

He had sent Josef to keep watch on Count Fedor and Sergei, knowing the brothers would attend Czar Alexander's inspection of his troops that afternoon. They might secretly despise the emperor, and even attempt to undermine his rule when possible, but they dare not publicly ignore his summons.

It seemed the perfect opportunity to discover if the Tarveks were hiding any nasty secrets.

Silently leaving the house by a side door, he gestured toward his servant and headed for the back of the stables, not surprised to discover Josef had hidden his horse next to his own dappled-gray mare in the overgrown bushes.

They had spent a number of years working together. Perhaps too many, he ruefully acknowledged, watching the wiry man round the edge of the stables. They were both reaching an age where they should be considering an occupation that did not include a noose or firing squad.

"That was speedy," he muttered. "The drills cannot have ended yet."

"Oleg is keeping watch on Tarvek and his brother." Josef's expression was sour. "I thought you would desire to know that Vanya Petrova was among the crowd."

"Alone?"

"Nyet. She has a young female companion with her."

Dimitri tensed, telling himself it was anger that made his stomach clench and his heart miss a beat. After all, he had specifically commanded Emma Linley-Kirov to avoid being seen when he had left her at Vanya's the night before. He had told her he would contact her when he decided what was to be done next.

"A female companion with honey hair and hazel eyes?"

"That is more than a mere man can say." Josef shook his head in disgust. "She is wearing one of those foolish bonnets that make it damned well impossible to know what's beneath the tangle of ribbons and feathers, but I would bet my last ruble it's the dragon from Yabinsk."

As would Dimitri.

Emma was stubborn enough to flaunt herself beneath the noses of the men who would kill her without hesitation.

"Damn. I'm beginning to believe she was sent to St. Petersburg to punish me for my numerous sins," he muttered, untying the reins of his horse from the bush. "Come along."

Josef grimaced, twisting the scar that ran down the side

of his face. The disfigurement terrified many, which suited Josef, but Dimitri knew he had received the wound protecting his sister from his drunken mother.

"I will remain and search the house."

"That will not be necessary. There are no females being held hostage in the cellar or convenient map to reveal their location. Although…"

Deliberately allowing his words to trail away, Dimitri mounted his horse and headed toward the narrow lane that led out of the estate. He knew his companion's curiosity would overcome his reluctance to mix among the nobles.

There was a muttered curse, then the sound of scrambling as Josef retrieved his horse and urged the beast to match Dimitri's steady pace.

"What did you find?"

Dimitri reached beneath the black multicaped coat he had chosen to cover his plain attire and riding boots. With a crowned beaver hat pulled low on his forehead and a heavy muffler wrapped around his lower face he was impossible to recognize. Even his stocky mare was unremarkable.

Being a successful criminal meant blending into the background when necessary.

"I found this in Tarvek's bedchamber," he said, pulling out a folded piece of parchment and handing it to his companion.

"Katherine Marie," Josef read out loud. "Friday at noon." He glanced toward Dimitri with a frown. "An assignation, no doubt."

"Quite possible," Dimitri readily agreed, urging his horse into a trot as they reached the paved street leading toward the Winter Palace. "But I recall finding a similar message in Pytor Burdzecki's desk."

Josef easily kept pace. "Katherine is a common enough name."

Which was precisely why Dimitri had dismissed

Burdzecki's note as inconsequential. The aging roué was known to keep several mistresses, not to mention the brothels he visited on a regular basis.

"Yes, but for both gentlemen to have an assignation on the same day, at the same time, with a woman with the same name defies the odds."

"You suspect this Katherine is a female they have abducted?"

"Or intend to abduct."

Josef was swift to realize the importance of Dimitri's words. "Then we can follow them. If they do snatch a female they will have to take her to their hidden lair."

Dimitri nodded, his expression grim as the traffic thickened and he was forced to slow his pace.

"That was my thought, as well. We need to keep a close guard on the men we suspect are involved with my father."

They traveled in silence as they weaved through the elegant carriages and small groups of pedestrians who were battling to make their way to the Palace Square. It was not that the crowds possessed an interest in the military drills or the poor soldiers expected to stand for hours in the cold as they prepared for the event.

But, it had become a rare occurrence for Alexander Pavlovich to make a public appearance over the past few years and the entire city was determined to catch sight of him.

"What's troubling you?" Josef abruptly demanded.

Dimitri smiled with wry amusement at his servant's perception. Yes. They had most certainly been working together for too long.

"Katherine Marie," he muttered, annoyed by a vague memory teasing the edge of his mind. "The name is familiar."

Josef shrugged. "As I said, it's common enough."

"Yes." Dimitri shook his head in frustration and abruptly

turned down a side street that would lead to the Summer Garden and the Field of Mars beyond. He knew a few tricks to avoid the worst of the traffic. "This way." Intent on reaching Emma, it took Dimitri a moment to realize his companion was beginning to fall farther and farther behind. He glanced over his shoulder with an expression of impatience. "Josef?"

The servant shifted uneasily in his saddle. He hated being in the finer neighborhoods. Understandable, of course. One misstep and a man could find himself rotting in the nearest dungeon.

"You wanted those noblemen to be watched. I'll find—"

"I have need of you," Dimitri firmly interrupted, returning his attention to the road.

"I knew that woman was going to be trouble the moment she threatened to geld Semyon with scalding coffee," Josef muttered, grudgingly returning to Dimitri's side.

Dimitri scowled. He was not pleased when he discovered Emma had been troubled by one of his own servants.

"Semyon should have been gelded, although I believe the flogging I gave him should be lesson enough in how to treat a lady."

"What do you intend to do with her?"

"That is a question that kept me pacing the floor most of the night," Dimitri said dryly.

Josef shook his head in sad resignation. "A wise man would pack his bags and flee at this moment."

"No doubt."

"And yet you intend to pursue her."

Dimitri shifted in his saddle, balking at the accusation. He took women beneath his protection and sheltered them from the cruelties of the world. He did not *pursue* them. Especially not those women who flouted his authority and deliberately placed themselves in danger.

"I intend to make certain that she does not ruin our opportunity to capture the bastards," he snarled. "If they recognize her, then they will become even more cautious. We will never be able to follow their trail."

Josef snorted. "And you are not at all fearful she might be in danger?"

Dimitri ignored the question, slowing his mount as they neared the Palace Square. Over the heads of the crowd, he caught sight of the soldiers marching past the emperor, who watched on horseback, his once handsome features lined with fatigue beneath the pale autumn sunlight. The duties of the crown sat heavily on Alexander Pavlovich's shoulders. At the czar's side was Herrick Gerhardt, his eagle gaze missing nothing of the milling crowd.

With a grimace, Dimitri turned his attention to the carriages that lined the square.

"Where did you last see them?" he demanded.

"Near the end of the Hermitage." Josef pointed across the Square. "What do you intend to do?"

He gritted his teeth, refusing to give in to the impulse to charge across the parade grounds and toss Emma over his shoulder as if he were a barbarian. Not only was it a ridiculous notion, but he would attract precisely the kind of attention he was hoping to avoid.

"You will ensure a note is delivered to Vanya that she is to return home without delay," he commanded.

Josef narrowed his eyes. "And you?"

"I will be waiting."

DISCREETLY STANDING behind Vanya, Emma attempted to concentrate on the passing crowd. She had, after all, been the one to plead with the older woman to discover a means she could catch sight of Count Fedor and his brother, Sergei. And she had promised faithfully she would do nothing that would allow others to believe she was other than a maid who was there to fetch and carry for her mistress.

But while she was desperate to discover if the count was the same Fedor who had stayed at her inn, she could not help being distracted by the stunning beauty that surrounded her. Over and over her gaze strayed to the imposing Winter Palace with its magnificent Corinthian columns and the statues that seemed to peer down at her from the roof. Almost as dazzling was the handsome emperor seated on his horse less than a stone's throw away, his large form attired in military splendor and his brilliant blue eyes seeming to regard his passing troops with a wistful gleam, as if he were wishing he could join the precise lines of soldiers and march away from the crowd that pressed around him.

For a woman who had never been more than a mile from her forgotten village in the wilds of Russia, it was a breathtaking vision she knew she would never forget.

With a shake of her head, Emma sternly returned her attention to the elegant women with their fur-lined capes and the gentlemen in their military finery as they jostled to gain a place near the emperor. None paid her the least amount of attention as she stood in the shadows, her face hidden beneath the oversized brown bonnet and matching cloak that fell from her chin to the tips of her toes. To the nobles she was a meaningless servant beneath their notice.

She was attempting to get a better view of the two gentlemen crossing toward an older man with silver hair and arrogant expression when a tiny boy dressed in ragged clothing stopped next to Vanya and shoved something in her hand.

Emma instinctively moved forward to protect the older woman, but she had barely taken a step when the urchin darted away, weaving his way with ease through the people.

"This is odd," the older woman murmured, glancing down at the crumpled note she held in her hand.

"What is it?" Emma asked.

"I suppose we shall soon discover. Will you be gravely disappointed if we leave?"

"Certainly not." Emma winced as a rotund woman nearly knocked her to the ground. "I doubt I could recognize anyone in such a crowd."

Vanya offered a comforting smile as they moved toward the waiting carriage.

"Do not fear, my dear. We shall find another means to cross paths with the gentlemen you seek."

The trip back to Vanya's home was speeded by the servants who walked ahead of the carriage and cleared a path, and within half an hour they were pulling to a halt. Allowing Vanya to be assisted by the waiting groom, Emma stepped onto the pavement behind her, unprepared for the ruthless hand that seemed to come from nowhere and clamp about her upper arm.

With a startled gasp, she whipped her head around to discover a man looming beside her, his face hidden behind a muffler.

"A word in private, Emma Linley-Kirov, if you please," he growled, his dark male voice and smoldering golden eyes all too familiar.

Dimitri Tipova.

She pressed a hand to her thundering heart. "Good Lord, you near scared the life from me."

Ignoring her chiding words, the exasperating man began hauling Emma toward Vanya's private rose garden.

"If you will excuse us, Vanya?" he belatedly tossed toward the older woman.

Vanya arched a silver brow. "Do I have a choice?"

"Not on this occasion."

Shocked by Dimitri's unexpected arrival, Emma allowed herself to be pulled through the gate and into the small stone grotto that hid them from view. It was only when he spun her to meet his furious gaze that she jerked her arm free of his slender fingers.

"You truly must overcome your habit of manhandling me, sir—"

"Dimitri," he bit out, removing his hat and muffler and tossing them on a nearby marble bench.

A chill inched down her spine at the hard expression on his beautiful face, but she held her ground, refusing to reveal her unease.

"I will not be bullied."

"Be happy that I have not turned you over my knee as I long to do," he snapped.

"I beg your pardon?"

"I suspected that you were headstrong and impulsive and inclined to follow your heart rather than your head, but I did not realize you were without sense."

"I do not have to remain here and be insulted by a—"

Her proud words were brought to a sharp halt as he reached up to tug the bonnet off her head, disregarding her angry protest as he dropped it on the ground.

"Did you truly believe that ridiculous concoction would protect you if you encountered the men who abducted your sister?"

"As a matter of fact, I do," she said, tossing back the thick honey hair that tumbled about her shoulders. "No one took the least notice of me."

"My servant recognized you from across the square."

"More likely he recognized Vanya Petrova and assumed I was her companion," she argued. "The men I am seeking have no expectation of seeing me in St. Petersburg and certainly not in the company of a noblewoman."

He stepped forward, his hands clenched at his side. "You took an absurd risk."

"I am quite at liberty to take whatever risks I desire. It is none of your concern."

"Emma, do not be a fool," he rasped. "Those men may hide among polite society, but beneath their fine clothing and excessively large homes they are no better than animals. If they decide you are a threat to them they will not hesitate to put you in a grave."

Emma bristled at his unwanted lecture, but there was something in his voice that tempered her fury.

It was understandable for any gentleman with the least amount of decency to be outraged at the thought of innocent young girls being abused. But there was something personal, perhaps even intimate, in Dimitri's anger.

Tilting back her head, she studied the chiseled perfection of his aristocratic features. This man was proving to be disturbingly complex.

"Herrick insisted that you were the best suited to assist me in finding my sister, but he did not reveal what connection you possess with these men."

His eyes darkened. "Do you wonder if I am a partner in their crimes?"

"No. Certainly not."

"I have confessed to be a sinner."

Without thought, she reached to place her hand on his forearm. "You might be a sinner, but you are not evil."

His gaze lowered to where her fingers lay against his coat. "There are those who would disagree."

She shrugged off his warning, bitterly aware that the opinion of others rarely had anything to do with the truth.

"Besides, if you were involved in their ghastly business you would hardly be eager to bring them to justice."

"Not justice." A terrifying anger burned in his golden

eyes. "I want them destroyed. I want their foul deeds exposed to the world so that they flee to the wilds of Siberia to hide from their shame. I want them to die alone and in complete despair."

Emma shivered at the stark pain that she sensed beneath his fury. "They hurt someone you love. Your sister?"

His jaw hardened and she thought he intended to ignore her question. Then, with a sharp movement, he turned away to gaze out the small window overlooking the nearby fountain.

"My mother."

Her heart squeezed with sympathy. "They abducted her?"

"There was no need. My mother was the daughter of a simple cobbler." His voice was as hard and frigid as the Siberian winter. "One day Count Nevskaya walked into my grandfather's shop and had his servant collect my mother and carry her to his waiting carriage."

"He just...took her?"

"He tossed a few coins on the counter in payment."

She swallowed the bile that threatened to rise in her throat. "And your grandfather did nothing to stay him?"

"It was a different time and the count was a close friend to Emperor Paul." The lines of his shoulders were rigid, his hands clenched at his sides. She had obviously stirred his deepest demons. "My grandfather could not risk the wrath of a nobleman when he had several other children to support."

Emma wrapped her arms around her waist, feeling cold to her very soul.

"How old was she?"

"Just turned fifteen."

It was worse than Anya. Dimitri's mother had been taken as if she were no more than an object that had been bought by a handful of coins.

"Where did he take her?"

"He owns a home near Novgorod. He kept her there for near six months, then…"

She unwittingly moved to his side, studying the bleak lines of his profile.

"Then what?"

"It became obvious she was with child so he dismissed her."

Her breath tangled in her throat as she abruptly realized she had been absurdly blind. She should have suspected the truth from the moment she had caught sight of his lean, noble features. Or at least after he'd attempted to bully her. That sort of arrogance had to be bred into a man.

"You are that child?" she asked softly.

He slowly turned to face her, his expression guarded. Emma sensed how difficult it was to speak of his past, as if the wounds were still raw and bleeding.

"I am."

She hesitated, unwilling to further his pain, and yet needing to know what happened.

"Did your mother return to her family?"

"They refused to take her back into their home. She was, after all, ruined in the eyes of the world. They could not hope to marry her off with a bastard child in tow."

Her cheeks heated with outrage. "But she was taken against her will."

Leaning against the fresco painted on the stone wall of the grotto, Dimitri studied her flush beneath his half-lowered lashes.

"You are not that naive, Emma."

No, she was not.

So long as women were kept powerless they were at the mercy of men, society and even fate that too often treated them with a ruthless cruelty.

"What happened to her?"

"What happens to most women forced onto the streets," he said harshly. "Once she gave birth to me she entered a brothel. Does that shock you?"

His wary gaze skimmed over her face, no doubt accustomed to others condemning his mother for the choices she was forced to make. Emma, however, felt only sympathy. And admiration.

"On the contrary, I admire her," she said with a steady sincerity. "She was obviously a woman who did whatever necessary to survive."

"From what I could discover she became reconciled to her fate and soon learned that her considerable beauty could provide her the necessary funds for a modest home." He grimaced. "A pity she could not be satisfied."

"What do you mean?"

"She was determined that I would have a proper education."

"It is what any woman would want for their child."

His features might have been carved from granite in the sunlight slanting through the grotto window.

"I did not ask for her sacrifice," he growled.

She frowned, puzzled by his lack of gratitude. Surely he must understand a woman was willing to sacrifice anything for the people they loved?

"Dimitri?"

His eyes grew distant, the muscles in his jaw knotted as he recalled his past.

"One morning she attired me in my finest clothes, which meant they did not yet have holes in the knees and elbows, and we walked for what seemed to be miles until we at last came to a magnificent palace. I will never forget marching up the front steps and ringing the bell as if we were welcome guests." His lips twisted. "I was terrified."

Emma smiled in understanding. Approaching Herrick Gerhardt's elegant home mere days ago had taken every bit of courage she could muster. And she was supposedly a mature woman.

"How old were you?"

"Eight, or perhaps nine." He shrugged. "Certainly old enough to realize we were not where we belonged."

She ignored the urge to reach up and stroke the sleek raven hair pulled into a ribbon at his nape. The wounded boy that lurked deep inside Dimitri made him no less dangerous. Indeed, the wave of tenderness that swept through her was far more disturbing than the potent attraction that tingled within her.

"Were you turned away?"

"No, my mother was quite determined, and my unmistakable resemblance to my father managed to get us over the threshold and into the count's private study." Shoving away from the wall, Dimitri paced to the center of the grotto. "I understood very little of the conversation beyond the fact my father did a great deal of shouting and my mother refused to leave. It was only later that I learned she had threatened to approach the count's wife and inform her that he had forced himself on a mere child if he did not see to my education."

Emma carefully considered her words. The tension in the air was tangible.

"Clearly her threat was successful."

His breath hissed through his clenched teeth. "It was successful in the sense I was sent to school in Moscow, but my father was far from pleased to be outwitted by a mere whore and set about destroying her life."

Emma winced, already suspecting that the poor woman had suffered for her bold courage.

"What did he do?" she husked.

"He had her evicted from her home, and then he ensured her wealthy patrons would no longer seek her companionship. It became more and more difficult for her to earn a decent living and she was forced to take rooms in the sewers of St. Petersburg." The golden eyes darkened with a bleak loss that tore at her heart. "It was only a matter of time before she had her throat slit and her body left in the gutter."

# CHAPTER SIX

As THE WORDS ECHOED through the grotto, Dimitri wondered what the hell he was doing.

He never shared his mother's tragic story. There were a handful of people who knew his mother had been a whore, and that she had been left to die in the gutter. And, of course, there was no denying his connection to the count.

But the sordid, intimate details...those he kept buried deep inside.

Until this woman. Emma Linley-Kirov stirred emotions he'd struggled for years to forget.

There was a rustle of wool and the light touch of slender fingers on his arm. Dimitri sucked in a startled breath. When had he developed an addiction to the scent of soap on warm, feminine skin?

"What happened to you?" she demanded.

He searched the wide hazel eyes, finding nothing but gentle understanding. Not that he was particularly surprised. While most women would be shocked by his mother and the life she had been forced to lead, Emma appeared almost...admiring.

And why would she not?

She possessed the same reckless courage and stubborn determination to risk her foolish neck for those she loved. His gut twisted with that same white-hot anger he had felt when he'd discovered she had been prancing about St. Petersburg for all to see.

"I was too far away to realize what was happening and

it wasn't until I fled the school when I turned fifteen that I realized she was dead," he snapped.

Her eyes widened at his blunt explanation. "You must have been devastated."

"I was infuriated." He grasped her shoulders, glaring down at her pale, fragile face. "If my mother had never confronted the count then she still would have been alive."

She met his gaze without flinching. "And you blamed her for leaving you on your own?"

"I blamed her for taking a stupid, unnecessary risk," he gritted, refusing to recall the endless nights he'd cried himself to sleep when he discovered his mother was forever gone from his life.

Emma frowned. "She loved you and wanted to do whatever she could to provide you with a future. You should be proud of her."

He tightened his grip, his eyes narrowed. "Do you think your precious Anya would be proud to learn you had died attempting to rescue her?"

She stiffened and met his glare with her own.

"I have to do this."

"For your sister?" he snapped. "Or for your own selfish need to be a martyr?"

She paled, her eyes suddenly appearing too large for her face. "So I am not only a bitter spinster, but a tedious martyr. It is fortunate your opinion means nothing to me."

Dimitri growled in frustration. "My opinion is that you are a stubborn minx who has mistakenly convinced herself that accepting help from others makes her weak. Return home, Emma, and allow me to search for your sister." He leaned down, whispering against her lips. "Or better yet, come with me and I will ensure your protection."

He heard her breath catch. "I doubt protection is what you offer."

Dimitri pulled back, his gaze sweeping possessively down her slender body.

"Once you are known to be mine there is no one who would dare harm you."

A frantic pulse fluttered at the base of her throat. "Except you."

Unable to resist, Dimitri skimmed his lips down the curve of her neck, lingering on that revealing pulse.

"I swear I would treat you with exquisite care." His voice thickened, his anger altering to a blaze of desire. "You would want for nothing."

She moaned, briefly melting against him before she abruptly stepped away to regard him with a leery frown. Her body might recognize that she belonged to him, but her mind was not yet ready to concede defeat.

"What I want is to find my sister and to return to our home together."

"Emma—"

"No." She shook her head, her hand pressed to her throat. "Do you believe your father is involved with the gentlemen who abducted Anya?"

Dimitri grimly restrained his need to yank her back into his arms. His experience with tender virgins might be limited, but he did know when a female was on the brink of bolting.

"Yes." He shoved his fingers through his hair, his body hard and aching. A distressingly predictable sensation when he was in the companionship of this frustrating woman. "His debauched taste for young girls has never diminished."

"Why did you not kill him when you discovered he was responsible for the death of your mother?"

Dimitri lifted his brows, startled by the blunt question. "He was a powerful nobleman and I was a mere boy," Dimitri reminded her, his tone dry.

"I cannot believe that is what deterred you."

"You think I was born a bloodthirsty criminal? Or perhaps you assume all bastards are without morals?"

A blush stained her cheeks, but she refused to be cowed. An unfortunate habit.

"I think you loved your mother and would move heaven and earth to avenge her death." She narrowed her gaze, studying him with unnerving perceptiveness. "So why do you hesitate?"

"Because death is not enough," he roughly admitted. "I want to make certain that Count Nevskaya and his cronies publicly suffer for what they have done."

The hazel eyes darkened. "And how many girls have been hurt because you were more concerned with humiliating your father rather than making certain he was unable to abuse helpless children?"

For perhaps the first time in his life, Dimitri Tipova was struck speechless as Emma turned on her heel and left him standing alone in the grotto.

THERE WAS A HEAVY, gray chill in the air as Dimitri left his horse in the shadows of a high hedge, and walked toward the plain black carriage that waited on the elegant street corner.

Wrapped in a heavy coat and muffler that served as his disguise, Dimitri cast a sour glance at the brooding clouds. Although St. Petersburg would always be his home, he often wondered if Czar Peter regretted his fierce determination to create an empire out of this wet, frozen landscape. The emperor had, after all, sacrificed an enormous number of his people, not only to the cold and disease and wolves as the city was being built, but also to keep his throne from a land-hungry Charles XII as well as uprisings from the Cossacks and even his own son, Alexei.

With a shake of his head, he dismissed his inane thoughts

and paused at the side of the carriage. Covertly glancing up and down the quiet street to ensure there were no prying eyes, he tugged open the door and climbed inside.

He settled on the leather seat across from Josef, who kept his gaze trained on the window that offered a perfect view of Pytor Burdzecki's town house.

"Well?" he demanded.

Attired in rough wool clothing more suitable for a dockhand than a man who had acquired a small fortune over the past years, Josef grimaced.

"Not so much as a leaf has stirred."

"And there has been no word from the others?"

"Nothing."

Damn. He had commanded two dozen of his most trustworthy cutthroats to keep watch on the homes of those gentlemen he suspected were involved in his father's nefarious amusements. The notes he had stumbled across had specifically mentioned noon, but unwilling to take any chances, Dimitri had demanded his employees hide themselves near the various homes before the crack of dawn.

"You made certain the household servants were to be followed?" he demanded.

With an offended expression, Josef reached for the nearby bottle of vodka and a large glass.

"You do not pay me because I am careless."

Dimitri could not argue. Josef possessed a meticulous cunning that had made him a successful thief long before Dimitri had taken him beneath his wing.

"Forgive me, Josef. I had convinced myself we could catch the bastards in the midst of their foul deeds." He clenched his hands, needing a means to vent his simmering frustration. "Now it seems they are to elude me yet again."

Josef gave a lift of his shoulder. "The messages you

discovered had no date. It could be they mean the next Friday."

"Or a Friday long past and once again I am too late," he snapped.

"Here." Pouring a large measure of the vodka, Josef shoved a glass into his hand. Dimitri swallowed the potent liquor, grunting as he lowered the glass and Josef leaned forward to refill it. "Another."

He arched a puzzled brow. "Is there a reason you are plying me with vodka?"

"I hoped it might sweeten your foul mood."

Dimitri scowled. "Of course my mood is foul. I do not appreciate being outwitted by a collection of aging reprobates."

"Those aging reprobates possess enough power to alter the course of history as they have too often proven," Josef said, his voice harsh with disgust. Many of the noblemen were personally responsible for squashing Alexander Pavlovich's attempts at reform in the early days of his reign. "Keeping a handful of peasant girls hidden would be a simple matter with a dozen estates and serfs who are too terrified to reveal the truth." Josef leaned back in his seat, his gaze watchful. "And your mood has been foul since you last met with Emma Linley-Kirov."

Dimitri grimaced, swallowing his instinctive denial. Why bother? Anyone unfortunate enough to cross his path since Emma had abandoned him in Vanya's grotto was painfully aware of his vile temper.

"She holds *me* responsible for her sister's abduction."

Josef sucked in a sharp breath. "Is she daft?"

Dimitri polished off the last of the vodka. He had spent the night trying to comfort himself with the notion that Emma Linley-Kirov was a provincial spinster who was too naive and too stupid to comprehend the complexities of his revenge. A wasted effort. Nothing managed to ease the nagging sense of guilt.

"She is annoyingly stubborn, headstrong and beautiful beyond reason, but I would never consider her to be daft."

"She must be if she would accuse you of harming children."

"She did not suggest that I personally forced a child into my bed, but rather that I stood aside and allowed others to continue with their loathsome deeds."

"What would she have you do?"

"Kill them."

Josef blinked, staggered by the thought of a sweet, innocent maiden harboring such bloodthirsty desires. Then he lifted the flask to take a large swig of the vodka.

"If she is so anxious to be rid of the bastards, then why does she not tend to the duty herself?" he muttered.

Dimitri's brows snapped together, a chill shivering down his spine. "Good God, do not say such a thing in her presence. She is quite capable of attempting murder if she thought it would save her precious sister."

"Perhaps she would discover it's not a simple matter to rid society of its vermin."

Dimitri tossed aside his empty glass, casting a jaundiced glance out the window of the carriage.

"Not simple, but not impossible, either."

"You have allowed the female to rattle your wits."

A humorless smile twisted his lips. Emma had rattled more than his wits. His long night of pacing the floor had not been solely due to her accusations. He had been hard and aching to bed the wench since she stormed into his office.

"Rattled wits or not, she was not mistaken. My desire for revenge has allowed my father to continue his debauchery."

Josef muttered his opinion of overbearing spinsters and the stupidity of men who allowed them to interfere in his business.

"The count is the villain, not you," he at last snapped. "How many women have you taken under your protection over the years? Only an arrogant ass would believe he could rescue them all."

Dimitri turned back to meet his loyal servant's scowl. "I can always depend upon you to keep me humble, Josef."

"I assume that is why you have kept me in your service for so many years."

"Well, it most certainly is not for your charm." Dimitri reached for the door of the carriage. It was obvious his hopes of discovering how his father and his associates kept the women they abducted hidden was doomed to failure. At least for today. "Return to your home, old friend."

Josef frowned as Dimitri stepped out of the carriage. "What of you?"

"Alexander Pavlovich is unveiling his latest portrait at the Hermitage this afternoon."

"God almighty, another one?"

Dimitri chuckled. Czar Alexander had avoided many of the Romanov's tendencies, but he was as vainglorious as his grandmother.

"Vanya Petrova is certain to attend and I do not doubt she will be brazen enough to bring her mysterious young maid with her."

Josef drained the last of the vodka, his expression sour. "You should be pleased. It is possible the female can be of service. People tend to be more willing to speak with a pretty young maid than a cutthroat."

"Pleased?" Dimitri clenched his fists, a dark fear churning through him. "If she has put herself in danger I intend to lock her in my cellar and never release her."

"You were right, Tipova," the scarred servant jeered. "Emma Linley-Kirov is not daft, you are."

EMMA FELT AS IF SHE were in a dream when Vanya's elegant carriage swept through the archway and halted in the courtyard before the vast Winter Palace.

How often had she dreamed of traveling to St. Petersburg and encountering a charming prince when she had been young and still naive enough to believe in childish fancy? Or of being draped in rich satin as she entered the vast palaces and curtsied before Czar Alexander?

Instead, she was dressed in the drab clothing of a proper maid and struggling not to stumble over her feet as Vanya led her into Jordan Hall with its grand columns and vaulted ceiling lavishly painted and rimmed with gilt moldings. She had a brief glimpse of the elegantly attired crowd sweeping toward the Jordan Staircase before Vanya pressed her toward a side hall, jolting her out of her brief moment of madness.

Maids did not belong in the upper rooms.

Which suited her perfectly, Emma sternly told herself, traveling through the spider web of corridors and shrugging off her sense of unreality.

Her journey to St. Petersburg was more of a nightmare than dream, and the sooner she found Anya so she could return home the better.

Besides, she was discovering that beneath the breathtaking beauty of the city and the grandeur of the nobility, there was a pervasive rot that lurked just beneath the surface. There was evil in shadows.

Shuddering at the unpleasant thought, Emma hurried toward the servants' quarters. The air was thick with a smothering heat that was no doubt necessary for the exotic plants she had glimpsed in the various salons and drawing rooms she passed, but hardly pleasant for the servants that scurried about their tasks. Ignoring the sweat that trickled down her spine, she followed the scent of baking bread, occasionally stopping to chat with the other maids that crowded into the kitchens.

She would question as many of the servants as possible before returning to the vast entryway and finding the best place to hide and watch as the guests departed the palace. If the men who had abducted Anya were attending Czar Alexander then she would see them leave.

But first…

Reaching the far end of the kitchen that overlooked the small enclosure with a handful of cows, she was nibbling on a plum and almond tart when one of the palace maids cautiously sidled next to her, a wary expression on her plump face that was framed by a halo of red curls.

"What is your interest in Count Fedor Tarvek?" she whispered, her gaze warily darting about the bustling room, as if terrified they might be overheard.

Emma slowly set aside the tart, careful to hide her flare of hope. The woman was as skittish as a dormouse, clearly uneasy at the mention of the man's name. She did not want to startle her into flight.

"My younger sister is seeking a position in his kitchens," she said, keeping her voice equally soft. "She is anxious for a job, but I have heard rumors—"

"You should warn your sister to seek a position elsewhere," the woman hissed.

"What do you know of him?"

The dark gaze again darted about the bustling kitchen, ensuring that no one had noticed them speaking.

"Nothing."

"Please." Emma reached to lightly touch the woman's arm. "Anya is young and headstrong and unless I can offer her more than vague warnings she is certain to ignore my fears. Did you work for the count?"

"No." She bit her bottom lip. "It was my cousin."

"What happened to her?"

"No one is certain. She told my Aunt that she was offered a position as parlor maid, but when she did not return home that night my uncle went in search of her."

A sick dread curled through Emma's stomach. "What did he discover?"

The woman's freckled face hardened with an impotent anger that Emma easily recognized. It was the same helpless frustration that had plagued her since discovering Anya was missing.

"She had simply disappeared. The count claimed that she had never arrived at his home, but my uncle was certain he found a ribbon belonging to my cousin in the hedge surrounding the estate."

"Dear Lord." Emma pressed a hand to her stomach. "You never heard from her again?"

"Nyet. And I have heard whispered she is not the only female to disappear."

"Do you…" Emma's words were cut short as the maid abruptly grasped her hand and nodded toward the window.

"The devil himself," she whispered.

Her breath was lodged in her throat as she leaned forward, staring at the two gentlemen who strolled past the window.

They were both elegantly attired in dark tailored jackets and breeches with high glossy boots that she would bet her last quid were worth more than her cramped cottage. Beneath their tall hats she could catch a glimpse of gray hair and lined countenances. That, however, was where the resemblances ended.

One man was short and stocky with a heavy jowl and an unmistakable paunch under his charcoal-gray jacket. The other was tall and lean with an autocratic profile and air of haughty superiority that annoyed her even from a distance.

Her gaze lingered on the shorter man, her heart skipping a beat as she recognized the debauched face.

"That is Tarvek?" she rasped.

"Yes. Filthy murderer."

Emma clenched her hands at her side. So, Dimitri's conjecture had proven right. Count Tarvek was the man who had stayed at her inn and snuck away with her sister.

She had a name for the bastard, now what did she do with the information?

"Who is that with him?"

"Count Nevskaya," the maid said, her eyes widening as Emma mouthed a startled curse as she realized she was staring at Dimitri's father. "Is something the matter?"

"I shall return in a moment," she muttered, heading for the nearby door.

The maid scurried behind her. "No, listen to me," she pleaded softly. "They truly are dangerous men."

"They will never know I am near," Emma promised, tossing the woman a reassuring smile before she slipped from the kitchen and headed for the back gate.

Count Tarvek and Dimitri's father. Two men who both possessed an evil lust for young girls.

It could not be coincidence they were together, clearly attempting to avoid others as they strolled along the paved lane.

Emma followed behind the two men, careful to keep a cautious distance. Despite Dimitri's low opinion of her intelligence, she had no desire to put herself in danger. But neither was she willing to ignore an opportunity to discover more of the men responsible for her sister's disappearance.

Staying in the shadows of the looming buildings, she shivered as the breeze tugged on her woolen cloak. After the oppressive heat of the palace, the chill of the gray afternoon was even more noticeable. Or perhaps it was a reaction to being led farther and farther away from the guests.

With her heart lodged in her throat, Emma followed the men through a stone archway, nearly stumbling over her feet as they came to an abrupt halt. Thankfully, neither glanced over their shoulders and she was able to scurry behind a bush as they stood closely together, pretending to study the nearby flow of the Neva River.

"The ship has sailed?" Tarvek demanded, his voice pitched low.

The tall, slender gentleman nodded, turning to regard his companion, and Emma's breath tangled in her throat. Good God. There was no mistaking he was Dimitri's father. It was in the chiseled perfection of his profile and arrogant thrust of his jaw.

Not that he could claim Dimitri's stunning beauty, she decided. There was a frigid lack of emotion in his eyes and a repellent sneer that twisted his thin lips. He reminded her of a snake. Cold, lethal and willing to strike without remorse.

"It departed on schedule," he was assuring his companion. "Soon it will arrive in London with our tender cargo."

Tarvek rubbed his fat hands together in a gesture that Emma remembered with a quiver of disgust.

"Tender, indeed," he husked. "I hope that our English friends were fortunate in their hunting. The last lot they delivered was barely tolerable."

Emma frowned in puzzlement. Tender? Hunting? Were they transporting live game? And if so, why would they go to such an effort to discuss their business so far from the other guests?

Dimitri's father shrugged. "They were not of the finest quality, but they brought a tidy profit."

"For you, perhaps," Tarvek growled. "My allotment was not nearly so generous."

"It is my ship that hauls the cargo and my crew who protects our investments. It was agreed I should have the larger profit." The older count slashed his hand through the air in a gesture of disdain. "Besides, you contributed only two of the females for our last shipment."

Tarvek shifted uneasily. "I cannot always control Sergei."

"It is unfortunate, but not my concern," Nevskaya said, his cold voice sending a chill of horror down Emma's spine.

With a gasp, she grabbed at the bush, feeling her knees threaten to buckle.

God almighty. The cargo was not wild game.

They were speaking of girls. Sweet, helpless children they considered of no more worth than animals.

And what did Tarvek mean that Sergei could not be controlled? Her stomach rolled at the mere thought.

"You should at least be pleased with my latest offerings," the villain said, a nasty smile of anticipation curving his lips. "Those were three of the most succulent females I have ever captured. It's a pity that they will be wasted on a boorish Englishman. Any man who would willingly live on that soggy island is barely more than a savage."

Emma's disgust was overwhelmed by a tidal wave of fury. Was Anya one of the three women? Was she even now being hauled far away from Russia? Her hands clenched. If she had a gun she would have shot both the monsters in the back.

Nevskaya laughed, unaware of the woman behind him plotting his imminent murder.

"So long as they fulfill their part of the bargain then I do not care if they mold in their dreary homes."

Lost in her violent imaginings, Emma was unaware of the shadow looming behind her, or the faint crunch of gravel beneath an approaching boot. It was not until a hand clapped over her mouth and a masculine arm wrapped around her waist that she realized the dangers of her distraction.

# CHAPTER SEVEN

IGNORING THE FRANTIC struggles of the woman held tightly in his arms, Dimitri hauled her away from his father and Tarvek. In truth, she was fortunate that the need to avoid attention kept him from tossing her in the nearby river.

He ground his teeth, his temper still smoldering at the sight of her crouched behind the bush, mere steps away from two of the most savage creatures to roam St. Petersburg's streets.

The aggravating wench was clearly determined to put him in an early grave.

"You will not be satisfied until you have managed to get that lovely throat slit, will you, *moya dusha*," he rasped close to her ear, rounding the corner of the palace where his horse and carriage waited.

With a jerk of her head, she managed to dislodge the hand he had clamped across her mouth.

"How dare you follow me?"

Dimitri conveniently ignored the fact he had not only followed her to the palace, but that he had scoured the damned place from the attics to the cellars before he had at last caught sight of her behind the bush.

He was not prepared to admit how desperate he had been to find her, not even to himself.

"Such vanity," he mocked. "Do you believe I am so taken with you I must trail behind you like a hungry stray?"

"I think you are the most irritating, arrogant, utterly vexing man I have ever had the misfortune to meet," she hissed.

He tightened his arms around her slender body, taking grim pleasure in the feel of her squirming form pressed against him. He was angry, not in his grave. Just having this woman near was enough to stir his desire.

"Careful, Emma, you will quite turn my head with such flattery."

"How did you find me?"

"I was searching for my father when I recognized a luscious backside where it did not belong," he glibly dissembled. "I knew it was only a matter of time before you were discovered."

"And so you charged to my rescue?"

"It is an unfortunate habit I seem to have acquired."

"And one you can leave off at any moment," she tartly informed him.

"Ah, if only it were that simple." He caught the gaze of his waiting driver and gave a nod of his head. Instantly, the carriage rolled forward.

"It is," she challenged. "Put me down."

"I have not yet completed my rescue," he said, reaching to yank open the door and tossing his wiggling bundle inside. Then, with a smooth motion, he was on the leather seat beside her, slamming shut the door.

"What are you—" Emma's angry words were forgotten as the carriage jerked into motion, racing over the cobblestones at a brisk pace. "Stop this carriage at once."

His lips twisted at her imperious tone. "I realize you are accustomed to giving commands in your isolated kingdom, Emma Linley-Kirov, but I am not one of your subjects."

Anger flashed through her magnificent eyes, but she was wise enough to realize he would not be bullied. Instead, she nervously shifted into the corner of the seat, as if that paltry space could dim the awareness prickling between them.

"Please, Dimitri," she stiffly pleaded. "Vanya will be frantic with concern if I disappear."

He shifted to face her directly, his leg stretched outward to prevent any attempt at escape. God knew she was idiotic enough to risk throwing herself out of a moving carriage.

"Word will be sent to Vanya that you are in my care."

Her lips thinned. "And that is supposed to reassure her?"

"Certainly it is preferable to having you left to your own devices, creating chaos among the fine citizens of St. Petersburg."

She muttered something beneath her breath that Dimitri suspected was comparing him to midden heap and glanced out the window, her brows drawing together at the elegant shops of the Gostiny Dvor they passed at a shocking speed.

"Where are you taking me?"

"I merely wished to speak with you in private." He diverted her question.

"Why?"

"What did you overhear between Tarvek and my father?"

She jerked, her eyes widening at his abrupt question. "You lecture me for being a reckless fool and now you desire me to share the information I have discovered?"

A slow smile curved his lips. "I do admire your intelligence."

With a snort she folded her arms over her chest. "I have no intention of telling you anything."

He leaned forward to whisper directly in her ear. "You will if you truly desire to find your sister."

Her hands lifted to press against his chest, but Dimitri didn't miss her revealing shiver. Or the leap of her pulse that fluttered at the base of her neck.

"Fine," she rasped. "I very much fear that Anya has been sent to England."

Dimitri reared back, his breath hissing between his clenched teeth.

"What did you say?"

Emma hesitantly repeated the conversation she had overheard, her wary gaze never straying from his grim expression.

A heavy silence filled the carriage as he considered the shocking information. How many years had he searched to find a trace of the women he suspected were being abused by his father and his associates? Christ, he had spent countless hours hidden in frozen gardens and dark alleys attempting to discover the truth. And worse, he had stumbled across the truth and he had been too blind to realize he held it in his hands.

"Dimitri?"

Shaken out of his dark thoughts, he clenched his hands with self-disgust.

"I have been unforgivably stupid," he gritted. "The *Katherine Marie*. I should have recognized the name."

"Who is she?"

"Not who. What," he corrected. "The *Katherine Marie* is my father's private ship."

"My God," she breathed, her face pale and her hands trembling as she folded them in her lap. "Then it's true. They have taken Anya away from St. Petersburg."

Dimitri resisted the peculiar desire to cradle her in his arms and offer her comfort. He protected women. He bedded them. He even supported a few. But there was something unnerving in the tug of tenderness Emma Linley-Kirov inspired.

Besides, she was as likely to slap him as to thank him for his effort. Emma was not a woman who appreciated having others witness her vulnerabilities.

"It would explain a great deal," he admitted.

He heard her draw in a deep, steadying breath, her chin tilting with the stubborn determination that was certain to give him nightmares.

"Such as?"

"I hire a vast number of people to keep me well informed. It seemed impossible that I was unable to discover more than vague rumors that young girls, and occasionally boys, were disappearing. I assumed they must take them from St. Petersburg, but it never occurred to me they would actually ship them abroad."

"I do not understand. If they—" she faltered, a flare of color staining her cheeks "—desire these girls, then why would they send them to England?"

He scowled, cursing the missing Anya for dragging her elder sister into the muck. For all her courage and tenacious strength, Emma possessed an innocence that was remarkably rare.

"Leave it be, Emma," he said roughly. "You have been forced deep enough into this sordid business—"

"I need to know."

"Emma."

She laid a pleading hand on his arm. "Please, Dimitri."

His gaze shifted to the window, absently noticing the aging palaces were being replaced by the classically designed homes preferred by Alexander Pavlovich's architect, Carlo Rossi.

"It would be my guess they transport the women to a select group of gentlemen in England who, in return, send back the females they have lured into their trap," he grudgingly revealed his suspicion. Now that he understood how his father had rid himself of the local females, it was a simple matter to deduce the remainder of his nefarious scheme.

Her brow wrinkled in confusion. "But why go to such a bother?"

"They did not in the beginning, as my presence in St. Petersburg is ample proof." He restlessly tugged off his hat and muffler, tossing them into the opposite seat. His gloves followed. "But Alexander Pavlovich has become remarkably pious as the years have passed and while he is not foolish enough to truly believe he can command his court to put aside their wicked pleasures, he has insisted they become more discreet."

"I still do not understand."

He reached to take her hand, not surprised to find her fingers were stiff with cold. Where the hell were her gloves? And her scarf? The foolish wench. She could shoulder the responsibilities of her business and her sister, but she was stunningly incapable of caring for herself.

Clearly she was in need of someone to protect her, regardless of her prickly independence.

"Allow yourself to imagine a very young and frightened English girl being smuggled into St. Petersburg," he said, studying the shadows that darkened her beautiful eyes. "She would be a world away from her family and friends, she would have no money and no ability to speak the language. She would be utterly at the mercy of her captors."

"She would not dare try to escape."

"Precisely."

She worried her lower lip with her teeth, too intelligent not to realize the dire fate awaiting such women.

"They cannot hold them captive forever."

"No. Once they…" He rubbed a hand over his face, hating the necessity of discussing such a repugnant subject with Emma. "Wearied of the girls, they no doubt sell them to brothels in Novgorod or Moscow."

She swayed, her face ashen. "Anya," she breathed. "I have to find her."

"Emma, we cannot be certain she was on the ship."

She met his gaze with an implacable expression that made Dimitri's gut twist with dread.

"There is only one means to discover."

HER WORDS WERE STILL ringing through the air when the carriage was pulled to a halt in front of a newly constructed house.

It was a home any gentleman would be proud to claim.

Built of pale stone, it boasted five bays with a central bowed projection that was most notable for the Venetian glass he had imported for the windows that flanked the double doorway. A sweep of stairs led to the wraparound terrace that overlooked the sunken garden arranged on both sides and the high brick fencing that offered a rare privacy.

For once, Dimitri did not experience the flare of pride at his creation. He was far more intent on scooping the startled Emma into his arms and climbing out of the carriage.

Predictably outraged at being carried through the gate and up the stairs, Emma smacked his chest, a stormy flush bringing welcome color to her cheeks.

"Have you taken leave of your senses?" She continued with her futile assault. "Put me down."

Dimitri crossed the terrace, smiling as the door was pushed open to reveal a broad man with the corded muscles of a laborer and the weathered features of a sailor. Hardly a typical butler, despite the distinguished mane of silver hair. In truth, Rurik looked exactly what he was. A pirate. And nothing could make him appear respectable. Not even the uniform Dimitri insisted he wear.

Dimitri shrugged. He had done his best to prevent panic among the neighbors.

"Caught a feisty one, eh?" Rurik demanded, a curious

glint in his blue eyes. Dimitri had never brought a woman to this house.

"Not intentionally," Dimitri gritted, entering the marble foyer and headed directly toward the massive cedar staircase that had been hand carved. "Now I must decide what is to be done with her."

"The dungeon is currently empty," Rurik offered.

Dimitri smiled down at the furious woman tucked in his arms.

"A temptation I must admit, but for the moment I will content myself with an undisturbed privacy. Would you ensure that dinner is prepared and kept warm in the kitchen?"

"Of course."

Emma's eyes widened as she turned her head to watch Rurik stride toward the back of the house.

"Wait." She jerked back to meet his amused expression as Rurik disappeared. "I see you have your servants trained to ignore the pleas of the poor women you kidnap."

Dimitri climbed the stairs, fully enjoying the sensation of Emma cradled in his arms.

"Rurik needed no training. He was a pirate who terrorized the seas until he was captured by the French during the war."

"If he was captured then what is he doing here?"

He reached the upper landing and headed directly for the main saloon.

"I take exception to fine Russian citizens being tortured by that French imposter."

She made a choked sound of disbelief. "You snuck into Napoleon's prison?"

"There are few men more loyal than those who have been rescued from the guillotine. And, of course, his wife happens to be the finest cook in the empire. When she promised her services in exchange for her husband's freedom I could not resist."

Her eyes narrowed, obviously suspecting the danger Dimitri had risked sneaking into the brutal French prison despite his nonchalant tone. Thankfully, her probing questions died on her lips as he stepped into the long saloon.

A tiny gasp escaped her as she studied the coved ceiling with gilded rosettes that framed the line of crystal chandeliers. The walls were covered in emerald satin panels with marble columns set between the high arched windows. The furniture had been purchased from the finest Russian craftsmen as had the parquet floor that was inlaid with cherry and teak. In all, it was a room that spoke of refined elegance.

"What is this place?" she asked as he settled her on the gold settee beside the massive black marble fireplace.

He moved to light the logs already stacked in the fireplace, chuckling at her astonished tone.

"My home."

"*Your* home?"

Turning, he leaned against the carved mantel and regarded her with a lift of his brows.

"Despite the rumors, I do not crawl from the pits of hell each evening."

She waved a hand toward the delicate jade figurines perched on a satinwood table.

"This hardly suits the image of the Beggar Czar."

"True—" he shrugged "—which is why I have several residences spread throughout the city. Each of them serve their own specific purpose."

"And what purpose does this residence serve? Your private brothel?"

"If that were true it would be an abysmal failure."

She jerked as if he had slapped her. "I suppose that is yet another insult at my lack of attractiveness?"

He frowned, prowling toward the settee. Was the woman demented? She was the most tempting, most exquisitely beautiful female he had ever encountered.

"On the contrary, *moya dusha,* it is the highest compliment." He sat on the cushion next to her stiff body, turning to study her wounded hazel eyes. "You are the only female beyond my cook to ever step over the threshold. In fact, there are less than a handful of people who even know of this house. I come here when I desire to be alone."

"Then why have you brought me here?"

With experienced ease, he reached to unbutton her cloak, tossing it aside, not at all surprised to discover her swathed in yet another layer of brown wool beneath.

"A dangerous question, Emma Linley-Kirov."

He felt her shiver as he turned his attention to the buttons that lined the gown from her chin to beneath the soft swell of her bosom.

"For goodness' sake, what are you doing?"

His blood heated as he slowly peeled back the heavy material to reveal the satin beauty beneath.

"Attempting to understand why you would believe for a moment I find you lacking in appeal."

"You have accused me of being a shrill-tongued spinster, a selfish martyr—" Her recriminations faded to a breathless sigh when he pressed his lips to the base of her throat.

"A delectable innocent who I have imagined unwrapping from your woolen layers a hundred times."

Her hands lifted to lie against his chest, but she made no effort to push him away.

"You complained when I did not hide myself."

"Of course." He stroked his lips to the hollow beneath her ear, his fingers continuing to unbutton the body of her gown. "Only I am allowed to enjoy your most intimate beauty."

"I think you enjoy mocking me."

"If you need proof of my desire I am happy to oblige."

"That is not—" She squeaked in alarm as he effortlessly pressed her back onto the cushions of the settee, following downward to cover her with his larger body. "Oh. Good Lord."

Good Lord, indeed.

## CHAPTER EIGHT

EMMA KNEW SHE WAS IN trouble as soon as he claimed her lips in a kiss that seared her to the tips of her toes. She was aware of being lowered to the cushions, and the pleasant sensation of his hard body pressed to her softer curves. More distantly, she could feel the friction of the wool gown as it was pulled slowly, yet relentlessly down her body. But the fear that should have had her shoving him away was overwhelmed by the excitement that jolted through her.

Clutching at his shoulders, she quivered as his tongue traced the seam of her lips, silently encouraging them to part. Hesitantly, she opened her mouth, shocked as he dipped his tongue between her lips. He tasted of cognac and danger, a heady combination that made her heart race.

Over and over he plundered her willing lips, his tongue tangling with hers in a beautiful dance.

She heard him groan, his hands expertly loosening her curls and gently spreading them across the cushions beneath her. His touch was tender, but she sensed the fierce hunger under the surface. It was etched in the taut muscles beneath her hands and the harsh rasp of his breath.

She shifted beneath him, her fingers biting into his shoulders. What was the odd restlessness that was plaguing her? The sense that her body was seeking a fulfillment that only Dimitri could offer?

"So sweet," he murmured, his lips drifting down the line of her jaw.

She instinctively tilted back her head, offering her throat to his skillful kisses.

"This is insanity," she muttered.

"Delectable madness," he readily agreed, his hands lowering to cup the soft swell of her breasts.

Emma shuddered in shocked pleasure, realizing her gown had been tugged down to her waist, revealing the plain shift she wore beneath. She could feel the heat of his hand branding through the thin material and when he bent his head to cover a straining nipple with his mouth, she nearly screamed. Dear Lord. The feel of the damp linen and the rough stroke of his tongue grazing her sensitive nipple were sending tiny darts of bliss through her.

She had never suspected a man's touch could offer such exquisite pleasure. Or that her body would respond with an aching need that overrode the whispers of alarm in the back of her mind.

"Dimitri?"

"Yes, *moya dusha*," he softly assured her, his lips continuing to torment her breasts as his hands slid beneath her, subtly tugging her heavy skirt upward. "Allow me to please you."

She trembled at the heady sensations that swirled through her. She felt as giddy as if she had drunk an entire bottle of champagne.

A moan was wrenched from her throat as Dimitri's slender fingers delved beneath her skirt to stroke up the back of her legs. Lightly, he traced the top edge of her stockings, making her lower stomach clench with a sharp pang of need.

Oh, this was…astonishing.

Her eyes squeezed shut as she instinctively allowed her legs to part. She could feel the hard thrust of his arousal against her hip and hear his fractured breathing as he buried his face in the curve of her neck, but nothing mattered apart from those clever fingers.

Allowing her hands to tangle in the thick satin of his

hair, she unconsciously arched her back, seeking relief from the tension coiling deep inside.

There had to be something...

"Please, Dimitri," she choked, not certain what she needed, but sensing he would understand.

As if capable of reading her mind, Dimitri brushed his fingers upward, seeking her damp cleft. At the same moment, he shifted to cover her mouth in a kiss that smothered her shocked scream of exhilaration.

Oh, yes, he understood perfectly.

Forgetting the necessity of breathing, Emma became lost in Dimitri's touch. With obvious experience he stroked his fingers through her moist heat, discovering a small spot that seemed to be the center of her pleasure.

Relentlessly, he continued his intimate caresses, his kisses becoming more demanding as her body tightened with a tension that was near painful. Her hands gripped his hair, her hips lifting of their own volition to meet his steady strokes.

She was straining toward an elusive peak, shivering as if she were in the throes of a fever. And then, just when she was certain she could bear no more, the pressure exploded, shattering through her with stunning force.

Dazed by the unfamiliar sensations, Emma lay shuddering beneath Dimitri, distantly aware of the soothing words he whispered in her ear.

How often had she assured herself that she was missing nothing by keeping men at arm's length? That she was content to remain a virginal spinster?

Only now did she realize just how bleak and lonely the endless nights were destined to be.

She shivered, her hands shifting to press against his chest with a sense of urgency.

"Dimitri, get up."

Slowly, he pulled back, studying her flushed face with

a brooding gaze. His lips thinned as he easily read the panic threatening to overtake her. He leaned down to steal a frustrated kiss before he straightened and watched her awkwardly tug her gown back into place.

Emma was acutely aware of his unwavering attention as she fumbled with her buttons and shoved the thick tumble of hair out of her face. His dark, beautiful features were tightly composed, but it was his unyielding scrutiny that made her shift uneasily into the corner of the settee.

A tense silence filled the saloon, then with a sharp motion Dimitri was on his feet and heading toward the door.

"Remain here."

Did she truly have a choice?

Emma lowered her head into her hands, attempting to sort through her baffled emotions. She was embarrassed, of course. She had behaved as a wanton in Dimitri's arms and he had every right to consider her no better than a tart. But the regret she should have felt was decidedly absent.

Indeed, there was a traitorous part of her that savored the vivid memories of Dimitri's every touch and caress, as if they were treasures she intended to harbor deep in her heart.

The thought was more unnerving than being trapped alone in this elegant house with a lawless scoundrel who could make her melt with a smile.

With a shake of her head, Emma shoved away her bewilderment and wrapped herself in the cool composure she had forged and tempered by a life of hardship. She would have ample opportunity to dwell on her reaction to Dimitri when she returned to her home.

For all that mattered now was finding the means to follow her sister to England.

She was busy sifting through her limited possibilities

when Dimitri returned to the saloon, a large tray balanced in his hands.

Her brows lifted in surprise as he set his burden on the low table in front of the settee. Good heavens, did Dimitri's cook prepare such a massive dinner every night?

Her stomach rumbled as her gaze took in the roasted veal, the pickled cucumbers and the traditional pancakes stuffed with mushrooms and rice. To drink there was a bottle of *medovukha* that had been made with honey, and for dessert were plates of *syrniki*, fried fritters garnished with sour cream and jam.

"I trust you are hungry?" Dimitri demanded, settling next to her and filling two plates with the delectable meal. "Irina left us a small feast."

She frowned. "I cannot remain here for dinner."

"You have a pressing engagement?" he demanded, forcing the plate into her unwilling hands.

Her mouth went dry as she glanced at his absurdly handsome face. During his absence Dimitri had removed his jacket and waistcoat, revealing the fine lawn shirt that was thin enough to hint at the muscular chest. His raven hair was still ruffled from her frantic fingers and the shadow of whiskers darkened his jaw. With his eyes glimmering like liquid gold in the candlelight he had never appeared more dangerous. Or beautiful.

"Vanya will be expecting me."

"I sent word that her little chick would be returned safely to her nest."

Her teeth clenched at his arrogance, a heat staining her cheeks.

"And, of course, it did not occur to you that I might not wish to have all of St. Petersburg know that I am here alone with a man?" she asked tartly.

He regarded her with mocking disbelief. "You have

flouted every rule of decorum since leaving your home and now you are concerned for your reputation?"

"It is enough that I must be a source of amusement, I will not also be considered a—"

She bit off her words, belatedly noticing the flare of fury in Dimitri's eyes.

"A whore?" he silkily demanded.

Her gaze lowered to the plate still clutched in her hands, regretting the painful reminder of his mother. No matter how angry Dimitri might make her, she deeply respected the woman who had sacrificed her life for him.

"Please, let me go," she whispered.

He heaved an explosive sigh, ramming his fingers through his tangled hair.

"Emma, there is no need to agitate yourself," he said, his voice carefully controlled. "Vanya is quite proud to be regarded as the most unconventional woman in all of St. Petersburg. She would approve of you doing whatever necessary to find your sister. And as for my servants…" He shrugged. "They would walk through the pits of hell before they revealed my secrets. There will be no one to judge you or what we choose to do in the privacy of my home."

"I still would prefer—"

"Why would you believe you are a source of amusement?" he overrode her, studying her with an unnerving intensity.

"Surely you must realize that young, unwed females are expected to remain in their proper place, not intruding into men's business by opening a coaching inn?"

"And how do they propose a proper female support herself and her sister?"

She shrugged. "I could beg on the streets or—"

"Or?" he prompted.

"Or accept a discreet arrangement with the local baron."

A murderous anger tightened his elegant features, reminding Emma he was a ruthless bastard who was rumored to cut off the hands of his victims.

"Give me his name."

"His name?"

"The baron who insulted you."

She shivered at his frozen tone. "Why?"

"I will kill him."

Her heart missed a beat. Despite the pain that Baron Kostya had inflicted, she had no desire to be responsible for his death.

"Is that not rather hypocritical?" She deflected his question. "You seemed eager enough to take me to your bed."

"I will take you wherever you want, but only if our desire is mutual." His eyes narrowed. "I do not use sex as a price to assist a woman in need."

She believed him. She doubted there was a woman born who would not tumble into his arms if given the opportunity. Not that she would ever give him the satisfaction of knowing just how irresistible she found him.

His arrogance was quite outrageous enough.

"Do you intend to take me to Vanya's?"

"After we have finished." He cut a piece of the tender veal and pressed it between her lips. "You cannot allow Irina's exquisite creations to go to waste."

She nearly moaned as the flavor of the succulent meat exploded on her tongue. Now she understood why a man would risk a French prison to earn the services of Rurik's wife in his kitchen. She was a genius.

Of course, she did not believe for a moment that was why Dimitri had risked his neck.

For a criminal he possessed a loyalty and honor that was far superior to most supposed nobles.

With a sigh, she conceded defeat, her hunger overcoming her common sense.

"Were you never taught the meaning of the word *no?*" she asked between bites.

He set about eating his own dinner. "I can't seem to recall. Perhaps you should remind me."

She shook her head. "I do not believe you are so desperate for a dinner companion. What is it you truly want?"

The golden gaze flared down her body with a tangible heat. "Never doubt my desire for your companionship, Emma Linley-Kirov."

She shivered as a heady excitement pierced through her. Already she desired the feel of his skillful hands; his warm, seeking lips…

She abruptly set aside her nearly empty plate. "And you have no other motive?"

"We need to discuss what you overhead between my father and Tarvek."

It was, of course, precisely what she had expected. For reasons she did not comprehend, Dimitri was under the mistaken notion he was at liberty to interfere in her life.

"What is there to discuss?" She conjured a meaningless smile. "I revealed all that I heard. Do you believe I am attempting to conceal information from you?"

"I am more interested in what you intend to do."

"At the moment it appears I have little choice but to share your dinner."

He made an impatient sound, his fingers cupping her chin and forcing her to meet his searching gaze.

"What I most admire about you, *moya dusha,* is your refusal to pretend you are less than intelligent. Do not begin now."

The edge in his voice warned he would have the truth from her, no matter how long it might take. Aggravating ass. She defensively squared her shoulders.

"I told you from the beginning what I intend to do," she grudgingly admitted. "I came to St. Petersburg to find my sister and nothing has changed."

His jaw knotted as he struggled to control his temper. "Not even you can be foolish enough to believe you can travel alone to London?"

"Why should I not?" she countered. "I speak perfect English and I have distant relatives I can contact should the need arise. Besides, I am certain Vanya must possess some acquaintance who intends to travel to England or even to Europe within the next few weeks." She folded her hands in her lap, her spine stiff with determination. "I am willing to become a companion or maid or whatever they might need."

"Whatever they might need?" he rasped.

"Within reason."

His bronzed features were rigid as Dimitri studied her with an expression of furious disbelief.

"Emma, you are not stupid. You must realize how vulnerable you would be traveling with strangers?" His fingers tightened. "What will you do when a bored husband decides you will offer a convenient diversion during the long voyage? Or when one of the sailors captures you alone?"

She forced herself to meet the blazing golden gaze without flinching. Dimitri Tipova might be the unquestionable leader of the St. Petersburg underworld, but he had no authority over her.

"A woman is always at risk of being abused by men, no matter where she is or what her station."

He arrogantly peered down the length of his nose. "Not if she is protected as she should be."

"I have learned to protect myself, Dimitri."

"Only because you had no other choice." His fingers eased their grip to brush over her pale cheek. "Now I offer you one."

Her eyes narrowed. "What precisely do you offer?"

"Stay here with me."

"As your mistress?"

He gently outlined her unsteady lips. "Call it what you will."

"And my sister?"

Concentrating on his tender caresses, Dimitri was seemingly oblivious to the dangerous sparks smoldering in her eyes.

"I will send my men to follow the *Katherine Marie* and rescue your sister."

"Tell me, Dimitri, if I refuse to become your mistress will you allow my sister to become another tragic victim of your father?"

He muttered an angry curse, leaning down until they were nose to nose.

"I told you that I do not barter for sex, Emma. With or without you in my bed I intend to capture my father's ship and return it to Russia so I can expose those involved."

Her stomach fluttered as his breath brushed her lips. A distant part of her understood the danger of provoking this man. Another part, however, was hurt and angered by his refusal to accept her desperate need to take part in rescuing her sister.

"So you can have your revenge?" she accused.

"Of course."

"While my sister—"

"Will be safely escorted to her home along with any other victims," he muttered, his fingers tangling in her hair as his lips skimmed down the line of her throat.

Her heart leaped with a treacherous excitement. "Dimitri."

"Yes, *milaya?*"

"What are you doing?"

He nuzzled the pulse that hammered at the base of her

throat. "I do not particularly care for your implications that my only means of persuading you to share my bed is with blackmail."

Her toes curled in her sensible boots, her body humming with sizzling awareness. Desperately, she pressed her hands against the hard muscles of his chest. This explosive reaction to Dimitri Tipova was a danger she did not know how to battle.

"I will not be distracted."

"If you believe all I desire is to distract you, then you are even more naive than I suspected." He breathed against her sensitive skin.

"No, Dimitri." She arched away from the tormenting kisses. "It is past time that I return to Vanya's."

The golden eyes narrowed, a slash of color staining his high cheekbones.

"We have not finished our discussion."

"I did not realize we were sharing a discussion. It seemed very much as if you were issuing orders and expecting me to obey them."

His brooding gaze lowered to study her lips. "If you will recall, I also offered you an invitation."

Her pulse gave an eager leap at the memory of his words. Despite her innocence she recognized the touch of a master. Dimitri would be an exciting, skillful, wholly consuming lover. The sort of lover that women would sacrifice husbands, riches, social standing—and all they possess to claim.

He would also be forceful and overbearing and convinced he would always know what was best for those under his protection. He would demand that she give away her hard-earned independence and that was a sacrifice she was unable to make.

Not when he would soon enough lose interest and leave

her to salvage her tattered life. She had been abandoned too many times to risk yet another loss.

Before he could guess her intent, Emma was shoving him away so she could hastily rise to her feet.

"The same invitation that I have turned down from other gentlemen who promised to protect me…"

"Do not compare me to that bastard." He fiercely overrode her words, his eyes blazing with frustration.

"Then do not insult me by treating me as if I am a foolish chit who must depend upon a man to survive." Collecting her cloak, she headed for the door. As humiliating as it might be to admit, she could not trust herself when Dimitri was near. One touch and she was lost. "I am perfectly capable of caring for myself and my sister."

She had reached the door when Dimitri was blocking her path, his hands reaching to grip her shoulders.

"Where do you think you are going?"

"To Vanya's." Emma tilted back her head, forcing herself to meet his dark glower. "I will walk if necessary."

His fingers tightened, his temper at the breaking point.

"Do not be a fool. My carriage will return you to Vanya."

"Thank you."

He hauled her against his chest, swooping down to kiss her with a brazen hunger.

"I will allow you to flee in fear tonight, but make no mistake, *moya dusha,* you are destined to become my lover," he murmured against her swollen lips. "And not because you need my assistance, or because I have forced you to my bed."

Dizzy from the pleasure of his kiss, Emma struggled to think clearly.

"Then why?"

"Because I have tasted your passion. You desire me."

His hand skimmed down her back, deliberately pressing her against the proof of his arousal. "Desperately."

Her mouth went dry, her heart thundering in her chest. "Good Lord. Your conceit is astounding."

A humorless smile tugged at his lips. "No more astounding than your ridiculous attempts to pretend you do not ache to be in my arms."

It was the biting truth of his words that gave her the strength to wrench out of his grasp and scurry down the hallway. She might yearn to melt in his arms, but she was not a fool.

At least, not a complete fool.

"Goodbye, Dimitri Tipova," she muttered.

"À bientôt," he called, his voice mocking.

It wasn't until she was safely stowed in Dimitri's carriage that she realized he had warned he would see her again rather than saying goodbye.

THE ST. PETERSBURG DOCK was bustling with activity as Vanya's carriage headed toward the end of a wharf where a sleek wooden vessel swayed on the white-capped waves. Winter was swiftly approaching and soon it would be only the staunchest sailors who would brave the frigid, buffeting waters of the Baltic. In the meantime, there was a frantic pace as sailors, merchants, dockhands and passengers darted among the looming stacks of cargo waiting to be loaded on the various ships.

Emma was relieved to leave the majority of the crowd behind as they halted near the edge of the water. It was unsettling enough to board a ship and sail so far from home without adding the worry of battling through the crowds.

Licking her dry lips, she peered out the window at the waiting ship.

When she had returned to Vanya's home three nights before, she had revealed all she had learned of her sister, as well as Dimitri's suspicion that Anya was being taken to London. The older woman had been sympathetic, but surprisingly reluctant to assist Emma in finding a means of following Count Nevskaya's ship.

Then yesterday morning, she had come to Emma's private chambers and revealed she had booked passage upon a ship bound for London. Emma had been caught between overwhelming relief and a natural fear at charging into the unknown. For all her pretense of courage, she was not indifferent to the many dangers that lurked once she left the protection of Vanya and Herrick Gerhardt.

And oddly, there had been a strange sense of regret.

She tried to tell herself that it was merely a reaction to the thought of traveling so far from home, but she knew she was not being entirely honest. That bothersome ache in the center of her heart was directly connected to Dimitri Tipova.

Damn his aggravating soul.

Hastily thrusting aside the unnerving thought, Emma turned her head to meet Vanya's searching gaze, managing to conjure a smile of appreciation.

"I do not know how to thank you, Vanya," she said, reaching across to pat the older woman's hand. "You have been so extraordinarily generous. It will take time to repay you, but I swear—"

"Nonsense," Vanya firmly interrupted, seemingly embarrassed by Emma's excessive gratitude. "You are not the only one who cares what happens to those poor girls, Emma. And if I were a few years younger I would be traveling to England at your side. As it is, I know that you possess the courage and strength to do whatever necessary to rescue your sister and the others."

Emma straightened, unashamedly pleased by Vanya's words. At least someone appreciated her determination, she told herself, smoothing her hand down her thick woolen cloak.

"Thank you."

"But you must promise that you will take the greatest care and quickly return to me," she urged. "Herrick Gerhardt will have my head upon a platter when he discovers I assisted you in leaving the country."

Emma hid her tiny shiver of fear. She would be strong for Anya. She had no choice.

"I promise."

"And this is the letter of introduction I promised. I have written to Leonida, so I trust she will have ensured there will be someone awaiting you at the London docks, but in the event you find yourself in need, you can use this to call upon assistance from the Russian Embassy."

Emma unsteadily tucked the envelope into the pocket of her cloak. Seated across from her, Vanya appeared to be yet another useless lady of society with her teal merino gown and pale fur shawl wrapped about her shoulders. But she had proven to be a woman with intelligence and compassion and an ability to take command when necessary. Emma could only hope she did not disappoint the older woman.

"This is so much more than I ever expected." She bit her bottom lip as she struggled to hold back a ridiculous urge to weep. "I do not know what to say."

Vanya leaned forward to gently pat Emma's knee that was currently hidden beneath several yards of brown wool.

"You do not always have to depend on yourself, Emma," she implored. "Accepting help from others does not make you weak."

Emma frowned, puzzled by the woman's peculiar manner. "I am accustomed to taking care of myself."

"As was I, but I have discovered that my independence was not nearly so threatened as I feared it would be when I

opened my heart to another." She appeared as if she desired
to say more, but as they both caught sight of the large man
attired in the rough clothing of a common sailor, she instead
settled back in the leather seat. "I believe this young man
is here to assist with your bags and to escort you to the
ship."

Emma sucked in a deep breath, refusing to acknowledge
the flutters of fear in the pit of her stomach.

"I will never forget what you have done for me."

"Hmm." Vanya shook her head. "I am not entirely certain that is a good thing."

"Vanya?"

"Just know that I have tried to do what I think best for
you."

"Of course, I know. I could not have asked for a greater
friend."

The door to the carriage was pulled open by Vanya's
driver and without giving herself time to hesitate, she
allowed herself to be assisted into the chill morning
breeze.

"Be brave, *mon enfant*," Vanya called softly.

# CHAPTER NINE

DIMITRI IGNORED THE shifting deck beneath his feet as he poured over the charts his first mate had spread across the bench.

It was not his first journey aboard his sleek Baltimore clipper. He occasionally felt the need to escape from the grinding demands of his role as Beggar Czar. There were few things more exhilarating than skimming across the water, surrounded by silence, and knowing that his duties were being left far behind.

Not that he had made such a large investment for the rare days of freedom. He was a businessman first and foremost. The ship had been built in the Americas to be the fastest on the waters and his crew had been hired in London from among the finest of all English seamen. As a result, he had made a small fortune in transporting various diplomats, noblemen, and even a few wealthy merchants who preferred to keep their travels confidential.

Which made it perfect for his current plans.

A grim smile curved his lips at the sound of approaching footsteps, and turning his head he waited for the large sailor with a thatch of black hair and weathered features to halt in front of him.

"Is our passenger aboard?" he demanded.

Andrew Simmons scowled, his hands shoved into the pockets of his wool coat.

"Safely stowed in her cabin as you ordered."

Dimitri narrowed his gaze. "You have no need to remind

me that you disapprove of having a female aboard the ship."

"Every sailor knows a wench is bad luck."

Although several stones lighter than the hulking sailor, Dimitri stepped forward, his hand deliberately caressing the handle of his dagger he had tucked into the waistband of his breeches.

"Andrew, allow me to offer a warning that you will share with the rest of the crew," he said with a lethal softness.

The man blanched. "Aye, sir?"

"Emma Linley-Kirov is an honored guest on this ship and if I discover a member of my crew has offered her anything less than utter respect they will be tossed overboard and left for the fish to enjoy. Do you comprehend?"

Sweat glistened on Andrew's forehead despite the noticeable chill in the air.

"Aye."

"Good. It would be unfortunate if there were any misunderstandings."

"There will be no misunderstandings."

"Then I believe we are ready to cast off."

"At once."

Stumbling over his own feet in his haste to obey Dimitri's command, Andrew headed toward the bow of the ship. Dimitri watched his departure as he regained command of his temper.

He had not been boasting. He would personally punish any man who dared to offer Emma an insult.

Refusing to consider why he still itched to pummel the large sailor, Dimitri at last turned on his heel and made his way to the lower cabins. With each step his annoyance transformed into a burgeoning sense of anticipation.

The past three days had been sheer hell. His empire might be made of thieves and scoundrels, but that did not make his responsibilities any less demanding. He had to ensure all his various businesses were operating smoothly before leaving the country. And of course, there had been the constant concern that Emma might foolishly attempt to slip away before he had completed his plans. The woman was as unpredictable as she was stubborn.

Most disturbing of all, however, had been the sleepless nights he had paced the floor of his bedchamber, his body on fire with the need to have Emma in his arms.

His pace quickened as he pushed open the door to his private cabin and stripped off his heavy coat, tossing it on the wide bunk. The room was built along the same sleek lines as the ship with table and chairs beneath the port hole and a chest of drawers attached to the paneled wall. He paused long enough to straighten his dove-gray jacket before heading toward the door that opened into the connecting cabin.

For a moment he stood in the doorway, his gaze unerringly finding Emma's slender body poised in front of the port hole as she watched St. Petersburg disappear into the mist. He would be able to sense her presence if he were blind.

The cabin was similar in design to his own, although constructed on a smaller scale as befitted a servant. Not that it mattered. Emma's place was at his side. And in his bed. And that was exactly where she was headed.

He stepped forward, his blood heating despite the ugly brown gown that offended his senses. He knew precisely what was hidden beneath the woolen layers.

"Surely you cannot be missing your home so soon?" he asked.

He heard Emma's gasp of horror as she spun around to regard him with an expression of stark disbelief.

*"You."*

Strolling forward, he flicked a finger over her pale cheek. "Yes, it is I."

Her lips parted, but it took a moment before she could speak.

"What are you doing here?" she at last managed.

"I did warn you that I intended to hunt down the *Katherine Marie*."

"No, you said you would send one of your servants in search of the ship."

His fingers shifted to tug the pins from her hair, breathing deeply of her warm scent as the honey curls tumbled about her shoulders. It did not matter if she were dressed in rags—she was the most beautiful woman he had ever seen.

"Ah, well, that was when I had hopes of a warm, delectable female to keep me distracted."

He felt her tremble, but her hazel eyes flashed with a predictable fury.

"And you wish me to believe that it was mere coincidence that you happened to choose the same ship as I did?"

"It is not so difficult to comprehend." He threaded his fingers through her hair, his body swaying in tempo with hers as the ship left the harbor and headed into open water. "This is the only ship currently bound for England that accepts passengers."

"And the cabin that connects to mine was the only one available?"

His lips twitched. "That is rather more difficult to explain."

"Yes, I can imagine it would be." She narrowed her eyes. "Not that it truly matters."

"No?"

"I will simply request that the captain offer me a different cabin."

"You believe there are an endless number of rooms aboard such a small vessel?" he taunted.

A dull flush stained her cheeks. "Of course not, but there must be one passenger who will be willing to exchange cabins."

He smiled wryly at her naiveté. "I would not be so certain."

"Your arrogance is truly astonishing, Dimitri Tipova," she snapped, her hands pressing against his chest. "You might be in command of St. Petersburg, but you have no authority aboard this ship."

He wrapped an arm around her waist and tugged her close, swallowing a groan as he accepted just how perfectly she fit against him.

"You should learn never to underestimate me, *moya dusha*."

She stiffened, a frown marring her brow. "And what is that supposed to mean?"

"It means that any pleas to the captain will fall on deaf ears."

"You cannot be that certain, unless…"

"Unless, what?" he softly prompted.

"Unless you have already bribed him?"

"There were no bribes, but considering the fact that I do pay his wages I should hope his loyalty would be to me." His gaze slowly roamed over her upturned face. "Of course, he has always possessed a weakness for beautiful women so perhaps we should not put him in such an uncomfortable position."

In the distance the sound of the rough shouts and boots pounding against the deck echoed through the air, but within the narrow cabin Dimitri was aware of nothing beyond the play of emotions that rippled across Emma's face.

"You pay his wages?"

"I pay the wages of the entire crew."

She licked her lips. "Why would you do that?"

"You know why, Emma."

The color leeched from her cheeks as she slowly began to realize she was completely and utterly in his power.

"This is your ship."

There was an uncomfortable tug on his heart as he gazed down at her pale, vulnerable face and the wide hazel eyes that were dark with apprehension. His jaw clenched with regret. Dammit, did she fear him? And why did the thought trouble him? Surely the stubborn female needed to be taught the dangers of her reckless behavior?

He shoved aside his momentary weakness and hardened his determination.

"It is."

She shook her head. "This is madness."

"My father is not the only man capable of owning a private fleet, although mine is considerably larger and far superior in design." A grim smile curved his lips. "With any luck at all we should reach London before the *Katherine Marie* docks."

"If you expect me to be impressed, then you are far off the mark."

Dimitri swallowed a sigh at her tart tone. How many women had fallen to their knees and tearfully praised him for his assistance? How many had offered whatever he desired in payment of his services?

"I am becoming resigned to your lack of appreciation for my stunning achievements," he dryly admitted, "but you could occasionally offer some well-deserved words of gratitude."

"Gratitude?" She jerked as if he had slapped her. "For what? For deceiving me? For luring me onto this ship under false pretenses?" There was a sharp pause, her hazel eyes darkening with pain. "Oh, my God."

"Now what?"

"Vanya knew this was your ship." She glared at him as

if he were responsible for the older woman's decision to conceal the truth from her. And…he was. He had insisted that no one know that he was in pursuit of his father's boat. Or that Emma was traveling with him. He would not risk alerting Count Nevskaya that he was in danger of having his sins revealed. "She was a part of your plot. How could she betray my trust? I thought she was my friend."

Gathering her hair in his fist, he tugged the satin strands until her head tilted back, revealing the flashing hazel eyes and the lush temptation of her lips.

"It is because she is your friend that she is determined to protect you," he growled.

He was tired of battling this woman. He wanted her in his bed. He wanted her beneath him as he parted her legs and sank into her feminine heat with a deep, hungry pace that would tumble them both into paradise.

As if sensing the sudden tension in the air, Emma sucked in an unsteady breath, a visible pulse fluttering at the base of her throat.

"By putting me at the mercy of a ruthless criminal?"

"At my mercy, eh?" Unable to resist temptation, Dimitri leaned down to touch his lips to that revealing pulse. "Mmm. Now that is a delicious notion."

Her hands pressed against his chest. "Dimitri."

"Yes, *milaya?*"

"I demand that you return this ship to St. Petersburg at once."

He nipped her sensitive skin, a smile curving his lips as she trembled in pleasure.

"Do you truly believe you are in a position to demand anything?"

"I mean it, Dimitri. Return me to St. Petersburg or—"

"Or what?" he challenged. "You will swim back to Russia?"

She arched her back, clearly attempting to avoid his

seeking lips. "Do not mock me. I will never forgive Vanya."

Pulling back, he studied her sulky expression, his fingers covertly unfastening the buttons that ran the length of her spine. He needed to feel the warm satin of her skin.

"Vanya is considerably older and far more experienced than you. Can you not accept she made a choice she thought best?" he coaxed. "And that she simply desired to protect you?"

"I can protect myself," she muttered.

His teeth clenched at her stubborn refusal to admit she needed him. Why did she have to be so damnably independent?

"Truly?" he rasped, easing the heavy gown down her body. "You have just admitted you are at the mercy of a ruthless scoundrel. And you have no one to blame but yourself."

Intent on their argument, Emma appeared unaware of his skillful disrobement, not even when the gown was pooled around her feet.

"I trusted Vanya," she hissed.

"You have relied upon blind luck since arriving in St. Petersburg." His gaze searing over her slender body. "And if not for the kindness of Herrick Gerhardt and Vanya you most likely would be a captive with your sister upon my father's ship or already sold to a brothel."

"And instead I am trapped with you."

Trapped? Could she possibly be more insulting?

He would prove that for all her spitting fire, she was eager to be *trapped* with him. Pressing her back against his body, he yanked at the ribbons that held up her linen shift.

"I could easily have ensured that you remained in St. Petersburg or were even returned to your tiny village," he rasped.

He heard her breath catch as his fingers skimmed the bare skin of her shoulders, her hands digging into his chest and a beautiful color returning to her cheeks.

"I was brought to this ship under false pretenses," she accused.

"Do you wish to rescue your sister or not?"

"Of course I do."

"Then put aside your ridiculous pride and accept that you are far more likely to bring Anya safely home with my assistance."

"It is not pride."

"No?"

Her lips tightened at his mocking tone. "I do not appreciate being manipulated."

And Dimitri did not appreciate desiring this woman with a consuming hunger that would not leave him in peace. If he had any sense he would have left Emma Linley-Kirov in St. Petersburg and concentrated on capturing the *Katherine Marie* so he could at last destroy his father.

Muttering a curse beneath his breath, he scooped her off her feet and headed toward the connecting door.

"It would not be necessary if you would be reasonable."

She squirmed in his arms, her eyes wide with shock. "What are you doing?"

"Taking you to our cabin."

"I have my own cabin."

He glared down at the face that had haunted his nights and intruded into his thoughts at the most inconvenient moments. He had not left her in St. Petersburg because he was unwilling to be parted from her. Annoying, but true.

"You belong with me."

With a frown, she smacked her hand against his chest. "You cannot simply decide I belong to you, Dimitri Tipova.

I am a person, not a bit of property you can collect and toss aside when you weary of me."

"How the hell am I supposed to weary of you?" He spread her across the narrow bed, his hands oddly awkward as he yanked off his jacket and waistcoat. His cravat and linen shirt followed. "You plague me no matter how I attempt to rid you from my mind."

She brushed aside the thick honey curls that tumbled across her face, her eyes widening with a wary excitement as he perched on the edge of the mattress and tugged off his boots.

"And you blame me?"

Shifting, Dimitri ran a hand over her slender foot and up the back of her calf, inching the thin shift upward and exposing the slender leg covered in a white silk stocking. Her undergarments were predictably prim, but ridiculously the sight of them made his gut clench with a savage lust.

He had tasted the delights of the most skilled courtesans throughout Russia and Europe, but while they had been delightful diversions, they had never made him so desperate to have them in his arms that he was willing to kidnap them.

"Of course I blame you," he husked, his fingers reaching the silken skin of her thigh at the top of her stocking. He groaned, his arousal heavy with a painful need.

Her eyes darkened with an awareness that slammed into him with potent force.

"For what?"

Beyond reasonable thought, Dimitri reached for her shift, ripping it from bodice to hem with one easy motion. She muttered something beneath her breath, but Dimitri barely noticed. Instead, he was lost in the beauty of her slender, perfect body.

The air was squeezed from his lungs as his gaze swept over her, the pink-tipped mounds of her breasts, the tiny span of her waist, and the sweet honey curls that hid the source of her most intimate pleasure.

"For daring to challenge me," he managed to rasp.

"I have done nothing but attempt to rescue my sister," she breathed, her tone distracted as Dimitri slowly lowered himself on the bed beside her. "You are the one who continues to interfere despite my pleas to be left alone."

He framed her face in his hands, his lips skimming over her flushed face.

"And that is what you desire? To be left alone?"

"Yes."

He chuckled as her hands instinctively smoothed over his bare chest, her body arching toward him in unmistakable invitation.

"I do not believe you."

"I…" Her words broke off with a shuddering sigh as his mouth traveled down the curve of her throat and feathered light kisses ever lower. "Oh, Lord."

His tongue circled the straining bud of her nipple. "Tell me again what you desire."

She cried out, her fingers shoving into his hair as she shifted restlessly beneath him.

"Dimitri."

"Do you wish me to halt?"

"No. God, no."

Raw relief surged through his body. He might very well have tossed himself overboard if she'd denied him.

With a driven groan, he suckled her nipple, peeling away what remained of her shift. She tasted of soap and sweet innocence and Dimitri cursed as he battled to remove the remainder of his clothing, his hands shaking. He was infamous throughout St. Petersburg as a skilled, talented lover willing to devote hours to a woman's pleasure.

At last rid of his clothing, he settled on the mattress and smoothed his hands down Emma's back, easing her toward his aching body. She briefly tensed, no doubt unnerved by the feel of his erection pressed against her lower stomach, but with a soft moan of capitulation she speared her fingers through his hair and urged his mouth toward the tight buds of her breasts.

Fiercely pleased to comply with her silent demand, Dimitri tugged her nipple between his lips, using his teeth and tongue until she was squirming with pleasure against him. His hands slid over the curve of her buttock and down the back of her thigh. With a small tug he had her leg draped over his hip, allowing his cock to press against her damp heat.

Raw lust slammed into him at the sensation of her warm, silken skin brushing against him, stealing his breath and making him quiver. Restlessly, he turned his attention to her other breast.

"Sweet Emma," he groaned, "I need you."

"Please, Dimitri."

He chuckled as his hand softly brushed the back of her leg, edging slowly upward.

"Trust me."

"Never," she breathed, but she readily cried out in pleasure as his fingers slid between her legs.

Dimitri clenched his teeth, staggered by his need to be inside this woman. She was so soft, so delicate, so utterly innocent...

Innocent.

His gut twisted. What he knew of virgins could fit in a thimble, but he did have enough wits left to realize he would have to take care not to hurt her.

Stroking a finger through her tender flesh, he found her tiny nub, teasing it softly while he shifted to capture her lips in a deep, demanding kiss.

Emma arched against him, her hands running a fitful

path down his back. She might be innocent, but her body was eager to be tutored.

Almost as eager as he was to tutor her.

With a smooth motion he rolled Emma onto her back, settling between her parted legs and continuing his persistent caresses. He heard her choked moan as he released her lips to trail a path of fevered kisses down her throat.

He cursed, trembling with the effort to not simply plunge into her and ease his craving. What had this woman done to him? His heart was pounding, his breath coming in sharp rasps and his cock so hard he feared he might come just trying to breech her maidenhead.

Pulling back, he studied her face surrounded by the spill of honey curls. The pale, creamy skin. The fan of lush lashes that lay against her flushed cheeks. The rose-tinted lips parted in invitation.

So beautiful, he thought, a flare of savage possession gripping his heart as he positioned himself at her entrance and with a slow, steady thrust sank into her heat. For a brief moment, Emma tensed and Dimitri forced himself to pause as her body adjusted to his invasion. Continuing to fondle her, he waited for her muscles to ease and her fingers to clutch impatiently at his shoulders before he at last pushed past her barrier.

His breath hissed through teeth at the exquisite sensations that jolted through his body. She was glorious. An enticing, splendid woman who had denied her own needs for far too long.

"Emma," he husked, his hips pulling gently back before sinking back into her welcoming body. "My sweet Emma."

"Yes," she sobbed, her nails raking down his back.

The tiny shock of pain was like a spark to his very short

fuse. With a groan of surrender he lost himself in the pagan tempo that was as ancient and powerful as the sea churning beneath them.

## CHAPTER TEN

EMMA SHIVERED AS Dimitri's ship slid silently through the eastern entrance basin into the Thames River.

It was a gray afternoon with a sharp breeze, but the docks were overflowing with ships vying to unload their cargo at the nearby warehouses. Tea, silk, fruit and tobacco was piled on the quays while spice merchants and pepper grinders plied their trade among the vast crowd of sailors, dockhands and passengers. It all combined to create an image of colorful chaos.

At any other moment she would have been thrilled with the sights spread before her.

How often had she lain awake at night dreaming of traveling to distant lands? Or begged her father to read her stories beside the fireplace so she could imagine being far away from their tiny village?

Now, however, she couldn't summon the proper appreciation for the busy docks, or the vast city that sprawled in the distance.

Not when her sister might be near.

Clutching the railing of the bow she leaned forward, indifferent to the breeze that tugged at her heavy wool cloak and the gray scarf she had wrapped around her head.

Too often over the past days she had allowed herself to forget the reason for her journey to England. Dimitri's fault, of course. It was not enough that he had spent their long nights seducing her with his wicked kisses and experienced touch, but he had also consumed her days, charming her with stories of his reckless youth that revealed far more of his true self than he realized.

He was loyal and protective and generous to those he had taken beneath his wing. He was also quick to guard his heart and to keep others at a distance. He would always need to be in command of a relationship, ensuring that no one was allowed to step beyond the boundaries he set.

Including her.

As if her thoughts had conjured him into being, Dimitri appeared at her side, a scowl marring his handsome face as he studied her.

"The air is brisk," he said. "You should return to the cabin."

Emma swallowed a rueful sigh, her heart fluttering with an unbearable excitement as he leaned against the railing. It was more than the elegant beauty of his bronzed face and astonishing gold eyes. Or the chiseled perfection of his male body beneath the tailored jade jacket and buff breeches.

It was the ruthless sensuality and sheer male power he carried about him with such ease.

Desperately, she fought to hide her ready response to his presence behind a cool smile. She could not make herself regret the nights she had spent in Dimitri's arms. Her destiny might be to live as a lonely spinster in a tiny Russian village, but she would have memories that would keep her warm for years to come.

Still, she could not allow the madness to continue.

Not only did she need to concentrate on discovering her sister, but she would not become a source of amused gossip once they were settled in London. It was one thing to be known as Dimitri's lover by his trusted servants, and quite another to have strangers speculating at her uncharacteristic behavior.

"And miss my first glimpse of London?" she demanded. "Do not be silly."

His scowl deepened at the cool edge in her voice. "The docks are hardly worth the risk of consumption. They are as foul and rat-infested as any other dock to be found in the world."

"Not all of us are jaded travelers who are incapable of appreciating the novelty of arriving in a city I never dreamed I would one day visit." She shrugged, ignoring the fact that she was shivering beneath her cloak. "Besides, it is no colder than it was in St. Petersburg."

With a sound of impatience, he grasped her arms and turned her to meet his searching gaze.

"You have no interest in London. You are hoping that your sister will be standing upon the docks, awaiting you to rescue her."

Her lips thinned with annoyance. It was bothersome that he could read her so easily.

"Whatever your opinion of my intellect, I am not entirely stupid," she snapped. "But neither am I willing to be hidden away when Anya has need of me."

His hands skimmed up her arms with an intimate gesture of possession.

"I will soon know if the *Katherine Marie* has recently docked. Until then I prefer no one know we have arrived in London."

With an effort, Emma shrugged his hands away and stepped back. How could she think clearly when she was distracted by the temptation of his touch?

"There is no one who could possibly recognize me."

His jaw tightened, but thankfully he contented himself with folding his arms over his chest and regarding her with a narrow gaze.

"Do not be so certain. I, better than most, know that there are eyes in the most unlikely places."

Emma didn't bother arguing. Of course Dimitri would know where danger might be skulking. It was one benefit of being a talented criminal.

"Do you intend to remain on the ship until we find the *Katherine Marie?*" she asked instead.

"No. I have requested the assistance of an acquaintance. He will be awaiting us once night falls."

She rolled her eyes at his vague explanation. "Is there any place you do not have acquaintances to offer you assistance?"

"My reach extends far beyond Russia." His brooding gaze swept down her slender form. "It is something you might wish to keep in mind."

A cold chill of premonition shivered down her spine. "Is that a threat?"

"I am not stupid either, Emma. No matter how many warnings I might offer, you will happily rush into danger if you believe it will help your sister. I intend to make certain you are not allowed to tumble into disaster."

The ship swayed as a larger vessel surged past them, sending Emma careening into Dimitri's waiting arms. For a moment she was lost in the heat and scent of the man who had taught her the meaning of ecstasy. Her mind might have decided that Dimitri was no longer her lover, but her body was eager to respond to the feel of his hard muscles pressed tight against her.

She sucked in a shocked breath as she hastily pushed away from his clinging hold. What was the matter with her? Was she truly so weak?

Grasping the rail to keep her balance, Emma glared at the man who was now smiling in smug satisfaction.

"On how many occasions must I remind you that you are not my keeper?" she said tartly. "If I wish to tumble into disaster then it is none of your concern."

He reached to cup her cheek in his hand, the golden eyes shimmering with a sinful temptation.

"As your lover it is my right to protect you. Even from your own stubborn nature."

"Dimitri, I am not, nor will I ever be a helpless female who must depend upon you to decide what is best. And you are not my lover."

"No?"

"No."

His lips twitched. "Then I imagined the nights you spent in my arms? And the taste of your sweet lips? And your soft moans when I enter you—"

Without thought she reached up to cover his mouth with her hand, her cheeks hot with embarrassment.

"Shh." Her gaze darted about to ensure the crew were scurrying about their duties. "Someone might hear you."

He stepped closer, his head lowering to whisper directly into her ear.

"Do not ever deny I am your lover."

She shivered, clenching her hands against the urge to tug the leather cord that held his hair in a tidy queue and run her fingers through the satin darkness.

"Dimitri, please," she husked. "What happened between us is a madness that must end."

His thumb gently caressed the chilled skin of her cheek. "It is too late for regrets."

"I do not speak of regret, merely a return to sanity." It took more effort than she cared to admit to knock his hand away. "I have traveled to England to find my sister, not to indulge in a meaningless affair."

His beautiful features hardened. "I assume you are deliberately attempting to stir my anger?"

She squared her shoulders, refusing to be browbeaten. "Why would you be angered? I am not the first woman who you have bedded, nor will I be the last. I should think you would be relieved that I am not so absurd as to attempt and cling to you."

"Instead you claim me to be meaningless and toss me from your bed?" His voice was as cold as the winter wind.

A treacherous part of her wanted to believe he was hurt by her rejection. Perhaps even distressed at the knowledge he would never again share her bed. But Emma was nothing if not sensible.

Dimitri had no doubt found it amusing to tutor an aging spinster in the arts of love to pass the tedious voyage. What else did he have to keep him occupied? His passionate seduction, however, had included a great deal of skill with a notable lack of emotion.

Which meant the only wound he suffered was to his pride.

"No doubt your acquaintances in England include a woman willing to take my place," she said, a matching chill in her tone.

His brows snapped together as if he were insulted by her words, but before he could speak one of the crew shouted a warning and they both turned to catch sight of the small boat being rowed in their direction.

"Emma, go below," Dimitri commanded. Then, as she stubbornly remained at the railing, he turned to grasp her hands in his. "Please, *moya dusha.*"

She held his unwavering gaze for a long moment, frustrated by his continual attempts to keep her sheltered. But even as she told herself she was not going to be dismissed as if she were a mindless child, she caught sight of Dimitri's nod toward his gathering crew.

He would have the rowboat turned aside before he allowed the strangers to board the boat with her on the deck.

With a glare that warned of dire retribution, Emma spun

on her heel and marched toward the stairs that led to the cabins below.

It was not that she did not appreciate Dimitri's concern. In truth, it had been so long since anyone had considered the possibility she might need protection that she could not deny the treacherous warmth that filled her heart.

Thankfully she was wise enough to understand the danger of undermining her hard-won independence. Dimitri was a passing presence in her life. Once she had rescued Anya they would return to Yabinsk and she would once again be alone to shoulder her responsibilities.

Besides, she instinctively prickled at the suspicion Dimitri desired to transform her into a helpless female that depended utterly on him. She could never become such a creature.

Deliberately she moved through the cabin she had shared with Dimitri and into the connected chamber. She would not allow herself to be distracted by memories of being seated before the built-in dresser as Dimitri brushed her hair, or her giggling pleasure as he had slowly and thoroughly bathed her in the copper tub, or the strength of his arms as he had carried her to the narrow bed.

Pacing the floor, Emma forced her thoughts to Anya. *Dear Lord, please let her be near,* she silently prayed. *And let her be unharmed.*

A surprisingly short period of time passed before she heard the sound of Dimitri's approaching footsteps. Turning, she watched as he entered the cramped space, his dark features unreadable.

"Has something happened?" she demanded.

"The *Katherine Marie* docked this morning."

She frowned. Dimitri had been confident they could outrun his father's bulkier ship, but only days out of port they had been hit by a storm that had thrown them off course and damaged the mast. Obviously, the delays had meant they'd arrived later than Dimitri had planned, but Emma could think of nothing beyond her vast relief that the *Katherine Marie* had made it safely to harbor, and that she hadn't been mistaken about the destination.

"Then my sister is here," she breathed.

"It would seem so."

"Thank God." She frowned at the frustration that shimmered in his golden eyes. "What is wrong?"

"Huntley placed servants on the docks to keep watch, but my father's crew managed to unload their cargo and slip past the guards unnoticed. She could be anywhere."

Her brief surge of hope began to fade as she realized the daunting task of searching London for a handful of girls. It could take days, even weeks. Always assuming they had not spirited Anya out of the city.

"Surely they cannot have gone far?"

As if sensing her growing distress, he moved forward to take her hands in a firm grip.

"We will find Anya," he murmured, his warm touch and low voice enough to soothe her fears.

Emma was unnerved by the realization of how deeply he affected her. Almost as if…no. She would not even think it. Dimitri Tipova had proven he could seduce her body, she damned well would not allow him to seduce her heart.

With an effort, she tilted her chin and met his gaze squarely.

"You said Huntley. Do you mean the duke?"

"Yes." He lifted his brows. "Are you acquainted?"

She grimaced. Did he truly believe a spinster from a tiny Russian village could be acquainted with a duke? Even with her English mother such a thought was absurd.

"Of course not, but Vanya said she had sent a message to the Duchess of Huntley and that she would provide me assistance." A pang of regret twisted her heart. "I suppose that was yet another deception."

"Quite likely she wrote to the duchess. And no doubt Leonida is prepared to offer you whatever assistance you desire without informing her husband of her promise." His lips curved in a mysterious smile. "She is as headstrong and unmanageable as you."

"How do you know an English duke?"

"I performed a small service for the duchess a few weeks ago."

Emma stiffened, an odd tightness squeezing her chest. There was husky amusement in his voice when he spoke of the duchess. As if he were intimately acquainted with her.

"What sort of service?"

He shrugged. "I fear it was a private matter that I am unable to discuss."

Without thought she yanked her hands from his grip, glaring into his handsome face.

"I see."

He appeared momentarily startled by her reaction, then his smile slowly widened.

"Ah. Are you jealous, Emma Linley-Kirov?"

She sniffed. He would, of course, be arrogant enough to presume she was jealous rather than...what? Furious? Outraged? Worried. Yes, of course.

"I merely am concerned that she will be too distracted to be of service," she bit out.

With a chuckle, he leaned down to brush his mouth over her lips. "Pack your belongings. I dare not wait until sunset to begin our search."

More in an effort to hide her flushed cheeks than to obey his husky command, Emma darted past him into the main cabin.

"How will you begin?" she asked, pulling her satchel from beneath the bed and filling it with her handful of possessions.

He leaned his shoulder against the paneled wall, watching her jerky movements with a rueful expression. Almost as if he regretted the end of their voyage.

She hastily shook off the dangerous thought.

"I will have my servants visit the local pubs."

She straightened in surprise. "You think my sister might be so near?"

"No, but the crew of the *Katherine Marie* will be eager to ease their thirst, as well as their various hungers, after such a voyage," he explained. "I hope they will be willing to reveal where the cargo was taken with proper incentive."

She nodded, wryly acknowledging it was a clever notion.

"And what of you?"

"Me?"

"If I have learned nothing else of you, Dimitri, it is that you are never without a plan to take advantage of whatever situation comes your way."

Without warning the golden eyes darkened and he prowled forward to wrap her in his arms.

"I would hope you have learned far more of me than my penchant for making plans," he growled softly.

She shivered in ready awareness. But with surprising resolution she pressed her hands against his chest in unmistakable denial.

"I know you detest losing, Dimitri, but I am not a challenge to be conquered."

His eyes smoldered at her direct challenge. "No, you are a treasure. One that I have claimed as my own." His gaze skimmed down to her slender body. "And I guard my treasure with great care."

Wiggling from his arms, she returned to her packing, pretending she did not notice his searing gaze.

"What do you intend to do once we are in London?"

There was a tense silence before Dimitri heaved a sigh of pure irritation.

"I will request that Huntley introduce me to society."

She dropped the stockings she was folding into a neat square. "I beg your pardon?"

He reached to pluck the silk stocking from the bed, absently sliding it through his slender fingers.

"It would be impossible to search all of London for your sister. I must attempt to bring her to us."

"And you intend to do that by prancing through society?" she accused.

"What I *intend* is to make it known that I am a gentleman of wealth who is in England for a short visit and willing to pay an extravagant sum to sate my particular lust for young females."

She paused to consider his words. "You think the men who are holding Anya captive will approach you?"

"If I offer the proper temptation."

"But it could be days before they approach you."

He nodded, his rigid expression easing with regret. "I am sorry, Emma, we must be patient."

Her jaw clenched. How could he say such a thing? She had been patient for weeks.

She wanted to rant and rage and curse in frustration at her inability to rescue her sister.

"And what of me?" she asked instead.

"You will be my wife."

"Wife?" Her heart came to a sharp, painful halt. "Have you taken leave of your senses?"

He shrugged. "I assumed you would wish to be included in the search."

"I do, but…" She stopped, licking her suddenly dry lips.

"Yes?"

"I could be a maid," she desperately offered. "In fact, it would be far easier if I could travel about unnoticed."

An unexpected anger flared over his bronzed features, and, tossing aside her stocking, he reached to frame her face in his hands.

"You could never be unnoticed," he rasped. "And listen well, Emma, you will not be traveling anywhere without me."

"It is not your decision to make."

"Do not be a fool, there will be far more doors opened to the wife of a wealthy Russian aristocrat than a foreign maid."

It was true. Certainly she could move about the seedier parts of London as a servant, but the elegant drawing rooms where the gentlemen who bought and sold young girls traveled would be closed to her. The knowledge, however, did nothing to ease the fluttering alarm at playing the role of Dimitri's wife.

"Even if I agreed to such a ridiculous notion, no one would believe I am a refined lady," she argued.

"There is no need for modesty. Whatever your father's occupation, it is obvious you were well educated and tutored in the manners of society." His thumb absently outlined the unsteady curve of her lower lip. "With the proper clothing there would be no one to question your disguise."

"Unfortunately I do not possess your acting skills."

"Very well. You can remain upon the ship if you prefer." His voice thickened with a wicked promise. "I vow to visit each night to keep the chill away."

She grasped the lapels of his jacket as her knees threatened to buckle.

"Absolutely not."

He smiled with insolent satisfaction. "Then let us be on our way, Huntley is waiting for us."

# CHAPTER ELEVEN

IN THE TRADITION OF MOST gambling halls, the Bacchus Club was a combination of opulence and depravity.

Tucked in a tiny cul-de-sac near Brook Street, the three-storied brick building was hidden behind a high fence guarded by two burly footmen. Inside, the tiny foyer led to a sweep of marble steps opening to a large, cavernous hall that was most notable for the floor-to-ceiling mirrors that reflected the light of the overhead chandeliers with dazzling zeal. A dozen small tables were scattered across the Italian marble floor, most of them already crowded with gentlemen who possessed the tense, hunted expressions that Dimitri easily recognized.

Addicts.

He had taught his servants to turn away such men. They inevitably caused trouble for his establishments, not to mention their poor families.

The Bacchus Club, on the other hand, was renowned for the debauchery of its clientele. It readily catered whatever sin might be desired.

He hid his grimace as the small steward scurried toward them. Beneath the scent of roast beef and cigar smoke was the unmistakable stench of desperation.

"Your Grace, such an honor," the man said with a deep bow. "Can I offer you a drink?"

At Dimitri's side, Stefan, the Duke of Huntley, peered about his surroundings in barely concealed disgust, seemingly unaware of the stir he was creating by his entrance.

Of course, Huntley had been creating a stir since leaving the cradle.

It was obscenely unfair that a gentleman who was born into wealth and power should also have been blessed with a tall, magnificent form and the finely chiseled features of his Russian-born mother. Combined with his dark hair and shocking blue eyes, he was a gentleman who commanded attention wherever he went.

Dimitri had become acquainted with the reclusive duke when the nobleman had been chasing his stubborn wife, Leonida, across Russia. It had only been with Dimitri's assistance that they had captured the villain who had been attempting to blackmail Leonida's mother.

"Cognac," the duke murmured.

"At once." The steward waved a hovering waiter forward and whispered in his ear before returning his avid attention to Stefan. Dimitri could appreciate the poor man's excitement. Stefan made no secret of his distaste for London society as well as the numerous gentlemen's clubs that had vied for his membership. If the Bacchus Club could claim him as a patron it would offer them an image of respectability that had been sadly lacking with their current members. "You will discover we offer whatever distraction that might strike your fancy, Your Grace. There is a light supper laid out in the hazard room and billiard tables down the hall. The cock fighting will not begin until later, but if you desire entertainment you are welcome to sample our delightful wares that await your pleasure upstairs."

Stefan waved a dismissive hand. "That will be all."

"Of course."

The servant bent low enough his pointed nose was in danger of brushing the marble floor before backing slowly away. Huntley watched the retreat, then turned to regard Dimitri with a jaundiced gaze.

"I did warn you the establishment was a sordid collection of reprobates," he muttered.

Dimitri chuckled, not nearly so fastidious as his companion.

"Did you expect a gentleman willing to rape young girls for enjoyment would choose a quiet evening at White's or Boodles reading the evening paper?"

"True." Huntley's expression hardened. He had not hesitated to offer his assistance once he discovered Dimitri's reason for being in London. "Where do you wish to begin?"

Dimitri glanced toward the curved staircase. "You mingle among the natives, I will return shortly."

Huntley arched a mocking brow, his gaze deliberately shifting to the buxom blonde who leaned over the wrought-iron railing with a provocative smile.

"I am not certain your wife would approve of such a tête-à-tête."

His hands fisted. *Wife.* It was a word that made most men shiver in fear.

Who desired to be forever tied to the same female who would no doubt consider it her duty to nag him into an early grave?

It was not fear, however, that made Dimitri shiver when he thought of Emma Linley-Kirov. Instead, it was an emotion that he refused to name.

"Then perhaps it would be best if she did not learn of it," he warned, already having endured a savage argument when Emma was forced to remain at the Huntley town house preparing for her introduction to London society.

"Women always have a means of discovering such things," Huntley drawled.

"There is nothing to discover. I am merely asking a few questions." His gaze narrowed. Huntley might be a powerful duke, but Dimitri had rightly earned his reputation as a

ruthless bastard. "And Emma will have no means of knowing unless you are incapable of guarding your tongue."

There was no mistaking the glint of humor in Huntley's
blue eyes. "As you say."

"You find something amusing?"

"I do indeed," the man admitted without apology.

Dimitri bit back his sharp words and instead heaved a
rueful sigh. Weeks ago Dimitri had taken a great deal of
enjoyment in watching Huntley being driven to distraction
by Leonida. Perhaps it was not so surprising the man would
appreciate witnessing Dimitri's bafflement when Emma
was near.

"You are a vindictive bastard, Huntley."

"And you are quite deserving of your inevitable fate."

Dimitri shook his head. "We are wasting time."

"I shall make a few discreet inquires among the guests,
but I prefer not to linger longer than necessary."

"I shall be swift."

"A wise decision," Huntley drawled as Dimitri headed
toward the stairs.

Dimitri ignored the taunt. He intended to question the
whores, not make use of their services.

Not that Emma could complain if he did, he told himself
as he climbed the polished steps. Had she not been the one
to claim their affair was at an end? As if their passion could
be so easily dismissed.

Perhaps she should be forced to consider the notion that
he had no need to beg for a woman in his bed. There were
always females anxious to enjoy his seduction.

Thrusting aside his lingering annoyance, Dimitri forced
himself to concentrate on the task at hand. He would deal
with Emma Linley-Kirov later.

He reached the top of the stairs, prepared for the garish
crimson sofas and crude paintings of naked women that
lined the walls of the saloon. The main focus was expected

to be the women sprawled upon the velvet cushions in vary-
ing degrees of undress.

His gaze skimmed over the females, barely noting the
sheer gauze that revealed more of their lush bodies than it
concealed or the sudden interest that brightened the heavily
painted faces.

"Well, well." The blonde who had been leaning over
the railing sashayed across the carpet, licking her lips as
she studied the manner Dimitri's garnet jacket molded to
his wide shoulders and the hard length of his legs in the
black satin breeches. Or perhaps it was the emerald stickpin
nestled in his cravat and the diamond on his ear that had
captured her attention, he cynically acknowledged. "Ain't
you the lovely one?"

"Here now, it be my turn, Edwina," a slender brunette
protested, sidling next to Dimitri to thrust her bosom into
prominent view.

"You never minded sharing afore," Edwina snapped.

"Be quiet." A commanding voice had both women hastily stepping back, revealing an imposing matron with her
auburn hair piled high on her head and her lush curves
encased in a jade satin gown striding in their direction.
"The gentleman will decide which one of you he fancies."
The brown eyes regarded him with a shrewd gaze. "Perhaps
you would like a small sampling before you choose?"

"That will not be necessary. I prefer a few moments
alone with you, Mrs....?"

The woman's expression hardened with suspicion. "Pickford," she grudgingly supplied. "Surely you would prefer
one of the younger girls?"

He conjured his most charming smile. "Not this
evening."

There was a long pause as she considered the lethal
danger etched onto his features. She was a woman who had

seen enough of the world to sense Dimitri's feral nature. At last she gave a shrug.

"Very well."

Waving away the curious cluster of females, the older woman led him down the long corridor, pushing open the last door to escort him into a sitting room that was filled with solid English furniture and gingham curtains that were distinctly out of place in a brothel. Dimitri felt a pang of regret at his insistence. This was Mrs. Pickford's home and he was an unwelcome intruder.

"This way," she stiffly urged, waving her hand toward the connecting door.

"Actually this will do," he said gently.

The woman turned to face him, her expression wary. "What is it you're wanting from me?"

"Nothing more than information."

"A dangerous commodity."

"I assure you that whatever you tell me in this room will go no further."

She snorted at his smooth promise. "And why should I trust you?"

"Because my mother shared your profession."

Mrs. Pickford sucked in a shocked breath at Dimitri's blunt confession, her suspicions slowly transforming into a shared understanding.

"What do you want to know?"

"A number of young girls were taken from St. Petersburg and brought to London. I intend to find them and take them home."

The brown eyes flashed in outrage. "If someone told you that they was here, then you've been taken for a fool. Nothing but good English girls here and none of them being held against their will."

Dimitri held up his hand in a gesture of peace. "Be at

ease, Mrs. Pickford, I do not suspect you of dabbling in the slave trade, but you are a woman of the world."

Her ruffled feathers soothed, the older woman allowed a faint smile to curve her lips.

"I suppose that's a fancy name for it."

"You, better than anyone, would hear rumors of those gentlemen who possess a taste for children."

Her smile faded. "Such gentlemen prefer to keep their tastes a secret."

"And yet these things have a way of becoming known to those in the business."

"If your mother truly was one of us then you should know that those who don't learn to keep their mouth shut find themselves floating in the Thames." Her lips tightened. "The Bow Street magistrate can claim to have made the streets of London safe, but a nobleman can do whatever he pleases with us lesser folk."

Dimitri sympathized with her concern. Hell, he better than anyone knew what happened to whores who spoke out of turn.

"I have promised that no one will ever know we have spoken," he gently reminded her. "You have my word."

With a shiver she paced toward the sideboard, pouring herself a whiskey that she downed in one swallow.

"It's too dangerous."

Regretting the necessity of pressing the older woman, Dimitri crossed the room to turn her to face him.

"Mrs. Pickford, it is obvious you are very protective of the girls in your care."

"Someone has to keep an eye on the foolish chits. They haven't the sense that God gave a goose."

"Precisely." He caught and held her wary gaze. "So you understand my desire to protect those I consider under my care."

For a tense moment, Dimitri feared that the woman

would refuse to help, then with a shudder, she determinedly squared her shoulders.

"I can offer nothing more than rumors," she warned.

"That is enough."

"It is said that Lord Sanderson has an unhealthy interest in young girls as well as boys."

"Does he live in London?"

"He has a town house in Mayfair."

Dimitri tucked away the information. Not that he expected to discover the girls being held captive in an elegant Mayfair town house. But Sanderson was unlikely to have developed his own father's caution. There might very well be something in the Sandersons' home that would reveal his secrets.

"What of his acquaintances?" he pressed.

Mrs. Pickford wrinkled her nose in distaste. "A Mr. Timmons and Sir Jergens."

"Do they possess similar tastes?"

"So it is said."

"Is there a particular location they could indulge their fantasies?"

"It is whispered there are…" The woman gave a nervous gasp as a log popped in the stone fireplace.

He grasped her hands, attempting to ease her distress. "What is it?"

The brown eyes darkened with a futile anger. "Secret auctions where the girls are offered to the guests who can pay the entrance fee."

An answering anger echoed in Dimitri. He was rarely shocked by the depravity that some men could sink to, but that did not lessen his desire to shoot them in the heart and leave them bleeding to death in a gutter.

"Do you know where the auctions are held?"

"It's never held in the same location." Her harsh laugh

filled the room. "Such men are too crafty to risk being caught."

"Not crafty enough." Reaching in the inner pocket of his jacket, Dimitri withdrew several coins and pressed them into her hand. "For your time."

Anxious to return to the Huntley town house and Emma, he had nearly reached the door when her soft voice halted him.

"Sir."

"Yes?"

He halted and turned to watch as Mrs. Pickford moved forward and quite unexpectedly tossed her arms around him in a fierce hug.

"I've been knocked about enough to figure most men ain't worth a bucket of spit, but I believe you might just prove me wrong."

A wry smile curved his lips. "Ah, if only everyone shared your kind opinion."

EMMA STUDIED HER reflection in the full-length mirror with a jolt of astonishment.

She had protested violently when Leonida, the Duchess of Huntley, had insisted she would have her dresser alter several of her gowns to fit Emma, but the beautiful woman with golden curls and blue eyes that were extraordinarily similar to those of Czar Alexander had insisted that it would take days, if not weeks, for a seamstress to create the proper wardrobe for Emma. And as for her determination to play the role of a maid…well, that been overridden with a gracious, but ruthless force by both Stefan and Leonida.

She smiled wryly. She had been initially overwhelmed when Dimitri had led her into the foyer of the Mayfair town house. Not even Vanya's beautiful home had prepared her for the double staircases that elegantly curved toward the formal landing with marble pillars and a Venetian chandelier that spilled light over the collection of Grecian statues.

The imposing entrance was only a taste of the luxury to be discovered in the vast house, and Emma had swiftly given up the effort to estimate what the oil masterpieces framed on the walls and the various objects of art spread throughout the home might be worth.

And then she had been introduced to the Duke and Duchess of Huntley.

Stefan, with his dark hair and lean, autocratic face that would cause any woman's heart to miss a beat. His dark blue eyes had held a cunning intelligence that seemed to pierce to her very soul. And at his side the lovely Leonida who had at first glance seemed as frigidly beautiful as the tundra in winter.

She would have fled in terror if Dimitri had not stepped close to run a comforting hand down her back.

Then, with a surprising laugh, the duke and duchess had moved forward, warmly welcoming her to their home and assuring her that they would do whatever possible to help retrieve her sister.

Leonida had whisked her away to her chambers where she had insisted on hours of fittings with her dresser while Dimitri had mysteriously disappeared with Stefan.

Now she gazed in the mirror in amazement at the transformation that Leonida had achieved.

The evening gown was a spangled crepe draped over a satin slip of shimmering silver. The bodice was cut off the shoulders with tiny puff sleeves and a silver velvet ribbon tied snuggly beneath her bosom. With her honey curls piled loosely atop her head and her cheeks flushed with pleasure she had never appeared more elegant.

Almost as if she truly were a proper lady, she acknowledged with a rueful sigh.

Hesitantly her hand reached to touch a diamond-crusted button.

"It is lovely, but—"

"No arguments," Leonida interrupted, turning Emma to meet her determined expression. "You look exquisite."

Emma grimaced. Since her mother's death she had precious little time to fuss over her appearance. Not that it truly mattered. She had more important concerns to occupy her attention.

"Hardly exquisite," she muttered.

Leonida shook her head in disbelief. "Emma, how can you not realize you are extraordinarily lovely?"

Discomforted by her companion's insistence that she might be more than passably pretty, Emma paced across the Persian carpet. She had fallen in love with the amber bedchamber with its canopy bed and lemonwood furnishings covered with English chintz the moment she had entered the room, but she was too restless to fully appreciate her surroundings.

She blamed her unease on being so far from her familiar village and in the home of an English duke. Any woman in her position would be unnerved.

A voice in the back of her mind, however, whispered that the skittish sensation was entirely due to Dimitri Tipova and his reaction when he returned to the town house to discover she had demanded separate bedchambers.

Chiding herself for allowing her thoughts to once again be distracted by the bothersome man, she turned back to meet Leonida's curious gaze.

"Anya has always been the beauty of the family," she admitted.

"No doubt because you were willing to disguise your own beauty and allow her to shine."

Emma shrugged. She never considered the sacrifices

she had made or allowed self-pity to embitter her. She was a great deal more fortunate than many people.

"Most would tell you I was born a tyrannical, ill-tempered spinster," she said ruefully.

Leonida smiled. "Well, there is no one who will mistake you for a spinster in this gown."

"Leonida speaks the truth, *moya dusha*," a dark, whiskey-smooth voice murmured. "There is not a man who will gaze upon you and not wish to possess you."

Sharp excitement jolted through her as Emma turned to discover Dimitri strolling into the room, his elegant ruby jacket and black waistcoat unable to disguise his raw masculinity.

"Dimitri," she breathed.

"You need not thank me for my efforts, Dimitri," Leonida drawled with obvious amusement. "It was a pleasure to assist Emma. She is a guest that I am glad to have in my home."

The smoldering golden gaze never shifted from Emma's wary face. "I will speak with Emma in private."

Leonida placed an arm around Emma's shoulders, making it clear she was willing to stand up to the dangerous cutthroat.

"Emma?"

"It is fine, Leonida," she assured her companion, wishing she felt as confident as she sounded.

Not that she feared Dimitri would hurt her. At least not physically. But that did not lessen the danger.

"I will be in my rooms just down the corridor if you have need of me," Leonida said, moving toward the doorway. She paused at Dimitri's side. "Take care."

Dimitri's lips twisted. "Your warning comes far too late, Your Grace."

Leonida chuckled. "Good."

"And I thought your husband vindictive."

"We are kindred spirits. It is a rare gift that Stefan and I were nearly too stubborn to appreciate." Leonida glanced toward Emma, her expression impossible to read. "I would hope you would be wiser."

With a cryptic smile Leonida left the room, closing the door behind her.

Alone with Dimitri, Emma swallowed the lump in her throat, shivering as his golden gaze seared over her body. Suddenly, she was acutely reminded of lying beneath him, his slender fingers tangled in her hair as he urgently made love to her.

"Is there something you need?"

He prowled forward. "You."

Instinctively, she backed away, her heart galloping at a mad pace as she bumped into the wall.

"Dimitri, no."

His hands slammed against the wall on either side of her shoulders.

"Why did you insist we have separate rooms?" he growled.

"I told you before we left your ship that our..."

"Affair?"

Absurdly, Emma found herself unable to say the word. As if by refusing to name the savage awareness that pulsed between them she could somehow banish the sensations.

"I told you it was at an end."

"And I disagreed." His eyes darkened as he buried his face in the curve of her neck. "Mmm. I missed you today."

Her hands lifted to his chest, her fingers grasping the lapels of his jacket as he nuzzled the hollow behind her ear.

"It was on your orders that I was forced to waste the entire day acquiring a new wardrobe," she complained, reminding herself of all the reasons she should be slapping this man's face rather than melting beneath his skillful touch.

"Never a waste." He pulled back to study her silver gown. "You are…breathtaking. Although I would prefer less of you on display. I suppose this was Leonida's notion?"

Before she could respond, he returned to his delicate caresses, his lips tracing a path of kisses down the line of her collarbone.

Her lashes fluttered downward, her body longing to press against him in silent invitation.

"Dimitri, we are expected downstairs for dinner," she forced herself to mutter.

He reached the edge of her bodice, her nipples tightening in anticipation as his warm breath brushed her skin.

"Huntley is besotted with his wife. It is quite likely dinner will be delayed."

She shuddered, a soft moan of surrender escaping her lips. Who was she trying to deceive? Her mind might be convinced that sharing Dimitri's bed was a dangerous notion, but her body was already aching for his touch.

Easily sensing her capitulation, Dimitri slid his arms around her waist, molding her to the hard muscles of his body as his lips continued their destructive path over the curve of her breasts.

Emma's breath caught in her throat, her hands trembling as she reached up to clutch at his shoulders. She briefly forgot her stern determination to keep Dimitri at a distance, and even that they would be expected to meet the duke and duchess for dinner within the hour. All that mattered was…

She abruptly stiffened as the unmistakable stench of cloying perfume assaulted her.

Fury exploded through her. How dare he? He had told her he was devoting the day to tracking down the gentlemen who might have purchased her sister.

Instead, he returned to her reeking of another woman.

Gritting her teeth, she shoved her hands against his chest, nearly toppling him backward as she stalked toward the door and yanked it open.

"Get out."

He scowled, a flare of color staining his high cheekbones as he studied her with a frustrated gaze.

"What is it, *moya dusha?*"

Her chin tilted. "You bastard."

"True enough, but you've known that from the beginning," he snapped. "Why are you so angry?"

"Do not ever kiss me when you stink of another woman."

# CHAPTER TWELVE

THE LONG, FORMAL GALLERY was predictably ornate, with marble columns topped by gilded capitals that framed the shallow niches where the Greek statues were displayed and a grand fresco painted on the vaulted ceiling.

At the far end a string quartet struggled to be heard over the gathered crowd. The elegantly attired aristocrats were far too intent on preening for one another to pay heed to the entertainment.

Not unless one considered entertainment to be scandal and seduction.

In no humor to appreciate the absurdity of London society, or the irony of pretending to be one of the aristocrats he so deeply despised, Dimitri leaned against a marble column and glared across the gallery at the honey-haired woman who was currently surrounded by a bevy of eager gentlemen.

And why would they not be eager?

Even among London's most celebrated women she sparkled with a fascinating beauty that had nothing to do with the emerald gown embroidered with pearls and everything to do with the creamy perfection of her skin and mysterious shimmer in her hazel eyes.

He snarled beneath his breath as one particularly forward gentleman angled so he could have a perfect view of Emma's scooped bodice. The savage need to march across the marble floor and publicly claim the stubborn female was like a punch to his stomach. Unfortunately,

Emma was quite likely to slap him in the face if he dared to approach.

"Perhaps it escaped your notice, Tipova, but it took a considerable effort to procure invitations to this particular soiree," Huntley drawled, coming to a halt at Dimitri's side. "Should you not be taking advantage of your proximity to Sanderson rather than hovering in the corner and glaring at your faux wife?"

Dimitri's gaze never strayed from Emma. "You are a duke. Every door is open to you."

"Open for me, but not my unknown Russian companion who has yet to prove to London society that he is not a barbarian who lives among the wolves and gnaws on bones."

Dimitri snorted, well aware that most of England believed that Russia was a land of savages. Granted the puffed up peacocks were willing enough to welcome Russian armies as allies in defeating Napoleon, but they certainly didn't believe the people were civilized enough for an English drawing room.

"Pompous asses."

"Do you wish to be introduced to Sanderson or not?" Huntley demanded.

Dimitri shook his head. "No."

The duke scowled, his hand waving toward the crowd. "Tipova, if you forced me to this repulsive gathering as a punishment—"

"Compose yourself Huntley," Dimitri drawled, his pride pricked. He might be floundering when it came to Emma Linley-Kirov, but he was perfectly capable of devising the best means to ensnare Lord Sanderson. Which was precisely why he had requested that Huntley procure them invitations to Sir Jergens's soiree. And why he was lurking in the shadows rather standing next to Emma where he belonged. Or better yet, sweeping the aggravating woman back to his ship so they could have a few hours alone. "You admitted that you have never made a secret of your dislike for Sanderson. Do you not think it would be suspicious if you were to approach him for the simple purpose of introducing me, and then I begin questioning him on his most private affairs?"

Huntley shrugged. "Please yourself."

"I always do." Dimitri stiffened as he watched Sanderson head toward the doors leading onto the terrace. On the point of following the rotund nobleman, he abruptly turned to stab his companion with a flat glare. "Huntley."

"Yes?"

"My thespian skills are without equal, but I will kill any man who dares to be overly forward with Emma." There was no mistaking the lethal intent in his voice. "You might wish to stay close enough to ensure I have no need to demonstrate just how barbaric this Russian can truly be."

Expecting a mocking smile, Dimitri was relieved when Huntley instead nodded with understanding.

"Do not worry, Tipova. No one will trouble her."

With a last glance toward Emma, Dimitri strolled with seeming nonchalance across the gallery, his lean body shown to advantage in the black jacket and silver waistcoat. He ignored open smiles of invitation from the women and wary suspicion of the men. His attention was solely focused on the gentleman disappearing through the French doors.

Stepping onto the wide terrace, Dimitri searched the darkness, a predatory smile curving his lips as he watched the flabby nobleman lean against the stone balustrade and pour the contents of his crystal glass into the garden below.

"It would seem that I am not alone in my distaste for inferior champagne," he murmured, striding across the terrace as he withdrew a silver flask from the inner pocket of his jacket. "Allow me."

The round face with heavy jowls and a protruding nose already turning red in the chill night air turned in his direction, Sanderson's deep-set eyes lingering on the diamond stickpin the size of a quail egg Dimitri had tucked in his cravat before shifting to the extended flask.

"What is it?"

"The finest vodka to be found in all of London."

Taking the flask, the nobleman drank deeply of the potent spirits before handing it back to Dimitri.

"So you're the Cossack?" he sneered.

Dimitri peered down the length of his nose, deliberately sweeping a frigid gaze over the burgundy jacket stretched painfully tight over the man's expanding stomach and the hint of wear on the leather pumps.

"I am Russian, yes."

The sneer faltered, and Sanderson nervously cleared his throat.

"What brings you to England?"

"Huntley invited me for a visit during his stay in St. Petersburg. He assured me that I would discover a number of diversions. Unfortunately…"

"Unfortunately?"

Dimitri leaned casually against the railing, stifling a yawn as he cunningly dropped the bait to lure his prey into the waiting trap.

"I have discovered the pious duke and I have very differing notions of entertainment," he mocked. "If I wished to devote my days to stuffy gentlemen's clubs and my evenings to tediously escorting my wife from one ballroom to another I could have remained in Russia."

Sanderson inched closer, a gleam of interest in his pale brown eyes.

"You have my utmost sympathy. Huntley has always been a self-righteous prig."

Dimitri hid a smile. He had depended upon the lesser man's predictable envy of Huntley.

"A pity." He adjusted the cuff of his jacket, ensuring the large ruby in his ring caught and reflected the moonlight. "A gentleman is offered such a wide variety of opportunities it is nothing less than a sin to deny himself the full bounty of pleasures."

His covert glance witnessed Sanderson licking his thick lips, an unmistakable greed tightening his expression.

"Such pleasures can often be quite expensive."

"What is the purpose of possessing money if it is not to enjoy life?"

"It would seem we are gentlemen of a like mind."

Dimitri arched a brow. "Are we?"

"If you wish, I could perhaps escort you to those amusements that Huntley would never approve of."

Dimitri hid his stark satisfaction. He was a gambler who understood never to overplay his hand.

"That is a generous offer, but you cannot wish to escort a foreign stranger about town," he said, a hint of wariness in his voice. It would be unnatural for him not to be suspicious of such an offer.

Sanderson offered an unctuous smile. "I consider it my duty as an Englishman."

"Duty?"

He tugged on the cravat tied about his fat neck. "You cannot return to Russia assuming all Englishmen are as pompously dull as Huntley and his ilk. We do have a reputation to uphold."

"And?" Dimitri prompted, folding his arms across his chest.

"What do you mean?"

He paused, narrowing his gaze. "Forgive me, I am by nature a suspicious man. I prefer to have the cards on the table, as you English say."

Sanderson's smile widened with approval. Clearly he appreciated Dimitri's blunt acceptance that the offer of companionship was not without cost.

"Very well." He stepped close, lowering his voice to make certain they could not be overheard by the few guests strolling across the terrace. "I believe we can be of service to one another."

Dimitri gritted his teeth. He longed to wrap his hands around the nasty man's throat and choke the truth from him. A pity he could not be certain Sanderson had any connection to his father or the kidnapped girls. For now he had no choice but to remain patient and hope the man would lead him to the truth.

"I am prepared to listen."

Sanderson cast a nervous glance toward the light from the gallery windows that spilled across the terrace. Understandable. Wicked deeds belonged in the shadows.

"You wish your visit to London to be a memorable event and I am familiar with an assortment of establishments that are willing to cater to a gentleman's every need."

"*Every* need?"

The nobleman leered in anticipation. "Absolutely."

Dimitri pretended to consider the offer. "And what would you desire in return?"

"I share your love for adventure, but like so many noblemen my current finances are in straightened circumstances."

"Ah. I would of course be happy to finance any expenses we might incur."

Sanderson's loathsome chuckle echoed through the garden. "When do you wish to begin?"

No one could have been more astonished than Emma to discover herself a source of fascination among the elegant English ton. In truth, she had anticipated her charade being exposed the moment she stepped over the threshold of the town house. Instead, she had been surrounded by a bevy of curious aristocrats who vied to capture her attention.

Oh, she comprehended that a measure of their interest was stirred by her arrival in the company of the Duke and Duchess of Huntley. And, of course, by being on the arm of Dimitri, who appeared to terrify society with his ruthless beauty and hint of savage danger in his golden eyes.

But she was female enough to accept that had she not been so frantic to discover some hint of her sister, she might have taken pleasure in the soiree.

Instead, she stood at Leonida's side with a smile forced onto her lips and waited for Dimitri to covertly trail Lord Sanderson onto the terrace. The man had confessed what he had learned in the brothel, but had adamantly refused to allow Emma to be a part of the search for Anya.

Which meant Emma intended to take matters into her own hands.

Leaning close to Leonida, she whispered into her ear. "It is time."

The duchess covertly tugged Emma away from the crowd, her beautiful face creased with concerned.

"Emma, please take care."

Emma hid her smile, having heard the story of Leonida's frantic flight from England to St. Petersburg that had included a kidnapping and near-death experience. The woman was hardly in the position to lecture Emma on being careful.

"I intend to do nothing more than question the staff. I swear I will be discreet."

"And quick." Leonida glanced toward the imposing duke, who stood near a marble column, his remote expression keeping away all but the boldest encroacher. "If Stefan discovers you are missing, then he will most certainly come in search of you. And I know from painful experience he is a difficult man to avoid. And as for Dimitri…" She grimaced. "I shudder to think of what he would say should I allow you out of my sight."

Emma did a good deal more than merely shudder.

She was well aware that if Dimitri discovered she was executing her own search for Anya he would have her hauled back to his ship and sent to Russia.

"I shall return before anyone suspects I am gone," she swore.

Weaving her way toward the entrance at the far side of the gallery, Emma ignored the attempts to capture her attention. Then, moving down the corridor away from the near-deafening chatter of the guests, she slowed her pace as she peered into the various rooms. They were all opulently decorated with rosewood furnishings and richly painted ceilings. Her stomach clenched. Did Sir Jergens afford his lavish home by selling Russian children?

She had nearly reached the back of the house when she spied the maid who was stirring the fire in what appeared to be a small parlor. Pausing in the doorway she bent down to rip the hem of her gown before she entered the room and headed directly toward the servant.

"You there."

The maid, with a round face and fuzzy brown hair that escaped her white cap, hurriedly rose to her feet, wiping her hands on her apron.

"Aye, my lady?" she breathed, bobbing a hasty curtsey.

Emma summoned a kind smile, hoping to put the maid at ease. "I fear a clumsy oaf has trod upon my gown and torn my hem. Would you be kind enough to assist me?"

"Of course. If you will follow me?"

The maid led her toward a window seat where a basket of darning had been tucked out of sight.

"Is it very bad?" Emma demanded.

The maid knelt on the carpet, reaching to pull out a needle and thread from the sewing basket.

"Not at all," she assured Emma, "I shall be done in a trice."

"I know it is not your duty…"

"Maggie," the girl shyly offered at Emma's prompting.

"Maggie, but my maid was forced to return to her mother in St. Petersburg and I have yet to replace her."

"I am happy to oblige, my lady."

Emma allowed the maid to concentrate on threading the needle and begin stitching the hem before she pretended to be struck by a sudden thought.

"Do you know, it has just occurred to me that you might be just who I need to speak with."

The maid glanced up in puzzlement. "Me?"

"Yes, I shall have need of a servant during the remainder of my visit and while I am certain an English maid would be perfectly qualified for the position, I must admit that I would prefer a Russian girl. Do you know where I might hire such a maid?"

The color visibly drained from the plump face. "Russian?"

The woman was obviously alarmed, but it was impossible to know if it was a mere reaction to being questioned by a supposed noblewoman. Emma considered her words.

"Well, most London domestic services only offer English or French servants. I had hoped you might be acquainted with a suitable girl."

"I…"

"Have I said something wrong?"

Maggie abruptly ducked her head, concentrating furiously on sewing the ripped hem.

"No."

"I would be willing to pay for your assistance, Maggie," Emma urged softly.

"I'm sorry, my lady, I don't know any foreign girls."

Emma bit her lip, studying the rigid line of the maid's shoulders and the tremble of her finger as she tied off the thread. The poor girl was truly frightened. Did she dare press her further?

"Then perhaps one of your friends would be able to recommend someone?" she at last asked.

The maid surged upright, a hectic glitter in her brown eyes. "There you are, as good as new."

"Maggie?"

"I must be returning to my duties." Without warning Maggie was turning to rush out of the room.

"Wait."

Cursing her lack of finesse, Emma belatedly followed in the servant's wake, not entirely surprised to discover that the girl had already disappeared. She was certain Maggie must know something. But what? And how did she force the poor girl to confess?

Ten minutes later, Emma came to a halt and glanced about the warren of rooms and hallways that made up the servant's quarters. Maggie was nowhere to be found and the servants who scurried past her were sending her the sort of curious glances that inevitably led to gossip. The one thing that Emma was determined to avoid.

Accepting that she had done enough damage for one evening, she gave a shake of her head and turned to retrace her steps back to the ballroom. It was only then that she realized that an extremely large man with a dark complexion had crept up behind her. Her eyes widened as she realized he was oddly attired with a scarf on his head and a matching loose white robe wrapped with a black rope that held it in place.

Who was he? And more important, what was he doing creeping about the London town house?

Instinctively, her lips parted to scream, but before she could make a sound the man had clamped a hand over her mouth and firmly wrapped an arm around her waist, plucking her feet far enough off the ground so he could back toward a nearby door.

Emma struggled as a surge of fear exploded through her. She might be several pounds lighter and barely tall enough to reach the man's shoulder, but that did not keep her from scratching at the hand over her mouth or desperately swinging her legs in an attempt to connect a blow to his knee.

The brute flinched and muttered beneath his breath, but he never hesitated as he used his foot to kick open the door and hauled her down a narrow flight of stairs into the abandoned rose garden.

Emma stilled her futile struggles. The man was too powerful for her to battle. Her only hope was to conserve her strength and pray she would be offered the opportunity to escape once he released his painful grip.

She shivered as a breeze whipped around the side of the house, easily cutting through the thin fabric of her gown. English winters might not compare to the brutal ferocity of Russia, but this was no weather to be prancing about frozen gardens without so much as a cloak.

The stranger carried her down the narrow path, heading toward the small grotto in the center of the garden. Then, stepping through the opening, he roughly set her back on her feet, making no effort to assist her when she stumbled into the darkness.

A slender male hand grasped her arm, gently steadying her before she fell to her knees. Emma was aware of the potent scent of exotic spices and warm male skin before the hand was removed and the darkness was pierced by candlelight.

She blinked against the sudden change from dark to light, then as her eyes became accustomed, she studied the slender man standing directly in front of her.

Her first thought was that he was as exotically male as his scent had been.

Although attired in English clothing with a black jacket fobbed with gold and white satin pantaloons, there was no mistaking the foreign beauty of his finely carved features and the rich glow of his golden skin. His hair was as dark as the midnight sky and cut close to his head, emphasizing his wide brow and the black, deep-set eyes that smoldered with a restless intelligence.

She shivered. The stranger carried with him the lethal allure of the desert. Scorching days beneath the incandescent sun and cool nights by the oasis, wrapped in a man's arms.

Emma's heart slammed against her chest as the stranger studied her for a long, disturbing moment, then his dark gaze shifted over her shoulder and he spoke to a man still standing behind her in a strange language.

There was a shuffle as the robed man left the gazebo and Emma was alone with the strikingly handsome man who set aside the candle and strolled toward her.

"Forgive me," he murmured, his smoky voice feathering down her spine. "I requested that my servant bring you to me and apparently he took my command quite literally."

Emma licked her lips, not fooled by his polished manners. She did not doubt for a moment that the servant had been commanded to bring her to the garden by whatever means necessary.

"So it would seem." She clutched her shaking hands together, glancing about the marble grotto with its pastoral scenes painted on the walls and benches set beneath the slotted windows. It was surprisingly spacious, but to

Emma's mind the stranger's presence seemed to overwhelm the circular space. "Who are you?"

He offered a half bow. "Just as you, I am a visitor to this country."

Which told her precisely nothing.

"And you believe that gives you leave to have me hauled about as if I am a bit of rubbish?"

A small smile curved his lips, emphasizing his dark beauty. "I have apologized."

Emma remained wary, but her panic eased. Surely if the man intended harm he would not be chatting with her in a grotto near enough for someone to hear her scream?

"But you have not yet introduced yourself, or told me why you have brought me to this excessively cold garden," she pointed out.

The dark gaze swept over her upturned face. "For now I believe it is best that we both guard our true identities..." He deliberately paused. "Emma."

"How did you know—"

"There are more dangers in London than you suspect," he overrode her startled question.

She shivered at his odd words. Did he know why she was in London? Was he somehow involved with those who had taken her sister?

"Is that a threat?" she breathed.

"A warning for you to take care," he corrected, his hand lifting to cup her chin in a gentle grip. "It would be tragic if you were to be harmed."

Acutely aware of the warmth of his touch and the tantalizing brush of his breath on her cheek, Emma resisted the urge to struggle against him. Dimitri Tipova had taught her to recognize a predator when one had her cornered.

"What do you want of me?"

"I have told myself that we could be of assistance to one another, but now that you are so near I wonder if I was not deceiving myself." His voice roughened as his gaze deliberately rested on her lips. "You are quite beautiful."

"Please...do not."

He ignored her unsteady plea, his fingers tracing the delicate lines of her face.

"Such exquisite skin. And soft, silken hair. And eyes that are the precise shade of my beloved cat." His head slowly lowered. "Fascinating."

"No." Emma pressed her hands against his chest, her cheeks flushed. "I will scream."

With a rueful grimace, the man pulled back, the dark eyes glittering with a wicked promise that their kiss had merely been delayed.

"You have no need to fear me," he promised. "I only wish to let you know that you are not alone in your search."

Her heart skipped a beat. "My search?"

He frowned as he abruptly glanced toward the door. "Someone approaches." He grasped her shoulders, his expression somber. "If you wish my help you will tell no one of this encounter."

"Why not?"

"Because, like the scorpion, I prefer to remain in the shadows until the moment is ripe to strike at my enemies."

Emma studied the proud golden features. This was a man accustomed to giving commands and having them obeyed. Not that a position of power made him trustworthy, of course. The men who had kidnapped her sister were supposed noblemen.

But she could not deny there was a part of her that was certain he was someone she could rely upon.

"And what if I have need of you?" she husked. "How can I contact you?"

The dark eyes flared with satisfaction and before

she could stop him, he had leaned down to steal a brief, possessive kiss.

"Do not worry, I shall always be near," he whispered.

Not entirely reassured, Emma shivered as he silently slipped from the grotto and disappeared into the shadows of the garden.

She was not at all convinced he was a gentleman she wished to have keeping watch on her, she acknowledged as she followed him out of the grotto and headed back toward the town house. Then again, if he could provide assistance in rescuing her sister, then he could lurk in the shadows all he desired.

Avoiding the servant's door where she had been forced into the garden, Emma instead hurried toward the terrace at the far edge of the house. She climbed the steps and was headed for the French doors when a familiar form stepped into her path.

"Emma." Dimitri glared down at her with obvious annoyance. "What are you doing out here?"

Emma jerked in surprise, her raw nerves not at all prepared to deal with yet another overbearing male. What had she done to be plagued with such creatures?

"I...I needed a breath of fresh air."

"Fresh air?"

"Yes."

The golden eyes narrowed with suspicion. "And you had no intention of attempting to overhear my conversation with Lord Sanderson?"

She breathed a soft sigh of relief at the realization he had presumed she had followed him onto the terrace. She might be a fool, but for now she had no intention of telling Dimitri of her encounter with the strange foreigner.

Not when he was certain to use the knowledge as an excuse to keep her locked in the Huntley town house, or worse, returned to his ship.

Besides, who knew whether the stranger might eventually be of service?

"There is nothing nefarious in my presence on the terrace, Dimitri. I took a brief stroll through the garden and now I am returning to the ballroom."

"Alone?" he drawled in disbelief. "Where is Leonida?"

"No doubt in the company of her charming husband."

"Ah." His expression softened as he stepped close enough to wrap his arms around her waist. "And were you jealous, *milaya?* Did you perhaps wish to be in the company of a charming, clever, excessively handsome gentleman?"

She trembled at his familiar touch, her body tightening with a sharp-edged hunger. In the flickering torchlight, with his hair ruffled in the breeze and his eyes dark with desire, he appeared enticingly uncivilized.

The desire to have him sweep her off her feet and carry her into the shadows of the garden was terrifyingly potent. Instead, she forced herself to step back, meeting his smoldering gaze with a tilt of her chin.

She would not be manipulated. Not by Dimitri Tipova nor by the stranger in the grotto.

"Yes," she admitted with a taunting smile. "Unfortunately, I have yet to discover such a man."

# CHAPTER THIRTEEN

DESPITE HIS BEST INTENTIONS, Dimitri found his thoughts drifting as Huntley discussed the various political implications from the recent Congress of Verona. It was not that he did not comprehend the dangers inherent in Spain's current instability, or France's proposed intervention. The mere fact that Alexander Pavlovich was offering to send one hundred and fifty thousand troops to Piedmont to dampen the uprising of Jacobins meant that there was a very real potential for war.

But on this winter afternoon, the squabbling between Metternich and Wellington and Chateaubriand seemed thankfully distant.

Instead, he gazed down at the terraced garden shown to full advantage by the row of floor-to-ceiling windows, his mood as dark as the threatening clouds.

At last sensing Dimitri's tension, Huntley rose from the heavy walnut desk and crossed the white marble floor of the library.

"How does your hunt go?"

"Slowly." Dimitri grimaced, reluctantly recalling the paltry entertainments he'd been forced to endure over the past days. Drunken boxing matches, seedy gambling halls, a dog fight and brothels that catered to any number of perversions. None, however, had offered the sort of young females he had demanded of Lord Sanderson. "I have hopes this evening I can convince my prey I am to be trusted with his secrets."

"It has only been a fortnight." The duke shrugged. "You cannot expect a miracle."

Dimitri's humorless laugh echoed through the vast room. The elegant library was large enough to house an army battalion.

"I cannot, but I assure you that is precisely what Emma expects."

"Understandable. It is obvious she is consumed with fear for her sister."

Dimitri clenched his hands. He fully sympathized with Emma's concern. He better than anyone knew the guilt that tormented her at Anya's continued absence, and her relentless determination to rescue her. No matter what the cost to herself.

Or to him.

But he couldn't deny his frustration at the impenetrable barriers she had surrounded herself with since arriving in London.

"I sympathize with her impatience, but I cannot allow her emotions to lead her to foolishness," he growled. "If she does not trust that I am capable of rescuing Anya, then she is most certain to take matters into her own hands."

Huntley smiled wryly. "I could have warned you of the dangers of entangling yourself with a headstrong female."

An icy dread gripped his heart as the haunting memory of his mother and her brutal death seared through his mind.

"There is no need for such warnings," he replied. "I am painfully familiar with the dangers. You are certain Leonida is keeping a close guard on her?"

Huntley arched a dark brow. "Why do you ask?"

With a sharp motion, Dimitri turned to pace toward a towering bookcase.

"I suspect Emma is keeping a secret from me."

"She is a woman. They are compelled by nature to keep a poor man baffled and suspicious."

"Not all women," Dimitri protested. And it was the truth. How many females had he taken into his care over the years? How many had eagerly allowed him to protect them from the cruel injustices that threatened them? "There are those who comprehend the need to depend on a man and to defer to him rather than constantly battling to assert her independence."

"If you say." Huntley at least made an effort to disguise his amusement. "Why do you believe she is keeping a secret from you?"

Dimitri continued his pacing, his brow furrowed with frustration. He had first assumed Emma's oddly furtive manner was caused by her annoyance at his refusal to allow her to chase about London in search of her sister. It was understandable she would desire to punish him.

But as the days passed, he was forced to accept that Emma was not a woman to harbor a grudge. If she were annoyed with him, then she would brazenly slap his face, not pout behind his back.

No. There was something occupying her mind. Something she was determined to keep hidden from him.

"It is those guilty glances when she thinks I am not looking," he muttered, acutely aware that he sounded a fool. "And those tiny flinches of surprise when I enter a room unexpectedly."

Huntley slowly smiled, crossing to regard Dimitri with an amused gaze.

"Have you considered her wariness in your presence is caused by the same affliction that has you pacing the floors and snapping at those foolish enough to cross your path?"

Dimitri tensed, not particularly pleased to be a source of entertainment for the duke.

"What affliction?"

"Desire."

"That is none of your concern," he growled, his voice edged with warning.

"I am not blind, Tipova," the man persisted. "It is obvious that the two of you have been intimate. Perhaps if you would return Emma to your bed then both of you could collect your composure and concentrate on your purpose here."

Dimitri gave a sharp crack of laughter. Did the duke believe that he was responsible for his enforced celibacy? Christ, he would sooner be tarred and feathered than spend another night alone in his bed.

"It was not my choice to have separate chambers," he proclaimed.

A hint of pity darkened Huntley's expression. "Ah."

Dimitri ignored the implication that it was his lack of talent that had driven Emma from his bed. He had no need to boast of his skill. Instead, he concentrated on making certain Huntley realized just how fragile Emma was beneath her facade of unshakable fortitude.

"Emma has been forced to take on responsibilities that would have crushed most women."

Huntley nodded. "I suspected as much."

"Then you must also have suspected that her unconventional choices have made her vulnerable to nasty gossip that has plagued her since her father's death. She would be deeply hurt if Leonida were to consider her less than a proper lady."

Huntley stiffened, obviously outraged by the suggestion they would deliberately harm their guest.

"Leonida is already extremely fond of Emma, as am I. We would never think less of her."

Dimitri shrugged. "Perhaps you could convince her. I have been unable to do so."

Huntley paused, studying Dimitri's guarded expression. "Why do I sense you have not made the attempt?"

Dimitri swallowed a sigh. The duke was annoyingly perceptive.

"Emma was a virgin before becoming my lover," he grudgingly confessed.

"You did not—"

"Force her? No," he snapped. "But in her mind I did seduce her. It appeased her conscience to tell herself that I took advantage of her innocence."

"And now?"

Dimitri shifted uneasily. What did the man want from him? A confession that his relationship with Emma had gone beyond a short tumble to ease his lust? That he needed her to be more than merely a reluctant lover?

"Now I wish her to accept her place in my bed because that is where she desires to be and not because I have lured her there," he muttered.

Huntley reached to clap him on the back. "Take the word of a man who has made his fair share of mistakes, Tipova, pride is a cold companion."

Dimitri headed toward the door, unwilling to discuss Emma and the baffling emotions that refused to leave him in peace.

"Sanderson will be waiting for me."

UPSTAIRS IN THE DUCHESS of Huntley's private parlor, the two women might have been poised for a painting.

Leonida was prettily settled on a brocade settee, her lilac gown a perfect complement to her golden beauty. Across the room decorated with painted mural scenes and boasting a coved ceiling, stood Emma attired in a blue-and-silver-striped walking gown with a blue velvet pelisse fastened with large silver buttons as she glanced out the bow window.

Neither woman, however, was remotely aware of the charming vision they created.

In truth, Emma was aware of nothing beyond the sight

of Dimitri striding through the back garden to the mews. Even at a distance he appeared absurdly handsome with his caped greatcoat emphasizing the width of his shoulders and the pale light slanting over the savage beauty of his bronzed face.

Her teeth clenched with a combination of unwelcome appreciation and sheer annoyance that he was once again spending the day hunting for her sister, while she was expected to remain quietly at home, awaiting his return like a well-trained dog.

"If the tea is not to your taste I could order you whatever you desire," Leonida murmured from behind.

Turning, Emma set aside her Wedgwood cup with a grimace. "Arsenic?"

"No man is worth dying for."

"Oh, I did not intend the poison for me."

Leonida tilted back her head to laugh with rich appreciation. "Oh, I do like you, Emma Linley-Kirov."

"Why did he bother to bring me to London if he meant to forget my very existence?" she growled, pacing across the Persian carpet to absently toy with the jade figurines that lined the mantel.

"If the burning glances he has been sending in your direction is any indication, he has not been capable of forgetting your existence for even a moment."

Emma could not contain her shiver. She was well aware of Dimitri's hot, lingering glances. How could she not be? The air itself seemed to catch fire the moment he entered the room. And she would be lying if she did not admit that she had spent more than one night aching for his touch.

But she had made her decision to bring an end to their affair. A decision that was only strengthened by the realization that she would never be capable of keeping her secrets hidden while sharing a bed with Dimitri Tipova.

How long would it be before the incorrigible man not only realized she was making her own inquiries throughout

London in an effort to locate Anya, but that there was a strange man supposedly keeping watch over her?

No. Whatever the temptation, she had to keep in mind that Dimitri had his own purpose in being in London. And if she, or Anya, had to be sacrificed to achieve that goal, then so be it.

"Desiring me in his bed and including me in his search for my sister is not at all the same," she said, her voice bitter. "He refuses to admit I might have some value beyond my body."

Leonida sighed. "Men are so sadly stupid."

"I doubt you would include your husband in your condemnation of the opposite sex."

"Of course I would," the duchess corrected. "Until I managed to properly train him, Stefan was as arrogant, insensitive and incapable of accepting a woman's ability to make her own decisions as Dimitri."

"Do you truly believe a man such as Dimitri Tipova could be trained by any woman?"

"You would not ask that question if you knew Stefan's brother, Edmond." Leonida set aside her teacup and rose to her feet. "I do not envy Brianna for the torment that man put her through before they wed. Of course now she is excessively happy."

Emma's heart twisted with an emotion perilously close to envy. She would be a fool to ever believe she shared more than a passing affair with Dimitri. Her destiny was a small coaching inn in Yabinsk. To yearn for more was only inviting disappointment.

"Enough of Dimitri Tipova," she snapped. "I am here for Anya, no other purpose."

"Certainly," Leonida calmly agreed. "How can I be of service?"

Emma sucked in a deep breath, regaining her composure. "Your maid was kind enough to discover that Lady

Sanderson enjoys a late morning stroll through Green Park."

"Good." With brisk steps, the duchess moved toward the door. "Then we should be on our way."

Emma hurried behind the woman as she headed down the long hall and then the marble sweep of stairs.

"There is no need for you to accompany me, Leonida," she protested. "You have done enough as it is."

"Nonsense." Pausing in the foyer, Leonida waited for a maid to scurry forward with a fawn cloak lined with fur and matching bonnet she settled on her golden curls. "I am going with you and there will be no arguments."

Hastily Emma pulled on a pair of warm gloves and a pretty bonnet trimmed with blue velvet ribbons.

"I cannot allow you to put yourself in danger."

"What danger can there be in a morning stroll through Green Park with two burly footmen to keep guard?"

Emma studied her companion's resolute expression, then she heaved a sigh of resignation.

"You are very stubborn."

Leonida chuckled. "So I have been told."

There was a brief wait as the groom scurried to bring around a black carriage with the Duke of Huntley's insignia painted on the side. But soon enough they were settled on the leather seats with blankets swaddled around them and warmed bricks beneath their feet.

Emma instinctively shifted to peer out the window as they rattled over the cobblestones, a sigh of appreciation escaping her lips as they turned onto Park Lane. Her gaze lingered on the palatial Grosvenor House with its stuccoed exterior and two-story bays that overlooked Hyde Park with aloof grandeur. And the less flamboyant Londonderry House that had been originally designed with a formal simplicity by Stewart and was in the process of lavish restorations. Leonida had whispered that Lady Londonderry was funding the alterations and desired to have a suitable setting to display her famous diamonds.

"London is perhaps not as elegant as St. Petersburg, but it has its own charm, do you not think?" Leonida murmured.

"I do," Emma readily agreed, a wistful smile curving her lips. "It is just as my mother described it."

"Yes, Dimitri mentioned your mother was English."

Emma nodded. The memory of her mother holding her tightly on her lap as she spoke of her homeland caused a bittersweet ache in the center of her heart.

"She often spoke of her home that she left behind to travel to Russia as a nanny. It made me long to visit." She grimaced. "Although not under such circumstances."

"Do you intend to contact your relatives while you are here?"

Emma shrugged. She had hesitated to contact her distant relatives after the death of her father. The last thing she desired was to be seen as a pathetic orphan in search of charity. And perhaps, if she were perfectly honest, she would have to admit that a small voice in the back of her head warned that there might be those among their relatives that might not consider her a suitable guardian for Anya. She would not take the risk her sister might be taken from her.

Utterly selfish of her, of course. And as she was discovering, utterly stupid.

Perhaps if she had allowed Anya to go to a traditional family with a stable home and a mother capable of devoting her time to her children, Anya might have outgrown her impulsive lust for attention.

"I might consider seeking them out once Anya is safe," she said, refusing to imagine the possibility that she would not find her sister. "It would be nice to meet our family. We have been alone a long time."

"You are not alone, Emma." Without warning, Leonida leaned forward to grip her hand. "Never again."

The warmth of Leonida's generous kindness helped to ease the icy dread that was lodged in the pit of Emma's stomach. It was odd. How often did the common folk in her tiny village complain of the cold disdain of the aristocrats, and how they cared for no one but themselves? And yet, her neighbors had done nothing to assist her when she needed help, while this woman who had been born into lavish luxury had not hesitated to extend a hand of friendship and to open her home to a perfect stranger.

"Thank you," she said, her voice brimming with sincerity.

The carriage rolled to a halt, a handful of grooms scrambling to open the door and pull out the steps.

"Here we are," Leonida announced, offering Emma a wink as they were carefully assisted from the coach and then discreetly followed by the burly guards as they passed through the gates.

A frown formed on Emma's brow as they strolled along across the frozen ground, her gaze skimming over the flat expanse of parkland that was surprisingly bustling with elegant pedestrians.

"Heavens! I had no notion it would be so vast," she murmured. "How will we ever find Lady Sanderson?"

"There are only a few paths that attract a lady of fashion." Leonida threaded her arm through Emma's and tugged her toward a line of trees. "This way."

"Where are we going?"

"The Queen's Walk. It passes by the basin." They walked in silence, both enjoying the sense of peace that was so rare in the bustling city, then Leonida turned to catch Emma's small smile. "What are you thinking?"

Emma sucked in a deep breath, acutely aware of the history that surrounded her. As beautiful as St. Petersburg might be, it had not yet acquired the centuries of stories and memories that shrouded London in mystery.

"My mother told me that Green Park was created by King Charles II and that it never was allowed to have flowers since his queen discovered him offering blooms to another lady while they strolled among the deer and temples."

Leonida chuckled. "Who is to say if it is true or not? I do know the temples were destroyed during the various celebrations over the years and, of course, there was a fireworks accident that caused a dreadful fire. Not that I am complaining. There is something very appealing in simple nature unmarred by man." Leonida leaned close to Emma's ear. "I believe the woman in the burgundy cloak with the yapping dog is Lady Sanderson."

Emma covertly glanced toward the woman who was struggling to maintain her grip on the leash holding a small, ill-trained dog. She stumbled in shock. Could that dumpy woman in a garish velvet cloak and matching bonnet be a lady of society? She looked more like the butcher's wife with her plump, ruddy cheeks and brown curls that escaped the limp bun at the nape of her neck.

"Truly?" she breathed.

"It is rumored she brought with her a considerable dowry, although Lord Sanderson has swiftly squandered her fortune. How do you intend to approach her?"

"I haven't the least notion." Emma ignored her companion's speculative gaze as they headed directly toward the woman who had halted to untangle her leash from a bush. It was not until Lady Sanderson had straightened and was watching their approach with astonishment that inspiration struck. "What a darling puppy," she cooed, squeezing Leonida's arm. "Is he not a darling, Your Grace?"

"Most handsome," Leonida readily agreed, managing to hide her grimace as the dog rolled in a patch of mud. "Wherever did you find him?"

The woman's mud-brown eyes widened with terrified shock at being approached by the elusive Duchess of Huntley.

"Your Grace, this is such a…" Lady Sanderson paused, making a visible effort to regain command of her shattered composure. "Lancelot was a gift from my father."

Leonida smiled graciously. "Lady Sanderson, is it not?"

"Yes. Yes, it is indeed."

"Sanderson?" Emma tilted her head to the side, pretending to be deep in thought. "Why is the name so familiar? Ah, of course. Your husband has kindly offered to escort Dimitri about town."

There was no mistaking the loathing that briefly flared through the older woman's eyes before she managed a stiff smile. Emma shuddered in sympathy. As difficult as her life had been, she at least had not been bartered off to a man she held in disgust. Not all the money, or exclusive parties or grand houses in Mayfair could compensate for that misery.

"Did he?"

"I believe they were also discussing some business or another."

"Business?" Lady Sanderson blinked in confusion. "I am sure you must be mistaken."

Emma giggled, ignoring the small pang of guilt at deceiving the poor woman.

"That is quite possible. Dimitri is forever scolding me for making a muddle of what I am told." She deliberately paused. "Still, I was quite certain that he mentioned Lord Sanderson was seeking a buyer for a piece of property that he wishes to sell."

"That is impossible. My husband's estate is entailed despite his efforts to have the will altered. He has no authority to dispose of his property."

"I do not believe it was a part of the estate. Indeed,

Dimitri implied it was a rarely used home or building," Emma pressed. The men had to be holding her sister and the other girls somewhere in London. And if Lord Sanderson was as stupid as Dimitri had implied then he was quite likely to have hidden them in a place of convenience rather than ensuring their presence could not cause him scandal. "Or perhaps it was a shop." She let loose another giggle. "There, you see? I am hopeless in recalling what I have been told."

"My father owns several warehouses in Cutler Street, but I can assure you they are not for sale." Obviously flustered by Emma's probing, the woman managed an awkward curtsey. "If you will excuse me, it is time for Lancelot's bath."

They watched in silence as the woman scooped up her dog and scurried away with surprising speed for a woman of her considerable girth.

"She is in rather a hurry," Emma said.

"So I noticed." Leonida stepped directly in front of Emma, reaching to grasp her hands with a worried frown. "Emma."

"Hmm?"

"I am willing to go to great lengths to assist you in your search for Anya, but you cannot search through warehouses on Cutler Street without protection." She squeezed Emma's fingers. "Do you understand?"

Emma forced a smile, silently apologizing to the woman who had offered her such kindness.

"Of course."

DIMITRI'S INSTINCTS that had been honed in the gutters of St. Petersburg were on full alert as the carriage pulled to a halt in the dark, narrow street.

The large, uninhabited buildings and maze of alleys were a perfect refuge for criminals. And an even more perfect location for a trap.

Discreetly, he shifted on the leather seat, slipping his hand into the pocket of his greatcoat. His fingers curled with an easy familiarity around the handle of his loaded pistol. He had also tucked a knife in a sheath at his lower back and another in his high, glossy boot.

If Sanderson were stupid enough to assume he was the typical effete nobleman, he was bound to be unpleasantly surprised.

"Are you certain you have the correct address?"

The nobleman lifted a bottle of brandy to his mouth, taking a deep swig. Dimitri curled his lips in the darkness. Only a simpleton would allow his wits to be dulled in such a neighborhood.

"Quite certain," Sanderson assured him, a hint of smug amusement in his voice as he shoved open the door to the carriage and blithely stepped onto the filthy street.

With a great deal more caution, Dimitri followed his gaze, searching the shadows even as he kept his fingers curled around the handle of his pistol. Sanderson might be stupid enough to get his throat slit, but Dimitri did not intend to be such a willing victim.

At last his gaze returned to the stark brick building, searching the narrow windows for an indication of danger.

"I have visited a number of brothels and none of them have resembled a warehouse that reeks of tobacco," he rasped. "I shudder to think of what sort of female would ply her wares at such a location."

Taking a last drink of the brandy, Sanderson casually tossed aside the bottle, swaying in the sharp breeze. Dimitri grimaced. He abhorred a man who could not hold his spirits.

"This is not precisely a brothel," Sanderson slurred.

"Yes, I had managed to surmise as much," Dimitri said dryly. "You promised this evening I should have the opportunity to taste of innocence. I do not appreciate being misled."

Sanderson wagged a fat finger moving to unlock a heavy wooden door.

"Have patience."

"Patience will not transform this decrepit building into an establishment worthy of my patronage. Nor will it offer me the sort of female I had hoped to ease my hunger."

Stepping through the doorway, Sanderson waited for Dimitri to join him before closing the door and lighting a gas lantern that had been set on a low bench. The dull glow revealed precisely what Dimitri had anticipated. A cavernous room filled with crates that had recently been unloaded at the East India Docks. The only thing that appeared to be missing was the guard that must surely keep watch on such valuable property.

Sanderson weaved a path through the stacked crates. "Now that is where you are mistaken."

"What do you mean?" Dimitri demanded, warily following in his wake.

"First I must swear you to absolute secrecy."

Dimitri snorted, coming to an abrupt stop at the man's ridiculous theatrical manner.

"There are gentlemen who might enjoy this pretense of mystery, but I am not one." An explosion of fury raced through him. He had wasted endless nights being led about London by this stupid clod. Nights that he could have devoted to Emma and returning her to her rightful place in his bed. And for what? To be dangled by vague promises of young girls just ripe for the plucking? "Nor am I foolish enough to be led into so obvious a trap."

Sanderson blinked, as if surprised by Dimitri's suspicions.

"'Tis no trap, I assure you."

"Then why are we here?"

Sanderson allowed a sly smile to curve his lips. "You

are not alone in your preference for tender young creatures. The more tender the better, eh?"

"As you say."

"Unfortunately, there are those in society who do not fully appreciate our choice of entertainment, so we must hide in the shadows."

"Understandable." Dimitri grimly squashed his surge of hope. The man had been making vague references to his ability to procure young girls for days. "It is best not to attract unwanted attention."

"Precisely." Sanderson leaned toward Dimitri, oblivious to the gas lantern that swayed dangerously close to a nearby crate. Ridiculous twit. "Which is why we have a number of young females transported from Russia to be auctioned for your pleasure."

Dimitri tensed. "They are Russian?"

"An odd coincidence, is it not?"

"Odd indeed." Dimitri's voice was hoarse, his mouth dry. Russian females? Could he at last be on the threshold of destroying Count Nevskaya and his accomplices? It seemed impossible after so many years of futile effort. "And they are to be auctioned tonight?"

"Actually, the auction is not until tomorrow eve, but with a generous offer I am certain I can convince my partners to give you first choice of the wenches."

"The females are in the warehouse?"

"They are." Sanderson offered a leering smile. "Would you care to meet them?"

"More than you could imagine."

# CHAPTER FOURTEEN

UNAWARE OF HIS COMPANION'S tense anticipation, Sanderson led Dimitri through a series of locked doors, then down a set of stone steps to a narrow tunnel below. Dimitri was not surprised by the secret passage. In fact, he was intimately familiar with such hidden cellars. Any gentleman who imported goods knew that it was vital to possess a public warehouse where the officials could inspect your legally transported cargo, and a separate location for those goods you prefer to keep away from prying eyes. He had several such places scattered throughout St. Petersburg.

"Follow me," Sanderson whispered, weaving his way through the damp tunnel.

Still conscious that he might very well be entering a trap, Dimitri remained on guard.

"I must admit I am curious how you managed to acquire Russian maidens," he prompted.

"It is a profitable exchange," the nobleman readily answered, the top of his high beaver hat nearly brushing the wooden beams that lined the ceiling and his glossy boots splashing through the occasional puddles. "We provide suitable English virgins to be sent to Russia and in return we are offered the tastiest of Russian fruits."

Dimitri hid a grimace, wondering how much of the business his father kept hidden from Sanderson. Count Nevskaya could not be so stupid as to offer more than the barest information to the babbling buffoon.

He could only hope it would be enough to convince Alexander Pavlovich to prosecute the nobleman.

"Very clever," he murmured. "I presume you have a colleague in Russia, so you need not make such a journey yourself?"

"We do, but of course, we are sworn to keep our identities in the deepest confidence."

"Granted a certain measure of caution is required, but surely there is no need for secrets among friends?" he urged with a chuckle.

"I doubt Count Nevskaya would agree," Sanderson grumbled, drunkenly unaware he had just revealed what Dimitri desired to hear. "He is obsessed with disguising his participation in our little scheme. There is a rumor he possesses an enemy that has pledged to destroy him. It has no doubt made him a tad skittish."

Dimitri smiled with cold satisfaction. "No doubt."

They had nearly reached the end of the tunnel where a heavy wooden door blocked their path when Sanderson abruptly turned to face Dimitri.

"A moment, sir."

Dimitri scowled with impatience. "Why are we stopping?"

Sanderson awkwardly cleared his throat. "Forgive me, but I wish to be assured you have recalled to bring along your purse. We are forced to hire rather dangerous ruffians to ensure the women maintain their innocence during the long voyage and they would not take kindly to a gentleman seeking to despoil a maid unless he had paid for the pleasure."

"I have come prepared." Dimitri reached beneath his coat to pull out the folded bills from his pocket, then he pulled his other hand out of his pocket just far enough to reveal the ivory handle of his pistol. "Fully prepared."

"So I see." Sanderson blanched, his hands unsteady as he turned to pound on the wooden door. "Valik, it is Sanderson. Open the door."

The door cracked open a sliver. "First I will see the money," a male voice thick with a Russian accent demanded.

A flush stained Sanderson's fat cheeks. He might be slow-witted, but he knew when he was being humiliated.

"Do not seek to rise above yourself, Valik," he growled. "The women are my property to dispose of as I wish."

"It is my duty to protect my employer's investment."

"Stand aside or I will have you hauled to Newgate prison and left to rot."

There was the sound of foul Russian curses, then with obvious reluctance the man pulled open the door and stepped back.

"Bring the females," Sanderson commanded as he swept regally into the cramped cellar.

Dimitri made use of the man's generous girth to covertly slide into the shadowed chamber unnoticed. A swift glance assured him that the room was empty beyond the hovering servant, but his tension did not lessen.

There was something oddly familiar about the Russian's bluntly carved features and small, deep-set eyes that glittered with cold intelligence. Dimitri's gaze lowered to take in the man's rough clothing that did nothing to hide the thick muscles and the pistol he held with ease.

He silently slid his own pistol out of his pocket, his body coiled and prepared to attack as the man approached Sanderson with a fierce scowl.

"First I will have payment…" He began, only to cease in shock as he caught sight of Dimitri over the nobleman's shoulder. Using his sharp instincts, he had his gun lifted and pointed at Dimitri's heart. "You."

Sanderson squeaked in terror as Dimitri roughly shoved him out of his way, his gun aimed at the Russian's head. He had discovered when he was a youth trying to survive on the streets that a shot to the heart was not always a killing blow. A hole in the head, however, was deadly.

"Bloody hell, have you taken leave of your senses?" Sanderson shouted.

"Stupid bastard," the servant growled, his gaze never wavering from Dimitri's grim expression.

"What are you doing?"

"Attempting to keep us from the gallows," Valik hissed. "Unless it was your intention to betray the count?"

Sanderson backed away, wringing his pudgy hands. "Do not be absurd. There must be some mistake."

"There is no mistake. Your fine Russian nobleman is Dimitri Tipova, the czar of St. Petersburg's criminals and sworn enemy of my employer."

Accepting that his charade was at an end, Dimitri held his gun steady as he calculated the best means of escaping the cellars that did not include a coffin.

"Sworn enemy?" he taunted, hoping that the temperamental servant could be prodded into recklessness. "Very dramatic."

"Lord almighty," Sanderson wailed. "We must do something."

"You will collect the girls and transport them out of England," Valik commanded with a composure at complete odds with his employer.

Dimitri was under no illusion which of the two was more dangerous. Which was precisely why his gun remained trained on the Russian even as he cursed the possibility of Sanderson slipping from his grasp.

"Now?" the nobleman rasped.

"Of course now, you idiot."

"But surely there is no need to panic? If you—" Sanderson waved his hands in Dimitri's direction. "Properly dispose of the threat then we can continue with the auction as planned. We are all interested in ensuring we gain a measure of profit before we ship the cargo."

Dimitri laughed with mocking amusement. "My father must have been desperate to have entered into business with such a buffoon."

The Russian grimaced. "I did warn him that his English partners were fools destined to ruin our scheme."

"How dare you speak of your betters in such a fashion?" Emboldened by his greed, Sanderson took a step forward, his double chins quivering with outrage. "Valik, you will kill this traitor and be rid of his body. I will continue with the auction as originally planned. Do you hear me?"

Fury tightened Valik's brutish face, his eyes glittering with a deadly hatred.

"All I hear is a braying ass who is determined to destroy us all," he snapped. "Do you believe that Tipova told no one he suspected you were involved in selling children?"

"Who would he—bloody hell," Sanderson gasped, pulling a lacy handkerchief from his pocket to dab at the sweat beading his upper lip. "The Duke of Huntley. I am ruined."

"It is not only Huntley who is aware of your debauchery, but the prime minister," Dimitri admitted with a cold smile. He had met with the gentleman only days after his arrival in London, thanks to Huntley's insistence.

Sanderson turned a pasty gray, setting aside the gas lantern as he swayed in horror.

"Liverpool?"

"To be honest I was taken aback by his eagerness to have you arrested. But then I realized a public trial at the Old Bailey might be a perfect means of assuring the unsettled populace that the nobles are not above the law." Dimitri ruthlessly pressed. "Perhaps your worthless existence might have some purpose after all."

"Oh, my God. Liverpool has hated me since we were

at Oxford together. A damned shame those Cato Street conspirators did not manage to kill the humorless prude," the distraught Sanderson muttered, clearly too ignorant to realize that had the radicals managed to assassinate the cabinet members as they had planned, they intended to overthrow the entire government, as well. And to be rid of noblemen such as Sanderson and his chums. "What the devil am I to do?"

"You will take the women from this warehouse and find some means to get them out of the country," Valik demanded.

Sanderson shook his head in panic. "No, I cannot."

There was a tense pause as Valik considered his limited choices. Then, catching both Dimitri and Sanderson by surprise, he withdrew a matching pistol from the pocket of his dark wool coat and shoved it into Sanderson's hand.

"Here."

Sanderson cursed, fumbling to point the gun in Dimitri's direction.

"What the devil are you doing?"

"Attempting to keep my head attached to my body," Valik admitted, backing toward the door that led deeper into the catacombs. "I will see to the girls."

Dimitri's teeth clenched as Sanderson's fingers tensed on the pistol. It was doubtful the damned nobleman could hit a target at ten paces if he were aiming, but it would be just Dimitri's luck that the bastard would kill him by accident.

"What of me?" Sanderson shrilled.

"You will…" Valik paused with a cruel smile. "Dispose of the problem you have caused."

"Wait…"

The servant disappeared into the shadows, leaving behind a tense silence.

Dimitri covertly shifted forward. If he could distract

the nobleman, he might be able to overpower him before the dolt could squeeze off a shot.

"Well, Sanderson, it appears that you have been left to bear the punishment for the sins of others."

"I will not—" Sanderson gave a dangerous wave of the gun as he noticed Dimitri's slow advance. "Stay back."

"I could be of assistance."

"Aye, you truly do believe me to be an idiot."

"I have no interest in you or your lack of intelligence, Sanderson," Dimitri soothed. "My purpose in coming to England was solely to destroy Count Nevskaya. If you cooperate, I will speak to Alexander Pavlovich in your defense."

Sanderson licked his lips. "What would you have me do?"

"Return with me to Russia."

"Russia? Why?"

Dimitri took another sly step forward. Still too far away to strike, but ever closer.

"I want you to confess all you know of the count's involvement in the slave trade."

The man jerked, his eyes wide. "We have never been involved with slaves."

Dimitri could not hide his revulsion at the ridiculous protest.

"Did I offend your delicate sensibilities?" he mocked. "Do you perhaps choose to refer to your sordid business as kidnapping defenseless children and selling them to be abused by disgusting lechers?"

Sanderson frowned in puzzlement. "They are just peasants. What good are they except to become whores?"

Dimitri stilled, his finger twitching on the trigger of his pistol. Unlike his companion, he was a deadly shot. One bullet and the twit would be a rotting corpse.

Then, he sucked in a steadying breath, reminding himself

that the only means to bring an end to the trafficking of Russian girls was to ensure his father was exposed as a monster and driven from society. And for that he needed Sanderson alive.

"I doubt the good citizens of England would so readily agree," he warned. "In their current mood they might very well stir up a riot if they are not satisfied with your punishment. Have you ever witnessed a man ravaged by a mob? It is a nasty means to die."

Sanderson trembled, the sweat dripping from his ruddy face.

"And what would traveling to Russia achieve?"

"If you confess to the czar, he might be willing to offer you sanctuary in Russia."

"So I can live like a heathen in some frozen village far from decent society?" Sanderson looked as if Dimitri had threatened to geld him. "Never."

"So you would rather be the source of scandalous ridicule as you are paraded through the streets on the way to the gallows?"

"No."

Overcome with his terror, Sanderson stumbled backward, his hand tightening on the pistol. Dimitri leaped to the side as the deafening sound of a gunshot filled the small chamber, but it was a heartbeat too late as the bullet sliced through his upper arm.

Landing on the hard ground, he struggled against a tide of blackness as the shocking pain ripped through his body.

EMMA WAS FULLY AWARE of the foolishness of sneaking from the Huntley town house dressed in the rough clothing of a stable hand that she had stolen from the laundry room. And for taking a hack to the nasty warren of streets where the Sanderson warehouses were located. And for hiding in a narrow alley as the elegant carriage came to a halt in the dark street and two gentlemen stepped onto the damp cobblestones.

It would no doubt serve her right if she were to have her throat cut and her body tossed into the gutter, she had ruefully admitted. But she had made the decision that she would do whatever necessary to rescue Anya when she had left Yabinsk. Even if that meant putting her life at risk.

Remaining in the shadows, her heart gave a sharp lurch as she easily recognized Dimitri standing in front of the warehouse. Despite the darkness she would know the broad set of his shoulders and the proud, perfect lines of his profile anywhere. There was no other gentleman in England who could match his dark, ruthless beauty.

And, of course, there was that disturbing awareness that swept through her body like a tidal wave. She would know Dimitri was near even if she were blindfolded.

So did his presence mean that her desperate hope that Anya and the other girls might be hidden in the warehouse was not utter insanity?

Gathering her ebbing courage, Emma silently crept forward as the men entered, waiting until she heard them crossing the wooden planks of the floor before slipping through the door. Her heart thundered in her chest, her mouth dry with fear. Whether it was the terror of being murdered by a ruffian, or of being caught by Dimitri was impossible to say.

Either posed a fate she intended to avoid.

She stepped into the large storage room, her nose wrinkling at the overwhelming scent of dried tobacco and spices. In the darkness she could make out the silhouettes of wooden crates stacked in neat rows, and in the distance the unmistakable glow of a gas light that was rapidly disappearing down a flight of stairs.

Not giving herself time to consider the countless reasons

she should be fleeing the warehouse with all possible speed, Emma cautiously crept past the crates, lingering at the opening to the stairs. She paused, ensuring that the men were not about to make a sudden reappearance. Then praying the wooden steps did not squeak and reveal her presence, she forced herself into the narrow stairwell.

She stumbled as she reached the bottom, startled by the black shroud of darkness that surrounded her. Not that she should have been surprised. Underground tunnels were as a rule dark and damp.

Reaching out her hand, she hesitantly made her way over the uneven ground, her rasping breath the only sound to break the thick silence.

Then, just as she began to fear that she was hopelessly lost in the dark, she heard distant voices. She shuffled forward, relieved by the dim glow of light that spilled from an open door into the tunnel.

Reaching the edge of the pool of light, she paused and pressed herself against the wall of the tunnel, clearly able to hear the raised voices of the men. For a moment she struggled to understand the argument, then her heart gave a violent leap.

Dear God, Lord Sanderson was holding Dimitri at gunpoint. And just as alarming, Anya was hidden somewhere nearby and that horrid Valik was rushing off to take her away.

Emma knew she had to do something. She had to…

Her shocked mind was still struggling to decide on a course of action when the air was shattered by the sound of a gunshot.

"Dimitri," she whispered, sheer terror holding her prisoner as Lord Sanderson suddenly stumbled past her and disappeared down the tunnel. But as Dimitri's low moan reached her, she thrust aside her fear and rushed into the room, discovering Dimitri lying on the floor, his beautiful face twisted in pain. With a small cry she sank onto her knees, her hand reaching to cup his cheek. "Dimitri, can you hear me?"

"Emma?" The thick curtain of his lashes lifted, revealing golden eyes that were shockingly lucid considering he had just been shot. And smoldering with fury. "What are you doing here?"

"It does not matter." She ran a frantic gaze over his body, spotting the torn coat sleeve and the blood already staining the fabric. "You have been hurt, we must get you to a surgeon."

Muttering under his breath, Dimitri sat upright, studying the wound beneath the heavy layers of clothing.

"It is no more than a scratch," he concluded, forcing himself to his feet.

Emma straightened, reaching to grasp his arm as he swayed. "Must you be so stubborn?"

He cast a smoldering glance over her wool coat and male breeches.

"Be assured we will have a thorough discussion regarding who is the more stubborn later, *milaya,* but for now I have to capture Sanderson before he can escape."

Emma frowned in puzzlement. For a moment the thought that Dimitri had been seriously wounded had driven everything from her mind. Now, the memory of the argument she had overheard seared through her mind.

"Sanderson?"

"He cannot have gone far."

"What does it matter where he has gone?"

"With his confession to Alexander Pavlovich, my father will at last be exposed to society as a monster."

"But we must go after that horrible Valik. He said he was taking the girls out of England," she argued.

Dimitri made a sound of impatience. "They will not be allowed to escape."

Emma's lips parted to inform him that she would go after the man alone if necessary when they both turned toward the door and the unmistakable sound of approaching footsteps.

"Emma?" a familiar male voice called.

Dimitri sent her a startled frown. "You brought Huntley with you?"

"Nothing so polite," the duke drawled, appearing ridiculously out of place in his elegant black coat and glossy Hessians. His stark expression, however, perfectly mirrored Dimitri's. "She snuck away the moment my back was turned."

Indifferent to the nobleman's fierce displeasure, Emma regarded him with a pleading expression.

"Please, you must help me, Your Grace. My sister—"

Her words were rudely interrupted as Dimitri firmly shoved her into the grasp of the duke.

"Return Emma to your town house and have her locked in her rooms."

Stefan had her arm in a vice grip before Emma could escape. "Very well."

"No!" Emma futilely struggled to free herself. "I am going to find Anya."

The two men ignored her.

"What of you?" the duke inquired.

"I must stop Sanderson from fleeing." His golden gaze shifted to Emma's mutinous expression. "Then I will make certain the girls are found and taken to my ship. They will be safe there."

Stefan dipped his head in agreement. "My servants will assist you."

"Thank you." His gaze never shifted from Emma's face, his own expression bleak. "Do not let her out of your sight."

In disbelief, Emma felt herself being ruthlessly urged

toward the door she had so recently charged through. Precisely the opposite direction she was desperate to go.

"Let go of me." She glared at Dimitri as she was overpowered by the large Englishman. "I will never forgive you for this, Dimitri Tipova."

His jaw tightened. "Emma, these men are vicious. They will kill anyone they believe threatens them."

"I do not care," she shouted. "Anya is here. I will not leave without her."

Dimitri turned his attention to the duke. "Huntley."

"You are certain?" the duke demanded.

"Yes."

"Forgive me," Stefan muttered, then with one powerful motion he had Emma tossed over his shoulder and was rapidly heading back down the tunnel.

Emma cursed and screamed and kicked, but her efforts to escape were ignored as she was hauled away like a bit of unwanted rubbish.

Why had she halted to see if Dimitri were alive or dead, she bitterly wondered?

Had she continued across the room and into the darkness beyond she might even now be rescuing Anya from harm. Instead, she had allowed her weakness for the captivating criminal to make her hesitate. And as punishment for her vulnerability she was once again unable to save her sister.

It was a mistake she would not make again, she swore.

Attempting to gather her badly shredded dignity, Emma ceased her struggles and allowed herself to be carried from the warehouse and bundled into the elegant black carriage. Stefan followed behind, settling his large body on the leather bench opposite her.

"This is for the best, Emma," he assured her as the carriage jerked into motion.

She clenched her hands in her lap, cursing the day she had ever encountered Dimitri Tipova.

"And what if it were your sister being held captive by ruthless beasts who intend to auction her to the highest bidder? Would you meekly return to your home and hope she be rescued?"

Stefan's expression gentled in understanding.

"I have been forced to swallow my pride and accept that another might possess the skills I lacked to confront a particular danger." He reached across to lightly touch her cheek. "You must trust Dimitri."

She turned to glare out the window, her heart aching with disappointment.

She had already put her trust in Dimitri. Naive fool that she was. Even when she had sensed that his lust for revenge was greater than his affection for her.

"Dimitri is driven by his need to punish his father," she said tightly. "He will sacrifice Anya if it ensures the humiliation of Count Nevskaya."

Unable to deny the truth of her words, Stefan heaved a sigh.

"Then trust my servants. They will not allow the girls to be taken from London."

"I trust no one but myself."

"Emma—"

"Please, no more lectures, Your Grace," she warned in raw tones.

A tense silence filled the air as they rumbled their way through the London streets to Mayfair. More than once Emma considered the desperate notion of trying to leap from the carriage and make her way back to the warehouse only to dismiss such foolishness.

Not only was it quite likely that the fall would break her neck, but she would not be allowed to go more than a few steps before Stefan's burly grooms would have her captured.

Arriving at the imposing town house, Stefan kept a tight grip on her arm as he escorted her into the elegant vestibule.

"My staff will be warned that you are not to leave the grounds," he declared in rueful tones.

Emma tilted her chin. "Then I am your prisoner?"

"My guest who I intend to protect, with or without your blessing."

"You must do as you think best." Turning on her heel, she headed for the nearby stairs. "As will I."

## CHAPTER FIFTEEN

THE BLUSH OF DAWN BARELY painted the sky when Emma heard the key being turned in her lock.

After being imprisoned in her bedchamber by the Duke of Huntley, she had spent the long night pacing the floor, dividing her time between cursing Dimitri Tipova for treating her as if she were a blundering idiot and praying that he swiftly returned with her sister.

How dare he send her away when she had traveled halfway around the world to find Anya? And how dare he put his need for revenge before the young girls who were at the mercy of those despicable animals?

As the hours had passed, her anger had swelled until she was trembling with the need to escape from her lavish prison. She had been taking care of herself for a number of years and she did not appreciate having her hard-earned independence snatched away.

So perhaps it was understandable that when the door slid open to reveal the foreign gentleman who had kidnapped her during Sir Jergens's soiree she did not scream. Or even attempt to race past him into the hall. Instead, she watched in weary curiosity as he offered a smooth bow.

"May I enter?"

"I…" She licked her lips, struggling to force her foggy brain to think clearly. A voice in the back of her mind warned that honest gentlemen did not sneak through a duke's town house and approach a maiden in her private chambers. But it was a voice she ignored as she met his steady black gaze. "Yes."

He hovered in the doorway, a faint smile curving his lips. "If you would be so kind as to close the curtains?"

"Why?"

"There are an inordinate number of servants lurking about the grounds. If they were to notice the shadow of a gentleman in your private chamber they would be certain to investigate."

Emma bit her lip, then gave a jerky nod. She understood the danger of allowing a strange man into her rooms, but she also knew that one scream and a dozen servants would rush to her rescue. The man had risked his life to seek her out in such an unconventional manner. Whatever he desired of her it had to be important.

"Of course."

She moved to pull shut the heavy curtains, inanely aware she was still attired in the rough breeches and linen shirt of a stable boy, her hair hanging in tangles and her face smudged from her adventure in the warehouse. The stranger, on the other hand, was elegantly dressed in a black jacket and satin pantaloons with a huge ruby twinkling in the depths of his cravat. As if he had just stepped out of an elegant ballroom.

Wrapping her arms around her waist, she watched as the darkly beautiful man entered the room and closed the door behind his slender form.

"What are you doing here?" she demanded.

Holding out his hands in a gesture of peace, he slowly approached her.

"As I suggested during our first encounter we have a mutual purpose in traveling to London."

"Surely it is past time for allusion and innuendo?" she snapped, her temper frayed and her nerves raw with concern for her sister. "If you have something to say, then please do so."

"Plain speech? Very well." He halted directly before

her, his exotic scent tantalizing her. "I know why you have traveled to England."

She stilled, wary he could be hoping to trick her into confessing her secrets.

"How could you possibly know?"

He reached up to pluck the hat off his head and tossed it onto a low table, the sable darkness of his hair glinting in the flames of the fireplace.

"With the proper enticement and enough patience a man can discover any information he desires."

She shivered, unable to believe that Dimitri's crew would be disloyal, no matter what the temptation. But then again, Dimitri had been forced to confide his purpose in coming to England to a number of government officials, including the prime minister. She doubted that their staffs would be above suspicion.

"And why would you be interested in my reason for traveling to England?"

His black gaze swept over her face, lingering on the lush curve of her lips.

"Beyond my fascination with your beauty?"

Her heart gave a nervous flutter.

"Please, do not," she breathed.

"Allow me to begin at the beginning." Pressing his hands together in a formal gesture, he offered a solemn dip of his head. "I am Caliph Rajih."

"Caliph?" Emma frowned, attempting to recall her studies of the near Orient—lessons that had been sadly vague when it came to foreign royalty. "You are a prince?"

"I am a leader of my people," he agreed.

The knowledge should perhaps have been shocking. After all, what sort of prince lurked in the shadows rather than take his place among the finest of London society? But Emma was more resigned than shocked. Had she not already suspected that he was accustomed to giving commands and having them obeyed? It was etched in the proud lines of his face and the arrogant carriage of his slender body.

"Where?" she demanded.

"Egypt."

Again, she was struck by thoughts of sunlight blazing over golden dunes and tents crowded about a small oasis. Men forged in the merciless desert were rumored to be as hard and unforgiving as the land that birthed them.

"You are a very long way from your home."

"As are you." His hand lifted to caress a stray curl resting against her cheek. "We are similar in many ways."

She hastily stepped away from his disturbing touch. "Why have you come to London?"

He studied her for a long moment, the dark eyes glittering with a wicked anticipation that sent a shiver of unease down her spine. Then, with a shrug, he paced toward the fireplace and leaned against the marble mantel.

"I will not bore you with the long and ofttimes tragic history of my country, but suffice it to say that we at last possess a powerful viceroy who is prepared to embrace the future rather than to smother us in the past," he said, reaching beneath his jacket to pull out a lacquered snuff box. His brows lifted as he caught Emma's sudden flare of amusement. "Why do you smile?"

Emma sank onto one of the sofas, weary after her endless night of pacing.

"You are obviously of the desert and yet there is something oddly English about you."

"Ah." With a practiced motion he flipped open the box and took a small pinch of the snuff, placing it neatly on his wrist before bending his head to inhale the perfumed tobacco. He returned the box to his pocket and met Emma's small smile. "My father sent me to school here when I was just twelve. He believed, as the pasha does, that a closer connection to the West is vital for our survival. I lived in this country until my father's death six years ago."

That certainly explained his ease with the English language.

"Then you are a diplomat?"

"When the occasion demands." He shrugged, his expression somber. "On this journey, however, my purpose is to bring to an end an ancient practice that has been a blight on my country's reputation."

"I fear I do not comprehend."

"The slave trade."

"Oh." She shook her head in confusion. "I thought…"

His eyes narrowed as she broke off her hasty words.

"You thought we were all savages who were so desperate for soft white flesh that we encourage the infidels to peddle their females in our markets?"

She wrinkled her nose, accepting she was very much in the wrong. How often she had to hide her outrage when she had overheard herself being referred to as a Russian savage? It was shameful that she would offer the same obtuse assumption.

"Forgive me."

He held up a slender hand, his expression rueful. "No, it is I who begs your forgiveness, Emma. For too long our corrupt officials have turned a blind eye to the traffickers. The pasha, however, seeks to improve our relationship with England as well as the Continent and he has made a vow to bar the peddling of females in our markets."

She nodded in sympathy. Despite the best efforts of the Romanovs, much of Russia still remained mired in the past. Change was never a simple matter for people to embrace, even when it might be for their own good.

"Does this have something to do with my sister?"

"I believe so. During the past few years I have noticed a number of Russian whores in the brothels of Cairo. I, of course, began my search for those responsible in Russia. You can imagine my frustration when I could discover no evidence of ships carrying unwilling females to Cairo."

Emma was quick to realize the truth. "Because they were traveling to England."

A pleased smile curved his lips, as if she had somehow fulfilled his expectation.

"You are intelligent as well as beautiful," he murmured. "Yes, the girls are taken from Russia to London and sold for the private pleasure of wealthy Englishmen. Eventually the men become weary of their trinket and wish to be rid of her with as little fuss as possible."

She ignored the sick dread in her stomach. If she allowed herself to dwell on all the horrible tortures that Anya might be enduring she would go stark raving mad.

Instead, she concentrated on the caliph's unexpected information.

It appeared that Dimitri had underestimated his father once again. They had assumed that once the Russian girls had been sold to the English roués that they would eventually be left in a local brothel. But if the caliph was right...

Dear Lord, she had to find Anya.

Emma surged to her feet, her hands trembling as she pushed back the thick curls that tumbled about her shoulders.

"You suspect they are taken to Cairo?"

His hooded gaze seared over her pale face before lowering to her slender body.

"They are no longer innocent, but there are a great many of my countrymen who harbor a lust for such pale, perfect beauty," he admitted, his voice low and husky.

Emma shivered, sternly refusing to allow her thoughts to stray from Anya and the beasts who held her captive.

"Do you believe the same men who have brought them to England also arrange to have them taken to Cairo?"

"Yes."

She pressed a hand to her heaving stomach. "Is there no limit to their depravity?"

"It would seem not." His dark features hardened, a lethal fury flaring through his eyes. "From what I have managed to discover, Count Nevskaya's servants remain in London until they collect the Russian females that have been returned to them, as well as the English girls that are their payment, and travel to Egypt. Once there, they sell the Russians in the markets before continuing back to St. Petersburg with the English maidens to pleasure the count and his friends."

"There is little wonder Dimitri was incapable of untangling their sordid business."

"Tipova," the caliph growled. "Do not speak his name in my presence."

She blinked at his fierce response. "Why?"

"I went to great trouble to prepare my trap only to have Tipova blunder into my snare and send my prey fleeing into the night." He straightened from the mantel and crossed to stand before her. "Along with your sister."

"Anya." Emma instinctively grasped his arm. "You know where she is?"

His warm hand covered her fingers, his male scent cloaking her in a musky spice.

"If she was among the females taken from the warehouse, then she is currently aboard a ship called the *Katherine Marie* and headed for Cairo."

The *Katherine Marie?* Emma would have fallen to her knees if he had not grasped her arms to keep her upright.

"Dear God, I failed her," she breathed, barely aware of being pulled into the caliph's arms and held against his chest. "It does not matter how I try, I always fail her."

Still holding her close, he bent his head to whisper in her ear.

"It is not too late, Emma."

She pulled back to meet the dark glitter of his gaze. "What do you mean?"

"My ship is being prepared as we speak. I intend to

sail for Cairo within the hour." He smiled with a blatant challenge. "Will you join me?"

A PRISTINE LAYER OF WHITE snow draped London as Dimitri wearily entered the Huntley town house.

In the distance a church bell tolled and the sound of the coal wagon rattled over the cobblestones, but a sleepy silence remained settled over the elegant neighborhood. It might be near ten in the morning, but society remained snuggled in their warm beds. It would be hours before they were primped and prepared to meet the day.

Worthless nitwits.

Allowing the waiting butler to take his outer garments, Dimitri shoved his fingers through his damp hair and climbed the steps.

His every instinct urged him to travel directly to Emma's chambers. The sight of the wounded fury burning in her eyes as Huntley had carried her away had plagued him the entire morning.

It was infuriating. He had only been protecting the stubborn minx despite her determination to get herself killed. God almighty, what sort of female would disguise herself as a stable boy and sneak about a neighborhood that would terrify the most hardened criminal? And then to attempt to charge after the Russian brute as if she were indestructible...

Obviously, Emma Linley-Kirov was in dire need of a man willing and able to restrain her dangerous impulses.

So why did he feel an overwhelming compulsion to seek her out and banish the shadow of betrayal from her eyes?

Climbing the marble steps, he was jerked out of his thoughts as Huntley appeared on the landing above him, clearly having lain in wait for his return.

"Tipova. At last." The duke wore a brocade gown with his dark hair tousled and his face unshaven, but his casual appearance did not lessen his imperious manner as he gestured for Dimitri to follow him into the book-lined study. He waved a slender hand toward the walnut desk as he crossed to toss another log into the fireplace. "The brandy is on the desk."

"I prefer my vodka," Dimitri said, pulling out his silver flask as he strolled to stand beside the bay window that offered a view of the snowy street below.

Stefan replaced the fire screen, then joined Dimitri at the window.

"You look like hell."

"Which is precisely how I feel," Dimitri admitted.

The duke's astute glance lingered on the bloody rip in Dimitri's coat.

"Shall I summon a surgeon?"

"I have recovered from far worse." He took a drink of the vodka. "Have you spoken to Emma this morning?"

"It is still early. She is asleep in her bedchamber."

Dimitri narrowed his gaze. Emma was frantic with her concern for her sister, not to mention anxious to stick a dagger in his heart, he would bet his last ruble she was pacing her floor as she awaited his return.

Assuming she had not found a means of slipping past Huntley's servants.

"Are you certain?"

Huntley grimaced. "I personally locked her in her rooms despite my wife's fervent protests. Any debt between us is now paid in full."

A sympathetic smile touched Dimitri's mouth. He had been subjected to Leonida's "fervent protests" during her stay in St. Petersburg.

"Agreed."

"Tell me what happened after I left," Huntley commanded. "Did you manage to locate Sanderson?"

Dimitri rubbed the aching muscles of his neck, still awaiting the sense of elation he had expected to feel. He told himself that he was too weary to properly celebrate his victory.

"I apprehended him as his carriage was leaving his town house. By the amount of luggage he had packed I assume he intended to be away from his home for a considerable length of time."

"Did he struggle?"

"He fell to his knees, weeping like a baby."

Huntley shook his head in disgust. "Spineless coward."

"He did manage one lucky shot," Dimitri muttered, his arm aching from the bullet wound. "The bastard."

"Where is he now?"

"Your message to Liverpool ensured the prime minister was prepared for my arrival with my captive. Liverpool swore that Sanderson would be well guarded until he could finish his confession to the king."

"And then?"

"Then he is to be given into my care to be taken to Alexander Pavlovich."

"What of the others?"

Dimitri shrugged as he turned to pace the floor. Despite the exhaustion that clung heavily to his body, he felt oddly restless.

Or perhaps not so oddly, he wryly acknowledged.

The incessant need to be with Emma was an itch that would not be dismissed. She was his to protect, a savage voice whispered in the back of his mind. Not Huntley's.

"The king's guards have been sent to capture Timmons and Jergens. They should be in custody by the end of the day," he muttered, unnerved by the primitive sensations that smoldered deep in his heart. "It will take weeks, if not months to gather the various servants involved."

"So it is done."

Dimitri turned back toward his companion, his expression grim.

"Not entirely."

"Ah." Huntley gave a nod of comprehension. "Anya."

"Your servants have been searching through the stews, but thus far they have found nothing."

"That is unfortunate."

Dimitri's sharp laugh echoed through the room. "It is more than unfortunate. Emma will hold me responsible if we do not find her sister."

Huntley offered a smile of sympathy, wise enough not to bother with absurd assurances that Emma would understand Dimitri was only doing what was best for her. They both knew the woman could not be reasonable when it came to her sister.

"They cannot hide forever, and I assure you that I have the roads leading from London being watched," he promised. "They will not slip past my guards."

"And the docks?"

With a shrug, the duke moved to pour himself a glass of brandy. "I have sent word that anyone seeking passage for a number of young ladies is to be detained."

Dimitri's brows snapped together. "Huntley, men who are in the smuggling trade do not purchase tickets."

"Perhaps not as a rule, but those men had no plans to flee London without notice. It is not a simple matter to arrange for a ship willing to sail with illegal cargo."

"True enough," Dimitri grudgingly conceded, still far from satisfied.

There were a large number of captains willing to turn a blind eye to smuggled goods with the proper incentive, but there were only a handful who were willing to dabble in the slave trade. It would surely take Valik a few days to arrange passage out of England.

Unless…

The flask dropped from his hand, the fine vodka spilling across the Persian carpet.

Huntley stepped toward him with a frown. "Tipova?"

"It is a simple matter if there is already a ship waiting," he gritted.

"What?"

"The *Katherine Marie*."

Huntley's eyes widened. "Bloody hell."

"Well, I hope the two of you are pleased with yourself."

As one they both turned to head toward the door, only to be halted as Leonida swept into the room, appearing remarkably beautiful in an ivory morning gown trimmed with sable and her golden hair artfully curled, but it was the angry flush on her cheeks and the tears glittering in her eyes that captured Dimitri's attention.

"Darling, now is not the best time..." Huntley began, then paused as his wife pointed a finger directly in his face.

"She is gone."

An icy dread sliced through Dimitri. "What did you say?"

Leonida turned to glare in his direction, her expression one of furious accusation.

"Since I refuse to starve my guests while they are being held as a prisoner beneath my roof I had a breakfast tray prepared," she hissed. "When I entered Emma's room I discovered her bed had not been slept in and that her belongings were missing. She is gone and you have no one to blame but yourself."

## CHAPTER SIXTEEN

EMMA STOOD AT THE BOW of the ship, watching the dancing waves that shimmered the color of mercury in the sunlight. In the distance, the coast of Alexandria was drawing ever closer, making her shiver at the exotic silhouettes of domes and obelisks that stood starkly against the vivid blue sky. Dear Lord, had she been a fool to come here?

It was a question that had haunted her since she had allowed Caliph Rajih to lead her from the Duke of Huntley's town house to his waiting ship.

Not that Rajih had given her cause for alarm, she conceded. In truth, he had behaved as a perfect gentleman during the voyage, joining her only for dinner in her private cabin before placing a chaste kiss on her lips and disappearing topside.

Emma could not discern whether his restraint was because the rough seas had demanded his full attention among the crew or because his flirtations in London had merely been a means to lure her onto his ship.

Or perhaps he considered her a female worthy of more than a convenient affair that would make her a source of amusement among his crew.

Unlike some gentlemen of her acquaintance…

Her hands tightened on the brass railing, her teeth clenching at the unwelcome thought of Dimitri Tipova.

No, she would not waste her time thinking of the man who had sacrificed her sister for his own revenge.

"Imposing, is it not?" a soft male voice whispered in her ear.

She turned her head to discover Rajih at her side, her eyes widening in surprise at the sight of him standing in his traditional white robes. Accustomed to seeing him in European attire, she could not deny a faint shiver of appreciation at the sight of his sophisticated facade stripped away to reveal the ruthless man of the desert beneath.

Of course, what woman would not appreciate the striking beauty of his dark, austere features and black eyes that burned with a restless intelligence?

Disturbed by her unexpected reaction to his presence, she abruptly turned to regard the vast citadel that Rajih was pointing out with obvious pride.

Constructed of pale stone, the large fortress consumed most of the island where it had been built to defend the city of Alexandria. Her gaze obediently skimmed fortified walls and forbidding castles that no doubt had terrified potential invaders.

"Very impressive."

"Yes, however it is a pity that the famed lighthouse that once stood in that precise location was destroyed. It was said to possess a vast mirror that could offer glimpses of distant cities and could cause attacking ships to be consumed by flames."

A portion of her tension eased at his light tone. As was no doubt his intention, she acknowledged with a faint smile.

"A most astonishing mirror."

"It was. But now it is lost like so many of our treasures." He shrugged, the anguished regret she sensed deep inside him at the callous plunder of his country tempered by a grim determination to regain command of Egypt's future. "But enough of the past." He swept his hands toward the busy quay. "This is the future."

Emma's attention turned toward the docks, momentarily dazzled by the large crowd milling along the banks of the river. Men with turbans, veiled women, sailors, fishermen, hawkers and children in all hues filled the air with a near-deafening clatter.

It was confusing and strikingly foreign and for a moment, Emma breathed in the brilliant sights and sounds. How different this was from her cold, barren cottage in Yabinsk.

Never in her wildest fantasies could she ever have considered the thought of standing at the bow of a ship with a handsome caliph at her side as they arrived in Egypt.

With a shake of her head she sharply reminded herself of the reason for her to be so far from home.

"Exquisite, but far more crowded than I expected," she admitted, her brow furrowed with concern. "How will we ever find Anya among so many?"

"It is doubtful the men will linger in Alexandria. They will earn a far better price for their merchandise in Cairo. For now there is nothing to be done but to appreciate the charms of the city." Rajih stepped closer, a smile curving his lips as she gave a sudden exclamation of delight. "Tell me what you see."

She pointed toward the strange animals kneeling at the edge of the water.

"I presume those must be the camels I have read of?"

He chuckled at her amazement. "They are as necessary to my people as the horses are to yours, but I must warn you they can be as temperamental and stubborn as a female."

She narrowed her gaze. "Indeed."

Capturing her hand, he lifted it to press his lips to her knuckles, then before she could protest his intimacy, he was pointing toward the horizon.

"There. Do you see the dome?"

"Yes."

"That is the seraglio of the pasha."

"Seraglio?"

"The harem." He smiled at her predictable frown before

smoothly turning her attention toward the towering obelisk. "And there is Cleopatra's Needle as well as Amud el-Sawari, or as the French have called it, Pompey's Pillar." His fingers brushed her cheek, his dark eyes lingering on the curve of her lips. "Perhaps if we have the opportunity I will take you to the catacombs. They are quite popular among the tourists."

Her heart missed a tiny beat. Only a female in her grave would fail to appreciate Rajih's potent attraction.

"But surely you do not intend to linger?"

"It will be morning before a boat can be arranged to take us to Cairo."

Her hands tightened on the railing. She had been certain they were gaining on the men who held her sister captive. Now Rajih was suggesting she tour Alexandria as if she were a silly tourist while Anya was taken ever farther away from her.

"What about those camels?" she demanded. "There must be a few we could—"

Rajih turned her to meet his somber gaze. "Emma, it will be far quicker, not to mention considerably more pleasant to travel by boat."

She made a sound of impatience. "I am not a pampered lady of society. I am accustomed to hard work and considerable discomfort when necessary."

"But it is not necessary." He laid a finger over her lips to cease her objections. "And while I do not question your fortitude you are not yet prepared for the unmerciful punishment of the desert. You must trust me."

Emma heaved a frustrated sigh. She did not want to trust Rajih. Or Dimitri. Or any other man.

She wanted to find Anya and return home where they both belonged.

Unfortunately, she had no choice but to depend upon the

caliph and to pray that he truly intended to help her rescue her sister from the monsters who had stolen her.

She returned to her cabin as they docked, pulling on a bonnet that was the precise shade of her pale orchid gown and arranged the veil to cover her face. Then, standing aside as her baggage was taken by a small boy wearing no more than a baggy pair of pants and sleeveless vest, she allowed Rajih to lead her off the ship and into a waiting carriage.

She settled on the leather seat, wincing at the turbaned servants who ran ahead of the vehicle, cudgeling the unwary who strayed in their path.

"Where are we to stay?"

"I own a house in Alexandria." Rajih waved a slender hand at the men who rushed to line the streets, shouting out what Emma presumed must be words of welcome. "It is far more modest than my home in Cairo, but it will offer a welcome comfort after such a rough journey."

On the point of demanding the precise nature of their living arrangements, Emma was distracted as their carriage was halted by a caravan of donkeys carrying men who beat small drums. Following them was a small crowd attired in silk robes trimmed with gold.

"Good heavens."

"Do not fear." Rajih placed a comforting arm around her shoulders. "It can be somewhat overwhelming for a visitor."

"Somewhat?"

"Customs and fashions, and even religion, might separate countries, but people are very much the same wherever you might travel."

She sucked in a steadying breath, her gaze skimming over the palm trees that lined the narrow lane and row of pale stone buildings that held shops, hotels and cafés where men sat around tables smoking tall pipes.

"I suppose that is true enough." Her gaze lingered on the

gentlemen wearing familiar tailored jackets and breeches strolling down the street as if they were royalty. "And to be honest, I am surprised to find so many Europeans."

Rajih shrugged. "It was not so long ago that the Sultan Kebir was in command of my country."

Sultan Kebir?

"Napoleon?" she deduced.

He nodded, the muscles of his jaw knotted. There was no need to ask his opinion of the French invaders.

"Yes."

"And you have yet to be rid of the infidel invaders?" she asked gently.

The dark eyes hardened in grim resolution. Caliph Rajih was a man who would sacrifice whatever necessary, including his pride, to resurrect his country from the ashes.

"For now we have need of their expertise," he forced himself to admit. "In ages past there was none who could compare with our scholars and engineers and scientists. We ruled without equal and none could stand in our path."

The carriage jerked back into motion, turning toward the outskirts of the bustling city.

"Do you intend to conquer the world?" she teased.

"Not this evening, but in time our glory will be restored."

Emma wrinkled her nose. Egypt had not been the only country to be invaded by Napoleon's forces, nor to have sacrificed the blood of too many good soldiers to be rid of his armies.

"Perhaps it is because I am a mere female from a forgotten Russian village, but I prefer peace to glory."

The merciless expression eased as he tugged a honey curl that had escaped from beneath her bonnet.

"As a *mere female?*" he drawled. "The crew of my ship was convinced you possessed the heart of a lioness with your golden beauty and fierce courage. You are as rare as the finest emerald."

His finger drifted down the curve of her neck, then scooped along the low cut of her bodice. She shivered, instinctively pulling away from the temptation of his touch. No matter what the caliph's attractions, she had given her heart to another.

Even if he was an ungrateful jackass.

"Rajih."

He smiled with a rueful resignation. "He is far away and yet still in your thoughts, is he not?"

A flush touched her cheeks as she attempted to feign indifference.

"He?"

"Your Russian thief."

"I have no desire to discuss Dimitri Tipova." She clenched her teeth against the jagged ache of loss. "He is a part of my past I wish to forget."

"And yet you carry his memory in your heart." Before she could guess his intention, Rajih grabbed her hand and pressed it to his lips. "Have no fear, beloved. I shall banish his ghost in time."

Having discovered it was impossible to argue with arrogant men, Emma sought to distract her companion instead.

"Goodness, why are those children darting into the road?"

The shimmer in his dark eyes revealed that he was aware of her ploy, but with a last kiss on her knuckles, he shifted to slide open the carriage window. At once a clutch of ragged boys ran forward, shoving tiny bundles into Rajih's outstretched hand. He tossed a handful of coins into the street before closing the window and turning back to Emma.

She watched in interest as he delicately unwrapped a fig leaf and revealed a small pile of dark fruit.

"Taste," he urged, lifting one of the delicacies toward her mouth.

"What is it?"

"Dates dipped in honey."

She took a tentative bite, sliding shut her eyes in appreciation as the sweetness exploded on her tongue.

"Mmm," she breathed, unconsciously licking her lips. "Ambrosia."

She heard Rajih's breath catch, his eyes darkening before he lowered his head.

"Allow me," he rasped, kissing the honey that clung to her mouth. "The sweetest of ambrosia."

His enticing scent cloaked around her, the exotic spice as heady a temptation as the strength in the hand that cupped her face. It would be easy to give in to Rajih's urging to replace Dimitri in her heart.

Not that she truly thought he could accomplish the impossible feat, but there would be undoubted pleasure in the effort.

Thankfully, she was a woman who learned from her mistakes.

She had allowed herself to depend upon Dimitri and had been betrayed. She would not allow another man the opportunity to disappoint her.

Pressing her hands to his chest, she pulled away from his kiss.

"We have halted."

His hand briefly tightened on her cheek, then with obvious reluctance he pulled back, a flush staining his cheekbones.

They said nothing as a servant in loose robes rushed forward to pull open the carriage door, and Rajih led her into the three-storied stucco home that was framed by palm trees and mimosa.

She noted the tiled floors and fountains surrounded by low divans as they moved through the foyer and into the inner rooms. She had no need for Rajih to tell her that the tapestries that lined the walls were ancient heirlooms or that the delicate pottery were priceless works of art. Even a peasant from Russia could recognize the exquisite craftsmanship of her surroundings, she wryly acknowledged.

They stepped through a set of towering doors into the square courtyard before Rajih at last came to a halt and turned to offer her a small bow.

"Welcome to my home, Emma Linley-Kirov," he said in an oddly formal fashion.

Her brows lifted as she studied the small stream of water that meandered through the dark greenery and the banks of flowers that filled the air with a thick perfume. In the center was a large fountain that sprayed water into the air and was surrounded by marble benches.

It was like a hidden jewel; all the more lovely because it was so unexpected.

"You consider this a modest home?" she demanded.

"It once belonged to my grandfather."

There was a sound overhead and she glanced up to discover birds of prey silhouetted against the brilliant blue sky. A small shiver feathered down her spine.

"Is there a harem?" she asked.

"Of course." His lips twitched as he deliberately stepped closer, his slender hand waving toward the profusion of brilliant blooms. "These gardens are a part of the seraglio. I believe you will find them suitably comfortable."

She licked her lips, belatedly aware that they were very much alone in the courtyard.

"Perhaps it would be best if I were to find rooms at a hotel—"

Rajih reached to tug off her bonnet, a heat flaring in his eyes as her honey curls tumbled about her shoulders.

"Do you fear I might lock you away as my concubine?"

"I would be a fool not to be concerned."

"Undoubtedly." He chuckled, brushing a light kiss over her lips before straightening to regard her with a steady gaze. "And I am a brute to tease you. Yes, Emma, during your stay our tradition demands that you remain in the women's quarters. It is for your own protection. But be assured that you will never be my prisoner."

DIMITRI PACED THE NORTH terrace of Windsor Castle, his gaze absently studying the frozen countryside spread beneath him. A servant had pointed out the Thames churning a path through the meadows, as well as the cluster of distant buildings he had proclaimed to be Eton College. He had also attempted to interest Dimitri in the history of the Round Tower standing in the middle ward that had been built by Henry II and the fine architecture of St. George's Chapel that he was assured possessed a fine stone-vaulted ceiling and a stained-glass window that was the finest in all the world.

At last accepting that the grim-faced Russian would not be coaxed into the warmth of the Grand Vestibule, nor impressed by the grand English castle, the servant had returned to his duties, leaving Dimitri alone with his dark thoughts.

He had not been offered an explanation as to why George IV had insisted that Lord Sanderson and Sir Jergens be brought to this castle to be held and questioned, although he suspected the portly king was anxious to suppress the revelation that proper English nobles were involved in the tawdry sex slave business. Such things were meant to be kept hidden from society.

But while Dimitri was anxious to be done with the royal formalities so that the men could be taken to Russia and their confessions heard by Alexander Pavlovich, that was not the reason he was restlessly pacing the frozen terrace.

No. The raw, gnawing fear that plagued him could be placed entirely at the feet of Emma Linley-Kirov.

His heart twisted in pain.

It had been three days since Emma had disappeared from Huntley's town house. Three days of futile searches through London. Of sending dozens of servants into the surrounding countryside, as well as to Paris and beyond to St. Petersburg to seek out any information of her whereabouts.

Of sleepless nights and endless bottles of vodka in an effort to dull the self-recriminations.

Perhaps he should accept that Emma had made her choice. He had done everything in his power to prevent her from her ridiculous habit of leaping into danger, had he not? If she were determined to get her throat slit, then there was nothing he could do to stop her.

Instead, he moodily vacillated between blinding fury that she would leave his protection and put herself at risk and a torturous knowledge that it had been his obsession to destroy his father that had driven her from his side.

Where the hell had she gone?

Was she alone? Had she found the trail of Valik and her sister? Had she been captured…?

The sound of approaching footsteps was a welcome distraction. Dimitri turned to watch Huntley's approach, hiding a smile as the duke irritably waved away the covey of servants attempting to straighten his caped greatcoat and wrap a cashmere scarf around his neck.

Dimitri had endured a similar battle when he had arrived at the castle, nearly forced to punch the aggressive footman determined to take his gloves and beaver hat. Thank God he would soon be back in St. Petersburg where he was never mistaken for a feeble nobleman incapable of putting on and taking off his own damned clothes.

Huntley's long stride never slowed as he headed toward the stone steps leading to the street below. Dimitri easily fell into step beside him, as eager as his companion to be finished with their business in Windsor and on their way back to London.

"It is done?" he demanded.

Huntley snorted in disgust, his breath visible in the chilled air.

"Between his bouts of wailing and pathetic pleas for forgiveness, Sanderson managed to confess the details of his sordid business."

"And Jergens?"

"He was equally forthcoming." Huntley shook his head. "A pity the guards did not discover Timmons until he had managed to take the coward's path."

Dimitri shrugged. Mr. Timmons had been discovered in his bedchamber with a bullet hole in his temple, obviously unable to face the sordid scandal that was about to spread throughout London.

"Did they reveal Count Nevskaya's participation in the nasty business?" he demanded.

"With glorious detail." Huntley's laugh echoed in the still air. "Indeed, they were both eager to claim that the count had approached them several years ago with the scheme and that they were no more than helpless dupes being manipulated by the evil Russian."

Dimitri waited for the torrent of exhilaration to overwhelm him.

This was the moment he had waited for since he learned of his mother's death.

The means to brand his father as a depraved fiend who preyed upon helpless children was in his hands. There would be none in society who would not turn their backs on him.

He would be an outcast. Alone in his shame.

Just as Dimitri had dreamed of for so long.

Any satisfaction he felt, however, was as cold and empty as his heart.

"I do not doubt the truth of his claim," he said, absently tapping his riding crop against his glossy riding boots as they moved down the steep incline toward the lower ward. "Sanderson does not possess enough wits to devise such a cunning plot. My father, however, has never suffered from a lack of intelligence."

"No, only a lack of morality."

"That is a rare commodity among noblemen."

Huntley lifted his brows at the less than flattering accusation. "I could say the same of thieves and scoundrels."

They followed the curve in the road, ignoring the snowflakes that drifted from the sullen clouds.

"Have you arranged with the king to have the men sent to Russia?"

"We are in…" Huntley paused, as if seeking the appropriate word. "Negotiations."

Dimitri muttered a Russian curse, his face hard with warning. "Huntley."

"Be patient, Tipova." Huntley slapped Dimitri on the back. "The king still harbors a bitterness at the perceived insults Alexander Pavlovich offered during his visit to England."

Dimitri's temper flared. He had not sacrificed so much only to have his opportunity for revenge threatened by a petulant peacock sitting on a throne.

"That was years ago," he growled.

Huntley lowered his voice, as aware as Dimitri of the numerous servants who scurried about the castle grounds. It never failed to astonish Dimitri how many nobles were blind to the people who served them. Such stupidity ensured that he was easily capable of discovering whatever information he desired.

And information was power.

"George might be king of England now that his father has died but that has not cured his unfortunate tendency to spiteful pettiness." Huntley grimaced. "As poor Brummell has learned to his regret."

"I do not care if Alexander Pavlovich pissed on your fat king's throne. I will not be denied my justice."

The duke grasped his arm and roughly hurried them both down the road to where their horses awaited them.

"Do not be a fool, Tipova," he muttered. "With a measure of diplomacy I will soon have the king convinced that the best means for him to be rid of a potential scandal is to send the men to Russia and lay the entire blame on Count Nevskaya. But not if you rile his temper. Be sensible."

Dimitri shook off the duke's hand, his expression sour. "I am in no mood to be sensible."

"Then be patient. It will be no more than a few days and you will have your revenge."

Dimitri gave a short laugh. "My revenge."

Huntley regarded him with a curious gaze. "It is what you desire, is it not?"

"So I have always believed." Dimitri glanced toward the moat that was filled with gardens rather than water. "For the past twenty years I have devoted my life to one purpose. The destruction of my father."

"No one can blame you for your hatred of the man who ruined your mother."

Dimitri winced. Would he ever be able to think of his mother without tormenting regret?

Regret that she had ever caught the vile attention of Count Nevskaya. Regret that she had been so stubbornly foolish as to attempt blackmailing him.

Regret that she had left him when he had needed her the most.

His heart gave another painful squeeze as he thought of another woman who had abandoned him when he needed her.

"No one but Emma."

"Ah."

"She holds me responsible for the loss of her sister."

The duke offered a sympathetic smile. "She was angry and not thinking clearly that evening. She is fully aware that you had no hand in the kidnapping of her sister."

"She might not hold me responsible for her sister's kidnapping, but she believes I allowed Anya to be shipped away beneath my nose." Dimitri's thoughts were jerked back to the night in the warehouse and his burning need to chase after Lord Sanderson before the fat fool could escape. "And she would not be wrong."

"They will be caught the moment they return to Russia," Huntley assured him, his imperious tone making Dimitri smile with wry humor. Huntley was one of the few noblemen that Dimitri did not wish had been drowned at birth, but the duke possessed the innate arrogance that allowed him to assume that his every wish would be granted. "Between Alexander Pavlovich's soldiers and your own servants there is nowhere they can hide."

"But they are not returning to Russia," a rough English voice broke into their conversation. With lethal ease, both Dimitri and the duke pulled their loaded pistols from the pockets of their coats and pointed at the man leaning against a low, stone wall. Swiftly, the stranger lifted his hands to reveal he was unharmed. "Here now, no need for guns and such. I'm a peaceable man."

Dimitri's aim never wavered. The man was small and wiry with the rough woolen clothing of a servant, but there was a cunning etched on the lean face and a hard glimmer of warning in the pale blue eyes that the man had lived the sort of life that made him dangerous. Dimitri had many such men in his employ—cold-blooded, ruthless and loyal to whoever was paying his salary.

"Who are you?" he rasped.

"Mr. Thomas Stroutt." He plucked the worn hat from his head and performed an awkward bow. "At yer service."

Huntley stepped forward, his pistol pointed directly between the man's eyes.

"I suggest you offer a compelling reason for eavesdropping upon a private conversation."

Thomas cleared his throat. "I believe I have information that will be of service to you fine gentlemen."

Dimitri sent his companion a glance that urged they hear the man out. He sensed Thomas Stroutt was too intelligent to approach the Duke of Huntley without a compelling reason.

"Speak quickly," Dimitri warned.

"I was hired by Mr. Peter Abrahams," the man said.

"Hired?"

"I am a man with a certain skill in discovering information others attempt to keep hidden."

Dimitri arched a brow. The man was a Bow Street Runner or a thief-taker.

In either case he was a man that Dimitri would wager missed very little.

"Who is Peter Abrahams?"

"He is the father of Lady Sanderson." Thomas replaced the hat on his dark hair. "A most powerful gentleman who is fiercely devoted to his daughter and her welfare."

"Why would Abrahams hire you?"

"The gentleman has become increasingly concerned that Lord Sanderson is connected to an unfortunate collection of shady characters."

"Shady is not the description I would have chosen," Huntley muttered in disgust.

Thomas turned to spit on the cobblestones, his expression dark.

"So we have discovered. Unfortunately, the information came too late to prevent poor Lady Sanderson from becoming a victim of the man's treachery."

Huntley gave a warning wave of his pistol. "You have yet to offer a reason I should not put a bullet in your brain."

The man shifted warily, wise enough to sense that the duke was not the usual coxcomb littering society.

"During my investigations I found that you were not the only men apart from Mr. Abrahams seeking the truth of Lord Sanderson's business."

Dimitri stiffened, far from pleased. He had spent a number of irksome hours in the company of Lord Sanderson. How was it possible he had been unaware there were others spying on the nobleman?

He was growing old and careless, he wryly concluded. Perhaps it was time he retired to his private estate and learn how to fish. Or were aging criminals expected to tend to their rose gardens?

With a shake of his head, he returned his attention to the man standing before him.

"Who else?"

"One of them Oriental sorts."

"Chinese?"

Thomas shrugged, revealing the predictable English contempt for foreigners.

"No, one of them Turks, I think."

"Do you have a name?"

"Caliph Rajih."

Huntley made a sound of disbelief. "You are certain?"

Thomas nodded. "Aye."

Dimitri turned to study the duke's shocked expression. "Are you acquainted with him?"

"We attended school together," Huntley admitted, his brows pulled together in a puzzled frown. "He is Egyptian, although he spent a good deal of his life in England and Europe until the past few years. From all accounts a favorite of Muhammad Ali Pasha."

Dimitri sympathized with Huntley's astonishment. "Why would he be interested in Sanderson?"

Thomas glanced about to ensure there was no one near. "When the females that Sanderson has been buying are no longer of value in London, they are taken to the slave markets in Cairo."

"Bloody hell," Huntley breathed.

A sudden chill arrowed down Dimitri's spine and, barely aware he was moving, he had reached to grab the woolen scarf wrapped around Thomas's neck, giving him a small shake.

"Where is the caliph now?"

With a practiced movement Thomas managed to free himself from Dimitri's grip, his expression knowing.

"He sailed away from London three days ago." The man rubbed his bruised throat, his eyes never straying from Dimitri's tight features. "Along with a female who looked remarkably like the woman posing as your wife."

# CHAPTER SEVENTEEN

MUCH TO EMMA'S frustration the journey from Alexandria to Cairo was postponed for three days as Rajih had revealed a sandstorm was sweeping through the desert without warning.

Her patience wasn't improved once they were aboard the shallow sailboat that carried them along the yellowish water of the Nile. There was a beauty to be found in the stunning scenery that slid past. The stark, reddish carpet of desert on one side and the rolling green fields on the opposite side. And most impressive of all the looming pyramids that made Emma want to pinch herself and ensure this was not all some strange dream.

At last they landed in Bulak and traveled to Rajih's home on the outskirts of the old city.

Or at least, what he called a home.

To Emma the sprawling three-storied building with mosaic-tiled floors and delicate tapestries, as well as ornate chandeliers was more a palace than a simple home. She had counted three formal courtyards, a private mosque and a domed pavilion before being hurried into the private gardens surrounding the women's quarters.

Behind the towering doors guarded by armed servants, Emma had found herself surrounded by a series of elegant apartments that framed the private baths. The floors were tiled with a lovely blue-and-ivory pattern while the walls were painted with frescoes that portrayed women bending at the feet of a long-forgotten caliph. Next to the vast gardens there was a charming room with low divans and gold-framed mirrors that reflected the vibrant colors from the blooms that spilled through the open archways.

Emma waited only long enough for Rajih to brush a light kiss on her cheek and warn her to stay out of the afternoon heat before sneaking out the back of the gardens.

Rajih was without a doubt a charming, well-educated companion who had treated her with tender care. In truth, he was precisely the sort of man she had dreamed of as a young girl in Yabinsk and if not for the aching concern for her sister, and of course, Dimitri Tipova…

She shut off her futile thoughts and quickened her step.

She was in Cairo for one purpose, and one purpose only.

Anya.

Clad in a traveling gown of pale lilac and a bonnet that possessed a thick veil to cover her face, she adjusted the small pistol she had brought from London that was tucked in the full sleeve of her gown.

She was not stupid. She understood that a woman traveling the narrow, dirt streets alone was foolishly dangerous, but what other choice did she have?

Rajih might be handsome and attentive and willing to indulge her in many ways, but to his mind she was a mere female who should bend to his will. He would conduct his search for Anya in his own manner and in his own time.

That was unacceptable.

Searching for the bazaars, Emma ignored the leers from the passing men as well as the shrill laughter from the women who leaned over wooden balconies to reveal their lush bodies barely hidden by the gauzy robes. In truth, she was more unnerved by the large dogs that darted among the crowd and the young men on donkeys who seemed intent on riding down hapless pedestrians.

A drop of sweat trickled down her back as she turned a

corner, reminding her of Rajih's warning that she was not yet prepared to endure the afternoon sunlight. Abruptly, she halted as she caught sight of the open gate that offered a glimpse of the covered bazaar beyond. Her heart gave a small leap as a potent perfume wafted through the air.

Was it possible?

Her scream went unheard as a hand was shoved over her mouth and an arm wrapped around her waist from behind. She struggled, but she was unable to halt herself being pulled back toward the street. Then, thankfully, she recognized the musky scent of Rajih's cologne.

"I believe that will be enough sightseeing for today," he drawled, bundling her into the waiting carriage with barely leashed anger. Settling her on the seat next to her, he yanked off her bonnet and tossed it on the floor. "I begin to sympathize with your poor Cossack. Do you possess no sense of self-preservation whatsoever?"

She folded her hands in her lap, attempting to hide her unease.

"I am here to search for my sister, not to be hidden away in your harem," she said, her chin tilted.

His dark, beautiful features were rigid with anger. "And you do not trust I am doing my best to make certain she is found?"

She shifted to glance out the window, seeking the words that would make Rajih understand the relentless need that burned deep inside her.

"Anya is my sister and my responsibility. I could not bear thinking I did not do everything in my power to protect her." Her hands curled into tight fists of frustration. "Is that so very hard to understand?"

There was a brief silence, then slender fingers cupped her face, gently turning her back to meet Rajih's dark, searching gaze.

"Do you know, *habiba,* I find myself quite envious of your sister," he said, his voice husky.

"Envious?"

His fingers tightened on her cheek. "You love so fiercely. Any man would be honored to have earned such a rare gift."

She grimaced, considering the few men who had bothered to pay her attention.

"Thus far the gentlemen I have known are not particularly interested in earning a place in my heart," she said, deliberately meeting his smoldering gaze. "Only my bed."

His thumb brushed her lower lip. "There are many men who can be extremely stupid."

"So I have discovered."

"And there are those men who find it far easier to reveal the desire of their bodies rather than confess the secrets of their hearts."

Her own heart gave a treacherous leap, warning her that a small part of her still longed to believe that Dimitri had considered her more than a convenient body in his bed. Which simply proved just how foolish she could truly be.

"It does not matter." She shrugged. "I have no interest in offering my heart to another."

"No?"

"My place is at Yabinsk, tending to my business and caring for my sister."

His gaze lowered to her lips, his thumb continuing to tease at the corner of her mouth.

"You do not truly believe you can return to such a mundane existence, do you?"

Emma shied from the thought of her small coaching inn and cramped cottage.

"What is my choice?"

"You could remain with me."

"As your concubine?"

He brushed a soft kiss over her lips. "Are you proposing a more formal arrangement?"

Heat flooded her cheeks at his teasing. "Certainly not. In fact, I presume you must wed for political gain."

Without warning his hand dropped from her face and his expression became guarded.

"I will bow to the pasha's will."

Emma regarded him with a frown, sensing that she had touched a source of distress.

"Does the thought of marrying for political gain trouble you?"

His smile was forced. "I have known I was to be a pawn from the moment my father sent me to England to be groomed as a diplomat."

"That does not answer my question."

The dark eyes narrowed, as if caught off guard by her persistence. And perhaps he was. Rajih was obviously unaccustomed to sharing his feelings. No doubt the burden of being born a caliph.

For a moment she could easily imagine Rajih as a young boy, forced to watch as his country was overrun with infidel invaders, and then the pain of being sent to England where he must have felt alone and terrified by his strange surroundings.

What man would not have learned to guard his emotions?

At last he offered a slow nod. "Yes, Emma, it troubles me greatly that my life is not my own to arrange as I would desire, but I accept my duty." His expression softened as his gaze swept over her upturned face. "And more important, I have discovered the importance of embracing happiness when it makes its rare appearance."

She ducked her head, unwilling to encourage his flirtations. She suspected that his gentlemanly restraint would be tossed aside with the slightest encouragement.

"Have you discovered nothing of my sister?"

Rajih heaved a faint sigh, then he pulled a curtain across the carriage window, thankfully blocking out the relentless sunlight.

"I have learned the *Katherine Marie* docked two days before we arrived at Alexandria and that the crew remained at least one night in the city."

Emma was torn between relief that she was still on her sister's trail, and the frustration that she continued to remain just out of reach.

"And when they left, did they come to Cairo?"

"That was their intention."

She stiffened as she heard the edge in his voice.

"What are you not telling me?"

"The Russian who was in charge of the girls was determined to flee Alexandria," he said. "Perhaps he sensed he was being followed."

She grabbed his arm, wanting to shake the truth from him.

"Rajih."

"As I told you, the most convenient means to travel is by boat, but it is also the most noticeable." He grimaced. "A smuggler could not risk attracting the attention of the pasha's guards."

His words made sense. The men responsible for kidnapping the girls had proven an undeniable talent for remaining invisible.

"So how did they travel?"

"By caravan."

Emma frowned. Since arriving in Egypt she had often seen the long line of camels and occasionally horses as they moved over the distant hills. It had not appeared a particularly comfortable means of travel, but it was not unusual.

"I do not understand—" Her words came to an abrupt

halt as she was hit by a sudden realization. "Oh, dear Lord. The sandstorm."

He gave a sharp nod. "Yes."

"Were they—"

"Nothing is known of their fate, Emma," he gently assured her. "It is quite possible they were disoriented by the storm and remain in the desert. I have sent word among the Bedouin tribes to search for them."

She bent forward, covering her face with her hands as her stomach clenched with a dread that was becoming all too common. Last night she had dreamed that Anya was still a baby and that she had gone to her cradle only to find it empty. She had raced about the dark cottage, screaming for help that had never come.

Had it been a premonition?

Was it possible that Anya was dead?

Without warning, the obstinate belief that she would rescue her sister and return them both to their home in Yabinsk wavered.

"It is almost as if fate is determined to keep me from Anya," she choked, tears filling her eyes.

She felt Rajih's strong arm circle her shoulders, pulling her against the hard muscles of his chest.

"They will be discovered," he murmured.

Her hands lowered as she tilted back her head to meet his concerned gaze.

"So I have been assured over and over, and yet I am no closer to Anya than when I left Russia."

He frowned, his thumb brushing away her tears. "Come, Emma, it is not in your nature to lose hope."

She shook her head, potently aware of the heat filling the carriage and distant chanting from the mosque. Never had Russia, and the life she had fought to build, seemed so far away.

"It is not so much a matter of losing hope as it is

accepting I do not have the skills necessary to be useful to my sister."

The carriage came to a halt, and with care, Rajih led her through the gardens to the seraglio, the whisper of his robes melding with the tinkle of the fountains in an oddly soothing sound.

"You are tired and hungry," he assured her. "By morning you will have regained your spirits and no doubt will have some new means to terrify me."

Emma nodded, realizing he was right. She could not recall the last time she had slept through the night.

"Yes, I am tired."

Halting at the arched entry into the harem's private gardens, he motioned toward a slender woman covered in veils who hurried forward.

"Put yourself in Samira's hands." He brushed his lips over her forehead. "She has a magical touch."

With an uncharacteristic sense of weariness, Emma allowed herself to be led into the cool shadows of the harem. Perhaps it was the heat, or the weeks of gnawing anxiety, or the long journey, but suddenly Emma felt in dire need of a few hours of peace.

Reaching the inner apartments, Emma allowed Samira to help remove her gown and undergarments. She sighed in pleasure as the heavy fabric slid away and she understood the logic of the loose robes and silken trousers preferred by the local women. It was far too warm for European clothing.

Once naked she allowed the servant to lead her into the sunken baths, stretching out her body and leaning her head against the tiled edge to study the glass dome that loomed above her.

Slowly the tension drained from her muscles and she cleared her mind of Anya and Dimitri and Caliph Rajih. For a few hours she desired only to forget her troubles.

A delectable hour later she left the baths and wrapped herself in a thin towel. Samira gestured for her to follow her into a shadowed alcove where velvet pillows had been piled in the center of the tiled floor. Arranged beside the pillows was a silver tray with various bottles of oils and burning pots of incense.

There was another flurry of gestures and Emma awkwardly lowered herself facedown onto the pillows, hiding her face in the velvet softness as she felt the towel being tugged aside. She was not a noblewoman accustomed to having servants seeing her naked, and certainly not touching her with such intimacy.

She heard a shuffle of feet and the clink of bottles before she sensed someone kneeling at her side. Warm oil was poured over her bare back, the intoxicating scent teasing at her nose and sliding sensually over her skin.

Still adjusting to the strange sensations, her breath caught in pleasurable surprise as warm male fingers stroked down the curve of her back. It felt…sinful. Decadent. And utterly wonderful.

"Rajih," she breathed, not needing to turn her head to recognize his scent.

"Does my touch please you?" he murmured softly.

"You should not—"

"Shh." He spoke directly into her ear, his fingers lingering on the rigid muscles at the base of her spine. "Allow me to ease your tension."

"I thought men were forbidden to enter the women's quarters unless they were…"

He chuckled as she stumbled over the word. "Eunuchs?"

"Yes."

"But I am not just a man," he said, his innate arrogance threaded through his dark voice. "I am caliph. I go where

I please. And it pleases me very much to be here with you."

She shivered, knowing she should send him away. "I will not become your concubine."

"Perhaps you should wait until you are asked to fill such a position, Emma."

"But you…"

Baffled by his reprimand, Emma shifted so she could glance over her shoulder, her words faltering at the teasing smile that curved his lips.

Rajih was always handsome, but with his robes loosened to reveal a glimpse of his golden chest and his carved features softened, he was near irresistible.

"I am offered the finest beauties to be found throughout the world," he reminded her, his slender fingers wielding their magic as they moved up her back. "Women with hair of fire or as dark and glossy as a raven's wing. Women who have been trained in the fine arts of pleasing a man or those who have been sequestered since they were babes to ensure their purity."

Despite the mocking shimmer in his eyes, Emma knew he was not boasting. He was a prince among his people, not to mention extraordinarily attractive, and she was quite certain any woman would consider it an honor to capture his attention. And, of course, in this part of the world, it would be very likely that the various sheiks and clan chiefs would offer the most beautiful of their women for his pleasure.

She smiled, astonishingly indifferent to her shameless lack of clothing and his brazen touch as she followed his lead.

"Some of them princesses, no doubt."

"Certainly."

"Hmm." Her gaze swept around the shadowed alcove. "And yet your harems remain empty."

Without giving her time to anticipate his intent, he bent down to brush his lips along the line of her shoulder.

"As you know, I have been away from my home for several weeks."

Her hands clenched the pillows, her body reacting to his skillful touch despite her reluctant heart.

"And your females managed to escape during your absence? How unfortunate."

He nibbled a path to her neck. "Do not fear, I have only to reveal my interest in seeking companionship to have the seraglio filled with graceful females, all eager to please their master."

She made a sound of disgust even as her body threatened to melt beneath his warm caresses.

"Master?"

He nipped the lobe of her ear, the heady scents of incense and precious oils making it difficult to think clearly.

"But of course. At heart I am still a savage."

"Then it is convenient I am not destined to be a member of your harem. No man shall ever be my master."

The moment her brave words echoed through the still air, Emma knew she had made a mistake. Rajih sucked in a sharp breath, his hands sliding into her damp curls and arching her neck so his lips could create havoc along the line of her throat.

"You challenge me to prove you wrong, *habiba*," he husked.

"I—" A burst of heat exploded in the pit of her stomach as he reached the sensitive spot at the juncture of her neck and shoulder. "Oh. That is not fair."

His laughter feathered over her skin. "Are there rules to our game?"

"You think this is a game?"

"A most delightful diversion."

Her toes curled as she struggled to think clearly. "Am I the prize to be won?"

"If you prefer, I am willing to be your reward," he chivalrously offered, shifting until his hard arousal pressed against her thigh. "Tell me what you desire."

Belatedly realizing that matters had progressed beyond what was comfortable, Emma stiffened.

"Rajih…"

She was not certain what she intended to say, but in the end it did not matter as there was the rustle of robes and a veiled servant was suddenly kneeling in the doorway of the alcove.

"Master," the woman murmured.

Swearing at the intrusion, Rajih wrapped Emma in the towel and shifted to block her from the view of the servant.

"I requested that we not be interrupted."

"Forgive me, Caliph, but your steward insisted you would wish to speak with Girard Bey." Her head was pressed to the tile floor. "He has information that is of interest to you."

For a moment Emma could feel the tension coiling through Rajih as he battled with the urge to send the servant away and his obvious curiosity about his unexpected guest.

At last he thrust his fingers through the dark satin of his hair and accepted the inevitable.

"Offer him coffee and assure him I will join him shortly," he commanded.

"Yes, Caliph."

In silence, the servant rose and vanished from the alcove. Rajih turned to offer Emma a tight smile, his eyes smoldering with a frustrated desire.

"Forgive me." He rose to his feet in an elegant motion,

straightened his robes. "I fear our entertainment will have to be postponed until later."

"Wait." Clutching the towel about her body, Emma rose and grasped his arm. "Please."

He covered her hand with his own, his eyes smoldering with promise.

"So eager, Emma? I promise not to keep you waiting for long."

She ignored his sensuous words, her thoughts returning to Anya.

"Does this man have information concerning my sister?"

His lips twisted, as if chagrined by her response, but his voice was gentle.

"No, Emma. Girard Bey is very much a gentleman of the city. I must depend upon those who consider the desert their home to locate the missing caravan." He lifted her hand to his lips before heading out of the alcove. "Return to the baths. I will join you as soon as I am able."

Emma forced herself to count to one hundred before she scurried to her private chambers and hurriedly pulled on the loose satin robes in rich blue and trimmed in gold that had been left on the low bed. It was odd to feel the cool satin brush her bare skin with no undergarments to act as a barrier, but she was in too great a hurry to consider modesty.

With quick steps she moved through the harem, ignoring the guards who stood at the doors and the numerous servants who gawked as she headed toward the formal quarters of the house. She was not certain whether or not females were allowed beyond the seraglio, but she was determined to follow Rajih.

It was not that she suspected he would deliberately lie to her, she assured herself. But she sensed he would be quite willing to hide information. Even if it concerned Anya.

It was the sound of voices that led her toward the large saloon on the opposite side of the house. Halting at a side door, she peered into the room, absently admiring the mosaic on the floor and the soaring ceiling that was painted with a lovely scene of a desert oasis. The low divans were crimson velvet with gold satin pillows and the high windows were shuttered against the sun, leaving the area bathed in welcome shadows. On one divan a middle-aged gentleman in a pale green, European-cut jacket and black breeches was settled, his thin face and small eyes reminding Emma of a rodent.

"Caliph," he was saying, his thick French accent revealing his heritage. "Forgive my intrusion."

Emma pressed against the door frame as Rajih appeared through an archway, a silver tray in his hands. A faint smile touched her lips. While the Frenchman was obviously dressed in the latest fashion, and possessed the air of a well-pampered nobleman, he was easily overshadowed by Rajih who was wearing what many men would consider little more than a dress and carrying a tray as if he were a common maid.

There was something harshly masculine about the Caliph that would cast any other man in the shade.

Well, any man but Dimitri Tipova.

She scrubbed the treacherous thought from her mind as she watched Rajih set the tray on a low table in front of the divan.

"My doors are always open to you, my friend," he said, reaching for the crystal decanter. "Sherry?"

The stranger leaned forward to grasp a small glass, and then—to Emma's shock—tucked a tidy pile of francs into the inner pocket of his jacket.

"You know my weaknesses too well," he said with an oily smile.

Rajih shrugged, seemingly accustomed to offering money along with his sherry.

"Pleasures are not weaknesses and it is my honor to ensure your stay in my country is one of comfort."

The man sipped his sherry. "So kind."

"I presume that you have information for me?" Rajih prompted.

*"Oui."* He set aside the empty glass. "You requested that I send you notice if I learned of any Russians arriving in Cairo."

"And?" Rajih demanded.

"I have reason to believe the Russian ambassador has just welcomed a small party into his home."

Emma frowned. Was it possible that the Russian ambassador was involved in the slave trade? And if he was, could he truly be so shameless as to have the girls brought to his home?

It seemed a needless risk when the pasha was so adamantly opposed to the barbaric practice.

"Do you have a name?" Rajih asked.

"Dimitri Tipova," the Frenchman said, unaware as Emma pressed a hand over her mouth to muffle her shocked cry of disbelief. "So far as I can determine he has no title, but it seems as if he is being offered a gracious welcome so he must be a favorite of the Romanovs. Is that the man you seek?"

Rajih dipped his head, his expression resigned rather than astonished. Almost as if he had been expecting Dimitri to travel to Cairo.

"It is."

The Frenchman grimaced. "It will not be an easy matter to have him removed from Cairo if he is under the protection of the ambassador."

"Do not trouble yourself, Girard," Rajih smoothly assured him. "I will deal with Dimitri Tipova."

## CHAPTER EIGHTEEN

DIMITRI WAS WELL AWARE that his ability to blend into any surrounding was his greatest talent.

He could move as easily through the gutters of Moscow as across the glittering ballroom of the Winter Palace. And with the proper clothing, no one would suspect he was an imposter.

Such a skill had allowed him to rise from a lowly pickpocket to the Beggar Czar.

Now, however, he felt distinctly disturbed.

It was not the Turkish robes he had donned in favor of his tailored clothing, or the small boys who stood at his side waving palm leaves in an effort to stir the stifling heat that filled the low brick house with its arched entryways and tiled floors. He had traveled through the near Orient on several occasions and had become accustomed to their traditions.

No, his unease was caused entirely by the fat gentleman sprawled on the low divan across from him.

Dimitri wasn't privy to Alexander Pavlovich's reason for offering Baron Koman the position of Ambassador to Egypt, but he suspected the czar had been anxious to rid himself of the vile man's presence. Why else would he send him to the most distant post possible, regardless of the fact he was utterly incompetent?

Dressed in loose robes and puffing on a water pipe, the rotund Russian lounged on his cushions, waiting for the pretty maid to refill his plate. His blond hair was thinning and his heavy features already red and swollen from his years of dissipation.

He reminded Dimitri of the decaying ruins outside of Cairo that were being swept away by the desert sands. He could only wish the same fate for Baron Koman.

Oblivious to Dimitri's seething dislike, Koman waved his full plate in Dimitri's direction.

"Oxtail?"

"Thank you, no." Dimitri hid a shudder as he rose from the divan and paced toward the fountain in the center of the floor. The heat and smoke from Koman's pipe were making his stomach churn. "I prefer to avoid a heavy meal so early in the day."

"Which accounts for your fine figure while mine…" The Baron laughed. "Well, it sadly reveals my love for my fine chef and my distinct distaste for bestirring myself. I blame the damnable heat. Only a savage would be foolish enough to dash about when a sensible man would seek the shade."

"The natives would probably be equally shocked to witness us tunneling a path through the snow."

"True enough, my boy." The baron licked his fingers, eyeing Dimitri with a curious gaze. So far as he knew, Dimitri was a favored friend of Alexander Pavlovich, as well as of the Duke of Huntley, who had come in search of Russian girls being sold in the slave trade. There was no need to explain that he was also a hardened criminal who was under threat of death in a number of countries… although not Egypt. At least not yet. "And there are benefits to living in a place that is not entirely civilized," Koman continued, a lecherous gleam in his eyes. "When you have finished your meal, we will travel to the bath where a man may find whatever pleasure he might desire."

Having visited a number of baths in Cairo, Dimitri was unfortunately aware of what pleasures were offered.

"An enticing invitation, but I am anxious to speak with the caliph."

"My dear Tipova, as I warned you last eve, a man cannot simply demand an audience with the caliph," the baron protested. "There is very rigid protocol that must be followed."

Not for the first time, Dimitri regretted his decision to call upon the ambassador. On the journey to Egypt it had seemed a reasonable decision to seek out the baron and request his hospitality for the duration of his stay. Huntley had warned Dimitri that rampaging like a madman through Cairo in search of Emma would not only make enemies of the locals, but would embarrass the woman he had come to claim.

Now he accepted that he had sadly miscalculated. The fat buffoon was never going to stir himself. Besides, Dimitri was in no mood for diplomacy. The need to find Emma was like a savage fire burning in his gut. He did not care if he had to sift the damnable country sand grain by sand grain to find her.

"I have a letter of introduction from the Duke of Huntley," he growled. "What more could I need?"

"Who is to say with these heathens? Best for me to approach the caliph when the timing is appropriate." The baron's tone was patronizing. "Until then I promise to keep you suitably entertained. You mentioned an interest in the local brothels? I know of a female who can dance the—"

"My only interest lies in finding the Russian girls who were stolen from St. Petersburg," he interrupted.

Koman heaved a deep sigh as he struggled to lift his considerable bulk off the divan.

"I would expect such a tedious lack of appreciation for the exotic pleasures from Alexander Pavlovich," the older man mourned. "But I had expected better from you, Tipova."

Dimitri smiled wryly. "It seems I am destined to be a disappointment to all I encounter. Have you heard rumors of Russian girls being sold in the markets?"

With a flick of his hand, Koman sent his servants scurrying from the room, leaving them alone to speak in privacy.

"In truth, Muhammad Ali Pasha's disapproval of the slave trade has made the traffickers meticulously cautious. The females are no longer paraded through the bazaar for a gentleman to purchase." The baron pulled a handkerchief from the sleeve of his robes, his gaze sliding uneasily away from Dimitri's. "You must receive an invitation to the private auctions."

Dimitri tensed. The bastard. It was obvious the man was intimately familiar with the slavers and their delicate wares.

"I am certain a gentleman of your standing could swiftly procure the necessary invitation," he said.

"Undoubtedly, but it would be such a bother. Far better to allow the officials to tend to such affairs." With a forced smile, the baron backed toward the entryway. "Ah. If you will excuse me?"

"Of course."

Dimitri made no effort to halt the idiot as he scurried out of the room.

Why bother? The baron was a worthless idiot who Dimitri was embarrassed to claim as a fellow Russian. But there had to be at least one person in the house who could be of use.

With that thought in mind, Dimitri left the smoke-filled room and dredged up memories of the brief tour he had taken of the house last eve. There was a separate counsel building near the pasha's citadel, but Dimitri recalled Koman waving a dismissive hand toward an office before leading him to his private quarters.

Passing the stairs that led to the upper rooms, Dimitri turned down a short hall and entered the large chamber that held a traditional desk and chair. Tall shelves lined with leather-bound books consumed the walls and a Persian carpet covered the floor. The double doors leading to the inner courtyard had been left open and Dimitri sucked in a deep breath of the fresh air. Although his profession meant he spent many nights in dark gambling houses filled with smoke and sin and lust, he found it increasingly unpleasant to mingle among the desperate souls.

Yet another warning he was growing old, he wryly accepted.

Stepping over the threshold, Dimitri halted as a thin gentleman with a thick mane of brown hair, dressed in a modest gray jacket and black waistcoat, rose to his feet. At first glance he appeared a somber man with unremarkable features and retiring demeanor. But Dimitri was accustomed to seeking the worth of a man beyond his outward appearance.

He, better than anyone, understood that a man could create any guise he desired.

"Stanislav, is it not?" he asked. "Baron Koman's secretary?"

Stepping around the desk, the man offered a deep bow, his brown eyes filled with a shrewd intelligence.

"Yes, my lord?"

Dimitri waved a dismissive hand. "Please call me Tipova, I am no gentleman."

"May I be of assistance?"

"That is my hope." Dimitri folded his arms over his chest. Stanislav was young, but there was an air of tidy efficiency about the office otherwise absent throughout the rest of the house. "There must be one person on the baron's staff who possesses the skill and ambition to ensure that Alexander Pavlovich is unaware that his Egyptian ambassador is a fat, lazy letch with no interest beyond his enormous appetites. I am betting that person is you."

The man paled, his gaze darting toward the door. "Sir—"

"Any deception came to an end the moment I stepped over the threshold," he warned his companion. "Now it is your decision whether my recommendation to Alexander Pavlovich includes the removal of the entire household or merely the baron."

Stanislav froze, his expression revealing his flurry of emotions—suspicion that Dimitri was attempting to lure him into a trap; fear that he might be tarnished with his employer's incompetency; and a burgeoning hope that his secretly nourished ambitions might at last be fulfilled.

It was the hope that at last triumphed, and with a small gesture, the secretary headed toward the private chamber attached to the office.

"If you will follow me?"

"You are a gentleman destined for a fine career," Dimitri murmured.

"I can only hope I survive to reap my just rewards." Once they were in the small chamber that held nothing more than a narrow bed and wooden armoire, Stanislav closed the door and turned to face Dimitri. "What do you desire of me?"

"You know why I am in Egypt?"

"I heard rumors that you seek a female who was taken from St. Petersburg by slavers and that you believe she was brought to the streets of Cairo."

Dimitri nodded in approval at the concise response. "What do you know of the woman?"

The man folded his hands behind his back, his expression clouding as he considered the question.

"There have been several Russian females sold in the slave markets over the past years." He shook his head.

"Unfortunately, the poor creatures are so broken by the time I can find them that they dare not speak of the men who have abused them. A pity. I can think of nothing I would enjoy more than having the animals drawn and quartered."

Dimitri smiled. "Do not fear, Stanislav, soon enough those men responsible for the theft of the girls will be brought to justice. If not by Alexander Pavlovich's hand, then by my own."

The young man arched a brow at the cold, lethal intent that was threaded through Dimitri's voice.

"I have heard that angering Dimitri Tipova is more dangerous than crossing paths with a wolf. Now I realize the rumors did not exaggerate."

He gave a sharp laugh. Certainly he had cast himself in the role of a dangerous wolf, stalking his prey with patient cunning. Only Emma had made him realize that he had been little better than those he hunted, willingly sacrificing young girls to sate his personal lust for revenge.

"A pity the rumors did not also claim I was man of intelligence."

The secretary frowned. "I beg your pardon?"

"Before I could detain those responsible they fled to England with several Russian girls."

"Ah." If Stanislav sensed that Dimitri was not being entirely forthcoming, he was wise enough to keep such thoughts to himself. "And you believe they were traveling to Cairo?"

"Yes. Can you discover if they have arrived?"

"Do you have the name of the slavers?"

"Valik."

"Russian." The secretary nodded, his absent expression revealing he was already considering the best means of acquiring the information Dimitri demanded. "That should narrow my inquiries. I will begin immediately."

"Stanislav?" Dimitri called as the man opened the door and prepared to leave the room.

"Yes?"

"I prefer discretion, but do whatever necessary to locate the girls."

"If they are in Cairo, they will be found, that I can assure you," the younger man promised without hesitation.

Dimitri smiled. "Czar Alexander is fortunate in his choice of diplomats."

DIMITRI WAITED UNTIL THE sun was setting before he made his way on foot through the crowded streets of Cairo to Caliph Rajih's palace.

With his dark coloring and traditional robes, he easily blended with the natives, capable of moving through the pedestrians without attracting attention. Not that his robes made him invisible. Unfortunate, since he had not had the need to sneak past guards since he was a lad.

Trusting his youthful skills, he slid along the high wall surrounding the palace, using the shadows to conceal his presence from the numerous guards. Then, reaching the back mews, he climbed over the wooden gate and dropped onto the cobbled yard near the stables.

A wry smile touched his lips as he realized he had managed to knock over a small marble statue, a mistake he would never have made as a lad, but at least he hadn't broken his fool neck. And for the moment, he hadn't alerted the entire household to his intrusion.

Aware his luck could change at any moment, he made his way to the gardens. His visits to Cairo taught him the women's quarters would be placed at the back of the house and surrounded by yet another wall. Egyptian men were fiercely protective of their females.

Actually, he had always considered them well beyond

protective. They were insanely obsessed with keeping their wives secluded.

He was dedicated to keeping women safeguarded, but why would a man desire a harem? The various females who drifted in and out of his life were enjoyable enough, but he had never felt compelled to lock them in his home. He had enough duties without adding a large number of wives he would have to tend to for the rest of their lives.

No, he had no urge to keep a female as his prisoner.

Not unless that female was Emma Linley-Kirov, a treacherous voice whispered in the back of his mind.

Clenching his teeth, Dimitri crushed the fury that threatened to overwhelm him.

From what he could discover Emma had gone willingly with the caliph aboard his ship. In fact, the dockhands they had questioned in London had been adamant in their assurance that the female in Rajih's company had not only been a willing companion, but had frequently urged him to hurry.

She would not be at all pleased if he intruded upon the household, tossing about demands and hauling her away from the palace.

For now he had no choice but to try and convince Emma that he was far more capable of assisting her in retrieving Anya than the caliph.

Hardly an easy task considering she held him responsible for allowing her sister to be taken from London.

Circling the shallow pond surrounded by lotus plants, Dimitri had just caught sight of the grilled gate that separated the women's quarters when a rustle had him spinning toward the fountain in the center of the courtyard.

His gaze narrowed as a dark, slender man with black hair and matching eyes stepped into view. Dimitri knew at once that it was Caliph Rajih. What other man would wear robes so richly trimmed? Or carry himself with the sort of arrogance that made Dimitri long to pummel his too-handsome face?

A mocking smile tugged at the man's lips as he offered a low bow.

"Welcome, Dimitri Tipova, I have been expecting you."

Swallowing a curse, Dimitri folded his arms over his chest and hid his frustration behind a mask of polite indifference.

"How very disappointing. I had not realized I was so predictable."

"Do not be too disappointed." The caliph strolled forward, his utter confidence warning Dimitri that he had several guards hidden nearby. "Most men are predictable when a beautiful woman is involved."

"You have Emma?" he asked, needing to be certain.

"She is an honored guest in my home," Rajih confirmed.

Dimitri struggled between relief that Emma was near and an irrational rage at the knowledge she had chosen to abandon him and place her trust in this man.

"Guest?" he gritted.

"Of course." Rajih chuckled. "Do you prefer to believe she is a prisoner that I forced to Egypt against her will? Perhaps you have imagined rescuing her from my harem and earning her undying gratitude?"

Dimitri made a sound of disgust. "You know nothing of Emma if you believe she would express any gratitude at being rescued, even if that was what she desired. She is more likely to blacken my eye and demand to know why I had not arrived sooner."

"Yes." The dark eyes flared with a genuine emotion that made Dimitri grit his teeth. "She is quite spirited."

"A polite means of saying she is willful, stubborn and

happy to toss herself into danger in the pursuit of her sister?" he demanded.

"I would never be so ungentlemanly."

Dimitri offered a sardonic laugh. "Thankfully, I was raised upon the streets of St. Petersburg and not the hallowed halls of Eton. I have a peculiar habit of speaking my mind."

Rajih waved a slender hand toward the gates of the harem. "If she is such a bother, I question why you would have traveled such a distance, not to mention risking my wrath by intruding into my home without permission, in pursuit of her."

"Because she is mine."

Silence filled the gardens at his stark words. Then, without warning, the caliph tilted back his head to laugh with rich amusement.

"I do not believe she would agree with your claim."

Dimitri stepped forward, shocked by the primitive sense of possession thundering through his blood.

What was the matter with him? He was a man who prided himself on his cold cunning and ruthless logic. Only fools allowed themselves to be ruled by their passions.

But there was nothing cold in his urgent desire to bury the dagger he had hidden beneath his robes in Caliph Rajih's heart.

"For now, I am more interested in ensuring that *you* recognize my claim," he growled.

"It would be a good deal more believable if she had not eagerly fled your company to be with me."

Dimitri's breath hissed through his teeth. "Emma is desperate to rescue her sister. She would bargain with the devil if she thought it would bring her closer to Anya."

"Yes, I am aware of the guilt and fear that haunts my beloved's heart," Rajih murmured. "And unlike you, Tipova, I am willing to do whatever necessary to ease her pain."

Dimitri winced, despite the knowledge the man was being deliberately provoking. It was true. He had failed Emma. Oh, he could claim any number of reasonable excuses for his decisions, but all that mattered was that Emma had turned to another man rather than believing he could be trusted to offer her what she most desired.

"What do you want of her?" he asked.

"Is that a jest?"

"Do you intend to keep her as your concubine?"

The caliph glanced toward the harem, his expression unwittingly soft with yearning.

"That would, of course, be the reasonable choice. She is beautiful and highly desirable, but she is also a foreigner with no connection to power and wealth. Even worse she is opinionated, ill-tempered and impulsive."

"Do not toy with me."

"Very well." Rajih turned back to meet Dimitri's fierce gaze. "The thought of taking her as my wife has become a near unbearable temptation."

His heart nearly stopped. "Never."

"You were given the opportunity to earn the fair lady's heart, but you cared more for your revenge," Rajih challenged.

"You know nothing of the matter."

"I know that Emma believes you betrayed her trust as well as her heart. She will never forgive you."

"That is for Emma to decide."

"Her decision was made when she stepped onto my ship." Rajih shrugged. "Accept your loss as a gentleman and walk away."

"I seem to waste an inordinate amount of time reminding others I am no gentleman," Dimitri snarled. "Emma will never be your bride."

"You have no means to stop me."

"I will see you in hell before I allow you to take Emma from me."

"I already have taken her," the caliph reminded him.

"Not for long."

Dimitri charged forward, fully intending to kill the bastard with his bare hands. Emma was his. No man, powerful prince or not, was going to steal her away.

He had taken a handful of steps when the garden was filled with burly servants dressed in robes and armed with curved swords that gleamed with a deadly promise in the torchlight. Still he continued forward, his calculating intelligence for once overwhelmed by primitive emotion.

Thick, muscular arms grabbed him from behind, then a large fist slammed into his jaw from the side, briefly making him lose consciousness. When he awoke it was to discover that he was framed by two of the servants, his arms held in iron grips as he was being roughly hauled through the back gate and tossed onto the street.

Rising to his feet, Dimitri dusted off his robes and lifted his head to discover Rajih standing just inside the gates.

"A small warning, Tipova," he drawled. "The next time you enter my home uninvited I will have you beheaded."

Dimitri narrowed his gaze. "You will regret standing in my path."

EMMA HID IN THE MIMOSA, watching the gates being slammed in Dimitri's face and Rajih leading his servants back toward the inner courtyard.

The sound of raised voices disturbed the night air, luring her from her private rooms, but by the time she had pulled on her robes and made her way out of the house, the servants had Dimitri in their hands and were tossing him out of the palace.

Now she stood in shadows, watching the man she had assumed she would never see again.

She had been shocked last evening when she had over-heard Rajih's conversation with the Frenchman. He had sounded as if he had been expecting Dimitri's arrival in Cairo. Which was absurd, was it not?

Dimitri had achieved what he desired. He had the wit-nesses he needed to stand before Alexander Pavlovich and swear that Count Nevskaya was involved in the slave trade. Why would he travel to Egypt rather than St. Petersburg?

The question badgered her throughout the sleepless night and restless day.

Now she watched as Dimitri slammed his hand against the sturdy wrought-iron gates, his face shrouded in shad-ows. Not that she actually needed to see his face to sense he was infuriated at having been so rudely tossed from Rajih's home.

He was a man who gave the commands and expected others to obey them.

A wry smile touched her lips as her heart fluttered and her blood heated. Despite the velvet darkness and the dis-tance between them, she could feel the tug of his compel-ling presence. It did not seem to matter that she was furious with him. Just the very sight of Dimitri was enough to make her tingle with awareness.

Waiting until Rajih had disappeared into the inner court-yard, Emma moved toward the gates, ignoring the tiny voice that whispered she was being a fool.

No doubt it would be far more sensible to return to her quarters and pretend that Dimitri had never arrived in Cairo. Surely she had enough troubles keeping Rajih at a proper distance and finding her sister?

But her curiosity would not allow her to simply walk away.

Or at least she told herself that it was curiosity.

Any other explanation was too dangerous to ponder.

"Why are you here?" she rasped, stepping into the pool of light from the nearby torch.

"Emma," he breathed, his expression impossible to read as his golden gaze swept over her. "Unlock the gate."

"No." She wrapped her arms around her waist, feeling oddly vulnerable in the loose silk robes, her hair tumbling about her shoulders. "Please answer my question."

"You know why I am here, *moya dusha*." His husky voice brushed over her like a caress, shivers of unwelcome pleasure racing through her. "I came for you."

"Then you have made a wasted journey."

"I would travel twice as far to be near you."

"That would be quite charming if I did not know you so well, Dimitri."

His lips twisted. "Somehow I do not think that a compliment."

"You did not follow me. If you are here, then it is for your own purpose." She took a step closer. "Did Sanderson manage to escape from your grasp?"

"So far as I know he is still in the custody of King George and his guards, although Huntley promised he would be taken to St. Petersburg to be questioned by Alexander Pavlovich."

She frowned, unable to accept he would allow Sanderson out of his sight before he was certain Count Nevskaya had been publicly humiliated.

"Then…" Her puzzlement disappeared as she was struck by a sudden thought. "Ah. Of course."

He narrowed his gaze, as if sensing he was not going to be pleased with what she had to say.

"Of course?"

"You will have need of Valik." She shrugged. "He is the obvious liaison between your father and Lord Sanderson. With his testimony there is no one who can doubt Count Nevskaya's guilt."

"It is true I intend to locate Valik." He lifted a hand to halt her angry words. "But only because he can lead us to Anya."

She stiffened. Did he truly believe she was so gullible?

"It is too late to feign concern for my sister. You could have rescued her in London, but you chose your obsession for revenge."

His expression hardened at her accusation. "I could defend myself by pointing out that by exposing my father, as well as Lord Sanderson and his cronies, I prevented a number of innocent girls from suffering the same fate as your sister."

Emma glared, not willing to listen to his arguments.

"Just go away, Dimitri."

His grip tightened on the gate, his eyes flashing with a warning that sent a chill down her spine.

"You will never be rid of me, Emma," he swore. "It does not matter where you go or how far you run, I will always be near."

## CHAPTER NINETEEN

EMMA SPENT THE NEXT DAY pacing through the harem, torn between the fear that Dimitri might actually storm the palace and attempt to take her by force, and a treacherous disappointment when he did not so much as make an appearance.

She was clearly losing what few wits she had left, she told herself. Dimitri Tipova had made his choice in London. Just as she had made hers.

There was nothing left for them to say.

As night began to fall she pulled on a silken robe in a soft shade of ivory that was richly embroidered with silver thread and tiny emeralds. Her curls were still damp from her bath and she left them loose to flow down her back. Then, with a dab of the jasmine oil that Rajih had sent to the harems that morning, she stepped into the gardens.

She was weary of her sense of isolation.

As lovely as her surroundings might be, she was accustomed to being endlessly occupied with one task or another and, of course, being among others. There was no privacy to be found in her coaching inn, or even the cottage with Anya and her friends constantly underfoot.

The hours of peaceful silence allowed her far too much time to imagine the horror and fear Anya must be enduring. Or worse, to ponder the memory of Dimitri as he stood at the gates of the palace, his presence still calling to her with irresistible force.

Entering the garden, she paced toward the fountain, pleased to discover the air had already cooled as dusk began to spread across the sky in dazzling shades of pink, peach and a vivid fuchsia.

She glanced in appreciation toward the distant sand dunes that appeared purple in the fading light. A line of camels stood silhouetted in the gathering shadows and the sound of exotic birds chirping filled the air. It was a vision out of a dream.

She bent down to run her fingers through the water pooling at the base of the fountain.

"Good evening, Emma."

Recognizing the rich, masculine sound of Rajih's voice, Emma straightened, her brows lifting as she caught sight of his lean form fitted in a dark uniform with gold braiding and several medals pinned to his chest. She had seen him in elegantly tailored clothing and the loose robes of his people, but the sight of him in full military dress was a sharp reminder of his power and position.

"Oh." She pressed a hand over her racing heart. "You startled me."

"Forgive me." He bowed before drawing closer to study her with a blatant sensuality. "As exquisitely beautiful as ever."

She smiled. "While you appear quite forbidding. Is there a special occasion for such finery?"

"Much to my dismay I have been commanded to make an appearance at my uncle's home."

An edge to his voice warned Emma there was more to his annoyance than the invitation to dinner.

"Has something happened?"

"My uncle indicated that he was entertaining several foreign dignitaries."

Her smiled widened. "Ah, so he wishes you to be at hand to charm them?"

"That would be my assumption under normal circumstances."

She tilted her head to the side, studying him with a searching gaze.

"Are these not normal circumstances?"

He stepped close, his hand cupping her chin and his thumb lightly stroking her lower lip.

"Not so long as Dimitri Tipova remains in Cairo."

"Dimitri?" She hid the sudden pounding of her heart, pretending nonchalance. "Is he in Cairo?"

The dark face was unreadable. "He is."

"And…" She licked her dry lips. "He is to be a guest at tonight's dinner?"

"I think it is more likely he arranged for my uncle to host the dinner and insist upon my presence."

She jerked in astonishment at the accusation. "How could he possibly have such influence among your family?"

"Tipova may not possess a title, but he has a vast fortune and he has made certain that the knowledge of that fortune is well-known throughout Cairo." Rajih grimaced. "Including those members of my family who are always eager to attach themselves to wealth."

Emma rolled her eyes. Of course. Dimitri was talented in the art of manipulation. Whether it was via money, power or sex.

"Even presuming that he was capable of arranging a dinner with your uncle, what would be the purpose?" she demanded.

"Obviously he wishes to keep me occupied."

"Why?"

Rajih shifted his hand to run his fingers through her hair, his touch gentle and yet possessive.

"To steal you away, of course."

"Absurd."

"There is nothing absurd in his determination to have you as his own." The dark eyes flashed with annoyance. "Nothing will deter him."

Emma folded her arms across her waist. Why was her senseless heart fluttering with excitement? She was still far from convinced that she was the reason that Dimitri had traveled to Cairo. Or that if he had followed her it was anything more than wounded male pride.

She would lay odds that the man had never had a woman willingly leave his bed. Not, at least, until he was done with the affair. And it would only make it worse that Emma had left with another man.

"If he is foolish enough to believe he can simply carry me off I shall soon disabuse him," she muttered.

He gently tugged her hair, his gaze scrutinizing her pale face. "Will you?"

"So far as I am concerned Dimitri Tipova is no better than any other man," she snapped. "He is willing to use me for his own pleasure without concern for my needs."

"Do not condemn all men, *habiba*."

She wrinkled her nose at the realization she had been excessively rude to the man who had offered her nothing but kindness.

"It is not a matter of condemning men, Rajih, but an acceptance that I would be a fool to depend upon anyone but myself." She touched his arm, a sadness settling in her heart. "I have been disappointed on too many occasions to offer my trust."

A silence settled over the gardens, filled only by the splash of the fountain and the soft flutter of wings as a bird settled on a nearby sycamore branch. Emma shifted uneasily, unnerved by his steady gaze. It was almost as if Rajih was attempting to see into her very soul.

"A reluctance to trust does not mean you have managed to banish Tipova from your heart," he said softly. "Your vehement reaction suggests that you still harbor feelings for the man."

Heat stained her cheeks. "I harbor a desire to have him carried into the desert and eaten by the jackals."

Rajih's lips twisted. "Ah, *habiba,* I regret I am incapable of inspiring such passion."

She frowned at his words. Had he not just heard her claim that she desired Dimitri to be eaten by jackals?

"Anger and passion are not at all the same."

"You are very innocent."

Anger sliced through her at his patronizing tone. With a sharp movement she brushed aside his lingering hand and stepped back.

"If that is a kind means of saying that I am stupid I readily agree."

Rajih shook his head. "I mean precisely what I said. There's a genuine purity about you that will remain untarnished no matter what happens in your life." He shrugged, his gaze skimming down her slender body. "Unfortunate for you, of course."

"Why unfortunate?"

"Because it is destined to attract the worst sort of bounders and scoundrels." Then he reached for her, pulling her hard against his sculpted torso. "You are irresistible to those of us with jaded hearts."

"Rajih."

He pressed a finger to her lips, sensing her reluctance.

"I will not press you, *habiba,* but I do demand a promise."

"A promise?"

"That you will not leave my home without first discussing your departure with me."

Emma considered before agreeing to Rajih's request. She would not give her word lightly. Not when she expected others to fulfill their vows.

"I promise," she at last agreed.

He brushed his lips over her forehead. "Thank you. I must go."

"Wait." She grasped his arm. "Have you heard nothing of my sister?"

"Not as yet," he said, genuine sympathy in his dark eyes. "But hold on to hope, Emma. They will be found."

She remained standing beside the fountain as Rajih bowed and turned to leave the garden.

*Hold on to hope...*

Such simple words, and yet they were increasingly difficult to cling to.

Lost in thoughts of her sister's torment, Emma did not hear the sound of rustling among the mimosa, or the soft tread of footsteps on the paved pathway. It was not until a pair of arms circled her waist and hauled her back against a hard chest that she realized the dangers of her distraction.

Her heart lodged in her throat as she instantly recognized Dimitri's warm scent. Not that she needed more than his touch to know who held her. There was no other man who could send thrilling quivers through her body at the mere brush of his hand.

It was wretchedly unfair.

No, there was no need to question that the man holding her captive was Dimitri. Nor to wonder how he had managed to enter the enclosed harem surrounded by guards. Dimitri could no doubt slip into the citadel and steal the pasha's jewels if he desired.

Splaying his fingers against her stomach, Dimitri bent his head to whisper directly in her ear.

"You play a dangerous game, *moya dusha*," he warned. "If I ever witness you in the arms of another man again I will kill him."

Emma struggled to breath, telling herself it was anger, not desperate longing, that made her tremble.

"So Rajih was right."

His arms tightened. "Do not speak his name."

"I will speak whatever name I might choose. You have no authority over me."

He tensed, then surprisingly, she felt his grip ease, his lips brushing the curve of her ear.

"Such courage, and yet you tremble," he taunted. "Do I frighten you?"

Excitement fluttered in her stomach, her toes curling as heat flowed through her veins.

It had been so terribly long since she had allowed herself to enjoy Dimitri's touch. Now her entire body ached with unfulfilled need.

Not that she was about to admit as much to the infuriating demon who was kissing a path of fire down the side of her neck.

"What woman would not be frightened when a man creeps into her private quarters and speaks of his intent to kill?" she accused.

"You must know I would never hurt you, Emma."

"But you did hurt me, Dimitri." The words tumbled from her lips before she could stop them.

Dimitri tensed, his warm breath teasing the delicate skin of her neck and sending jolts of pleasure down her spine.

"That was never my intention."

Angered as much by her reaction to his touch as by his ridiculous words, she arched away from the potent heat of his caressing lips.

"Yes, it was. You have always known you would allow nothing to come between you and your revenge," she hissed. "Certainly not me or my poor sister."

"And if I tell you that I regret my choice? That I would make a different decision if we were back in that warehouse in London?"

She shook her head, refusing to consider his words

sincere. "I would say that it is very convenient to claim such regret now that you have what you desire."

His grip tightened and with relentless determination he turned her in his arms to meet the blazing gold of his eyes.

"But I do not have what I desire," he rasped, his hands gripping her hips and pressing her against the swollen thrust of his arousal.

Dangerous warmth pooled between her legs. "Stop now."

"Emma, have you no regrets?"

She turned her head, unable to think clearly when he was so near.

"Of course I do," she muttered.

He placed a hand against her face, firmly turning her face to meet his tense expression. For the first time she noticed the shadows beneath his remarkable eyes and the pronounced jut of his cheekbones, revealing that he had lost weight since she had last seen him. An annoying pang of sympathy tugged at her heart.

"Then surely you can find it in your heart to forgive me?" he asked.

"I do not wish to forgive you," she said, as much to convince herself as Dimitri Tipova. "All I want is to find my sister and return home."

"Your home is with me."

Her heart faltered at the sheer certainty in his voice. "No."

The golden gaze blazed over her face. "Yes, *moya dusha*."

She pressed against his chest. It was so simple to swear she was done with Dimitri and his persuasive kisses when he was far away. But when he held her so close against him…

Emma shook her head in denial. "I have no need of you."

"Perhaps I have need of you."

Her sharp laugh echoed through the gardens. There was only one reason Dimitri would need a woman.

"To warm your bed?"

"I will not deny I am desperate to have you in my arms. But it is more than mere lust. You are meant to be at my side."

"For as long as I please you."

"For so long as we please one another." In one fluid movement, Dimitri swept her off her feet, cradling her against his chest as he carried her toward the arched entrance of the women's quarters. "Allow me to please you, *milaya*."

Her heart raced with a combination of anger and searing need.

"No. Rajih…"

Her words were brought to a shocking halt as he covered her mouth with a tempestuous kiss that stole her breath.

He tasted of vodka and male desire. A heady combination that made her entire body clench with an aching hunger.

"I warned you not to speak that name," he muttered against her mouth. "The only man on your mind or your lips will be me."

She would have denied his stark claim of possession if he hadn't kissed her again, her barely restrained desire flowing through her like molten lava. Instinctively, her arms lifted to circle his neck, her lips parting in silent invitation.

Distantly, she was aware they had entered the seraglio and he was headed toward the private apartments. She could smell the burning incense and the precious oils beside the baths, but she made no effort to struggle from his grasp.

Why bother?

She wanted Dimitri.

Desperately.

Finding her apartments with unnerving accuracy, Dimitri stepped into her bedchamber where a fire already burned against the chill of the approaching night. He shut the door behind them and slid her down his body until she was standing directly in front of him.

"You have plagued my every dream, *milaya*," he rasped, a flush staining his cheeks and his eyes glittering with a hectic fire. "I have never wanted a woman as I want you."

A renegade warmth flooded her heart. Dear Lord, how many nights had she cried herself to sleep after being treated as if she were little better than a leper by the men in her village? Or scurried from the local shops after overhearing her neighbors laughing at her threadbare gown and haggard appearance?

To the world she had offered an impervious composure allowing her to tend to her business and protect Anya from the censure of others. But inside…

Inside she had hidden the wounds that never healed.

Not until Dimitri, a tiny voice whispered.

He had been the first to see beyond her ugly wool gowns and prickly independence to the vulnerable woman beneath. And more important, the first to make her feel as alluring and desirable as any other woman.

It was a rare gift she would always treasure. Even after he was gone from her life.

She thrust aside the jagged pain threatening her heart.

In this moment she did not want to think of the inevitable loneliness in her future or the past betrayals. Tonight she would accept the pleasure Dimitri offered.

"This means nothing," she muttered, more for herself than for her companion.

Then, before she could falter, she reached to pull the silken robes over her head, tossing the heavy fabric aside to reveal she wore nothing but slippers beneath.

Dimitri's breath hissed through his teeth, his body so stiff he looked as if he had been transformed into a statue. Although no statue had eyes that blazed with a pure gold fire.

"Emma," he rasped, his voice thick with longing. "You have missed me, have you not?"

"No."

A sudden smile curved his lips at her refusal to admit her inner emotions, and with hands that were not entirely steady, he hastily rid himself of his own robes before tugging off his soft leather boots.

"Your body tells me otherwise," he husked, his gaze on her beaded nipples as he prowled toward her.

She shivered, already anticipating the feel of his hands on her bare skin.

"I do not deny that I desire you." She bravely met his smoldering gaze. "But there is nothing more."

Dimitri cupped her face in his hands, a hint of pique tightening his features. Almost as if he were disturbed by her indifference.

Which was ridiculous, was it not? What interest did he have in her beyond the use of her body?

"Do you wish me to beg for your affections?" he asked in a rough voice.

"You beg?" She laughed at the mere thought. "You would not know how."

"You wrong me." He leaned downward, softly teasing her lips with his. "It was one of my finer talents before I was sent to school. All I had need of was a cane and a rag to tie over my eyes and I could make a small fortune."

She squashed the thought of Dimitri as a small boy

struggling to survive on the streets of St. Petersburg. She was already far too vulnerable.

"Do not remind me how talented you are in deceiving others," she husked.

He swore at her stubborn resistance, then parting her lips with the tip of his tongue, he plundered her mouth with unrestrained passions.

Emma's pulse raced as his tongue slipped into her mouth and, arching against the hardness of his chest, she shoved her fingers into the thick satin of his hair. He groaned, wrapping her in his arms as he urged her backward. Still holding her mouth captive, he tumbled them both onto the wide divan.

All thoughts were lost as he landed on top of her, his heart beating a rapid tattoo against her tender breasts.

He should have been too heavy, too overwhelming, too… male. Instead, she savored the feel of being pressed into the velvet cushions and the rough scrape of his hair against her skin.

This was no gentle seduction. No sweet love play.

This was a raw craving that refused to be denied.

"Emma…" Breathing heavily, he brushed heated kisses over her face, his hands outlining the curve of her hips. "It has been too long."

It had been too long. Far too long, she admitted to herself, arching beneath him in a silent plea for relief from the need clawing deep inside her.

"Then why are you wasting our time together with conversation?" she demanded, her voice strained.

He growled, his mouth trailing down her throat and over the upper curve of her breasts. Emma had no notion where her brazen manner was coming from, but she was too impatient to worry over it. She had spent too many nights dreaming of being in Dimitri's arms to squander a moment.

"As you wish, *moya dusha*," he rasped, his hands shifting to cup her breasts so he could ravage them with his lips and tongue and teeth.

She cried out in pleasure, her legs parting so he could settle between them. The hard length of his arousal pressed against her inner thigh. She shuddered, already damp with longing.

"Dimitri."

"Patience," he urged, his lips moving down the soft swell of her stomach, his hands slipping beneath her backside to lift her to his seeking mouth.

"Dear…Lord," she breathed, trembling beneath the onslaught of sensations.

He was wicked, decadent and as beautiful as a bronzed god in the flickering firelight.

What woman could possibly resist?

Certainly not Emma.

Biting her lower lip to keep her moans from filling the harem, she felt Dimitri shift until his mouth could nibble on the flesh of her inner thigh, his hands holding her still as she squirmed in pleasure.

His lips stroked ever higher, at last finding the very source of her desire. She closed her eyes in appreciation, her fingers clutching his hair as he stroked his tongue through the heart of her femininity.

Her head spun and her soft pants filled the air. That exquisite pleasure was beginning to build in her lower belly and still he continued with his caresses. Over and over he teased the tiny nub, seeming to take delight in her muffled groans.

At last she tugged at his hair, hovering on the edge of pure bliss.

"Please," she begged, her voice barely recognizable.

His head lifted to meet her dazed gaze, his eyes glowing with a fierce craving.

"What would you have of me, Emma?"

*Your love.*

The words whispered through her mind only to be roughly shoved aside.

She would not ruin this night with impossible dreams.

"I need you," she whispered.

"Yes."

Surging upward, he entered her with one smooth thrust.

Emma sucked in a sharp breath, her hands sliding down the rigid muscles of his back as he set a relentless pace that had her soaring toward the stars.

# CHAPTER TWENTY

TUCKING EMMA AGAINST HIS side, Dimitri breathed deep in an effort to slow the thundering pace of his heart.

A task that would have been considerably easier if his potent awareness of her was not still rampaging through his body and urging him to take advantage of their rare moment together.

It had been too long.

Far too long.

And the need to drown himself in the pleasure of her sweet desire was nearly overwhelming.

Unfortunately, he could not ignore the manner Emma's body was stiffening as sanity returned, her tiny hands reaching to press against his chest.

"I have missed you, *milaya*," he whispered, pressing his lips to her hair as he sought to temper the palpable regret in the air.

"This was—"

"Exquisite?" he interrupted. "Astonishing? A miracle?"

"A mistake."

"No, Emma, the only mistake was attempting to leave me. We belong together."

Her eyes shimmered like the finest emeralds in the firelight.

"I did not leave you, Dimitri."

His fingers stroked the satin skin of her shoulder, his body already stirring at the feel of her warm curves pressed against his body.

"No?"

"No." She shifted to meet his gaze with a somber expression. "I followed my sister. Something you attempted to prevent me from doing."

His grip unwittingly tightened. "My only desire was to keep you safe."

"That was not what I wanted of you."

"I understand your need to rescue Anya," he said. "I even admire your courage."

"And yet you locked me in Lord Huntley's house while you allowed Anya to be taken from London."

He swallowed a sigh. How many years had it been since he had explained his decisions to anyone? Quite likely it had not been since his mother's death.

And most certainly he did not apologize. Not ever.

At least, not until Emma Linley-Kirov.

"For how long do you intend to punish me for my impetuous decision?" he asked, his voice low.

She shifted on the cushions, a faint color staining her cheeks.

"I am not attempting to punish you. I am merely explaining why we cannot possibly be lovers."

His brows lifted as he swept a glance down her naked form.

"And yet we are."

She arched away, her features hard with a frustrating denial.

"No."

"Emma, I have apologized for not putting Anya before my revenge scheme, but I truly believed we would easily be able to find the girls once Sanderson was captured." He struggled to maintain his patience. Why did she have to be so damnably stubborn? "What more would you have of me?"

She tilted her chin. "Your promise that you will let me

make my own decisions even when you do not agree with them."

"You mean I am to turn a blind eye when you wish to charge into danger?"

"It is my right."

"It is madness."

With a sudden surge, she wiggled out of his grasp and slid off the bed, grasping her satin robe and pulling it over her beautiful body before he could halt her. His lips twisted as he rose to his feet and pulled on his own clothing.

With her exotic surroundings and strange garb, she looked moons away from the prudish spinster who had entered his coffee shop in St. Petersburg. He wondered if she realized just how much she had transformed over the past weeks?

"You comprehend how impossible this is?" she was demanding, tying her hair in a braid with shaking hands.

His brows snapped together at her husky words. "Dammit, Emma, you seek to unman me."

"Because I will not become a meek, biddable creature who is grateful to obey your every command?"

Biddable? He swallowed his instinctive laugh. He had never encountered a woman less biddable than Emma Linley-Kirov.

"Because you will not allow me to protect you."

"I do not want your protection. I want—"

He stilled as she hastily bit off her words, a hint of panic in her eyes as if she had nearly revealed something she was determined to keep hidden from him.

"What do you want?"

She turned away, pacing toward the towering Oriental vase that was set in the corner of the room.

"It does not matter."

With three long strides he was at her side, grasping her upper arm and turning her to meet his searching gaze.

"Tell me, *moya dusha*. What do you want of me?"

She shook her head, her eyes dark with an unreadable emotion.

"What you cannot offer."

Dimitri refused to be bothered at the conviction in her voice. He would regain this woman's fragile trust. Eventually, she would put the past behind them and look toward a future together.

He would accept no less.

"Do not be so certain." He skimmed his hand up her arm, cupping the back of her neck in a possessive motion. "I have not traveled such a distance to return home without you."

She shivered, the pulse at the base of her throat fluttering with an unmistakable reaction to his touch.

"The choice is not yours."

He allowed a wicked smile to curve his lips. "Perhaps not, but there is nothing to curb me from convincing you that your place is at my side."

She studied him, her delicate features troubled. "Why?"

Dimitri paused, sensing the question was important to Emma.

"What are you asking?"

"You have had lovers before me."

"Do you wish me to apologize for them?"

She grimaced, and Dimitri harbored the hope that she was bothered by the thought of him with another woman. God knew that he had been tortured by Caliph Rajih.

"Of course not," she denied. "But I find it difficult to imagine you are always so reluctant to end an affair."

He shrugged. It was true enough. He had never sought to prolong an affair. There was always the danger that his lovers would begin to hope that they could claim more than a temporary position in his life.

Of course, he had never before had a woman who continued to stir his interest, not to mention his desire, long after he should have tired of her companionship.

A part of him was terrified at his need to keep her near.

Any man instinctively understood that the moment a female became as necessary as breathing that he was in deep trouble.

The larger part, however, didn't give a damn if he were in trouble or not. The mere thought of his life without Emma was unbearable.

He brushed his lips over her forehead. "None have ever been like you."

He heard her breath catch, but she obstinately pulled away from his touch, her expression set in grim lines.

"No doubt because they did not resist your need to be their savior," she accused. "If I were foolish enough to give in to your urgings and return to St. Petersburg, you would soon grow weary of me."

His anger stirred. Perhaps because there was a hint of truth in her words? He could not deny he made a habit of rescuing damsels in distress. And that he took pleasure in their feminine gratitude. It eased his guilt at his inability to save his mother.

But Emma had long ago transformed from a female in need of rescuing to the one female who could fill his heart with joy.

"Savior?" He shook his head, refusing to let her believe for a moment he considered her anything but a beautiful, desirable woman that he was determined to have in his life for all eternity. "Not even my dearest friends would believe I am anything other than a selfish pirate who takes what he wants and damn the consequences. And I assure you, I never intend to grow weary of you."

She backed away, her arms wrapped around her waist. "It would not be a matter of whether you want to or not.

Once I am safely in your care you would have no reason to consider me as anything other than a burden you would be anxious to be rid of."

Dimitri studied her guarded expression, sensing the hollowness of her words. Her fear went deeper than him losing interest in her.

"Do you know, Emma, I believe I at last begin to understand you," he said slowly.

She touched the tip of her tongue to her upper lip. "I very much doubt that."

"You are afraid."

"Certainly, I am," she hastily admitted. "I have been afraid since I discovered Anya missing."

"You are afraid of your feelings for me." He brushed a stray curl off her cheek. "That is why you continue to devise ridiculous reasons to keep me at a distance."

Her face paled in the flickering firelight, the scent of incense nearly overwhelming.

"Your arrogance truly is astonishing," she rasped.

His fingers lingered on her cheek, savoring the warm satin of her skin.

"Listen to me. You can trust your heart to my care. I will not abandon you as others have done."

He felt her tense beneath his fingertips, her eyes wide and dark with wounds that she struggled so hard to keep hidden.

"Why would you say such a ridiculous thing?"

A dangerous tenderness swept through him. He desperately longed to scoop her in his arms and take her someplace where she could never be hurt again.

"Because those you loved and depended upon died, leaving you alone to shoulder burdens that have been far too heavy." His thumb outlined her lower lip. "It is little wonder you protect your heart with such ferocity."

For a brief, breathless moment Emma swayed toward

him, as if he had at last managed to convince her of his
sincerity. Then, with a frightened shake of her head, she
again stepped back, her spine stiff.

"Please just go away."

Dimitri muttered a curse, fully intending to remain
precisely where he stood until he had exhausted Emma's
arguments. For all her protests he had not missed the brief
glimpse of yearning he had seen shimmering in her eyes.

Emma might claim she wanted nothing more than her
independence, but he had seen the truth of her heart.

It was the appearance of a robed servant who gestured
at him from the arched doorway that ruined his plan.

Hurriedly hiding his disbelief behind a resigned expression, he brushed his lips over her cheek before stepping
back and smoothing his tousled hair.

"Perhaps you are right," he said.

She blinked, her defensive anger faltering beneath his
unexpected capitulation.

"I beg your pardon?"

"This is not the time or place for such a discussion," he
forced himself to say.

"You are leaving?"

He smiled despite his annoyance at the ill-timed interruption. Emma could not entirely hide her disappointment
at his announcement.

"It is what you desire, is it not?"

She hunched her shoulders. "Of course it is."

With a chuckle, he leaned down to lightly kiss her lips.
"Dream of me."

He had reached the door when a delicate porcelain figurine
went sailing past his head to smash against the stone wall.

"You are…impossible," she shouted after his retreating
back.

His smile remained as he followed the retreating servant
toward the back of the harem.

It was odd that he had known dozens of beautiful women who were not only compliant, but eager to please him, and yet none had stirred more than a passing interest.

Perhaps fate had decided to punish him after his years of sin.

Only it did not seem like punishment. He stifled a groan as he recalled the explosive pleasure he had so recently enjoyed. For all the irritation that Emma offered, being with her was as close to paradise as a man could possibly find.

The servant slipped through a narrow door into the gardens beyond, and with an effort Dimitri shoved aside his thoughts of Emma and concentrated on the servant who slid to a halt in the shadows of the high wall surrounding the harem.

At a glance there was nothing about the veiled servant to capture his interest. There were at least a dozen females attired in precisely the same manner throughout the palace, although this particular servant was taller than most.

It was only Dimitri's familiarity with Josef and his willingness to go to any length to slip about unnoticed that allowed him to recognize the slender Russian man. And, of course, his ugly countenance that no veil could entirely disguise.

Reaching up a hand, Josef tugged aside the thin veil, and headdress, a taunting smile curling his lips.

"Yet another satisfied lover, eh, Tipova?" he mocked. "You have a remarkable talent with women."

"My talent does not extend to appearing as one," Dimitri teased in return, allowing his gaze to skim down the robes his servant wore with remarkable ease. Joseph was a magnificent actor who could play any role required. "You are exquisite."

"Take care, Tipova. I have several daggers hidden beneath these robes," the scar-faced man warned.

They both tensed as the distant sound of voices echoed through the gardens, reminding Dimitri they were standing in the gardens of a man who had only yesterday threatened to have him beheaded.

As if reading his mind, Josef silently turned toward the wall, running his hands over the smooth stones until there was a faint click and a portion slid open.

"Through here," the man urged.

Ducking through the opening, Dimitri glanced about the dark street that ran beside the palace, abruptly realizing that Josef had managed to discover a secret entrance through the ancient walls.

"You never cease to amaze me, Josef," he muttered as his companion joined him.

With swift, efficient motions, Josef rid himself of his robes to reveal a rough tunic and loose breeches worn by Turkish servants.

"I prefer a more tangible reward than mere amazement."

"What of my heartfelt appreciation?" Dimitri laughed as his servant grunted his disapproval. "Do not fear, you will be properly rewarded." His amusement faded as he glanced up and down the narrow street, ensuring they could not be overheard. "What have you discovered?"

"There was a man who resembled Valik's description who was seen in a café near the citadel."

It was precisely what Dimitri had hoped to discover when he requested Josef make contacts among the natives of Cairo. After all, a man involved in an illegal trade might do his best to avoid soldiers or those in authority, but he would never notice the thousands of commoners who filled the markets and cafés and public baths. Such people always made the best spies.

"Have you visited the café?"

"I went there earlier to enjoy a small pastry."

"Did your pastry include any information?"

"Not so much as I would have desired." Josef's grimace was barely visible in the wash of moonlight. "There were several patrons who recalled a large man, possibly Russian, who briefly visited the café, but he left long before I arrived and no one knew where he was staying."

Dimitri swore. "So we are still in ignorance."

"Not entirely. I made a search of the neighborhood."

"And?"

"I discovered three brothels within walking distance of the café."

Dimitri shrugged, not willing to leap to conclusions that might blind him to other possibilities. He had already allowed Anya to slip through his fingers once. It would not happen again.

"The auctions needn't be offered at a brothel. It is quite possible that the girls are being held in a private residence."

"It is possible, but with the pasha's current disapproval of the slave trade there are fewer citizens willing to risk the citadel's dungeons by being so intimately associated with the traffickers," Josef reasoned. "If they are hidden in a brothel then all involved could plead to have no knowledge of the auction. Besides, we must begin somewhere."

"Yes," Dimitri readily agreed, sensing there was something his companion was keeping from him. "Is that why you intruded on my private evening with Emma?"

Josef discreetly shifted back, a certain indication that he had been indulging his love for daring gambles.

"I made a brief sojourn to each of the brothels to discover the various pleasures offered."

Anger jolted through Dimitri at the grudging confession. Damn, the obstinate fool. After Josef had risked his neck to bring an end to a foul murderer who had kidnapped the Duchess of Huntley, Dimitri had decided his old friend had reached an age when his lust for adventure needed to be curtailed. He had brought him to England and then Egypt for his cunning, not to charge recklessly into danger.

"You entered the brothels alone?"

Josef jerked a head toward the nearby harem. "As you just mentioned, you were otherwise occupied."

"You should have waited until I could accompany you," he growled. "I did not bring you to Cairo for you to have your throat slit and your body tossed into the Nile."

"If I desired a mother hen, Tipova, I would find one considerably more attractive than you."

Dimitri glanced toward the pile of robes that Josef had so recently shed.

"You are hardly in a position to toss about insults."

The slender man snorted, his lips twitching with amusement. "Do you wish to know what I learned or not?"

Dimitri heaved a sigh. What was the point in chastising the man? Josef had spent a lifetime tossing dice with the devil. It was going to take a more than a lecture from Dimitri to curtail his dance with death.

"I do," he admitted.

"Two of the brothels were eager to welcome me inside and introduce me to their females. They even allowed me the opportunity to search the establishments."

"I thought we agreed not to stir unnecessary curiosity?"

A smug smile spread across his face. "I explained that I was seeking a respectable brothel for my wealthy employer and that he suffered a peculiar fear of fleas. What could I do but inspect the rooms?"

"I assume you found nothing?"

"Fleas."

"Charming." Dimitri shuddered. He was far too familiar with the filth and squalor to be found in cheap establishments. "And the third brothel?"

"Oddly enough they claimed that they could not accommodate my employer for the next week."

Dimitri's interest was instantly piqued. "Did they offer an explanation?"

"I was told that there had been a fire in the private chambers and that they were making repairs."

Dimitri gave a decisive shake of his head. "There is no brothel that would turn away a potential customer even if the place was *still* on fire."

"My thoughts exactly."

A thick silence descended as Dimitri glanced down the empty street and then toward the looming palace.

On the other side of the thick walls Emma was no doubt still cursing his name and tossing priceless artifacts at the door, and yet he desired nothing more than to return to her private quarters and drag her into his arms.

But if there were even a slim possibility that he could discover Valik and the innocent females he was holding prisoner then he had no choice but to put aside his personal desires and pursue the bastard.

"Damn."

Josef smirked, seeming to enjoy Dimitri's reluctance to leave Emma.

"If you want to return to the lady I will search the brothel," he taunted. "At your age you really should avoid situations that demand agility."

"The traffickers are not the only ones who can toss you into the Nile, my friend." He pointed down the dark street. "Lead me to the brothel."

## CHAPTER TWENTY-ONE

EMMA WAS INFURIATED.

She told herself that it was Dimitri Tipova's intrusion into Rajih's palace and his brazen seduction that made her long to toss every breakable object in the vast palace. Had she not made it clear the last time they met that she wanted him to leave her in peace? He had no right to force his company on her.

But while she might be in a temper, she was not utterly unreasonable.

If she had truly been disturbed by Dimitri's arrival then surely all she need have done was call for one of the countless servants? Dimitri was a dangerous, even lethal, adversary, but not even he could fend off a half dozen large eunuchs.

Besides which, there was no means to convince herself that the seduction had been anything but mutual.

A shameless excitement jolted through her body. She had wanted Dimitri with such fervor that nothing could have kept her from his arms. And if he had not so rudely abandoned her, then she would no doubt be willing and eager to be seduced again.

And that was the cause of her anger, she ruefully acknowledged.

Not because Dimitri Tipova had intruded into the harem grounds, but because he had left them.

Stepping out of the seraglio that suddenly threatened to smother her, Emma breathed deeply of the perfumed air, glancing up at the sky spattered with twinkling stars.

She was a fool, of course. She had been adamant that she would never forgive Dimitri for his betrayal, and yet, he had only to kiss her for her to toss aside all common sense and melt in his arms.

She shivered, startled by the bittersweet pang of yearning that pierced her heart without warning.

She wished she was home in her shabby cottage.

Perhaps it was not so surprising.

Since her mother's death her life had never been easy. Not only had she faced the duties of the household and caring for Anya, but she had been forced to toss aside her own dreams of a future. But for all her sacrifices, she had never felt as…lost as she did now.

In Yabinsk she knew what each day would bring.

Now she felt as if she were floundering through a blizzard with no notion of where she was headed, or what was awaiting her at the end of the road.

Consumed by her disturbing thoughts, Emma welcomed the soft sound of slippers on the path. Turning her head she watched as the veiled servant hurried toward her.

"There you are, mistress," the girl said, her voice soft but edged with surprising urgency.

"Samira." She stepped toward the servant. "Is there something you need?"

"Yes. The caliph is waiting for you."

"He has returned?"

"He is waiting in a carriage behind the seraglio."

Emma frowned in confusion, disturbed by the odd chill that crept down her spine.

"I do not understand. Why would he be waiting in a carriage?"

"His message merely said that I was to request you join him." The woman cast a furtive glance around the garden, as if fearful of being overheard. "Do you wish me to inform him that it is inconvenient?"

"No. I…" She shook her head. There was no reason to be uneasy. Rajih would never harm her. And it might very well be that he had discovered information that could lead them to Anya. "Of course I will join him. Thank you, Samira."

There was the briefest hesitation before the servant bowed, then she turned to lead Emma through the banks of mimosa.

"This way."

They traveled through the garden in silence, Emma occasionally glancing over her shoulder to ensure that Dimitri was not lurking among the shadows.

Against her will she wondered where he had gone and why he had left so abruptly.

Had he somehow been alerted to Rajih's return and left before he could be discovered? Or had he simply achieved what he wanted with her and was now seeking fresh entertainment?

She stumbled, shocked by the pain of the thought of Dimitri enjoying the pleasures of another woman.

No. She would not think of Dimitri or the manner he could infuriate her one moment and send her pulse fluttering the next. Not when such a task did nothing but leave her with an aching head.

Far better to concentrate on Rajih and his mysterious request.

Samira paused to unlock the back gate, motioning Emma through with a wave of her hand.

Emma absently smoothed her hands down her robes, acutely aware of her mussed appearance. Would Rajih suspect the reason for her wrinkled robes and flushed cheeks?

Her brief flare of unease was forgotten as she stepped past the high wall of the palace to discover the dark carriage waiting for her.

Another chill trickled down her spine.

Rajih had a stable full of carriages as well as the strange contraptions that were placed atop a camel to ride through the desert. But his vehicles were all sleek and elegant and noticeably expensive.

Nothing at all like the black, bulky carriage that was built for function rather than beauty.

Emma paused, unwilling to deny her prickling sense of alarm. She might not understand the strange premonition plaguing her, but she was not going to ignore it.

She turned on her heel, intending to rush back into the safety of the harem. Instead, she discovered a large man with thick features and small, terrifyingly cold eyes waiting for her.

Her lips parted to scream, but before she could make a sound the stranger had his beefy hand wrapped over her mouth and a heavily muscled arm wrapped around her waist.

"So kind of you to join me, Emma Linley-Kirov," he muttered in Russian.

Emma's heart froze in fear. The man had to be one of the slave traders. What other Russian would be staying in Cairo and dare to attack a guest of Caliph Rajih?

But how had he found her? And more terrifying, what did he intend to do with her?

As if reading her mind, the brute tightened his arm around her waist, hoisting Emma a few inches off the ground to haul her toward the nearby carriage. Emma struggled, her legs flailing and her arms reaching over her head to yank at her captor's hair.

He ignored her pitiful efforts, easily bundling her into the carriage and forcing her onto the worn leather seat. Then, with an efficiency that spoke of years of practice, he jerked her arms above her head and snapped the steel manacles that were attached to the roof around her wrists.

Once he was certain she was securely imprisoned he took the seat opposite her and gestured to a servant hovering outside the carriage. The door was slammed shut and Emma realized there was no handle on the inside of the door just as the vehicle jerked into motion.

Her heart painfully began palpitating, slamming against her ribs as she accepted she was completely at the mercy of her kidnapper.

Forcing her horrified gaze from the manacles that bit painfully into her flesh, she regarded the man seated across from her.

The sight of him did little to ease her terror.

Not only was he large and thickly muscled, but there was a lack of emotion on his broad face. He was a man obviously accustomed to holding women as his hostages. And no amount of tears or pleading would sway him.

All she could do was pretend a confidence she was far from feeling.

"You will regret this," she warned.

He appeared remarkably unconcerned. "This is what you have wanted, is it not?"

"It most certainly is not."

"Then why have you been chasing after me for weeks?"

His mocking words stole any hope that this was nothing more than a terrible misunderstanding.

"You are Valik?"

His small eyes glittered in the faint torchlight that slipped through the barred windows of the carriage as they turned onto a crowded street and slowed to a mere crawl. Emma could hear the chatter from busy cafés and the call of the vendors, but she knew that she might as well have been alone in the world with the man seated across from her.

For now there was no escape.

"Obviously we have no need for introductions."

"Where is my sister?"

"Have no fear." A cruel smile touched his lips. "The two of you will soon be reunited."

Emma ignored the threat, more concerned with Anya's welfare than her own.

"Has she been hurt?"

"She is alive." He shrugged. "Which is all that concerns me."

"You—"

"Careful," he growled, revealing his first hint of emotion. "You don't want to say something you might regret."

Emma deliberately tilted her chin, sensing the hideous man took pleasure in intimidating women. She would be damned before she gave him the satisfaction.

"You are a fool, you know," she said tartly. "Lord Sanderson has already made his confession to King George and even now is traveling to Russia to appear before Czar Alexander."

He regarded her with an unnerving intensity. "Which is why I decided to have you join your precious sister."

"I do not understand."

"It is fairly simple, kitten." He leaned forward, wrapping Emma in the stench of stale vodka and unwashed body. "I might have been born in the gutters, but I've always had a preference for a more luxurious life."

She wrinkled her nose, wishing his preference included a bath and change of clothing.

"By kidnapping and selling children?"

He settled back in his seat, his leer sliding over her with a repulsive thoroughness.

"It happens to be a career that pays quite well," he boasted. "Far better than begging for a handful of coins on the frozen streets of Moscow."

"There are honest professions," she rasped.

"Not for a bastard serf." His short laugh echoed through the carriage. "So far as the empire is concerned we have no use but to be conscripted to the army or buried in the mines of Siberia. Neither fate appealed to me."

Unfortunately, Emma could not argue. Those in Russia who were born into poverty were rarely given the opportunity to better their lives. In truth their existences were often grim, brutal struggles for survival.

"You implied you had a reason for kidnapping me." She diverted the conversation back to more important matters.

"Beyond the charm of your companionship?" he mocked.

"Yes."

"You, kitten, are to be my revenge."

"Revenge?"

The beady eyes flared with shocking hatred. "Dimitri Tipova has ruined my very lucrative arrangement and that's not a thing a man forgets. I had to give thought to a proper punishment."

Emma's breath caught in her throat. Absurdly, she had never considered the possibility that the demented brute would seek to hurt Dimitri. After all, it didn't take a great deal of intelligence to realize that a man did not rise to be the czar of the criminal world without the ruthless skill to defeat any opponent.

Now she struggled not to allow a wrenching surge of fear to overwhelm her.

"You have no idea what he is capable of," she warned. "He will destroy you if you do not flee before he discovers you are in Cairo."

"Oh, I intend to flee," he drawled. "Once I am certain that Tipova knows that I have stolen his lover and intend to share her with the most depraved men to be found in Egypt."

She shifted on the seat, her arms aching from being held above her head. Her mind, however, was racing. This horrid man would not be allowed to hurt Dimitri.

The mere thought of him being injured, or worse, was unbearable.

"You are mistaken."

"Am I?"

"Yes." She cleared her throat, forcing herself to meet his malevolent gaze. "I hired Dimitri Tipova to help in my search for Anya, but he is no more than my employee."

"The Beggar Czar a mere employee?" He snorted in disbelief. "Don't treat me as if I'm an idiot."

She managed a disdainful sniff. "Obviously he had his own motives for assisting me, but they had nothing to do with being my lover. I am a proper lady."

"Even a proper lady becomes a tart when given the opportunity."

Heat stained her cheeks. "You are offensive."

"And you are a liar." He reached to grab her chin, his fingers bruising. "I saw the two of you together in that warehouse in London. The man is so besotted with you that he will go stark raving mad at the thought of you being used as a common whore. I might even let my guards have a turn or two. They so rarely get the chance to taste the wares."

Despite her best intentions, her brittle courage faltered beneath his vile threat.

"Do you have no conscience whatsoever?" she husked.

"None. You would do well to remember that." The carriage came to a halt and reaching beneath his jacket, Valik pulled out a pistol. With a grim expression he pointed it directly in her face. "We have arrived. I would suggest that you not fight my servant. I prefer to savor my revenge, but I will shoot you if I must."

"I hope you rot in hell, you monster."

"Bitch."

THE HOUSE WAS BUILT IN a narrow street and nearly hidden behind the large palm trees. On the front a balcony hung over the street with grilled windows, no doubt used for the girls to lure potential customers. In the back a wooden pavilion was swiftly falling to ruin and a narrow alley was filled with rubbish.

It appeared to be like any other brothel in Cairo if not for the guards posted at every entrance. And, of course, the pack of mangy dogs that had nearly mauled him when he first approached the building. Dimitri had taken refuge on the side terrace, leaving Josef to deal with the savage curs.

Nearly twenty minutes later the wiry servant shimmied up the trellis to join him, his bare feet barely making a sound as he crossed the wooden terrace.

"You disposed of the dogs?" he demanded, his voice a low whisper.

Josef nodded. "The kitchen of the local café was stocked with a nice supply of meat. They were easy enough to lure away." He gestured toward the narrow window that Dimitri had already used to enter the house and search for the girls. "What did you discover?"

"The bottom floor has four rooms. A front parlor, an office, the kitchens and a pantry. The second floor has six small bedchambers." He grimaced. "The upper floor contains the attics, but the doors and windows are barred. I assume that if the females are here that is where they are being held."

"Interesting." Josef glanced over the edge of the terrace to the shadows below. "Guards?"

"Far too many for a mere brothel. I have counted five so far."

Josef rubbed the tip of his nose, considering their few options.

"A dangerous situation. Perhaps we should wait until later in the evening. The guards will eventually seek a place to hide from the employers and enjoy a bottle of raki together."

Dimitri chaffed at yet another delay. He wanted to expose the slavers and rescue the females so he could concentrate on Emma. Surely once he had her sister she would agree to leave the damnable harem and return to St. Petersburg where she belonged?

But he was not a fool.

If he acted too hastily he risked sending the bastards fleeing before they could be captured. Or worse. He could stumble into a trap.

Still undecided, Dimitri shifted toward the edge of the terrace as he heard a noise in the alley.

"What is that?"

Josef peered into the shadows. "A carriage."

They both tensed, knowing that a vehicle would never willingly choose to travel through the filth of the alley unless there was a need for secrecy.

Was it possible the auction was already beginning?

He scowled, debating how long it would take to convince the authorities to send soldiers. It would be far more efficient to gather his own servants and attack the brothel. Unfortunately, he was not certain that the pasha would approve of a foreigner shedding blood on the streets of Cairo.

Not when the gentlemen attending the auction were quite likely wealthy citizens who could create any number of political difficulties.

Dimitri bent down as a servant hurried toward the carriage, opening the door and reaching inside. His eyes narrowed as he heard the low sound of male voices, then the unmistakable shriek of a furious female.

Had they been keeping the women at another location and were only now bringing them to the brothel?

That complicated matters since he couldn't know if Anya had yet arrived.

Leaning forward, he watched as the servant stepped back from the carriage, his arms wrapped around a furiously struggling woman. For a moment he was distracted by the sight of the large Russian who stepped from the carriage, instantly recognizing him as the man from the London warehouse. Then, as he heard Josef suck in a shocked breath, he returned his attention to the female who continued her futile fight for freedom, the moonlight shimmering over her honey curls and delicate features.

"Emma."

All logical thought ceased as he vaulted off the terrace, overwhelmed by his savage need to gut the man who dared to put his hands on her.

God, he had to reach her. He had to…

Without warning, he was tackled from behind, landing awkwardly on the hard ground. He cursed as Josef grasped his arm and wrenched it to a painful angle behind his back, effectively holding him captive.

"Damn you, Tipova, do not force me to hurt you," the servant hissed.

Dimitri struggled, but the smaller man had the leverage to keep him trapped, not to mention enough force on his arm to threaten to snap it in two. Something Dimitri was quite certain his friend was prepared to do if necessary.

Turning his head, he spit out the dirt and watched in the distance as Emma was hauled into a side door of the brothel, followed by the hulking form of Valik.

Any hope of a hasty rescue was slipping away.

"Let me up," he commanded.

"You promise you will not do anything stupid?"

He trembled with fury. "Josef."

"You may release him," a soft voice ordered. "I promise to shoot him if he takes a step toward the brothel."

Josef leaped off his back, his gun pointed at Caliph Rajih as he appeared from the shadows of the pavilion. With less grace, Dimitri surged upright, his hands clenched at his side as he glared at the slender man in a dark uniform, a curved sword in his hand.

"I should have suspected you were involved in this vile business," he rasped, his body rigid with a combination of anger and anguish. Emma was in the hands of slave traders, and while his blind thirst to reach her was being tempered by the realization he might very well endanger her by barging into the situation without considering the consequences, he was still tormented by his frantic urgency. "Your presence in London, not to mention your interest in Emma, was far too convenient."

Ignoring Josef's pistol pointed directly at his heart, Rajih stepped forward, his expression hard.

"You ever again accuse me of being involved with the slave trade and I will have your head on a pike," he warned, the sharp edge of his sword glinting in the moonlight. "Believe me, that is not an empty threat."

Dimitri stepped forward, his hands clenched with the fierce need to strike out.

"You think we are stupid enough to believe your presence here is a mere accident?"

"I could ask the same of your presence, Tipova. What are you doing at this brothel?"

The two men glared at each other, both seeking to prove their dominance. Like dogs snarling and snapping at one another. At last it was the realization he was wasting precious time that Dimitri swallowed his pride.

He would sacrifice whatever necessary to save Emma.

"My servant heard rumors that a large Russian man was seen in the neighborhood," he confessed, his tone pitched so it would not carry on the night air. "He investigated and found that this particular brothel had supposedly suffered a fire."

Rajih glanced toward the building that was shabby, but unmarred by flames.

"A fire?"

Josef shrugged. "So I was told."

"Not a particularly convincing lie," Rajih said.

Josef rolled his eyes. "The servants did not impress me with their swift wits."

"I have explained my presence, Caliph." Dimitri folded his arms over his chest. "Now I will hear your story."

"There is no…story." The dark eyes narrowed. "I returned to my home after enduring a tedious dinner party, which I believe I have you to thank for my invitation."

Dimitri could not halt the cold smile from curling his lips. He had considered himself quite clever in arranging Rajih to be absent from the palace so he could spend the evening in Emma's arms.

"I sent no invitation," he protested.

"We will settle that debt at a more convenient moment."

He waved aside the threat. "You said you returned home."

"Yes, and when I discovered Emma was missing I gathered my servants so I could question them."

"What did you learn?"

"I learned that I had more than one uninvited guest during my absence," Rajih said, his tone promising retribution. "Yet another grievance I intend to settle with you later. For now it only matters that one of my female servants confessed to accepting a bribe to lead Emma to a carriage waiting near the stables."

"Perhaps you should take greater care in hiring your staff."

Something like remorse flared over the dark face. "Samira was jealous of my obvious affection for Emma. She now deeply regrets her behavior."

"Not so deeply as she will regret her behavior if Emma is harmed."

The caliph moved the sword just enough to remind Dimitri it was in his hand. A subtle warning.

"I am capable of punishing my own servants."

"Tell me precisely what she said."

"She knew very little." Rajih shook his head. "A Russian man approached her in the bazaar earlier in the day and urged her to join him at a local café. Samira knew it was wrong, but she was angry and agreed to his request."

"Valik," Josef muttered.

"Whoever he was, he offered Samira several drachmas if she would lead Emma to the carriage at precisely ten o'clock," Rajih continued. "He told her that Emma was his sister who had fled from home and he was anxious to return her to Russia and her family."

Dimitri glanced toward the house, every passing moment grating against his nerves.

"That still does not explain your presence here," he snapped.

"The carriage left only moments before my arrival. Once I had a description of the vehicle, it took little effort to catch up with it in such heavy traffic."

"This makes no sense." Josef interrupted the conversation without warning.

Dimitri glanced at his servant in surprise. "What do you mean?"

"Why would Valik kidnap her?"

"Obviously, he discovered Emma had followed him to

Cairo and was afraid she would reveal his sordid business to the pasha."

"If he had managed to find out that Emma was in Cairo, then he most certainly knew you were here," Josef reasoned. "After all, you have made no effort to hide your presence while the woman has been hidden in a harem. Considering you pose the far greater danger to him, Valik would be a fool to hazard stealing Emma from the caliph's palace when he could quite easily shoot you in the back."

"Not to mention the pure satisfaction," Rajih murmured.

Dimitri shot him a dark scowl before returning his attention to Josef.

"Just say what is on your mind, Josef."

"The only reason a man is willing to risk his neck is for love or—"

"Hate," Dimitri finished for his companion, his thoughts racing.

Josef's words made sense. He better than anyone understood the effectiveness of manipulating others with threats to their families. A man might refuse to pay a gambling bill even after a savage beating, but he would beg, borrow or steal the necessary funds to protect his wife.

And if you wanted to sincerely hurt a man...

Well, you threatened his lover, not him.

"He no doubt holds you to blame for interfering in his profitable affairs," Rajih pointed out the obvious.

"Yes." His gut twisted in icy fear. If something happened to Emma he would be destroyed. "What better revenge?"

Josef stepped forward to grab his arm, his face tight with concern.

"Or trap."

"Yes," Dimitri slowly agreed, his gaze shifting toward the brothel as a plan began to form. As much as he might long to charge into the house and shoot anyone who might stand in his path, he had enough sense to know that Emma would be killed before he could ever reach her. No, he had to convince the damnable Valik to release her unharmed. And there was only one means of persuading such a man. "Of course, it ceases to be a trap once you recognize it for what it is," he husked.

"Damn," Josef muttered. "You're going to do something stupid, aren't you?"

Dimitri turned back to meet his companion's accusing glare.

"Yes, and you are going to assist me."

## CHAPTER TWENTY-TWO

"Ow." EMMA GLARED AT the large servant who carried her through the filthy brothel, his expression stoic despite the fact he had just smacked Emma's head into the door frame of the parlor. "If I must be carried then could you at least not ram me into the walls?"

Leading them past the low divans and stacks of pillows tossed about the bare floor, Valik glanced over his shoulder with a mocking smile.

"You are wasting your time if you hope for a response from my servant. I cut out his tongue when I hired him."

Emma fought to control her panic. "My God, you are demented."

"Cautious." The large man shrugged, angling toward the narrow staircase. "No matter how much I might be willing to pay a man to keep my secrets I can never be certain of his loyalty. It is far more effective to make certain he can't speak at all."

The man carrying her through the dark room with a low ceiling and heavy scent of incense appeared indifferent to being discussed as if he were no more than an animal. Perhaps his spirit was too broken to care.

"The world will be a far better place when Dimitri hunts you down and kills you," she hissed.

Valik chuckled, pausing at the base of the stairs to turn and regard her with a smile of evil anticipation.

"If he is reckless enough to seek me out, then he will quickly discover that he is the prey, not the hunter."

"You are…" Realization hit with shocking force and

Emma felt her stomach clench with an icy dread. "Oh, my God. You are hoping he will come after me."

The man's smile widened, his hand waving about the seemingly empty room. No doubt he had a dozen guards hidden about the place.

"Let us just say that I am prepared should he choose to rescue his woman. And if he doesn't…well, I at least have the satisfaction of knowing that for the remainder of his life he will blame himself for your painful and degrading destiny."

She struggled to hide her fear, knowing that was precisely what he desired.

"You know nothing of Dimitri. He will kill you and there is nothing you can do to stop him."

"Such faith in your lover," he taunted. "It's heartwarming."

"I have faith in the knowledge you are not half the man that he is."

Fury flashed through the beady eyes, and turning on his heel, Valik stomped heavily up the stairs.

"It's no wonder your sister was so eager to flee your sour nature," he growled. "I would have smothered you in your sleep."

"Anya? Is she here?"

"You wish to join her? It is my pleasure," he muttered, continuing up a second flight of stairs to the attics. He paused to unlock a heavy door, pushing it open to climb yet another short flight of stairs. At the top there were two doors on either side of the narrow hallway. He unlocked the one on the right-hand side, thrusting it open with a grim smile. "Enjoy your reunion. It is to be of a short duration. You are both to be sold tonight."

Emma cursed as the servant dumped her over the threshold, slamming the door shut and locking it before she could react. Rising to her feet, she rubbed her bruised hip and glanced around the cramped room.

There was not much to see.

The ceiling was low and flat with a small ladder that led to a narrow opening in the roof. There were a few pillows scattered over plank wooden floor and an oil lantern billowing smoke and a grudging light on an upturned barrel in one corner, but no furniture and nothing to ease the bleak emptiness. Across the narrow room a piece of fabric was hung in a doorway, concealing the room beyond.

Where were Anya and the girls that Valik was holding hostage? If they were near she should surely hear something from them?

Were they bound and gagged? Were they being forced into silence by guards?

Were they...

She squashed her increasingly panicked thoughts, stepping toward the center of the room.

"Anya?" she called softly. "Anya?"

There was a rustle of fabric and Emma watched as the curtain across the door was thrust aside and her sister stepped into the room.

She sucked in a sharp breath, her anxious gaze running over her sister's loose curls that were several shades lighter than her own and the pale face with a pair of large blue eyes that Emma had always envied.

Despite being clad in odd baggy trousers and a small embroidered vest that left her stomach exposed, she looked precisely as she did the morning she had disappeared and Emma felt a pang of surprise tug at her heart.

Perhaps she had expected Anya to look...different.

As if her terrifying adventure should have altered her in some visible manner.

Instead, she regarded Emma with a familiar petulant expression, her chin jutted to a stubborn angle.

"Emma?" Her voice was sharp. "What are you doing here?"

Emma blinked back her tears of joy, telling herself that Anya's less than welcoming reaction was merely shock at her unexpected arrival.

"It was my intention to rescue you," she said, her voice choked with emotion. "Unfortunately, it would appear that I am to be hoisted on my own petard."

"Hoisted on a what?"

"It does not matter. Where are the other girls?"

Anya shrugged. "They are being prepared for the auction in the rooms across the hall."

Unable to reign in her need to touch her sister and assure herself that she truly was unharmed, Emma rushed across the room, wrapping her arms around the startled Anya. "Oh, dear Lord, it is so wonderful to see you."

"Emma, release me," Anya commanded. "I cannot breathe."

"Forgive me. I am just so relieved to know you are alive. You cannot imagine how terrified I have been." Emma pulled back, her hands running over her younger sister as she had done when she was little and had taken a tumble from a tree. "Come, let me look at you. Are you hurt? Have they…"

"For God's sake, Emma, would you just stop your tugging on me?" Anya snapped, shoving away from Emma's lingering touch with obvious impatience.

Emma bit her lower lip, wondering if Anya was fearful that she was about to be scolded on being so foolish as to have run off with virtual strangers. Her sister resented being in the wrong and tended to strike out in defense.

"Of course," Emma said, gently tucking one of her sister's curls behind her ear. "At least assure me that you are well."

"I am perfectly well." Anya pushed Emma aside. "Or I would be if you would stop fussing over me."

Emma wrapped her arms around her waist, attempting to hide her pain at Anya's dismissive manner. She did not expect her sister to gush in delight that she had risked her life to come in search of her. Or even to offer a simple gesture of gratitude.

But should Anya not be at least a tad relieved she was no longer alone with the bastards who had kidnapped her?

"I cannot help myself," Emma said slowly. "I have been frantic to find you since you left Yabinsk."

"Well, as you can see, I am fine."

"Yes, I suppose so." Emma shook her head, accepting her sister's words. Which allowed her to turn her thoughts to the question that had plagued her since she had discovered her sister missing. "Anya, why did you…"

"You know why I left, Emma," Anya interrupted the hesitant question, pacing the small space with jerky steps. "You might have been content being an eccentric spinster who everyone mocks behind your back, but I would rather die than be cursed with your fate."

Emma winced at the brutal description. "I never expected you to share my fate. There is no reason you cannot wed a decent man and have a home and family of your own."

"A decent man?" Anya tossed her head, her golden curls shimmering in the lamplight. "You mean Boris Glavori who buried his first wife after forcing a dozen children on her? Or perhaps the butcher who came to call on me with blood beneath his nails?"

"Surely anything would be preferable to being taken captive by slave traders?"

"You know nothing."

Emma shook her head in growing confusion. "Then explain it to me."

Anya hunched her shoulders, refusing to meet Emma's gaze. "It is true that Count Tarvek and his brother proved to be hideous creatures who should be beheaded without delay. I do not comprehend how they could ever claim to be gentlemen."

"I assure you they will soon reap their just rewards," Emma promised.

"But not all the men in their employ are evil."

Emma froze, a sense of dread lodging in her heart. "What are you saying?"

With a sudden movement Anya turned away, heading back toward the curtained doorway.

"You should never have come after me."

"But you must have known I would." Emma followed in her sister's wake, baffled. This was not going at all as she had imagined it would. Where were the other girls? And why was Anya behaving as if Emma were an unwelcome intruder rather than a savior? "You are my sister. I love you, Anya. I would protect you with my life."

They entered a room barely as large as a closet with a narrow cot and a chipped washstand. Bending down, Anya yanked a leather satchel from beneath the bed and clutched it to her chest.

"Well, it is because of you that Mikhail and I have not yet managed to escape," she said. "I can only hope that you have not yet again ruined our plans."

"Who is Mikhail?"

"One of the guards." Anya's chin tilted at Emma's horrified expression. "He happens to be desperately in love with me."

"He is a trafficker?" Emma rasped.

Anya sniffed. "I should have known you would find fault without even knowing him."

Emma itched to grab her sister and give her a violent shake. As relieved as she might be to have at last found her, there was no doubt Anya had not changed a wit. She was still stubborn, impulsive and utterly selfish.

"Have you taken leave of your senses?" she gritted. "My God, he is responsible for kidnapping children and selling them to monsters."

"He has kept me safe when others would have harmed me and he intends to take me to his home in Austria."

Emma swallowed her angry words. Why bother? Anya had never listened to anything she had to say before. And perhaps she should try and consider what her sister had endured.

After all, she must have felt scared and alone when she realized she had fallen into the hands of slave traders. If this guard had shown her a bit of kindness and had sheltered her from the others, then it was perhaps not surprising that she would have attached herself to him.

"My dear, you are not thinking clearly," she said gently. "Only to be expected after all you have endured. Once we have returned home—"

"Never." Anya stepped backward, a sulky pout tugging at her lips. "I will never return to Yabinsk and you cannot force me."

"Perhaps we can visit England before returning to Russia," Emma coaxed, refusing to acknowledge the possibility they might not find a means to escape from Valik's clutches. "We do have family there, after all."

Anya stomped her foot. "You have not listened to a word I have said."

"Certainly I have listened, but you cannot expect me to allow you to remain at the power of a slave trader. It is insanity."

"He is a good man."

"Even if I could be persuaded to believe he is a saint I would not let you be with him." Emma grasped Anya's shoulders, willing the foolish girl to recognize common sense. "You are a child, Anya, and you belong at home with me."

The moment the words tumbled from her lips she wanted to call them back. Over the past months Anya had become increasingly sensitive to being seen as a girl rather than a woman.

Whirling on her heel, she stormed back into the larger room, her cheeks stained with color.

"You always ruin everything."

"Anya, this is ridiculous." Emma clenched her hands, following behind her sister. "I have traveled from St. Petersburg to London to Cairo to find you. Once we find a means to escape then we will discuss your future."

Anya never slowed as she headed to the back of the attic. "I no longer have to obey you, Emma Linley-Kirov."

"Did you ever?"

"I am a grown woman and I will make my own decisions." Reaching the small ladder, Anya turned back to glare at Emma. "I will never return to that horrid cottage."

Emma faltered, her heart twisting with distress. Had she not sacrificed everything to ensure her sister could have a stable home?

"Was it truly so bad?" she rasped.

"It was horrible. Like being caught in a poacher's trap." Anya shuddered, her pretty features hard with disgust. "God, there was nothing but snow and mud and ignorant villagers who had nothing better to do with their days than to make life a misery for others."

"But we had each other."

"Each other?" Anya's shrill laugh grated against Emma's tender nerves. "No, I was just another cross that St. Emma had to bear."

"Anya," Emma breathed, studying her sister as if she had never seen her before. And perhaps she hadn't. Before their father's death he had warned Emma that she was spoiling little Anya and that it would be better for the young girl to take on a few of the responsibilities around the cottage. Emma, however, had wanted to protect her sister from the tedious chores. Now it seemed that her effort to help Anya had only created resentment in the younger woman. "That is not true."

"Of course it is." The blue eyes darkened with a simmering antipathy. "You have reveled in your role as martyr since mother died. Do you know how often I was scolded to be properly grateful that you had sacrificed yourself for me?"

"Would you have preferred that I had abandoned you?" Emma wrapped her arms around her waist, as if she could protect herself from Anya's cutting condemnation. "Or taken you to an orphanage?"

Anya sniffed. "You could have sought help from our relations. There had to have been at least one family member who would have offered to provide us with a decent allowance so we did not have live as though we were no better than serfs."

Emma grimaced. "I could not beg for charity from complete strangers."

"Only because your pride was more important than my happiness. If you had considered my feelings at all then I would never have allowed the count to lure me away from home."

Emma shifted uneasily. How could she deny the charge? She had allowed her pride to prevent her from seeking assistance from the family she had never known. Of course, she could hardly have suspected that Gerhardt Herrick would be so kind. Or that he would have been so willing to acknowledge a distant relative.

At the time she had only known that it was her responsibility to find the means to support her sister and she had done the best she could.

"Anya…" Her soft plea was interrupted by the sound of a slamming door from below and the rumble of male voices. Emma stiffened, an icy fear flowing through her veins. Valik had warned that the auction would be held tonight. Was it beginning? "What is that?"

"Yet more trouble. No doubt because of you."

With a last glare, Anya turned to climb the stairs.

"Where are you going?" Emma demanded.

"I told you that Mikhail intends to take me to his home."

"How do you intend to escape?"

"He promised he would tend to the details." Reaching the top of the ladder, Anya reached up to push open a trap door. "I am to meet him on the roof."

Emma tilted back her head, unable to believe after all that had occurred that her sister could still behave in such a reckless fashion.

"You are placing your trust in a slave trader who has not even shared his plan of escape?" she rasped, reaching to grab the skirt of Anya's gown. "For God's sake, he will have you completely at his mercy."

Anya kicked out, dislodging Emma's hand. "Let go of me."

"Please, Anya, listen to me."

"No."

Anya shoved her satchel through the small opening before scrambling behind it, pulling herself out of the attic and onto the roof.

Emma grabbed the ladder and prepared to climb after her sister. "Wait."

Anya peered through the opening, her curls tumbled about her pale face.

"I am sorry, Emma, but you cannot come with us."

Emma's eyes widened in stunned disbelief. "You intend to leave me here to be sold in a slave auction?"

"You should never have followed me."

"Anya."

The trap door was slammed shut and Emma listened in amazement as there was the sound of scraping, as if something were being shoved over the door to keep it from opening. Still, Emma remained poised on the ladder, refusing to believe her sister would actually abandon her in the attics while she made her own escape.

No matter what happened in the past, Anya could surely not be so heartless?

It took nearly a quarter of an hour for Emma to accept that her sister could indeed be that heartless. She had climbed the ladder, pounding on the trap door that would not budge and futilely calling for her sister who refused to answer.

At last she had been forced to accept defeat.

"Dear God," she muttered, laying her head against the wooden rung of the ladder and closing her eyes in weariness. "I have been so stupid."

With an annoyed impatience, Dimitri allowed the two guards to roughly drag him through the brothel, at last shoving him onto a low divan in the parlor.

It had taken three attempts to at last be caught by the ridiculous fools. He had all but approached them and requested a waltz before they had noticed him pretending to pick the lock of a side door. He could only assume that the men had grown weary of guarding females who had yet to earn a single ruble for them.

Now, he turned his head to watch as Valik entered the room, his hair tousled, as if he had run his fingers through it more than once. The expression on his beefy face, however, was smug. No doubt he was preening at the mistaken belief he had accomplished something no other man had managed.

"Ah, Dimitri Tipova," the Russian drawled, halting directly before the divan. "You cannot know how I have longed for you to pay a visit."

Dimitri settled more comfortably on the cushions, stretching out his legs and crossing them at the ankle.

"I should have visited you much sooner if you had not been fleeing from me in terror." He flicked a glance toward the two guards who both stood like mindless statues. "Not that I am surprised. Those men who peddle in the flesh trade are by nature spineless cowards who skulk in the dark and prey on the weak."

"You dare to lecture me?" Valik gave a sharp laugh. "You command every criminal in St. Petersburg, including a dozen whores. Christ, you chop off the hands of anyone who irritates you. And you look down your nose at me?"

Dimitri shrugged. "I do not force anyone into a life of sin, I only demand that they obey my particular laws, and in return I offer them my protection from those predators who are without honor."

"Arrogant bastard."

"So I have been told."

"You may think you are better than me, but I am the one who came out the victor. I captured the notorious Dimitri Tipova."

Dimitri lifted a mocking brow. "Surely you cannot believe that I stumbled into such an obvious trap? I did not rise to my current position by being stupid...." His gaze returned to the hulking guards. "Or careless."

The sneering smile faltered and Valik waved a dismissive hand toward his companions.

"Leave us," he commanded, waiting until the men had lumbered from the parlor before returning his attention to Dimitri. "You cannot fool me. You are desperate to rescue your lover."

Stark, brutal fury speared through Dimitri at the

realization that Emma was even now in the filthy brothel, being held against her will and no doubt terrified.

"Oh, I fully intend to rescue Emma," he said, his soft voice only emphasizing his lethal intent. "It is in your hands whether you end this encounter with enough wealth to begin a new life. Or as a corpse."

Dimitri hid a smile as the man took an instinctive step backward.

"You are in no position to threaten me," he snarled, obviously angered by his display of cowardice.

"You think not?" Dimitri smiled. "I assure you that you have only moments to decide whether you wish to conduct a profitable business arrangement with me or be escorted to the pasha's citadel by Caliph Rajih's guards."

Dimitri watched in satisfaction as Valik paled at the threat.

Rajih had not been pleased when Dimitri had insisted that he enter the brothel alone, insisting that they wait until he could call for his servants and they could surround and attack the brothel in a coordinated effort. And Josef had treacherously agreed with the bastard. But Dimitri had refused to yield.

There would be no guards, no attacks and no shots fired until Emma was safely in his hands.

"You are bluffing," the large man rasped.

"If you have heard anything of my reputation then you should know that I never bluff."

Valik clenched his hands, suspicion tightening his features as he paced the floor.

"The caliph knows nothing of me or this brothel."

"How do you think I found you?"

He shot Dimitri a skeptical frown. "You want me to believe he sent you here?"

"Do not be an idiot," Dimitri retorted. "The caliph dared to steal Emma away from me while I was occupied in

London and brought her to this godforsaken country." He did not have to pretend his surge of annoyance. "I intend to punish him, not become his lackey."

The beady eyes narrowed. "I did wonder why the woman was in the caliph's harem."

"A mistake I had every intention of correcting."

"So if you are not friendly with the caliph, then how would you know he is planning to send his guards to this brothel as you claim?"

"I called upon the palace earlier in the evening." Dimitri allowed a faint smile to touch his lips. "Of course, I took the precaution of slipping in unnoticed."

Valik snorted. "Of course."

"Why trouble the servants?" Dimitri lifted his shoulder in a nonchalant movement. "I am perfectly capable of opening a door. Or window, if necessary. It allows me to discover information that might otherwise have remained a secret."

Valik returned to his pacing, his expression hard as he sensed his opportunity for revenge slipping away.

"What information?" he growled.

Dimitri unconsciously tapped his fingers on the cushions of the divan. It was one thing to be cautious, but did the fool intend to spend the entire evening chatting?

Rajih's patience would not last for long, and as for Josef... well, if the fiercely loyal servant became convinced that Dimitri was in danger, he would do whatever necessary to rescue him.

Including putting Emma at risk.

"The most interesting was the tearful confessions of a female servant who spoke of a Russian man who bribed her to lure Emma into a waiting carriage behind the harem," Dimitri said, coming straight to the point.

"Bitch."

"It was then the caliph sent a servant to trail your

carriage through the heavy traffic while he gathered his guards and prepared an assault on those who had dared to kidnap his favorite concubine." Dimitri leaned forward, not bothering to hide his smoldering frustration. "I followed the servant so I could arrive before Rajih and slip Emma away."

Valik shoved his fingers through his hair, his expression harassed.

"Are the two of you demented?" he muttered. "The woman is a sharp-tongued vixen who any man with a thimble of sense should be delighted to be rid of."

Dimitri's hand instinctively slid up the sleeve of his robe where he had a dagger strapped to his forearm. He had another dagger tucked in his soft leather boots and a pistol in the holster beneath his left arm. The guards had been fools not to search him more carefully for weapons.

Unfortunately, he was not yet in a position to slice Valik open and leave him for the jackals. That particular pleasure would have to wait until he was certain Emma and the other girls were well away from the bastard.

"If that is true then you will be relieved to give her into my care."

"No." Coming to a halt, the Russian scowled in frustration. "You have destroyed my life, you smug bastard. Now you shall witness your woman used by every male who attends the auction this evening before I put you out of your misery." He paused, his expression gloating. "Perhaps I should warn you, some of the men can be excessively rough. I doubt Emma will survive the experience."

Dimitri slowly rose to his feet, refusing to react to the taunt despite the savage fury churning in his heart.

He had discovered as a youth on the streets of St. Petersburg that it was the man who refused to be goaded who survived.

Cold logic was always superior to mindless anger. Just as intelligence was always superior to brute strength.

He would eventually have the opportunity to make this man suffer. The sort of slow, agonizing suffering that could only end in death. But for now he had to convince the bastard that there was only one means for his survival.

"Are you deaf?" he taunted. "There will be no auction, Valik. Already the caliph is preparing to attack."

Sweat bloomed on the man's forehead, his breathing heavy. "Then I will kill you both and escape."

"Escape to where?" Dimitri pressed. "You are in a foreign country and I will bet my last drachma that you have little money. And worse, your wealthy associates are too consumed with their own survival to lend you assistance." He glanced toward a grilled window where the sound of braying donkeys and the distant howl of jackals were poignant reminders of how far from home they were. "A pity."

"I will sell the females," he stubbornly insisted.

Dimitri gave a bark of laughter. "You can sell a pack of terrified young women while fleeing from the caliph's guards? I doubt that even you are that talented."

Valik's bravado faltered beneath Dimitri's ruthless prodding, his hand swiping at the sweat that dripped down his brow.

"What do you offer?" he demanded at last.

Dimitri folded his hands over his chest. "You will allow me to leave the brothel with Emma and the other females. In return I will give you five hundred rubles."

"Five hundred?" The man licked his lips. "A paltry sum for a man in your position."

Dimitri had deliberately chosen a sum that would be large enough to tempt the man without being overly excessive. Valik was too cunning not to suspect a trap if Dimitri were willing to offer a fortune.

"It is what I have at hand and certainly it is enough to purchase a ticket upon a ship leaving Egypt," he said. "It offers you hope."

"You have the money with you?"

Dimitri narrowed his gaze. "I did just tell you that I was neither stupid nor careless. My servant is waiting at the Al-Hakim mosque. He will give you the money once he is certain I am safe."

Valik was shaking his head before Dimitri finished, his expression hard with suspicion.

"I am not a fool, either. What is to keep your servant from simply shooting me in the heart?"

Dimitri shrugged, already prepared for Valik's refusal. He preferred to issue commands and have them obeyed, but he could barter with the skill of a merchant when necessary.

"Then we will travel to the mosque together," he offered. "With me as your hostage my servant will not dare harm you until I am released."

Valik frowned, silently pacing and weighing the undoubted danger of accepting Dimitri's offer against the potential benefits.

Dimitri held his tongue, realizing if he pressed too hard the man might give in to his primitive desire to simply shoot him in the heart. He did, after all, hold Dimitri responsible for destroying his very profitable business.

Besides, Dimitri had little more to offer. His plan had been hastily conceived with none of his usual attention to details.

At last the man came to an abrupt halt, a fevered color staining his face.

"No."

An icy dread lodged in the center of Dimitri's gut. "No?"

"No." Valik moved to grab Dimitri's upper arm in a bruising grip. "I have a better idea."

# CHAPTER TWENTY-THREE

WITH HER HARD-EARNED ability to put the latest disaster out of her mind and concentrate on the troubles at hand, Emma efficiently searched the attics for a means to escape, and then when it was obvious she was trapped, she searched again for a potential weapon.

What was the point in giving in to her disappointment at Anya's betrayal? Or to allow herself to be consumed by the fear of being brutally raped?

Neither would help change her situation.

Instead, she had to keep her thoughts centered on the best means of escaping.

Unable to find any sharp object, she settled for breaking off one leg of a stool she had discovered beneath Anya's cot and moved to hide behind the door. Eventually someone would come to get her, and she intended to be prepared.

She did not know how much time passed before she heard the heavy sound of approaching footsteps. Ignoring her cramped muscles, she gripped the wooden stool leg. She did not believe for a moment she could overpower a man twice her size and weight, but she hoped to catch the monster off guard. All she needed was enough of a distraction to dart through the door before the man could catch her.

And then…

Well, her plan didn't extend beyond the door, but for now that was enough.

Lifting the weapon above her head, she held her breath

as the door was pushed open. Then, as the large form of Valik entered the room, she launched herself at his back.

The stool leg shattered as it hit the man's broad shoulder, but it did not have the impact she hoped for. Instead of sprawling to the ground, the man whirled on his heel, his face an ugly shade of puce as he lifted a meaty hand to hit her.

"Damn you, bitch."

Braced for the impact, Emma was unaware of the second man who entered the attic. It was not until strong arms wrapped around her from behind and clamped her to a wide chest that she realized the danger.

"No," the man rasped, surprisingly turning to protect Emma from the blow.

Instantly recognizing the voice, Emma glanced over her shoulder in shock.

"Dimitri?" she breathed, wondering if he were a mirage. Rajih had warned her that the desert was a treacherous place, offering her heart's desire only to reveal it was all no more than an illusion. Still, he seemed real enough. If he were a figment of her imagination, surely he would not be scowling at her as if he were infuriated by her attack on Valik, or his arms would not be holding her so tightly she could barely breathe? "What are you doing here?"

The golden gaze shifted to Valik, who was angrily pacing through the attic.

"A discussion for later, *milaya*," he muttered.

Valik ripped aside the curtain that separated the two rooms.

"Where is your sister?" he growled.

Emma licked her lips, hastily conjuring a lie to cover Anya's absence. Whatever Anya had done, she was still her sister. Her only family. And Emma would protect her with her dying breath.

"A guard came by a few minutes ago to take her from the room."

She ignored Dimitri's searching gaze as Valik stepped toward them.

"What guard?"

"How would I know? It is not as if we were in a position for introductions."

Perhaps sensing Emma was hiding the truth, Dimitri shifted until he was standing between her and the slave trader.

"You have no time to linger, Valik," he warned. "Not if you want to keep your head attached to your body."

"Fine." In one smooth motion, Valik reached into the pocket of his jacket to remove a pistol he promptly pointed at Emma. "Do not forget for a moment that your lover's life depends on you. You attempt something foolish and she dies."

Dimitri's expression hardened, but he said nothing as he tucked Emma close to his side and led her down the stairs. Too terrified to protest, Emma barely noticed as they moved through the silent brothel.

She had no notion if Dimitri had followed her to the brothel or if Valik had captured him. She didn't know where they were headed, or what was going to happen when they arrived. And for the moment, she did not care.

All that mattered was that Dimitri was in danger and it was entirely her fault.

Sick with dread, Emma stumbled through the narrow door that led to the back alley. A strange prickle made the hair on the nape of her neck rise, as if she were being watched from the shadows, but she dared not glance around with Valik pressing the pistol to the center of her back.

"The carriage," Valik growled, steering them past the pavilion to the waiting vehicle and yanking open the door. "Get in."

Already suspecting what was about to occur, Emma grudgingly climbed into the dark interior, her mouth dry as Dimitri settled on the seat opposite with a grim expression. She sensed that it would take very little to prod him into a foolish bout of heroism.

Her fear was confirmed when Valik reached inside the carriage, yanking her hands over her head to lock them in the dangling manacles.

"No," he snapped, surging forward.

A pistol pressed against her temple. "I warn you, Tipova, sit back."

Emma tensed, not out of concern for herself, but the horrifying fear that Dimitri would be injured.

"Dimitri…please," she whispered between lips that were stiff with foreboding.

His eyes flashed with golden fire, but with a grudging motion he settled back on the leather seat and turned his glare toward Valik.

"That is not necessary."

"We play this game by my rules, Tipova." Valik stepped back with a humorless smile and slammed the door.

Dimitri muttered a few of the more foul Russian curses as he noticed the lack of a handle, accepting that they were well and truly trapped. Then, he cursed again as they felt Valik climb onto the driver's seat and with a jerk, they were rattling down the narrow alley.

"How did you find me?" she demanded, as much to distract her dangerously infuriated companion as to ease her curiosity.

Dimitri's jaw knotted as he waged a battle to maintain his composure. He had ruthlessly devoted the past twenty years to carving a place for himself in the world where he was always in command of the situation.

To be at the mercy of another had to be worse than torture.

"I didn't," he said, his words clipped. "I was at the brothel before you arrived with Valik."

Emma narrowed her eyes, forgetting the painful steel biting into her wrists and the jarring sway of the carriage. Discovering that Dimitri had already been at the brothel was not at all what she had expected.

"Why would you be there?"

"It was not for the reason you are so clearly imagining," he retorted, shifting so he could peer out the narrow window. "Josef learned that a large Russian man had been seen in the neighborhood and he suspected he had some connection to the local brothel. He wished me to join him so we could investigate."

"Is that why...?"

His gaze flicked back to study her wary expression. "Why?" he prompted.

She blushed, wishing she could call back her impulsive words.

"Why you left the harem?"

The golden eyes warmed, as if he were savoring a particularly pleasant memory.

"I certainly did not leave willingly, but I could not ignore the potential to find Anya," he husked, his handsome features somber in the light that flickered from the torches that lined the streets. "I have learned my lesson."

Bittersweet misery settled in her heart at the unwelcome reminder of her sister. For all her relief that Anya seemed safe in the care of the guard, Mikhail, it would take time before she could think of her without the aching sense of loss.

"Anya," she breathed, lowering her lashes to hide the pain.

She heard the creak of leather as Dimitri shifted forward. "You managed to speak with her, did you not?"

"Yes."

"Has she been hurt?"

The manacles holding her captive rattled as she shrugged. "She claims she is unharmed."

"Do you fear she is trying to spare you the truth of her injuries?"

"Sparing me?" Emma's sharp laugh filled the carriage. "No, that certainly was not her intention."

There was a short pause, then Dimitri's hand cupped her chin and tilted her face to meet his piercing gaze.

"Emma?"

She tried to be angry with him. Her relationship with Anya was a private matter. What right did he have to press her?

But his gentle touch was sending comforting warmth through her that eased the pain of Anya's treachery, and she found the words tumbling from her lips before she could prevent them.

"I should have listened to your warnings."

"You begin to worry me, *milaya*." A faint smile curved his lips, but his expression was troubled. "Have you taken a blow to the head?"

"I simply realize that my efforts to care for Anya have done nothing but push her away." She blinked back the hot surge of tears. "As you said, I have no one to blame but myself for being abandoned by those I love."

His fingers tightened on her chin, his brows pulling together in a frown.

"Halt that."

"Why? I would think you would be pleased to know you were right."

He studied her for a long moment, his unnerving stare seeing far too much.

"Tell me what happened."

"Does it matter?"

"Please, Emma." His warm breath brushed her cheek. "Tell me."

She briefly closed her eyes, savoring the sensation of having him near. She was horrified he had put himself in danger, but a weak part of her wanted to wrap herself in his arms and be surrounded by his strength.

Where was her proud sense of independence now?

"Anya was in the attics when I was brought to the brothel," she confessed, grudgingly opening her eyes to meet his smoldering gaze. "Let us just say she was not pleased by my attempts to rescue her."

"Why not?"

"She already had planned to escape with one of the guards. I was an unwelcome interference to her elopement."

A dangerous tension filled the carriage, sending a shiver down her spine.

"A guard?"

Emma hesitated, still reluctant to reveal Anya's perfidy. Perhaps because she feared it would reflect on her failure to instill proper morals into her sister, she ruefully conceded. Then she winced as they turned a sharp corner, the manacles biting into her flesh as a reminder of their dire situation.

Dimitri had risked everything to rescue her. He deserved the truth.

"She swears that he is in love with her," she muttered. "He promised to take her to his home in Austria."

His fingers stroked over her cheek, his tone cautious, as if he were afraid of causing her more distress.

"I assume that you attempted to convince her of the stupidity in trusting such a man?"

Emma's lips twisted, remembering how she had pleaded with her stubborn sister.

"Of course, but she refused to listen to reason. She is

quite convinced that there is no worse fate than returning to Yabinsk with me."

Sympathy briefly softened his features. "She is very young, *milaya*. If you are patient, she will eventually come to appreciate all you have sacrificed."

Emma shook her head. It had taken Anya's agonizing rejection to force her to accept that she had been willfully blind over the year.

There was nothing she could do, nothing that she could offer, that would be enough for her sister.

Nothing.

"No, she is lost to me."

"Emma, listen to me," he urged, his voice lowering to ensure it did not carry past bars that blocked the windows. Not that it was likely Valik could overhear anything over the clatter of the crowds that filled the streets. How late was it, she inanely wondered? Midnight? Certainly Cairo was still bustling. "Caliph Rajih is waiting outside the brothel. As soon as he is certain you are safe he will rescue the girls and capture the remaining guards," Dimitri assured her. "As much as I might hate the bastard, you can trust Anya to his care."

Emma felt a surge of relief that girls being held captive would at last be safe, but shook her head at Dimitri's belief that Anya would be among the rescued women.

"You do not understand, Anya is already gone."

He stilled, his eyes narrowing at her words. "I remember you said that a guard had come to take Anya from the attics," he said slowly. "I sensed then you were lying."

"It was all I could think of to keep him from going in search of her."

His hand cupped her cheek. "Where is she?"

"I had only been in the attics for a few moments when she gathered a satchel and escaped through a trap door in the roof. She claimed that her beloved was awaiting her."

"And you remained behind?"

She turned her head, unable to watch the dawning comprehension in the golden eyes.

"Obviously."

"Why?"

"Surely we should be discussing how we are to escape?" she demanded, watching the light flickering beyond the carriage window. How much farther to the mosque? Surely they had to be close?

Dimitri firmly turned her face back to meet his ruthless scrutiny.

"Why did you remain in the attics, Emma?"

"Because Anya locked the door behind her," she snapped. "Are you satisfied?"

Emma was not surprised by the furious outrage that rippled over his beautiful face. Dimitri Tipova might be considered a criminal by most, but he possessed an unwavering sense of honor and a loyalty to those who depended on him. He would consider Anya's abandonment the worst sort of treachery.

"No, I am damned well not satisfied," he growled, a violent anger glittering in his eyes. "Do you mean to tell me that the ungrateful brat not only deserted you so that she could flee with her lover, but that she blocked a means for you to escape even knowing you were to be sold as a whore?"

Emma shrugged, weary of the bitter disappointment that spilled through her heart like acid.

"It no longer matters."

"When I manage to capture that bitch—"

"Please, Dimitri," she husked, unwilling to hear his opinion of Anya.

"I do not care if she is your sister or not, if she ever hurts you again, she will answer to me."

"She was my family," she reminded him, telling herself

that his fierce threat did not send a jolt of satisfaction through her. She could surely not be so petty. "Now I am alone."

The raven brows lifted at her husky words. "Is that a jest?"

"It is the truth."

His jaw tightened, revealing an unexpected annoyance. Why? With both her parents dead and Anya gone, there was no one left in her life.

"Then you must inform Herrick Gerhardt who has publicly claimed you as his cousin, as well as Vanya who considers you a beloved friend." His voice held a sardonic bite. "Ah, yes, and there is Leonida who threatened unmentionable harm on my manhood if I did not return you unharmed to the Huntley town house."

"It is not the same as—"

"I suppose I should also include Caliph Rajih, may his soul rot in hell, who is willing to risk the displeasure of this pasha to make you his wife," he relentlessly overrode her protest.

Her cheeks burned. A part of her accepted that Dimitri was not merely offering false comfort. Since leaving Yabinsk she had discovered that there were truly good people in the world willing to offer her assistance. Still, after so many years of having no one but herself to depend upon, it was difficult to put her trust in others.

"He is not thinking clearly," she said.

"No, he is not." The golden eyes flashed with an unnerving determination. "If he was, then he would know that you belong to me."

Her heart slammed against her ribs as she jerked away from his lingering touch.

"I do not belong to you, Dimitri Tipova."

"Of course you do." He settled back in his seat, his arms

folded across his chest. "You are not alone, Emma. Not ever again."

A perilous yearning tugged at her heart. He could so easily make her weak when she needed to be strong.

Stronger than she had ever been in her life.

"Do you have a plan for our escape or not?" she rasped.

His frustrated sigh filled the carriage. "It is more of a bargain than a plan. Josef is waiting for us at the mosque with money that I will offer to Valik for our freedom."

She frowned, wondering if he were disguising his true plan.

"You intend to bribe him?"

His lips twisted at the unmistakable disbelief in her voice. "It seemed the best means to ensure you were not harmed."

"And after you give him the money?"

He shrugged. "We shall hopefully never again be forced to endure his unpleasant company."

"You will allow him to flee?"

He caught and held her suspicious gaze. "If it means that you are safe."

She studied his somber expression, unable to stay her flicker of distrust.

"What of your revenge?"

"How often must I tell you that there is nothing more important than you?" He leaned forward, claiming her lips in a punishing kiss. "Nothing."

She forgot the discomfort of having her arms trapped above her head and the fact they were both at the mercy of a heartless slave trader. Instead, she sank into the persuasive demand of his kiss, needing the reassurance she was not to be betrayed and abandoned once again.

It was only when the sway of the carriage lessened that she pulled back, her heart squeezing with a surge of fear.

"We are slowing."

He swore, unable to hide his concern.

"Emma, I have no means to make certain that Valik will not attempt something desperate."

"What do you mean?"

The carriage halted and Emma heard the sound of Valik leaping to the ground and striding around the vehicle.

"As soon as Valik has released you I have told Josef to put you in the carriage and leave." He glanced toward the window before turning back to stab her with an urgent gaze. "No matter what might happen."

"You believe Valik intends to betray us?"

He paused, clearly caught between the desire to reassure her and the knowledge that she would prefer the truth.

"For the moment he is desperate to escape, but once he has the money in his hands, he will recall that I am to blame for all his troubles," he admitted. "At such moments men tend to toss aside good sense and allow their emotions to rule them."

Her eyes ran a lingering glance over his beautiful face, drinking in every line and curve that was indelibly engraved on her mind.

"Men such as you?" she asked softly.

"I never let my emotions rule me."

A sickening dread welled through her heart as she heard Valik's approaching footsteps.

"If that were true you would not have tried to rescue me. And you most certainly would not be in this carriage."

He shrugged. "It was a logical decision."

"It was insanity." Her voice was thick with emotion. "Dimitri, if something were to happen to you—"

"Emma, I command hundreds of cutthroats, thieves and pickpockets, all of whom are far more dangerous than Valik," he reassured her. "So long as I know that you are out of danger I am capable of besting a mere slave trader."

She bit her lower lip. "You are not so invincible as you believe."

"Of course I am. You will not be rid of me so easily."

They both stiffened as the door to the carriage was slowly pulled open.

"Dimitri," she breathed, her mouth dry with fear.

"Remember," he urged harshly. "You are to go directly to Josef and do not leave his side."

Valik stood beside the open doorway, his pistol pointed directly at Dimitri.

"Out, Tipova. Slowly." The large man watched Dimitri climb out of the carriage, his expression wary and his large face damp with sweat. Then, he lifted his hands to unlock the manacles holding Emma captive. "Now for you."

"Valik, if you leave a mark on her skin I will make certain your next profession is being a eunuch," Dimitri drawled, the lethal edge in his voice unmistakable.

The man made no response as he grabbed Emma's arm and roughly hauled her from the carriage. She could hear the rapid rasp of his breath and feel the tremble of his body. Valik was near a state of panic. Which could only mean disaster.

Feeling as if her heart were being crushed by a giant fist, Emma sent Dimitri a frantic glance, silently willing him not to do anything that might startle the growingly desperate fool. Dimitri, however, ignored her silent warning. Instead, he was watching Valik with the eyes of a predator preparing to strike.

Maintaining his bruising grip, Valik jerked Emma around the end of the carriage, allowing her a glimpse of the nearby mosque.

Constructed of bricks with a stone facade, the mosque had been built by Fatimid Caliph al-Aziz in 990 and, according to Rajih, it had recently been used by Napoleon as a fortress despite the insult to the faithful citizens of Cairo.

From her vantage she could see the central portal and the two corner minarets that marked the entrance to the courtyard framed by open arcades, but it was too dark to fully appreciate the beauty of the ancient structure.

And of course, it did not improve matters that she was currently being held captive by a dangerous lunatic.

"Where is your servant?" Valik demanded.

Dimitri paused, perhaps sensing Valik's growing apprehension, then, turning toward the mosque, he gave a low whistle.

There was a tense moment before a black carriage turned the corner and rolled to a halt on the opposite side of the street. A slender servant in a linen shirt and loose trousers leaped from the driver's seat and tied off the reins. He had reached the middle of the street when Valik lifted a warning hand, perhaps unnerved by the sight of the man's hard face marred by a scar running along his cheek, or the barely leashed violence that glittered in his eyes.

"Do not come any closer."

"Josef." Dimitri shifted to stand beside Valik. "You have the money?"

"I do." The servant held up a leather purse.

"Give it to me," Valik commanded.

"No," Dimitri snapped. "We will do this exchange by my rules."

Emma felt the slave trader stiffen in outrage, the rasp of his heavy breathing and the sour scent of his fear sending a prickle of warning over her skin.

"You may command the streets of St. Petersburg, Tipova, but I do not take orders from you," he said, his voice thick with hatred.

"You will if you want your money."

"What do you want?"

"Release Emma. Once she is in the carriage, Josef will toss you the purse."

"I don't trust you."

"Josef, open the purse," Dimitri ordered. On cue, Josef loosened the leather drawstrings and opened the purse so the torchlight could flicker over the silver rubles inside. "You see?" Dimitri said. "It is just as I promised."

"And as soon as you have the female you will have me shot," Valik muttered, jerking Emma against his foul body and wrapping a thick arm around her waist. "No. Give me the money and I will leave the woman near the citadel."

## CHAPTER TWENTY-FOUR

DIMITRI SWALLOWED HIS curses and struggled against the pounding fury that beat through his body at the sight of Emma being manhandled by the filthy creature.

His instincts dictated a leap forward and wrench her away before gutting the bastard. Instead, he was forced to grit his teeth and wait until Valik was properly distracted. He could not risk Emma being injured because of his primitive urges.

The plan, after all, had been nothing more than a hasty prayer that he would rescue Emma from the looming auction, hopefully without provoking the nervous Russian into killing them all.

"Calm yourself, Valik," he soothed. "We had a bargain."

Valik shifted away from him, pointing the pistol against Emma's temple.

"I am negotiating a new bargain."

Dimitri tensed, fighting to contain his raging emotions behind icy composure. There had never been a moment more vital to think with a calm detachment.

Calling upon the brutal discipline that he had honed after his mother's death, he cast a discreet glance toward Josef. This was far from the first dire situation he had shared with his servant, and over the years they had developed an unspoken ability to know precisely what the other was thinking. At times it was almost frightening.

"You are not stupid," he said, his voice as cold as a

winter's night in Siberia. "You know I will not let you leave with Emma."

Valik licked his lips, his beady gaze shifting to Josef as the slender man deliberately strolled forward, his hand reaching into the pocket of his jacket to remove a pistol.

"Take another step and I will kill her," he rasped.

"Josef," Dimitri pretended to chastise his servant, using Valik's distraction to shift a step closer.

"I wager I can put a bullet between his eyes before he can shoot the woman," Josef taunted.

"There will be no need," Dimitri drawled, taking yet another step. "I am certain Valik intends to be reasonable, do you not?"

As expected, the agitated man did not allow his gaze to waver from Josef, or the gun he was currently pointing in his direction.

"Give me the money."

Josef held up the purse and allowed it to dangle from the tips of his fingers.

"This money?"

"Tipova, I would suggest that you command your servant to give me what I want," Valik snarled. "Otherwise your lover is going to suffer a very nasty fate."

Dimitri could barely hear over his thundering heart, but his hands remained steady as he reached beneath the sleeve of his robe to retrieve his dagger.

For the moment, he was utterly focused. The scent of the perfume makers, the sway of the palm trees, the bray of a nearby donkey and the chill of the night breeze all faded away as he gripped the handle of the dagger. All he needed was the smallest opportunity. Just a breath of a chance.

And he would strike.

"Josef rarely listens to me," he said. "It is only because he amuses me that I allow him to remain in my employ."

Josef waved his pistol, keeping Valik's attention without being overly threatening.

"I thought it was because of my talent for disposing of the corpses you leave behind?"

"Not all those corpses were my doing," Dimitri protested.

"Yes, but I tidy my own messes." There was another wave of the pistol. "I suppose I will be expected to dispose of this fool, as well?"

"It is not as if we are in St. Petersburg where you must dig through layers of ice. You can toss him into the desert and leave him for the vultures."

Josef ran an assessing glance over Valik, his expression sour.

"Perhaps you have failed to notice that he is as large as an ox? You'll have to hire me help to drag him out of the gutter."

"There are a number of monkeys scurrying about who might be of assistance."

Valik nervously shifted. "You cannot fool me into believing you do not care about the woman."

Realizing that the slave trader was about to turn and discover how close to his back Dimitri had moved, Josef gave a wild laugh as he stumbled toward him.

"I don't," he called. "And since I am the one with the pistol…"

Startled by the sudden movement, Valik allowed his fear to overcome him. Removing the pistol from Emma's temple he instead pointed it in Josef's direction.

"I told you to stay back."

A cold smile curved Dimitri's lips as he attacked.

The bastard had made two mistakes. The first was assuming that Josef was the more dangerous adversary. And the second was turning his gun away from Emma. It had been his one guarantee that Dimitri would not dare to strike.

Plunging the knife deep in Valik's back, Dimitri wrapped an arm around his throat and yanked him to the side, effectively dislodging Emma from the man's grasp. Only then did he drive the larger man to the dirt road, digging the knife deeper into his flesh.

Valik grunted, briefly caught off guard. Dimitri was swift to take advantage, jerking the dagger free only to slam it low in the man's back, experienced enough to avoid the ribs so the blade could dig deep into his body.

Dimitri felt warm blood rush over his hand, cursing Valik's massive size and ruthless thirst for survival. A lesser man would have conceded defeat, realizing he had been mortally wounded.

Valik, however, refused to accept fate without a fight and with a sudden roar he swung out a beefy arm. His elbow connected with Dimitri's chin with shocking force, briefly blinding him with pain.

Dimitri cursed, his hold on his opponent loosening. It was enough for Valik to roll away, shrieking in pain as Dimitri grimly held on to the dagger while it was ripped from Valik's flesh.

For an odd, timeless motion the two of them lay on the road, face-to-face with the spectrum of death hovering between them. Valik's eyes glittered with demented fury, flecks of blood visible on his lips. In contrast, Dimitri was coldly determined, quite willing to die if it meant saving Emma.

Then, as one, they both moved to put an end to the violent encounter.

Pulling back his arm, Dimitri swung it in an arc, surprised when Valik made no effort to deflect the blow. It was not until the explosive sound of a firing pistol nearly deafened him that he realized the man was still holding his gun. And that he had shifted to aim the weapon directly at him.

He oddly felt no fear. Only a wry acceptance that he was at last to be punished for his wicked ways. And regret. A sharp, biting regret that he would be leaving Emma far too soon.

Of course, if he were going to hell, he had no intention of going alone. Putting the full force of his body behind his strike, Dimitri drove the dagger directly into the center of Valik's heart.

He felt the blade slide easily through Valik's chest and at the same moment he felt as if a large, very angry horse had just kicked him in the shoulder. The breath was jerked from his body as the bullet slammed into his flesh, the force of the blow sending him rolling across the road.

Distantly, he heard the sound of Josef's curses and Emma's screams, but it was difficult to think through the sudden fog that was clouding his mind.

There was pain. Red-hot, searing pain. And a frustration that his body refused to respond to his commands, so that he could make certain Valik was dead as he was supposed to be and not preparing to shoot again. But there was also the shocking realization he was not about to make his inevitable journey to hell.

How many times had he been shot in his lifetime? A half dozen? Certainly often enough to recognize a flesh wound from a mortal injury.

He wasn't going to die.

Well, at least not in the next few moments.

The relief had barely passed through his mind when there was a flurry of footsteps and Emma sank to her knees at his side. Welcome warmth filled his heart at the sight of her pale face leaning over him.

Surely that was terrified concern for him simmering in her beautiful green eyes?

"Dimitri, damn you," she choked, her gaze shifting to the blood staining his robe. "I knew this was a ridiculous plan."

He smiled at her, savoring the feel of her fingers gently smoothing the hair from his brow, even as her knee pressed against his arm to send a blaze of agony through him.

"I told you it was a bargain, not a plan," he reminded her.

"It was still ridiculous."

"My sharp-tongued vixen." His gaze skimmed over her delicate features framed by a halo of honey curls. "Should you not be offering a kiss to ease my pain rather than lecturing me on my botched rescue? Which was highly successful despite your complaints."

"Successful?" She regarded him as if he'd taken leave of his senses. And perhaps he had. He was lying flat on his back, bleeding onto a dirty Cairo street from a gunshot wound to his shoulder—his second gunshot wound in the past month—with his assailant only a few feet away, but all he could think of was the wonderment that his time with this lovely woman was not yet at an end. "You have been shot."

"But you are safe," he said softly.

She frowned, shaking her head in frustration. "You are the most aggravating—"

She was interrupted as Josef appeared at her side, a pistol held loosely in his hand.

"What of Valik?" Dimitri demanded.

"Dead," the servant assured him. "What do you want me to do with the body?"

"Leave him for the jackals to enjoy," he muttered, his pain making it difficult to think clearly. "For the moment I am more interested in bleeding somewhere other than a filthy street."

"We must find a surgeon," Emma breathed.

Dimitri shuddered. Any man who had traveled through the world knew one of the greatest dangers was putting his health in the care of the local doctors.

They inevitably caused more damage than they cured.

"Are you so anxious to see me dead?" he rasped.

She frowned in confusion. "Of course not, but you have just been shot."

"I wouldn't take my dog to the local surgeon," Josef muttered.

"But—"

"Josef is experienced in stitching my wounds." Dimitri headed off her arguments.

She grimaced, casting a jaundiced glance at his servant. "I suppose he has had a great deal of practice?"

"Enough," Josef readily admitted.

"It is nothing to be proud of." She returned her harried attention to Dimitri. "What if the bullet is still in your shoulder?"

Josef shrugged. "Then I will dig it out."

"And risk it becoming inflamed?"

Ignoring his pain, Dimitri reached to grasp Emma's hand. She was stubborn enough to go in search of a damnable doctor if she thought it best for him.

"I needn't worry," he said, his voice strained. "I will have you to nurse me back to health, *milaya*."

Her eyes narrowed at his teasing, but the stroke of her fingers on his brow was exquisitely tender.

"How can you be so certain I will not leave you for those vultures you spoke of earlier?" she demanded.

"Because it is in your nature to care for others, even when they do not deserve your concern."

Misery flared through her eyes and he silently cursed his thoughtless words.

The last thing he desired was to remind her of her worthless sister.

"Perhaps I have learned that caring for others is a dangerous emotion that is not worth the pain," she said, her voice so low he barely caught her bitter words.

"Emma—"

"Guards are coming," Josef snapped, his hand tightening on the pistol and his slender body tense as he prepared for trouble.

Dimitri ignored Emma's protest as he struggled to lift his head.

"The caliph's?"

"The pasha. And they do not look pleased."

He managed to sit upright despite the agony that jolted down his arm.

"Damn."

Seemingly indifferent to the approaching soldiers who were fully armed with both rifles and swords, Emma carefully shifted to put a bracing arm behind his back. Dimitri swallowed a rueful sigh. The ridiculous woman would always be more concerned with the welfare of others than her own safety.

Which was precisely why he intended to devote the rest of his life to protecting her.

"Surely that is good?" she asked. "We have done nothing wrong."

Dimitri battled against the wave of dizziness, his gaze taking in the determined approach of the five soldiers. His heart sank at the sight of their military precision and obvious ease with their weapons.

This was no ragtag group of mercenaries.

They were trained fighters who had tasted war.

"We have shed blood on the streets of Cairo," he absently murmured. "I doubt the pasha will approve."

"Valik is…" Emma caught her words, glancing toward Valik's unnaturally still body. "He was a slave trader. A criminal."

"And what am I?" he demanded wryly. He turned to meet Josef's calculating gaze. "Can we flee?"

"You can." He nodded toward the nearby carriage. "I will distract them."

"No." Dimitri's tone was commanding. He would not risk his most loyal servant. "I doubt the pasha's mood will be improved if we were to kill his soldiers."

He heard Emma suck in a sharp breath. "You are going to allow yourself to be captured?"

"There does not seem to be much choice." He swiftly considered his severely limited options. There was no avoiding the soldiers. Not without putting Emma in danger. He could only hope that the pasha would offer a reasonable hospitality until he could find the means to escape. "Josef, slip away and gather the men. Take them out of the city and if we have not been released within the week—"

"Wait," Emma interrupted, her expression grim. "You will need Josef. I have a better plan."

His brows snapped together. "Emma."

"Trust me."

Without giving him the opportunity to stop her, Emma surged to her feet and darted toward the nearby palm trees before becoming lost among the shadows.

Dimitri gritted his teeth, and Josef muttered his vile opinion of females who were too stubborn for their own good. Neither, however, were foolish enough to risk drawing the approaching soldiers' attention toward the fleeing woman.

Instead, they exchanged a resigned glance and prepared to be arrested by Muhammad Ali Pasha.

EMMA RAN THROUGH THE streets of Cairo like a mad woman, utterly indifferent to the drunken men and roaming packs of dogs that threatened her. All she could think of was finding help before Dimitri could be taken by the approaching guards.

A futile hope, she discovered as she at last reached Rajih's palace only to be told he had not yet returned.

Not knowing where else to turn, Emma allowed herself to be escorted into the harem to await his arrival.

It was not as if she could approach the pasha and demand that his soldiers release Dimitri.

Could she?

Pacing the tiled floor, she impatiently counted the passing minutes. For once the soft tinkle of the fountain and the faint scent of incense did nothing to soothe her frayed nerves. Nor did the expensive wine that was left near the baths on a silver tray.

It seemed like an eternity before she at last heard the sound of voices in the inner courtyard. With a small cry of relief she darted from her private rooms, only to be forced to halt as she realized Rajih was not alone.

Standing behind one of the carved-marble columns, she watched as Rajih directed his servants to care for the five young girls huddling together in obvious fear.

She was briefly distracted as she studied the pale, dirty faces of the poor females who were dressed in gauzy trousers and tiny vests that revealed more of their shivering bodies than they concealed.

They looked so terrified. As if they could not allow themselves to believe they were actually safe in Rajih's care.

And who could blame them? They had spent weeks being held hostage, forced from one place to another with the constant threat of being raped, or worse, hanging over their heads. It might very well be they would never again be able to trust in others.

Her heart constricted with unbearable pity, fiercely glad

that Dimitri had managed to put a dagger in Valik's black heart.

It was only a pity that the other men involved in the hideous business were not destined for a similar fate.

She waited until the robed servants had led the wary girls toward the back of the harem before she stepped from behind the column.

Sensing her presence, Rajih spun on his heel, his eyes widening in surprise as she launched herself forward, straight into his welcoming arms.

"Emma."

"Oh, Rajih, thank God," she husked.

He brushed his lips over the top of her head before pulling back to study her with a searching gaze.

"Should I be delighted by such a fervent greeting or alarmed?"

"Are those the girls from the brothel?"

His dark eyes shimmered with regret. "They are."

"What will happen to them now?"

"Tipova implied that the current Russian ambassador is not to be fully trusted with young, vulnerable girls, so I will have my personal servants return them to St. Petersburg."

She managed a small smile. If not for Dimitri Tipova, she was quite certain she would have lost her heart to this man.

"That is very generous," she said. "You are a good man, Caliph Rajih."

He shook his head, his fingers tucking her tangled curls behind her ear.

"You might wish to withhold your kind opinion," he warned. "I fear I have unfortunate news."

She pulled back, belatedly recalling he had put himself in danger to rescue the girls. Who knew how many guards Valik had left behind at the brothel?

"You were not hurt, were you?"

His dark features softened at her impulsive concern. "No, I am fine."

"Then what has happened?"

He paused, clearly reluctant to reveal what was upon his mind.

"Emma, your sister was not among the girls I rescued from the brothel," he at last disclosed. "I questioned the females but they claimed that Anya has been kept separate from them since they left England and they have no knowledge of where she is." His arms tightened around her, as if fearing she might suddenly bolt into the night. "I have servants searching for her, but for the moment it seems that she has simply disappeared. I am sorry, I should have been quicker to send in my guards."

Emma grimaced, regretting that Rajih was torturing himself with guilt at having failed her.

"No, Rajih, Anya fled before you were able to enter the brothel," she swiftly reassured him. "All that matters is that you managed to rescue the other girls."

"She fled?" Rajih frowned in confusion. "Alone?"

Emma shook her head, hunching her shoulders against the tide of sick betrayal.

"She was with one of the guards," she said. "They are supposedly on their way to Austria."

Rajih stilled, clearly sensing her distress. "Do you want me to send my guards after them?"

"No, she had made her choice."

"Emma—"

Swallowing the lump in her throat, Emma pulled out of his comforting arms and tilted her chin. Now was no time to fret over her sister's astounding selfishness. Not when Dimitri was depending upon her.

"Please, Rajih, I do need your assistance, but not for Anya," she pleaded softly.

"What do you need?"

"Dimitri has been taken captive by Muhammad Ali Pasha's guards. We must free him."

A thick silence filled the courtyard as Rajih considered her confession, then slowly he folded his arms over his chest.

"Tell me what happened."

As concisely as possible she revealed their carriage ride from the brothel to the mosque and Valik's refusal to release her. She briefly faltered as she described Dimitri's attack on the horrid man. There would not be a night when she was not haunted by the vivid image of Dimitri being shot, not knowing for an agonizing moment whether he was alive or dead.

With effort she gathered her composure and finished explaining Dimitri's dire situation, emphasizing the very large and heavily armed guards who had been rapidly approaching.

Once she was finished, Rajih turned to pace through the perfumed shadows of the courtyard, his expression impossible to read.

"How badly is he injured?"

"The shot was to his shoulder, but I fear the bullet may still be in the wound and he lost a great deal of blood."

"Do not fear," he muttered absently. "The pasha has a number of healers."

She snorted. "If Josef will let them near."

Rajih halted, turning to regard her with a warning gaze. "The choice will not be his to make."

A shiver inched down Emma's spine. There was an edge in his voice that sharply reminded her that they were in a foreign country with its own laws and traditions. For the moment, Dimitri and Josef were at the complete mercy of the pasha.

"Is Dimitri in danger?"

"I am not entirely certain." Rajih thankfully knew her well enough to speak the truth. In this moment she could not bear to be treated as if she were a mindless, shrinking violet in need of tender care. "The pasha will not be pleased that a foreigner committed murder on the streets for all to see."

"But Valik was a slave trader, not to mention he was holding me hostage," she protested.

"True, but the officials prefer that such matters be dealt with discreetly." Rajih grimaced. "The pasha possesses a dislike for explaining violent deaths of the foreign consuls."

Emma possessed a small measure of sympathy for the ruler. His country was too often at the mercy of invaders. He could not risk offending potential allies.

That did not mean, however, she would meekly stand aside and allow Dimitri to become a sacrifice to his political weakness.

She stepped forward and laid a hand on Rajih's forearm. "Can you speak with the pasha and convince him that Dimitri is innocent?"

The dark eyes lowered to study her fingers that lay against the fine fabric of his jacket, a mysterious smile curving his lips.

"I could, but it would hardly be to my benefit," he murmured.

She frowned. "Rajih?"

"If I am not mistaken, Tipova intends to take you away from Egypt."

An uncomfortable sensation tugged at her heart. Something that might have been regret.

"With or without Dimitri I intend to return to Russia."

His eyes lifted to stab her with a relentless gaze. "Why?"

"It is my home."

With a gentle care, Rajih covered the fingers that rested on his arm, his gaze sweeping over her upturned face.

"No, Emma, Russia is the place you were born," he corrected. "Your home is where you choose to be."

A dim, nearly forgotten memory of her parents seated before the fireplace in the cottage rose to mind. There had been nothing special about the evening. At least nothing that she could recall. But the image of her mother and father snuggled closely on the sofa, their hands entwined and their faces soft with love, had created a warmth in her young heart.

That was what created a home.

"I suppose that is true."

As if sensing her bittersweet memories, Rajih shifted to cup her face in his hands, his expression somber.

"I want you to stay with me."

"As your concubine?"

"As my wife."

*Wife.* She blinked, regarding him with disbelief.

For goodness' sake, was he touched in the head?

He was, after all, a shockingly handsome man with a ruthless virility that would make any female weak in the knees. She had seen how women fluttered when he stepped onto the streets of Cairo.

And of course, there was the tiny matter of him being a wealthy caliph with a number of estates spread throughout Egypt.

The mere notion he could desire an aging spinster with an evil temper and sharp tongue was…

Without warning, her laughter was spilling through the dark courtyard.

"This is absurd," she choked.

His brows drew together, his pride obviously offended.

"You find my proposal amusing?"

"I find it astonishing. I…" She bit her bottom lip, struggling to regain command of her fragile composure.

He stepped forward, grasping her shoulders in a firm grip. "Emma?"

"For most of my life I have either been the source of pity or amusement," she confessed, anxious to assure him that she was deeply honored by his proposal. "It is not a simple matter to accept that a gentleman could consider me worthy to be his wife. Certainly not a gentleman who is offered the most beautiful women in the world."

His expression eased at her words, his hands stroking a warm path down her back.

"You are a woman of rare courage and loyalty," he said. "These are qualities that I would desire for my sons."

Her heart missed a beat, and she sharply turned away. She had never allowed herself to consider the possibility of children. Not when she knew she was destined to be an old maid.

It was simply too painful.

"That is why you wish to marry me?"

"You know why I want you as my wife," he husked, his arms wrapping around her slender waist and his head lowering to bury in the curve of her neck. "The question is what do you want, Emma?"

# CHAPTER TWENTY-FIVE

DIMITRI HAD A VAGUE memory of being surrounded by angry soldiers and roughly carried to the citadel. Thankfully, he had lost consciousness only moments after passing through the great round towers built into the walls guarding the fortress.

He preferred to stay unaware of his humiliation of being hauled to the dungeons as a common criminal.

Unfortunately, there was no means of remaining senseless when his servant was using a large dagger to dig out the bullet that remained in his shoulder. Hell, that sort of pain would have awoken him if he were dead.

Wrenching open eyes that felt as if they were filled with a good measure of desert sand, he glared at the slender man kneeling beside the low divan that Dimitri was stretched across.

"Damn you, Josef," he said, annoyed when the words came out as a thin whisper. "That is my shoulder you are poking and prying, not a slab of meat from the butcher."

With a last brutal twist of the dagger, Josef sat back on his heels, a smile touching his scarred face as he held up the bullet he had just removed.

"The pasha did offer one of his numerous females to tend to your injuries." Setting aside his tools of torture, the servant grabbed his silver flask and poured a generous measure of brandy into Dimitri's wound. "No doubt they would be gentle enough for your delicate nerves."

Dimitri ground his teeth against his shout of agony.

Why was it that a bullet always felt worse coming out than it did going in?

Sensing the encroaching darkness that threatened to overwhelm him, Dimitri grimly tried to focus on his surroundings.

Above him the vaulted ceiling was magnificently decorated with blue-and-white tiles, the superior craftsmanship unmistakable. Far too exquisite for the dungeons. Which was an improvement on this rotten day.

With a small movement, he turned his head far enough to sweep a glance over the large room filled with the divans and large pillows that were preferred among the natives, covered in yellow-and-green silk. The walls were covered with finely carved wooden panels, and there was a massive fireplace with a green-marble mantel. At last he shifted his attention to take in the arched windows where the early morning sunlight tumbled through the grilled screens.

He grimaced, realizing he had been unconscious more hours than he initially suspected.

Where was Emma? And most important, was she safe?

"They would certainly be preferable to gaze upon," he absently muttered.

Packing the wound with clean linen, Josef efficiently wrapped a narrow strip of fabric around his shoulder to hold it in place.

"Do you want one fetched?" he demanded.

With his thoughts still on Emma, Dimitri managed a painful laugh.

"You just dug a bullet out of my flesh, in an unnecessarily painful fashion I might add. I do not relish the thought of having another removed."

Josef snorted, washing his hands in the ceramic bowl filled with water.

"I doubt any of the females in the pasha's harem carry loaded pistols."

"No, but Emma would be eager to put another in my tender backside should she discover I allowed a beautiful female to put her hands on me."

A completely unexpected fondness flickered over his servant's narrow countenance.

"She is too honorable to shoot you from behind. She is far more likely to stab you in the heart with a dagger."

"That is most reassuring." Bemused, Dimitri struggled to sit upright, relieved to discover that the worst of the fiery pain seemed to be fading from his shoulder. Of course, he did not protest when his servant helped him slip on a pale blue robe and pressed a flask into his hand. "You surprise me, Josef," he admitted, drinking deep of the fiery spirits.

"Why?" Josef gathered the bloody rags and dagger, dumping them on a silver tray. "I have stitched you back together more times than I can recall."

"No, I am astonished that I am not forced to endure a lecture on the stupidity of men who fall victim to a female's snare."

Josef straightened, carrying the tray to set it on a low table inlaid with bronze.

"You know my opinion."

"Then why are you not scolding me as if I am a witless idiot?"

"If you must dangle on some female's leash then you could do much worse than Emma Linley-Kirov."

Dimitri was genuinely shocked. He had known Josef since they were both scrawny youths, struggling to stay alive in the gutters of St. Petersburg. In all that time the man had never revealed more than a bitter distrust for the opposite sex.

The predictable result of a boy beaten nearly to death by his mother and left in the rubbish to die.

"Good Lord, surely you cannot approve of a mere female?" he teased.

Josef turned to meet Dimitri's amused gaze. "She is different from most."

Dimitri's lips twisted. "True."

"Did you see her standing in the street as cool as you please, while Valik held a pistol to her head?" Josef smiled. "I could not have done better myself."

A stab of remembered terror made his heart forget to beat. "It is a vision engraved on my mind, I assure you."

"Most women would have swooned or at least been sniffling and begging for their life. But not Emma."

Dimitri nearly rolled his eyes at the admiration in his companion's voice. It was all very well for Josef to approve of Emma's impulsive courage. He was not the one who lived in constant fear she would plunge into some disaster he could not save her from.

"No, not Emma. She would spit in the eye of the devil," he admitted wryly. "Just like my mother."

"That is surely a good thing?"

"I had convinced myself that I preferred females who understood that it was a man's responsibility to offer her protection. Not a woman who—"

"A woman who would make a man proud," Josef finished with a lift of his brows.

Dimitri attempted to appear resigned, even as a smug satisfaction flared through his heart.

Yes, he would always be proud of Emma.

She was utterly unique.

"It is a pity she is destined to put me in an early grave."

"It is not too late to walk away."

"It was too late from the moment she arrived in St.

Petersburg." Dimitri lifted the flask to his lips, wincing as the bandages tugged at his injury. "Damn."

Josef moved back to the divan, scowling down at his employer.

"How does it feel?"

"As if I have a hole in my shoulder, but I will no doubt survive." Dimitri raised the flask in a toast. "Yet another fine job, old friend."

Josef grimaced as the faint sound of voices penetrated the large double doors at the far side of the room.

"Let us hope that I did not remove the bullet so that the pasha could have your head removed," he muttered.

Dimitri struggled off the divan, grasping Josef's arm as a wave of dizziness threatened to buckle his knees. He would meet his fate on his feet.

"We haven't yet been taken to the dungeon, which means we are still considered guests and not prisoners."

"Do not be so certain," Josef muttered. "There are two very large guards on the other side of the doors. It will not be easy to escape."

"For now I prefer to avoid insulting our host," he said, a hint of warning in his voice. It would not take long before Josef decided he had wearied of the pasha's hospitality and took matters into his own hands. "It is quite possible we will be released once I have the opportunity to explain to the pasha why there is a dead Russian in his gutter."

Josef grunted. "Or he might decide we would make a tasty meal for his pet tiger."

Dimitri hid his sudden smile, not bothering to correct his servant's odd belief that Egypt was filled with tigers and lions and any number of other dangerous animals.

"Highly doubtful."

"So you say."

Dimitri's hand tightened on Josef's arm as the doors were pushed open to reveal two slender female servants attired in nearly transparent robes with tiny jewels dangling from their noses.

"Patience, Josef."

SIX HOURS LATER, DIMITRI had managed to forget his decision to behave as a rational, law-abiding gentleman.

It was not that he had been ill-treated. Quite the contrary, in fact.

The females that had led them to the baths had been beautiful and anxious to please. Rather too anxious, he wryly admitted, recalling their shock when he had refused to allow them to wash him with their scented oils. And when they had returned to their room, it was to find a sumptuous feast had been left on trays.

Once he had eaten, Dimitri forced himself to lie back on the pillows and rest. His shoulder was rapidly healing, but it would take some time to regain his strength.

As the hours passed, however, his attempt to calmly await his fate evaporated like wavering mists of a mirage. He might be in luxurious comfort, but he had no assurance that Emma was not in trouble.

She had run into the night alone, traversing the dangerous streets of Cairo with nothing but luck to protect her.

The worry was like an aching thorn in the center of his heart.

Pacing the floor, he at last moved to stand beside the grilled window overlooking the southern enclosure of the citadel, his gaze lingering on the massive green dome of the Hall of Justice. Beyond it was the black-and-yellow marble palace built by An-Nasir Muhammad where the pasha conducted his daily business of ruling his empire.

Surely the pasha had to be near? How difficult could it be to send for him and demand an explanation for the death of Valik?

With a muttered curse he turned on his heel to glare at Josef, who was busy with his own pacing.

"Where the hell is the pasha?" he burst out.

Josef flashed him a jaundiced frown. "You were the one to counsel patience."

"I need to know that Emma is safe."

"Do not worry, Dimitri Tipova," a voice drawled from the door. "Emma is under my protection."

Dimitri jerked his head to view Caliph Rajih strolling across the delicate carpet. His gaze skimmed over the man's white robe heavily embroidered with gold trim and the matching turban, a scowl marring his brow as he lingered on the curved sword belted to his waist.

It was more than an ornamental weapon. That was obvious from the well-honed edge and worn leather of the hilt. There was also an ease in the manner Rajih wore the sword that suggested he was familiar with using the lethal tool.

Dimitri, on the other hand, had awoken to discover his pistol and knives had been taken while he slept. And even the dagger that Josef had used to cut the bullet from his shoulder had disappeared.

He did not like feeling vulnerable.

Or perhaps it was the smug smile curving the man's lips that he did not like.

All he knew was that he had a sudden urge to wrap his hands around the bastard's throat and squeeze the life from him.

"Where is she?" he snapped.

"She is visiting the pasha's seraglio."

Dimitri's stark relief that Emma was indeed safe warred with his outrage at the thought of her being within the pasha's harem.

"You brought her to the citadel?"

"Do not hold me accountable." Rajih shook his head.

"She refused to remain at the palace and threatened to come on her own if I did not allow her to accompany me."

"Ah." Despite his annoyance, Dimitri smiled at the man's obvious frustration. "You have my sympathy."

"I should no doubt have chained her to her bed, but I feared yet another of your enemies might be lurking about to snatch her while I was gone."

Dimitri refused to react to the deliberate taunt. Soon enough he would be whisking Emma back to St. Petersburg, and his newly constructed town house, where she belonged.

"My supposed enemies will be fleeing Cairo like rats from a sinking ship."

"Do not be so certain."

Dimitri tensed, not missing the edge of warning in the man's voice.

"What do you mean?"

"Despite my preference that you remain conveniently locked behind these walls, Emma was quite insistent I make a personal plea for your release."

Dimitri grinned. "She must have been quite persuasive."

"She is aware that I would do whatever necessary to please her."

"And what pleases her is my release? That must be a painful disappointment for you."

Rajih waved a dismissive hand. "Emma has a tender heart and she blames herself for your situation. She will eventually see the error of her ways and accept that I offer far more than a Russian criminal can, no matter how great his wealth."

There was enough truth in the caliph's accusation to send an unwelcome chill down Dimitri's spine.

He took pride in what he had accomplished over the

years. Why not? How often did a ragged beggar boy actually manage to create his own empire?

But for all his accomplishments, there was no denying that he was the bastard son of a whore and worse, a ruthless criminal who was, for all his fine estates and vast fortune, no better than a common serf.

What woman with the least amount of sense would not prefer a handsome caliph who could not only offer her wealth, but an opportunity to mingle among the finest of society?

Then, squaring his shoulder, he dismissed his unnerving doubt.

Most women would indeed leap at the opportunity to become Rajih's bride, but not Emma.

She desired many things; a family, a sense of independence, a home, but never wealth and certainly never social standing.

Those were the things that he could offer.

"She will never be yours," he grated, his hands clenched as he stepped toward the damned intruder.

"Tipova, perhaps you can postpone your urge to challenge the man who is here to plea for our release?" Josef stepped between them, poking Dimitri in the chest. "At least until we are away from this place? There are few prisons I cannot escape from, but this is a fortress."

Dimitri growled low in his throat, his predatory nature fully aroused. Unfortunately, he could not dismiss Josef's warning.

For the moment, he had to swallow his pride and accept whatever assistance Rajih was willing to offer.

"Have you spoken with the pasha?" he asked between gritted teeth.

The Egyptian smiled. "I have."

"You explained that Valik was in this country to auction young girls?"

"Yes."

Dimitri narrowed his gaze, sensing that Rajih had not come to announce he was at liberty to leave.

"And?"

Rajih moved to the tray on a side table, pouring a drink from the decanter of brandy.

"Unfortunately, I was not the only petitioner to approach the pasha concerning your presence in Cairo."

"Petitioner?" Dimitri stiffened in shock, wondering if the word had a different meaning in Egyptian politics. "What precisely does that mean?"

Rajih emptied his glass in one swallow. "When I was brought before the pasha to proclaim your innocence another arrived to swear to your guilt."

So, it was precisely what he feared.

But how could anyone possibly know he was currently being held captive by the pasha? And why would they come as a petitioner to proclaim his guilt?

"Who?"

"Baron Koman."

"The Russian ambassador?" He frowned, a fury exploding through him. "Damn his black soul."

Rajih smiled, not bothering to hide his amusement at Dimitri's frustration.

"I assume the two of you are acquainted?"

"Unfortunately." Dimitri paced across the floor, brooding on the unexpected complication. "The bastard must have discovered my intention to speak with Alexander Pavlovich to have him removed from his position."

Rajih made a choked sound of surprise. "You have such influence with Czar Alexander?"

"It is not a matter of influence. The man is an incompetent fool."

"Not entirely incompetent," Rajih countered. "He made quite a compelling argument that you are an infamous

Russian criminal who had recently decided to take command of the slave trade."

Dimitri came to a sharp halt, unable to dismiss the sensation that there was far more to his current troubles than an indolent, half-witted Russian nobleman.

"If that were true then why would I have killed Valik and allowed the girls to be released into your care?"

"It was suggested that it was a battle for power." Rajih shrugged. "You would, after all, need to destroy the current business before establishing your own."

Dimitri paused, his suspicions becoming certainty. "Koman made this suggestion?"

Rajih set aside his glass, sensing the sudden danger that prickled in the air.

"Why are you so surprised?" he asked. "You admitted the man has reason to wish you harm."

Dimitri prowled forward, his expression hard. "Yes, but he is a lazy, stupid man who is barely capable of summoning the ambition to leave his divan."

An age-old bitterness flared through Rajih's dark eyes. "He resembles every other foreign diplomat in Cairo."

"The crux of the matter is that Koman might pout and complain and even threaten retribution, but he would never summon the initiative or the temerity to approach the pasha," he growled, fiercely regretting his lack of weapons. "And he most certainly does not possess the intelligence to devise such a clever means of implicating me as a slave trader."

The dark eyes narrowed. "I assure you that it most certainly was the baron I just witnessed testifying to your guilt."

"I do not question his presence, only his motive," Dimitri replied, his voice cold. "There has to be more than revenge that compelled him to the citadel."

With a glare at Dimitri's bristling manner, Josef attempted to ease the rising hostility in the room.

"What could be more powerful than the desire for revenge?" he demanded.

Dimitri folded his arms over his chest. "Fear."

Josef absently stroked a finger over the scar marring his cheek.

"You believe he fears the loss of his position as a diplomat?"

"No," Dimitri readily denied. Koman was a self-indulgent pig who cared for nothing beyond his own pleasure. "It has to be a greater threat than his career."

"His wealth?"

Dimitri nodded. "Or his life."

Rajih made a sound of impatience. "You make no sense, Tipova. What possible gain could be in forcing Koman to testify against you?"

Dimitri's attention snapped back to the caliph, his suspicions a hard knot in the pit of his stomach.

"Tell me what the pasha has decided."

"Obviously, he has been put in an awkward situation." Rajih paused, as if carefully considering his words. "He has long considered me a trusted advisor, but he cannot be seen to ignore the accusations of the Russian ambassador who also happens to be a powerful nobleman."

A cold, humorless smile curved Dimitri's lips. His cunning mind was already devising various plans of escape that did not include the pasha or Caliph Rajih.

"I sympathize with his dilemma, but that does not reveal what he intends to do with me."

"Or me," Josef muttered.

"He has sent an advisor to St. Petersburg to speak with Czar Alexander before a decision is made."

Dimitri exchanged a startled glance with Josef. Was his mysterious enemy unaware that Alexander Pavlovich owed him several favors and assumed the czar would be happy to leave Dimitri rotting in a foreign prison? Or was this simply a delaying tactic?

He had first assumed that Koman's petition to the pasha was an attempt to punish him. It could be an opponent who desired him to be distracted for some nefarious purpose.

And he knew precisely who would desire him to be distracted.

"A tidy means of avoiding responsibility," he mocked.

Rajih silently studied Dimitri's forbidding expression, his hand instinctively reaching to curl around the hilt of his sword.

"You should be grateful. It was within his power to have you executed."

Dimitri was in no mood to be appreciative. "Am I to remain a prisoner while the advisor is in Russia?"

"A guest."

"A guest who is unable to leave the citadel?" he growled.

Rajih shifted his weight, his fingers tightening on his sword.

"An unfortunate necessity."

Dimitri refused to be intimidated, regardless of the stupidity of confronting an armed man with nothing more than his bare hands.

"It is also a predictable response."

Rajih narrowed his gaze. "Predictable?"

"The pasha had little choice but to insist I remain under guard after a prominent ambassador accused me of trafficking and murder."

Josef cleared his throat, his gaze nervously darting between the two men.

"Who would want you trapped here?"

Dimitri's gaze moved with a slow deliberation over Rajih's poised body.

"There is one gentleman who comes to mind."

With the elegant ease of a trained swordsman, Rajih had the sword pulled from his belt and the tip pressed beneath Dimitri's chin.

"If I wished to be rid of you, Tipova, I would not bother with such an elaborate scheme," the Egyptian warned. "The desert is littered with the bones of my enemies."

Dimitri was vibrantly aware of a faint breeze wafting through the grilled windows, the perfumed oils that clung to his robe and the trickle of blood that ran from his chin down his neck.

One misstep and he would be skewered.

"Perhaps you did not want me dead, but merely unable to return to Russia with Emma," he snapped, "With me locked in the citadel, you will be at liberty to offer her…" His jaw tightened. "Comfort."

The sword dug deeper, making Dimitri flinch, but he ignored the pain. Instead, he concentrated on the outrage that smoldered in Rajih's dark eyes.

That was not the expression of a man attempting to hide his guilt.

No. He was clearly offended.

Dangerously offended.

"You insult both Emma and myself," Rajih gritted. "I am not so desperate that I need to trick a female into my arms, and Emma is not so weak she must cling to whatever gentleman happens to be at hand."

With a grudging reluctance, Dimitri accepted that Rajih was not responsible for his current dilemma.

A pity.

He would have enjoyed wreaking vengeance on the arrogant son of a jackal.

"You are right," he managed to mutter. "I apologize."

"Are you taunting me?"

"No." Dimitri grimaced. "My particular business

demands that I be able to discern when someone is lying or telling me the truth. You cannot feign wounded pride."

With obvious annoyance he would not be allowed to remove Dimitri's head, Rajih lowered his sword and stepped back.

Josef moved to pour a large glass of the brandy, his expression revealing he held Dimitri entirely responsible for the near disastrous encounter. He downed the liquor in a single swallow.

"If it's not the caliph, then who?"

Rajih shrugged. "There are others who would wish you to be…indisposed."

Actually, there was an endless list of potential enemies. He had not achieved his position without cunning, treachery, coercion and a vast amount of brute force. But how many of them knew he was in Cairo? Or in the custody of the pasha?

And how many were powerful enough to force Baron Koman to do his bidding?

He gave a frustrated shake of his head. There was still something he was missing.

"Who do you suspect?"

"Valik's guards bolted the moment he left the brothel," Rajih offered. "They would be delighted to have you locked away while they attempt to make their escape from Egypt."

"It is possible."

"Or perhaps it is an unknown adversary who is manipulating matters from the shadows." Rajih smiled. "You seem to have a talent for creating enemies."

Josef set aside his empty glass. "We can discover the identity of the enemy once we are away from this place."

Dimitri paused before giving a discontented nod. "How long before you can convince the pasha to release us?" he demanded of the caliph.

"There is nothing to be done until Czar Alexander has responded to the pasha's request for assistance."

Dimitri's brows snapped together. "Impossible."

"There is no choice."

"Then I will find my own means of disappearing."

"Do not be a fool, Tipova." Rajih deliberately lifted his sword, his warning unmistakable. "If your servants are caught attempting to slip into the citadel they will be put to death immediately. Just as you will be killed if you are caught trying to escape."

"You cannot expect me to remain trapped here like a rat...."

Dimitri bit off his words as he was struck by a haunting reality.

Trapped.

Yes, that was precisely what he was.

Trapped and all but helpless.

If he were the mysterious enemy why would he want his prey trapped and helpless?

Rajih stepped toward him, regarding him with a suspicious expression.

"What were you saying?"

Dimitri forced a grim smile to his lips. "Very well."

Josef swore, reaching to grasp Dimitri's arm in a punishing grip.

"Tipova—"

"Josef, it is obvious we must wait for Alexander Pavlovich to demand our release." He overrode his servant's protest.

Josef glared at him with a sour disapproval. "You are assuming he won't tell the pasha to have us fed to his tiger."

"Tiger?" the caliph asked in confusion.

"It is of no importance," Dimitri muttered, swallowing

his pride as he contemplated the most pertinent dangers of his situation. "I must demand a favor of you, Rajih."

Dimitri had to appreciate the manner in which the man hesitated before offering his promise. He might never be friends with Rajih, but he did respect his integrity.

"That depends upon the favor," he admitted.

"I assure you that it does not include storming the citadel."

Rajih heaved a resigned sigh. "I am listening."

"I wish for Emma to be returned to the safety of St. Petersburg."

The other man stiffened, a stubborn expression settling on his lean face. Not that Dimitri was surprised. Rajih made no secret of his desire to keep Emma for himself.

"That is her decision."

"No, you must be firm with her," he insisted. "We both know how stubborn she can be. She will remain so long as she fears I am in danger, regardless of the fact that my enemies might very well use her to punish me."

"You do not believe me capable of keeping her safe?"

Dimitri crushed his possessive instincts. For now all that mattered was that Emma was whisked far away from Cairo.

"Once she is in St. Petersburg, she will be under the protection of Herrick Gerhardt, the czar's most trusted advisor. And more important, she will be too far away to be an effective pawn. That is the only true means to keep her safe."

There was a pause as Rajih considered Dimitri's request, then with a wry smile, he offered a dip of his head.

"I will do my best, but I do not perform miracles."

"That is all I ask."

The caliph turned to walk across the floor, pausing as he reached the heavy doors.

"It has been many years since I visited your country,"

he murmured, his voice filled with a blatant anticipation. "It will be delightful to spend a few weeks at the Summer Palace."

Dimitri clenched his hand, watching as the caliph stepped out of the room and the door closed behind him.

He should have stabbed the bastard with his own sword.

Indifferent to Dimitri's brooding desire for blood, Josef moved to stand directly before him, his hands planted on his hips.

"Have you gone completely mad?"

# CHAPTER TWENTY-SIX

THE SERAGLIO WAS TRULY a place of wonderment.

Although recently refurbished, it maintained the charm of ages past with a domed ceiling decorated with blue-and-gold tiles to form a night sky slumbering above a large fountain carved into the center of the marble floor. The inner wall was covered by fine tapestries with a doorway that opened to the private gardens, while the arched windows on the opposite wall were covered by golden grills.

The furniture, however, was surprisingly European with several scrolled settees and an applewood writing desk situated beneath a framed mirror.

It was all very beautiful, but Emma was acutely aware of the heavily armed eunuchs patrolling the spiderweb of corridors and private rooms. It would be all but impossible for a person to slip unnoticed out of such a formidable fortress.

A knowledge that weighed heavily on her heart.

Ignoring the various refreshments served to her by veiled servants, Emma anxiously paced the floor, awaiting Rajih's return.

Not that she was particularly reassured when she was at last led to the lower stables where Rajih hurried her toward the waiting carriage. Not after he revealed that Dimitri was to remain a guest of the pasha until Alexander Pavlovich could be convinced to demand his release.

"No." With a jerk she freed her arm from Rajih's grasp, her chin jutted to a stubborn angle. "I am not leaving until I am certain that Dimitri is safe."

Regaining his grip on her elbow, Rajih steered her around the edge of the black carriage and away from the numerous servants milling about the stable yard.

"I promise that he is at considerably less risk as the guest of Muhammad Ali Pasha than in St. Petersburg where he no doubt possesses any number of enemies," he said.

"But he is not a guest," she hissed, "he is a prisoner."

Rajih grimaced, casting a covert glance toward a passing groom.

"Emma, I beg that you keep your voice down unless you wish both of us to share his fate."

She bit her lower lip, well aware she owed this man a debt of gratitude that could not be repaid.

Not only had he risked his life to rescue the poor girls from the brothel the previous evening, but he had sacrificed his pride to request Dimitri's release, even though he would as soon cut out his tongue.

And there was no escaping the knowledge that he had done so for her.

Just as so many others had suffered to assist her.

"Forgive me, Rajih, I never intended to put you in this awkward position," she said. "I have caused enough trouble for others."

Rajih frowned, cupping her chin to lift her face so he could study her suddenly subdued expression.

"None of this is your fault, *habiba*."

She could only wish that were true. Perhaps then she would not be plagued with a relentless guilt.

"If I had not been so stubbornly determined to chase after Anya, then Dimitri would be enjoying his life in St. Petersburg and you would not be forced to jeopardize your friendship with the pasha to plead for his release."

"The fault lies with the men who kidnapped the girls to sell like animals, not you."

"Still—"

He placed a finger across her lips, his gaze sweeping over her face with an odd yearning.

"Emma, the past cannot be altered. We must consider the future."

She sucked in a deep breath, ignoring the stench of horses and unwashed body that tainted the air. Her regrets would have to wait until she had the time and opportunity to make amends. Instead, she grabbed Rajih's hand and regarded him with a determined expression.

"You are right, of course, but that does not mean I am willing to abandon Dimitri."

The dark eyes simmered with something that might have been disappointment before he had smoothed his features to an unreadable expression.

"I am not suggesting that you abandon him, but rather that you use your own influence to ensure that he is found innocent," he said, his voice smooth.

She stepped back, suddenly wary. "You want me to speak with the pasha?"

His brows lifted at her impetuous words. "No, as charming as our leader would no doubt find you, this is a country that believes a woman should remain silent behind the walls of the seraglio. He would not allow you to testify on Tipova's behalf."

"Barbaric."

"It is the way of my people."

"Then how can I help?" She twisted her hands together in frustration. She detested the sense that she was helpless to rescue Dimitri. "You just admitted that Baron Koman has proven to be a traitor."

"Yes." Rajih's expression hardened, warning that Koman could expect to be punished for his treachery. "A most unexpected complication."

"Does Dimitri know why the baron would claim he is guilty?"

Rajih shrugged. "He says he does not."

"Maybe he is a part of the trafficking and now hopes to deceive others into believing Dimitri is responsible," she absently mused.

"It would be a convenient means to make another pay for his sins," he agreed. "But Dimitri is convinced there is another forcing the baron to do his bidding."

She snorted. "Dimitri is not always so infallible as he wants others to believe."

His lips twisted. "I will readily agree with Tipova's bloated arrogance."

Emma glanced toward the looming citadel, shivering despite the heat of the late-afternoon sunlight and the heavy ivory-colored robe that was richly embroidered with pearls.

"If I am not to approach the pasha or Baron Koman, then who am I supposed to influence?"

"Czar Alexander."

Emma's mouth dropped open in disbelief. Had Rajih just suggested that she blithely call upon the emperor of Russia and demand that he have a notorious criminal released from the prisons of Muhammad Ali Pasha?

"Are you jesting?" she breathed.

"Not at all."

She shook her head, swallowing her urge to laugh. "I fear you have a mistaken notion of my importance, Rajih."

His expression softened as he lifted a hand to brush a stray curl from her cheek.

"That is not possible."

"But it is," she insisted. "You met me in London in the companionship of the Duke and Duchess of Huntley, but that is only because they owed Dimitri some mysterious debt. I am not the lady of society I pretended to be."

Amusement smoldered in the dark eyes. "For which I am

eternally grateful, considering you were posing as Tipova's wife."

She ignored his teasing, determined that he would know the truth of her.

"What I mean is that I am not the person I pretended to be."

"Then who are you?" he asked, his voice soft.

"I am..." With a sharp motion she turned away, hiding her troubled expression. "Nobody."

Rajih's hands settled on her shoulders. "Emma."

"No, it is true." Her gaze absently lingered on the stunning sight of Cairo spread below. "I am a mere commoner from an unremarkable village in Russia. And even there I am a source of mockery. I have no influence."

She was not certain what she expected, but it was not his breathy chuckle as he lowered his head to speak directly into her ear.

"You could not be more mistaken, *habiba*. I am quite certain that within moments of being in your company, Alexander Pavlovich would be willing to demand the release of every prisoner in Egypt." He deliberately allowed his lips to brush her cheek. "But that will not be necessary."

"What do you mean?"

"Tipova mentioned that you are related to Herrick Gerhardt."

Caught off guard by the unexpected words, Emma stepped from his lingering touch. Turning, she regarded him with a wary frown.

"He is a distant relative," she admitted, "but we had never met until I came to St. Petersburg to seek his assistance in finding Anya."

"Distant relative or not, he is a well-respected advisor who has the ear of the czar."

"Herrick has been very kind, but I am not certain he

would be willing to speak with Czar Alexander on my behalf."

Rajih frowned, sensing her hesitation. "What is it Emma? Do you find it difficult to ask others for help?"

She was briefly distracted by his perceptiveness, even if it was misplaced on this occasion.

"To be honest, I used to find it impossible." She wrinkled her nose, all too easily recalling her stiff-necked refusal to seek out those distant relatives who might have been of assistance. "I considered it essential that I be able to survive on my own. After all, what could possibly be more important than my independence?"

"Anyone who has endured your loss would seek to gain a sense of control over their lives." He glanced up at the birds of prey circling overhead, his jaw clenched with suppressed emotions. "I understand better than most."

"Of course." Sympathy tugged at her heart. "You have lost both your parents."

His gaze shifted to the distant outline of the pyramids that stood with ageless splendor among the sand.

"And my country," he murmured. "Now I would do whatever necessary to protect it."

A bittersweet smile arched her lips. Until her sister had left her stranded in that brothel, she had believed that there was no sacrifice too great to keep her family safe.

"You do understand," she murmured. "A pity Anya was not so forgiving."

His expression hardened at the mention of Anya. "You cannot continue to punish yourself for the failures of your sister. You have done all that was possible to offer her a stable home. Her future is now in her own hands."

"Yes."

"So, will you overcome your reluctance and ask for Herrick Gerhardt's assistance?"

She paused, unconsciously shifting her feet. "Of course. I will do whatever possible to help."

"And yet you hesitate."

A wry smile curved her lips as she met his deliberately bland gaze.

"Because I am not utterly stupid," she said, her eyes narrowing in warning. "I know very well that Dimitri demanded that I be rushed away from the dangers of Cairo and returned to Russia."

His lips parted, as if he were debating the ridiculous notion of lying to her. At last he reached to take her hand in a comforting grip.

"Emma, there is nothing you can accomplish by remaining here. A female, especially an unwed female, has no power or freedom in Cairo." A suddenly wicked promise smoldered in the dark eyes. "Unless you prefer to remain hidden in my harem?"

Conceding that she had been neatly outmaneuvered, Emma gave a rueful shake of her head.

Rajih spoke the truth.

What could she possibly achieve if she lingered in Egypt? It was not as if she had a small army at her disposal to overrun the citadel. Or even the skills to slip past the guards and secretly free Dimitri.

And while she was far from convinced her plea to Herrick Gerhardt would be more than a waste of breath, she was willing to make the attempt.

"I am beginning to suspect you are attempting to be rid of me," she teased.

With a mysterious smile, Rajih lifted her fingers to his lips.

"Quite the contrary.

"What do you mean?"

"I intend to escort you to St. Petersburg."

WAITING UNTIL THE DINNER trays had been removed and
the servants had finished preparing the beds for the night,
Dimitri gathered several pillows from the outer chamber
and arranged them beneath the silk sheets.

"This is a very bad plan," Josef muttered as he stuffed
his own bed with pillows.

Dimitri smiled wryly. His servant had been grumbling
and moaning for hours. Not that he blamed his companion.
They were very much the pasha's prisoners, even if they
were not locked in the dungeons. But, Dimitri was familiar
enough with his long-time friend to know it was not being
held in the citadel that was causing his foul mood, but
fear that Dimitri's suspicions might not be as stupid as he
wanted to believe.

Josef would stand before the firing squad without batting
an eye, but the thought of someone he cared for in danger
nearly unmanned him.

"It is not a plan at all," he pointed out. "Merely a hasty
attempt to avoid being murdered in my bed."

Josef snorted. "I still don't understand why you believe
we are going to be attacked."

"It is the only explanation that makes sense."

"Sense?" Josef straightened from the bed, throwing his
hands in the air. "What sense is there in trying to keep you
locked behind this fortress if someone wants you dead? It
is much easier to shoot you in the back if you are walking
down the street."

"Yes, but the benefit is knowing my precise location."

"So would kidnapping you."

Dimitri smiled, recalling numerous traps meant to destroy him that he had efficiently avoided. There were many
on the streets of St. Petersburg who would swear he possessed magical powers.

"I am not so easily captured, as many men have discovered over the years."

Josef grunted, unable to argue with his logic. Not that he was satisfied. The servant would be snarling and snapping until they were far away from Egypt.

"But how could any enemy know you would kill Valik and that the pasha's guards would bring you to the citadel? Do you think they are fortune-tellers?"

Dimitri stepped back, regarding the narrow bed. At the moment it appeared to be a sheet pulled over a line of pillows. But in the dark and at a distance, the lumps beneath the sheet should give the impression of a body.

Or at least that was his hope.

All he needed was for his enemy to be distracted for a few moments to launch his ambush.

Dimitri returned his attention to Josef, accepting he had done all that was possible with no weapons, no notion of who or how many might attack, and a wounded shoulder that still ached like the very devil.

"No fortune-tellers, merely a man swift to take advantage of the situation," he said. "After all, no one attempted to have me arrested before now—"

"That we know of," Josef interrupted.

"That we know of," Dimitri conceded. "But now that I am trapped at the citadel, it obviously occurred to someone that they could use my confinement to their advantage."

"To kill you?"

Dimitri restlessly paced to blow out the candles that burned in the candelabras. The light from the fireplace should be ample enough to see any intruder without revealing his bed was empty.

"Who is to say?" he muttered. "It could be for the simple enjoyment of watching me suffer, or an attempt to flee before I have the opportunity to interfere in their plans, or any number of plots…including the desire to put me in my grave." His jaw clenched. "I intend to be prepared."

Josef's lips parted to continue his arguments, then

recognizing Dimitri's stubborn expression, he heaved a resigned sigh.

"What do you want of me?"

"It appears that the doors are the only entrance to the room, but I prefer not to take a risk of being caught off guard." He waved a hand toward the elaborate gilded-iron grills he had inspected earlier. So far as he could determine they appeared to be firmly attached to the stone of the citadel, but he had not survived so long without a good deal of caution. "I want you to remain near the windows."

Josef grimaced, but he readily moved to crouch near the edge of the windows.

"This is going to be a tedious night."

Dimitri extinguished the rest of the candles and moved to stand beside the door.

"It is preferable to listening to you snore."

They fell silent as they waited.

And waited. And waited.

As the minutes, and then hours, passed, however, he did not abandon his post or ease his vigilance. He was accustomed to thieves, cutthroats and pirates who did their business at night and on their own schedules.

Besides, if there were an assassin, he would want to wait until he was confident that Dimitri was asleep before entering the room.

Shifting his weight from foot to foot to keep alert, Dimitri froze at the sound of the door being slowly pressed open.

A fierce satisfaction jolted through him. Not at the sight of the slender man who slipped into the room and crept toward the bed with a pistol in his hand. In truth, it was unnerving to witness his potential murder from a distance. But at the knowledge his suspicions had been justified.

His instincts remained honed to razor sharpness, even if his lust for his career had begun to wane.

Waiting until the intruder had nearly reached the bed, Dimitri slid silently forward, approaching the man from behind. With one swift motion, he had plucked the pistol from the intruder's hand and pressed it to his temple. His other hand he wrapped around the man's neck, jerking him against his chest to cease his struggles.

There was the faint sound of shuffling from across the room before Josef was lighting the candles to show that the intruder was an Egyptian attired in a European-styled uniform that revealed he was one of the pasha's guards.

"Do you speak English? Russian?" Dimitri's fingers tightened on the man's throat, grimacing at the sour stench of fear that clung to him. Whoever he was, he most certainly was not a hardened criminal. "Answer me or I will crush your throat."

"I can discover the truth." Josef prowled forward, bending downward to uncover the knife strapped to the man's ankle. Then, with an evil grin that emphasized his scar, he pressed the tip of the knife to man's groin. "Answer the question."

"Bastards," the man spat in a thickly accented English.

"Who are you?" Dimitri asked.

"Fawzi."

"Well, Fawzi, perhaps you would not mind explaining what you are doing in this room?"

Fawzi shuddered, his breath a heavy rasp and his heart thumping so hard that Dimitri could actually feel its pounding beat.

"Please."

Sensing the fool was about to become hysterical, Dimitri glanced down at his servant.

"Josef, I believe our companion is prepared to be reasonable."

"Yes, yes." Waiting until Josef had removed the knife

from his most tender parts, Fawzi swallowed heavily. "It is nothing more than an unfortunate mistake."

"I will agree with unfortunate, but it was no mistake," Dimitri mocked.

"No, no. A big mistake. I thought I heard a noise and I entered to make certain you were not ill."

"How very considerate."

"The pasha was insistent you be comfortable during your stay at the citadel."

With a sudden movement, Dimitri shoved the man until he was turned to face him, pointing the pistol at his heart. He needed to see a man's face to know when he lied.

"Then perhaps we should join the pasha," he suggested. "He will be pleased to know how dedicated you have been to my welfare."

Fawzi licked his lips, his eyes darting toward the distant door.

"He will be in his bed."

"I do not mind awakening him."

Beneath his bronzed skin the man paled. "No."

A hard smile curved his lips. He was at least reassured that the nefarious plot to see him dead had not come from the pasha.

"Josef, would you discreetly discover what has happened to our guards?"

With a silence few men could match, Josef glided across the room and after a covert peek into the hallway, he disappeared through the door. A handful of minutes passed before he returned, his expression unreadable.

"They are both on the ground."

"Dead?"

"Drugged."

Dimitri returned his attention to Fawzi, his finger tightening on the trigger.

"It would be a simple matter to drug the dinner sent

from the kitchens." His gaze bore into the man's wide eyes. Fawzi was terrified at being caught, but Dimitri sensed a desperate cunning beneath his fear. He was like a rat, all the more dangerous for being cornered. "Especially if the tray was delivered by a fellow guard."

"Yes, I think we really must wake the pasha."

"Please." Fawzi held out his hands in a pleading motion. "What do you want of me?"

Dimitri studied the narrow face with its sunken black eyes and scraggly black beard.

"Why did you drug the guards and sneak into this room?" He gave a deliberate wave of the gun. "The truth."

The man hesitated, clearly weighing the danger of being caught in a lie. At last he grimaced.

"I came here to kill you."

Dimitri's lips twisted. That was certainly blunt.

"Is there a particular reason you wished me dead or do you simply hate all infidels?"

"A man approached me on my way back from a visit to my mother and offered me a fortune if I would put you in your grave."

"What man?"

"I don't know." Fawzi pressed his hands together in a gesture of entreaty. "No...wait. He called to me from a carriage as I was about to enter the citadel. He kept the curtain across the window so I never saw his face."

Frustration settled in the pit of his stomach.

Of course Fawzi never saw the man's face. Why would discovering the truth become a simple matter at this late date?

"Was he an Egyptian?"

"No, a foreigner. Like you."

"Russian?"

Fawzi shrugged. "Maybe."

"What did he say?" Dimitri took a step closer, his expression hard with warning. "I want every word."

"I can't remember every word."

"Try very, very hard."

Sweat dripped from the man's face as his gaze lowered to the pistol a short distance from his heart.

"He asked if I was a guard at the citadel and if I had the means to enter the room of the pasha's two foreign prisoners. When I admitted I could move freely about the citadel he promised me a purse filled with silver."

Dimitri lifted his brows in astonishment. "And you believed him?"

"He gave me a few coins to prove his sincerity," the man muttered, his expression sullen. "He said I could have the rest when I brought him proof that you were dead."

"What proof?"

The man nervously cleared his throat. "I was to cut out your eye and bring it to him."

"God almighty," Josef breathed.

"He claimed he would recognize it, so I was not to try and fool him," the man hurriedly explained.

Dimitri was forced to swallow a sudden lump in his throat. His life had been one of upheaval and violent survival. He had assumed that nothing could shock him.

Now, however, he was stunned by this ruthless confession. Who could hate him with such passion?

"Did he give a reason he desired my death?" he rasped.

"No."

Dimitri regarded the bumbling assassin with distaste. "You were willing to kill a man in his sleep and cut out his eye for no other reason than a purse of silver?"

An unctuous smile curved his lips as he pressed a hand to his chest.

"My mother is ill. I need the money for her medicine."

"Of course. Your poor, sick mother," Dimitri drawled, his eyes narrowing as he realized the pathetic louse might actually be of worth. "Then we had best go and collect your reward."

Without warning Josef moved to grab his arm.

"Have you lost all sense?" he demanded.

"We shall soon enough discover." Dimitri's gaze never shifted from Fawzi. "Where were you to meet your mysterious patron?"

## CHAPTER TWENTY-SEVEN

DIMITRI WAS CAREFUL TO keep the pistol prominently displayed as Fawzi led them through the sleeping citadel. It seemed wise to remind the man just what would happen should he be foolish enough to attempt an escape or to alert the guards that prowled through the dark corridors.

Depending upon Fawzi's familiarity with the maze of rooms, they were soon out of the main building and moving through the servants' quarters. Dimitri demanded that they pause long enough for Josef and him to change into the rough linen tunics and loose breeches of stable hands before they were leaving the main building and heading toward the massive tower that guarded the nearest gate.

There was a tense moment as they were halted by the sentry, his expression skeptical as Fawzi babbled in Arabic. Unable to follow the conversation, Dimitri could only trust that the knife Josef had discreetly pressed to the man's back would discourage any attempt to attract unwanted attention.

At last they were through the thick walls that surrounded the citadel and moving down the hill to the city below.

Dimitri sucked in a deep breath, astonished that they had truly managed to escape the fortress.

Of course, if he were thinking clearly he would knock Fawzi senseless and flee Cairo with all possible speed. Instead, he poked the slender man in the back with his pistol and urged him toward the clump of palm trees.

Once they were lost in the thick shadows, he grabbed

Fawzi's arm and yanked him close enough he could whisper in his ear.

"Is that his carriage?"

He pointed toward the black vehicle that was parked before an abandoned building. At a glance he could determine no more than it resembled nearly every other carriage in Cairo and that there was one burly Egyptian groom standing next to the horse, lazily smoking a cheroot.

A closer glance, however, revealed the occasional twitch of the curtain that covered the carriage window, as if whoever was inside was growing impatient, and the slouched inattention of the groom.

His sheer negligence was a silent invitation to be hit over the head.

Obviously, whoever was plotting his death clearly had no military training and few skills necessary to survive the streets.

"Yes," Fawzi said. "I recognize the servant."

Josef moved to stand at his side. "Do I need to remind you that this is perhaps the most stupid decision you have ever made, Tipova?" he growled. "Including the night you dueled with three swordsmen at the same time."

A reminiscent smile touched his lips. Over the years his authority had often been challenged. His polished manners and preference for elegant attire convinced some fools that he could not possibly be as dangerous as his reputation implied.

In the past, he had enjoyed proving his worth.

Thankfully, he had reached an age where he was ready to put such reckless stupidity behind him.

No doubt because he now had something, or rather someone, to live for.

"I won, did I not?"

Josef narrowed his gaze, clearly not amused by his teasing.

"Damn you. We have escaped. Allow me to gather the others and we can be far away from Cairo before the pasha realizes we are no longer his guests."

Dimitri shook his head, his attention returning to the carriage across the road.

"Not until I discover who is so anxious to see me dead."

"What does it matter so long as they do not succeed?"

"Because they will quite likely try again." His gaze shifted to the nearby buildings, searching for hidden dangers that might be lurking in the shadows. "I do not intend to spend the remainder of my life in fear."

"You always have enemies wishing you harm," Josef muttered. "It has never troubled you before."

Dimitri turned to meet his servant's frustrated glance, his expression somber.

"I now have another's welfare to consider," he said, his tone suggesting that he would not compromise when it came to protecting Emma. "I will not leave here until I have brought an end to the threat."

"But…"

"My decision is made, Josef," Dimitri interrupted. "Fawzi."

"Yes?"

He pointed across the street. "I want you to approach the carriage and pretend that you have accomplished your mission."

"No, I have done all you have asked of me," Fawzi whined in alarm. "If I go to the man without the proof he demanded I will be shot."

Josef waved his knife in front of the man's face. "If it is an eye you are wanting then I can make certain you have what you need."

Not surprisingly, Fawzi fell back with a squeal, his face drenched with sweat.

"Josef." Dimitri sent the servant a warning glare. "I have need of him."

"Why?"

"He can provide a distraction while you dispose of the groom."

"And what of you?"

"I intend to join our mysterious lurker."

Josef clenched his jaw, his disapproval etched on every line of his face.

"Don't be a fool," he gritted. "We have no notion how many men might be in the carriage."

Dimitri grimaced. That was an unfortunate risk. But what choice did he have?

"No, but I will have the element of surprise."

Josef snorted. "Surprise will not halt a bullet to your heart."

"Trust me."

The men exchanged glares, then at last accepting that nothing would prevent Dimitri from confronting the unknown enemy, Josef heaved a frustrated sigh.

"Damn you, Tipova."

Keeping his firm hold on the Egyptian, Dimitri urged him toward the edge of the palm trees.

"Fawzi, I want you to count to twenty and then approach the carriage."

"And when he asks if you are dead?" the man rasped.

"Use your imagination. Just keep him occupied." His grip momentarily tightened, biting into Fawzi's arm with a warning pressure. "Oh, and Fawzi?"

The Egyptian swallowed heavily. "What?"

"If you attempt to reveal our presence, I will not only shoot you, but I will have you chopped into pieces and delivered to your poor, sick mother." He smiled with a cold cruelty that had frightened men far more courageous than Fawzi. "Do you understand?"

It took a moment for Fawzi to regain enough composure to give a shaky nod.

"Yes."

"Good." Dimitri gestured toward his servant. "Josef, the guard."

Muttering curses in various languages, Josef silently disappeared and headed down the street so he could approach the groom from behind. Dimitri followed several steps behind him, waiting near the corner for Fawzi to stumble and sway his way across the street.

Dimitri grimaced at the man's craven lack of discipline, but at least his peculiar manner had attracted the attention of the guard who remained oblivious as Josef approached and whacked the back of his head with the hilt of his knife.

With a grunt, the man tumbled to the ground, and Josef smoothly took the reins of the horse, keeping it from jarring the carriage. At the same moment, Dimitri moved forward, his gaze locked on Fawzi who was leaning toward the curtained window, speaking softly to whoever was inside.

He took a moment to make certain his pistol was primed, then with one smooth motion he had the door open and was surging into the carriage to press his gun against the chest of the man seated near the window.

"I suggest you sit very still and lift your hands so I can see them," he commanded, waiting until the stranger had raised his arms over his head before he used his free hand to search the man for weapons. Predictably he found an ivory-handled dueling pistol in the pocket of the caped greatcoat and a smaller gun tucked in the top of the glossy Hessians. He suspected there might be more hidden about the carriage, but for the moment he was satisfied that there were none near at hand. Keeping the pistol pointed at his companion, he settled in the opposite seat and offered a small smile. "Now, I believe introductions are in order."

There was a tense silence before the man slowly reached up to grasp the brim of his high beaver hat and toss it onto the seat beside him.

"While I would say they are superfluous," he drawled.

Dimitri stiffened, an icy shock momentarily halting his heart and squeezing the air from his body.

Although the inside of the carriage was dark, the curtain had been pushed aside to allow a spill of silver moonlight to wash over the man's gray hair and the elegantly carved features. Features that were heavily lined from a life of self-indulgence.

No. He grappled to make sense of what he was seeing. It was not possible.

And yet…

And yet, it could be that this moment had been destined since the day Count Nevskaya had forced the innocent child of a local cobbler to his bed.

The golden eyes that were a mirror image of Dimitri's flashed with a familiar hatred, jerking him out of his fog of disbelief.

"Father," he drawled, his voice cold and perfectly steady. Despite his shock, he had developed the ability to confront any situation with utter composure. Besides, he was beginning to suspect that fate had offered him a rare opportunity he would be an idiot to squander. "What an unpleasant surprise."

"I heartily return the sentiment," the count sneered. "You were supposed to be dead."

"While you were supposed to be rotting in Czar Alexander's prison."

With a tight smile, Nevskaya adjusted the signet ring he wore on his pinkie, seemingly indifferent to the gun pointed at his heart.

And perhaps he was.

Dimitri had devoted years to governing his feelings. It

had been a necessary skill to survival. He suspected his father, however, was not disguising his emotions. Count Nevskaya was simply devoid of all but anger and hatred.

How else could he have tossed his pregnant lover into the gutter? Or abused children without remorse?

"Clearly we are both doomed to disappointment," he murmured.

"What are you doing in Cairo?"

"Valik sent a messenger to St. Petersburg to warn me that Dimitri Tipova had followed him to London and was busily destroying the business I worked for years to create."

Dimitri's lips twisted. "Do you expect an apology?"

Nevskaya wrinkled his nose as if there were a foul smell in the air.

"I expect you to tend to your criminal activities and leave me in peace."

"But I do not wish to leave you in peace," he informed his father, his gaze never wavering from the face that had haunted him for too many years. "I want you to suffer exquisite agony each and every day of your miserable existence."

"Such melodrama." The count waved a dismissive hand. "You are so regrettably like your mother."

Dimitri's finger tightened on the trigger of his gun, only distantly aware of the sound of footsteps as Fawzi grasped his opportunity to escape.

How satisfying would it be to put a bullet in the reprobate's black heart?

"I happen to consider that a compliment," he gritted. "My mother was a beautiful, courageous woman who was destroyed by a disgusting letch." He flicked a contemptuous gaze over his father. "You are not worthy to speak her name."

"She was a peasant who was fortunate to have won my attention."

Oh, yes, definitely a bullet straight into his heart.

"Quite fortunate," he snapped. "She was raped, impregnated and then tossed into the gutter to die. I cannot fathom why she was not overwhelmed with gratitude."

"Bah."

Dimitri bit back his angry words. He was wasting his breath if he hoped to make his father suffer the least amount of guilt. The only means of truly wounding him was to attack his insufferable pride.

He forced himself to lean back in the seat, his expression sardonic.

"Of course, she did manage to outwit you."

"Absurd."

"How furious you were when she arrived on your doorstep and demanded that you pay for your son's education." Dimitri chuckled, genuinely enjoying the memory of his mother's boldness, her spine stiff and her head held high as the count threatened any number of vile retributions. "But she would not be bullied or cowed."

"I should have had you both disposed of like the vermin you were," his father bit out.

"Yes, it is a pity you were a pathetic coward who allowed yourself to be manipulated by a mere whore."

Fury flared through his father's golden eyes as an ugly color crawled beneath his skin. Dimitri braced himself, willing the man to attack. He might have qualms about shooting an unarmed man, no matter how deserving of death he might be, but he would not hesitate to defend himself.

Then, with an obvious effort, the count wrapped himself in his haughty composure.

"She soon enough regretted her temerity," he taunted. "I heard that she died in the gutter."

Dimitri smiled, grimly refusing to react. "And now you are about to share her fate."

Nevskaya's gaze covertly shifted toward the gun before returning to Dimitri's face. It was no more than a flicker. But it was enough to convince Dimitri that his father was not quite as impervious to the dangers of his situation as he would have him believe.

"You think I fear death?"

"Yes, I think you fear it very much," Dimitri said slowly. "But who could blame you? Men who prey on children are destined for the deepest pits of hell."

"I am a nobleman," he announced with cold disdain. "I am above tedious morals."

Dimitri grimaced. He might have laughed if not for the knowledge Nevskaya truly believed his social position gave him liberty to commit any sin with impunity.

And worse, he was not alone in his arrogance.

Despite Alexander Pavlovich's best attempts to rid Russia of its barbaric reputation there remained a blatant belief among the nobles that they possessed the God-given right to treat serfs however they pleased. Indeed, it was rumored the czar's own military advisor had recently beat to death one of his peasants.

Still, there was a growing disapproval toward such outlandish behavior as the czar became increasingly pious, filling his royal court with his more conservative supporters.

He shook his head, turning his thoughts to more important matters.

"You have not yet explained why you are in Cairo."

The older man shrugged. "Once I discovered that Sanderson had been arrested I knew it was only a matter of time before the idiot revealed my part in the—"

"Trafficking of children?" Dimitri supplied.

"Arrangement."

"I do not understand." Dimitri tilted his head to the side, a goading smile on his face. "If noblemen are above morals, then what do you care if your sins are exposed to the world?"

"Unlike his proud ancestors, Alexander Pavlovich is a weak, ineffective ruler who has allowed himself to become a tedious prude." His words echoed Dimitri's earlier thoughts. "His father would have been ashamed to know he had spawned such a spineless bore."

Dimitri shuddered. Czar Paul had been a brutal, stupid man, and a notoriously corrupt leader who had been increasingly unstable before his timely demise.

But then again, it was predictable that his father would prefer the man who had repealed Catherine's laws intended to protect the peasants.

"Hardly spineless." He settled more comfortably on the leather seat. "Alexander Pavlovich did, after all, manage to take the throne when he was still little more than a lad. A bold stroke."

"A knife in the back is the behavior of a coward."

"A rabid dog has to be put down by any means necessary."

The count made a sound of disgust, typically more concerned with his perverted sense of honor than the most basic morality.

"*You* would certainly think so. Peasants have no notion of honor."

Dimitri studied the man seated across from him, shifting through the confusing emotions that battered him.

For so many years Count Nevskaya had been the demon who haunted his life. The choices he had made, the sacrifices he'd suffered and the ruthless hunger to achieve a place in the world where he could never be a victim had all been due to his father.

Now as he sat across from the blackguard, he wondered why he had ever given him such power over his existence.

Not that he didn't still hate him with a violent passion. Or wish him into the fiery pits of hell.

But he was beginning to realize that Count Nevskaya was a cold, insignificant fool who had condemned himself to a life of lonely misery years ago.

A man who no longer had the power to hurt him.

A heady sense of relief raced through his blood. As if a heavy weight had been taken off his shoulders.

Or perhaps it was his heart.

"Do you truly believe yourself superior to me simply because of an accident of birth?" he demanded.

His father sniffed, offended by the mere question. "I am Count Nevskaya, an ancient and noble title. The blood of royalty flows through my veins."

"And yet, for all your grand titles and royal blood you have squandered your fortune and have become a common beggar, pleading to your wife's brother to keep your roof from tumbling onto your head." Dimitri took pleasure in reminding the pompous twit. "And of course, you are forced into kidnapping helpless children with the assistance of ridiculous buffoons such as Sanderson to support your debauchery." A cold smile curved his lips. "I, on the other hand, have amassed a vast fortune and purchased more than a dozen estates that are all fully staffed with loyal servants."

"You are an uncouth savage," his father snarled.

"And yet, I am welcomed at the Winter Palace while you have now become a source of embarrassment," Dimitri pressed. "No one in society would allow you across their thresholds."

Nevskaya flinched before he could stop the revealing movement, his gaunt face unnaturally pale.

Satisfaction warmed Dimitri's heart. For a man with his father's bloated pride it was unbearable to be shunned by his peers.

"This scandal will pass in time," the older man muttered.

"Not if you are locked in Czar Alexander's prison. Which is precisely why you fled when you discovered that Sanderson was revealing your sordid secrets."

"You know nothing."

Dimitri shrugged. "It is true I am confused why you would choose to flee to Cairo."

"It is none of your damned business."

The sound of a cart rattling down the dirt road filled the carriage as Dimitri considered the various possibilities.

Egypt was a convenient country to disappear in.

So long as a man had money he could live in comfortable seclusion. Still, he could not imagine the fastidious Count Nevskaya choosing to live among the savages.

He regarded his father with a frown. "Did you hope that Valik would take you in like a poor stray?"

"Those females belong to me."

Of course. How had he been so stupid?

"You were hoping to locate your servant so you could auction the girls and claim the full profit before you attempted to disappear." He shook his head in sheer revulsion. "Where did you hope to go once you had your money? The Indies? America?"

"Does it matter?"

"No, I do not suppose it does." Dimitri breathed in deeply, reminding himself the girls were safely out of the reach of this vile creature. "Not after I managed to ruin your scheme yet again," he taunted, his voice thick. "How very frustrating it must be for you to be constantly outwitted by your bastard son."

Fury darkened his father's golden eyes. "You may have escaped the pasha's guards tonight, but you will never be allowed to leave Egypt. Eventually you will be returned to the citadel."

Being returned to the citadel was the least of Dimitri's concerns at the moment, but the threat did put in mind a nagging question.

"That reminds me. However did you force Koman to crawl off his divan and petition my guilt before the pasha?"

There was a moment of sullen silence, then the older man absently smoothed the folds of his cravat, his fingers lingering on the ruby stickpin that shimmered like a drop of blood on the crisp white linen.

"The baron possesses a young daughter who resides with her mother in St. Petersburg."

"And?" Dimitri prompted.

"And I pointed out that such a gently reared female would be worth a fortune in the slave market."

Dimitri's breath hissed through his teeth. Whatever his dislike of the fat, indolent baron, no man deserved to have his daughter threatened with rape.

"And *I* have been branded a coldhearted bastard. Have you no conscience whatsoever? Ah..." His lips twisted in a sneer. "Of course. I was forgetting that noblemen have no need for common decency."

His father waved away Dimitri's mocking criticism. "I merely made a suggestion. It was Koman who assumed that it was a threat."

"You are truly remarkable. Do you take responsibility for nothing?"

His father leaned forward, his eyes glittering with a cold hatred.

"You are in no position to judge me," he hissed.

"Why? Because I am the son of a whore?"

"Because you are not so different from me."

Only years of rigid discipline kept Dimitri from pulling the trigger of the pistol.

"You compare us again, and I will yank out your tongue,"

he said, his frigid tone revealing he was prepared to follow through on his threat.

The count's lips twisted in an ugly smile, taking obvious pleasure in Dimitri's outrage.

"But we are. You have devoted your life to plotting your revenge upon me. And we both know you would have committed any sin, no matter how evil, to destroy me." He leaned forward. "I have done nothing less."

In the moonlight Dimitri could see the haunting likeness between them.

The wide forehead, the aquiline nose, high cheekbones and full lips.

He had always assumed that those physical similarities were all he had in common with Count Nevskaya. After all, the man was a depraved monster who had destroyed countless children. How could he bear to think they were related by more than blood?

But a tiny voice whispered that he had nearly allowed himself to become as empty and bitter as his miserable father.

His dark crusade for revenge had consumed his life. And the count was not mistaken when he claimed that Dimitri had been willing to do whatever necessary to destroy the man who he held responsible for his mother's death.

He had almost sacrificed his own heart.

In the end, it had been Emma who rescued him.

She filled his heart with love, banishing the hatred that had nearly destroyed him.

He allowed a smile of smug satisfaction. "The difference is that my revenge has succeeded whereas yours has failed miserably."

A malignant anger twisted the count's lean features. "Do not be so certain. You have not yet escaped Egypt."

Dimitri shrugged. "Even if I were to be captured and returned to the citadel it will be no more than a momentary inconvenience. We both know that Alexander Pavlovich will soon demand my release."

"Until he does, however, you will be trapped." The older man narrowed his gaze, a muscle in his jaw twitching. "And I can assure you that Fawzi was not the only man I hired to see you dead. Eventually one will succeed."

Dimitri had to admire his father's tenacity. Even when he had to realize his plot for revenge had been ruined, he continued to search for a means to salvage his pride.

"I do not believe you."

"Why would I lie?"

"If there were truly more assassins you would have kept them a secret," Dimitri countered. "To reveal them to me would steal away their greatest power."

"Power?"

"The power of catching me off guard." Dimitri shook his head. He had played chess often enough to know when he had his opponent in checkmate. "No, you are defeated, Father. Utterly and completely defeated."

His father abruptly stiffened, his icy composure crumbling as he at last accepted that he had been bested by his own son.

In that moment he was not the sophisticated Count Nevskaya. Or the cunning power behind the slave traders. Or even the father who had glared down his nose when Dimitri's mother had hauled him to the elegant town house.

No. This was a man facing ruin.

The golden eyes smoldered with a demented fire and spittle formed at the corners of his mouth.

"You will pay for this," the count spat, his hand fumbling toward the door of the carriage.

For a moment, Dimitri assumed his father was attempting to escape.

He was not, after all, the sort of man who would face his guilt with dignity. Had he not fled St. Petersburg like a gutless deserter, leaving behind his comrades to be charged with his crimes?

Then, he realized that Nevskaya was instead digging into a side pocket.

The world slowed as Dimitri watched his father with an odd detachment.

He knew what the man was searching for. He had similar pockets sewn into his own carriages to make certain he had a loaded pistol conveniently at hand. The streets could be a dangerous place. Who knew when you might have need of a hidden weapon?

His finger tightened on the trigger, but still he hesitated. So far as Dimitri was concerned, his quest to destroy his father was at an end.

What did the past matter when his future promised to be a glorious adventure with Emma Linley-Kirov?

As long as Dimitri made certain that the pasha knew the count was in his country and that he was responsible for the traffickers, eventually his father would be served his just rewards.

But even as he shoved himself toward the far door of the carriage, the count had the gun in his hand and was swinging it in Dimitri's direction. Dimitri had a brief moment to wryly accept his father had possessed none of his qualms as he swiftly fired a shot, the bullet grazing his already wounded shoulder.

Dimitri instinctively returned fire, his own shot far superior as it hit his father directly in the center of his chest.

It had been years since he had missed his target.

The stench of gunpowder filled the carriage and with a sense of inevitability, Dimitri watched as his father sprawled across the seat, the gun dropping from his lifeless fingers.

He knew that he should feel something.

Triumph. Sorrow. Relief.

Instead, his only thought was that he hoped his newest bullet wound was healed before he reached St. Petersburg. Emma would not be pleased if she discovered he had managed to be shot once again.

His inane musings were interrupted as the door to the carriage was yanked open and Josef stuck his head through the opening, his knife clutched in his hand.

His gaze darted about the carriage, settling on the motionless form of Nevskaya even as he reached down to snatch the pistol from the carriage floor.

"Damn you, Tipova, you nearly frightened me into my grave," he growled, waving the gun at the count. "Is he…"

"Dead," Dimitri said in clipped tones, waving his friend from the door so he could climb out of the carriage.

Once he was standing on the street, he sucked in a deep, cleansing breath.

He was vaguely aware of the Arabian jasmine-scented air and the distant passage of guards returning to the citadel, but he paid them no heed.

He was anxious to put the exotic splendor of Egypt behind him.

Moving to his side, Josef nodded his head toward the carriage.

"What do you want done with the body?"

Dimitri shrugged. "Leave it for the vultures."

"Fawzi disappeared, of course. Vile little rat," Josef muttered. "Did you want him tracked down?"

"No, I am done with revenge."

There was a short silence as Josef studied him with a narrowed gaze.

"Now what?"

"Now, Josef, we go home."

## CHAPTER TWENTY-EIGHT

*St. Petersburg*

WITH A BREATH OF RELIEF, Emma slipped into the blessed silence of a small breakfast room at the back of Vanya Petrova's town house. A brief glance revealed walls covered in green damask panels with birchwood furnishings, but it was the view of the sunken rose garden that attracted her attention.

The hem of her ivory gown richly trimmed with gold lace brushed the parquet floor as she walked and her hands absently stroked the lovely fabric.

Vanya had surprised Emma with the dress earlier that morning. Obviously, the wily noblewoman had already suspected that Emma intended to use the excuse of having nothing appropriate to wear to her wedding to hide in her rooms.

A faint smile curved Emma's lips. She was, of course, delighted that Vanya was at last exchanging vows with her devoted lover, Richard Monroe. And deeply touched that the older woman had gone to the trouble of postponing the ceremony until Emma had returned to St. Petersburg.

After all, it was not as if she were a part of her family. Or even a close friend. She was simply a common peasant who imposed herself on the poor woman.

The realization had nagged at her with growing persistence over the past few days.

What reason did she have to linger in St. Petersburg?

Without warning, the image of a dark, lean face with

golden eyes seared through her mind. Dimitri. The damnable man who had yet to make his glorious arrival.

A savage pain sliced through her heart before she was ruthlessly thrusting aside the worthless emotion.

Although she had heard from Herrick that Dimitri had managed to escape from the pasha, and had been forced to kill his evil father, she had received no more than a terse note that might have been sent from a stranger.

Which was perfectly fine with her, she told herself.

Had she not already decided that she and Dimitri Tipova were utterly unsuitable?

Now if she could just convince her traitorous heart.

Ignoring the distant sound of laughter floating from the formal parlor, Emma studied the garden that slumbered beneath the pale February sunlight. Absently, she rubbed her bare arms, a strange chill crawling over her skin. No doubt it was a mere reaction to the cold after the heat of Cairo.

It was not as if she believed in premonitions.

The stern warning had barely passed through her mind when the sound of footsteps had her spinning about, her heart lodged in her throat.

For a breathless moment she expected Dimitri to step through the door. Ludicrous, of course. Even if he had returned to St. Petersburg there was no reason for him to make an appearance at Vanya's home.

No reason whatsoever.

Thankfully unaware of Emma's stupid sense of disappointment, the Duchess of Huntley entered the room, appearing stunningly beautiful in a pale blue gown that perfectly matched her eyes with silver netting that was sprinkled with a king's ransom in sapphires.

"What a beautiful wedding," she said, moving toward Emma with a determined smile.

Emma did not have to be told that Leonida had been

the one chosen to seek her out and ensure that she had not sunk into a fit of melancholy.

Over the past few days, she had been acutely aware of the worried glances from Herrick and Vanya, and even the haughty Duke of Huntley had chided her for the shadows beneath her eyes and the pallor of her skin. As if she were to blame for her sleepless nights.

"Yes." She managed a smile, knowing that Leonida only had her best interests at heart. "And Vanya made an exquisite bride."

"It makes one wonder why she tortured poor Richard for so many years by refusing to be his wife. It is obvious she adores him."

Emma shrugged. She was only vaguely familiar with the complicated courtship between Vanya and Richard, although she had heard several stories of Vanya's cunning plots over the years to protect Alexander Pavlovich's claim to the throne.

"Perhaps she was not yet prepared to sacrifice her independence."

"True. She is a remarkably intelligent woman who has led a most fascinating life." Leonida chuckled, the sunlight shimmering in her pale golden hair. "I hope someday she will be inclined to confess a few of her more thrilling adventures."

Emma glanced toward the delicate vases that Vanya had acquired on her journey to China.

"I deeply admire her."

"As do I." Leonida paused, a speculative glint in her eyes. "Still, a woman does not necessarily have to sacrifice her independence when she weds."

Even suspecting the conversation was destined to be shifted in the direction of Dimitri, Emma tensed.

"You say that only because you were blessed with a husband who is devoted to your happiness." She absently brushed aside a curl that had come loose from the elegant knot on top her head. "Most women have little choice but to bow to a man's will, regardless of her desires."

"Which only means that a woman must take care in choosing her husband."

Emma shook her head. A woman might be able to choose her husband, but she had little control over who she fell in love with.

"If only it were that simple." She sighed.

With a frown, Leonida reached to take her hand. "What is troubling you, Emma?"

"Nothing." Emma determinedly squared her shoulders. "In fact, my life is at last settled. I shall soon be returning to my cottage in Yabinsk."

"Oh." A frown tugged at Leonida's brows. "So far away?"

"I have promised both Vanya and Herrick Gerhardt that I will return to St. Petersburg to visit."

"And what of Dimitri?"

Emma tugged away from Leonida's grasp, spinning on her heel to pace to the ceramic stove set in the corner of the room.

"I do not know what you mean."

"I am not blind," Leonida said. "He loves you. And I am fairly certain you return his feelings."

Emma bit her lower lip, knowing it was futile to lie. Despite being a pampered lady of society, Leonida was far from stupid. And it was not as if Emma were skilled in disguising her emotions.

Unlike others.

"What if I do?"

"Love is a rare gift, Emma." Leonida moved to her side, her expression troubled. "Why would you turn your back on Dimitri?"

"I am not turning my back on Dimitri. I am…"

"Yes?" Leonida softly prompted.

Emma hunched her shoulders, wishing Leonida would rejoin the other guests. As much as she enjoyed the woman's charming friendship, Emma was unaccustomed to sharing her emotions with anyone.

"We could never be happy together," she muttered.

Leonida hesitated, as if carefully considering her words. "Does it trouble you he was forced to become a criminal?"

"Oddly enough, no." Emma smiled ruefully. Perhaps if she were a more righteous person she would be shocked by Dimitri's past, but life had taught her not to judge others. Not when she had endured the endless censure of her neighbors. "Oh, I am not naive. I know that he has suffered a brutal life and that he has profited from the sins of others, but I also know that he has a kind and generous heart and that he would give his life to protect those he considers his family."

"He also happens to be superbly handsome and indecently wealthy," Leonida teased. "What more could you desire?"

"It is not what I desire, but what Dimitri desires," she said, her brows lifting as Leonida suddenly laughed. "What is so amusing?"

"Dearest Emma." Leonida reached to pat her arm. "You need only see Dimitri's expression when you enter a room to know that it is taking all his restraint not to toss you over his shoulder and haul you away like the pirate he is."

A hot flush stained her cheeks. Not at the knowledge Dimitri had been so blatant in his passion for her. What woman would not be pleased to have such a handsome gentleman regarding her as if she were the most beautiful woman in the world? Instead, it was the memory of the vivid dreams that had plagued her.

She awkwardly cleared her throat. "I was not referring to Dimitri's lust."

"No?"

"I meant his passion for protecting those he loves."

Leonida wrinkled her nose, as if intimately familiar with domineering males.

"Ah, it is unfortunate, but there is no man who does not possess the urge to protect others," she admitted, a glimmer of sly humor shimmering in her blue eyes. "A wise woman allows him to fuss and then do precisely as she pleases."

"That might be well enough for most men, but not Dimitri." Emma wrapped her arms around her waist as she shivered with an aching sense of loss. "He blames himself for his mother's death."

Leonida sucked in a sharp breath. "How dreadful."

"The belief has tortured him his entire life."

"Which is all the more reason he needs you to help heal his wounds," Leonida urged gently, unaware her words were like a dagger to Emma's heart.

"No." She shook her head. "What he needs is a woman who is happy to depend upon him without question and does not mind having her life controlled by another."

"Actually, I think I should be allowed to decide the sort of woman I prefer, Emma Linley-Kirov."

A shocked silence filled the room as both women slowly turned to watch the handsome, raven-haired gentleman stroll toward them.

Her gaze slid down his slender form that was shown to advantage in a Persian-blue jacket with silver waistcoat and black pantaloons. His cravat was precisely knotted with a diamond stickpin tucked among the folds and his hair smoothed into a queue at his nape.

Emma's heart squeezed with a painful excitement. He was so splendidly, dangerously beautiful.

"Dimitri," she breathed.

At her side Leonida cleared her throat, a mysterious smile curving her lips.

"If you will excuse me, I promised Stefan I would save him a waltz."

Emma barely noticed the woman's discreet departure. In truth she was not certain she would have noticed if the ceiling had tumbled onto her head.

Not when her knees were threatening to give way and her breath annoyingly elusive.

He halted directly before her, his golden eyes watching the emotions rippling over her face with unnerving intensity.

"Did you receive my message?" he demanded at last.

His words helped to shatter the odd sense of unreality, reminding Emma that she had waited day after painful day for this man to reveal that he had not forgotten her existence.

"*Wait for me* is not a message," she informed him stiffly. "It is a command."

His lips twitched. "What I have to say to you could not be put into a letter."

Emma lowered her gaze, belatedly realizing she was giving away more than she had intended. Hurriedly, she sought to turn the conversation.

"Herrick revealed that you…"

Her words stumbled to a halt as she struggled to find a delicate means to offer her sympathy.

"Shot my father through the heart?"

She lifted her gaze to study his guarded expression, her tender heart rebelling at the thought he might blame himself for his father's death.

"That you were forced to protect yourself," she corrected.

A rueful smile curved his lips, his hand reaching to tuck a stray curl behind her ear.

"You would, of course, assume the best of me."

"If you wished to kill your father you could have done so anytime in the past twenty years." She paused, wondering if he were truly as calm as he wished her to believe. "Did he follow you to Cairo?"

The golden eyes darkened with a sudden impatience, his hands cupping her face as he regarded her with a sudden determination.

"Count Nevskaya no longer matters. Indeed, nothing matters but you."

Emma scrambled away, her heart fluttering as she sought to confront him with a measure of composure.

"Wait," she husked. "There is something I must tell you."

He stilled, his eyes narrowing as he watched her nervously tug at the sapphire ribbon threaded beneath her bodice.

"Why am I certain I am not going to like what you have to say?"

She licked her dry lips. "I am leaving in the morning for Yabinsk."

Emma braced herself for a furious response. Dimitri, after all, was a man who expected to make the decisions for others and have them obeyed.

Which made his rigid control all the more frightening.

"Why?"

"It is my home."

"You intend to spend the rest of your life alone in your cottage?"

With an effort, Emma hid her flinch at the stark truth in his accusation.

*The rest of her life alone…*

It was her worst fear, but what choice did she have?

"I have my coaching inn to keep me occupied and Anya might come to her senses and—"

"Anya will never return to that cottage and we both know it," he overrode her, shifting to block her path to the door.

How had he suspected she intended to flee?

"There is no need for you to be so cruel."

Frustration flared through the beautiful golden eyes. "Obviously there is every need. You are stubborn beyond reason."

Her chin tilted as she regarded him with a hint of outrage. Deep inside she knew it was foolish to hope that Anya would return to the cottage. And in truth, she was not certain if she could ever fully forgive her sister for her betrayal.

But Dimitri Tipova had no right to criticize her decisions.

"If that is what you believe then you will be pleased to be rid of me," she muttered.

Dimitri stepped forward, his hands lightly grabbing her upper arms as his features softened with regret.

"*Moya dusha,* please forgive me, but you must realize that returning to the cottage will not bring back your family."

A familiar pain tugged at her heart. "I am well aware that my family is gone. You have no need to remind me."

"Then why are you leaving?"

She heaved a resigned sigh. This man dared to claim that *she* was stubborn.

"I cannot remain in St. Petersburg."

"Have you developed a dislike for the city?"

"Really, Dimitri," she snapped with impatience. "You must be aware that Vanya was wed earlier today."

He grimaced with rueful amusement. "I could not fail to

notice since she devoted the past quarter of an hour lecturing me on my ill manners in missing the ceremony."

"Then you must realize it would be impossible for me to remain beneath the roof of newlyweds."

"They are not precisely the traditional newlyweds," he pointed out. "They have been lovers for the past twenty years or more."

Emma refused to be swayed. Vanya's wedding was, after all, no more than a convenient excuse to leave St. Petersburg.

"I am still intruding."

They glared at each other for a tense moment, then a slow, worrisome smile tugged at his lips, his brooding gaze gliding over her wary face and down to the scooped line of her bodice.

Emma shivered, her skin prickling as if she could feel the heat of his gaze.

"Vanya would not agree, but it was never my intention that you should reside here."

"*Your* intention?" She stiffened at his nonchalant tone. "You have no say in where I live…"

With his typical arrogance, Dimitri ignored her stern warning, his hands tightening on her arms as he yanked her against his chest. In the same motion his head swooped downward, claiming her mouth in a kiss of brazen possession.

Tiny jolts of pleasure raced through her, heating her blood and causing her toes to curl in her ivory slippers. He tasted of champagne and untamed male as he teased his tongue between her lips, his grip easing so his fingers could lightly caress her bare arms.

Emma shuddered as anticipation fluttered in the pit of her stomach.

She had ached for weeks for this man's touch. His hard, lean hands exploring her body, his seeking mouth stirring a wicked need, his low voice whispering encouragement in her ear.

Now she was forced to swallow a whimper of disappointment when he pulled back to study her flushed face.

"If you prefer the country I have an estate near Moscow and another just beyond Kiev," he murmured.

She blinked, struggling to follow his words while her body trembled with desire.

"You want me to live with you?"

"Of course." He peered deep in her eyes. "We belong together."

She shook her head sadly. "I cannot be the woman you want."

"No," he readily agreed, "you are the woman I need."

She paused, uncertain. "Need?"

"Before you came into my life, I thought it was enough to surround myself with those in need, filling the emptiness in my heart with a hatred for my father."

"You should not dismiss what you have accomplished," she chided. "Herrick has told me of those you rescued from the streets."

"I am a sinner, not a saint, Emma." He gently brushed her cheek with the back of his hand, his expression somber. "And I have begun to realize that a part of my need to be the savior is because it allows me to keep others at a distance."

"I do not understand."

With a sigh he dropped his hands and turned to pace toward the center of the room. Emma frowned, startled by the hint of vulnerability she had glimpsed in his eyes.

"When people depend upon me, all I need offer them is my protection. There is no danger to my heart," he confessed. "But you refused to accept my rules."

"Which is why we are so unsuited."

He swung back to meet her puzzled gaze. "No, it is why we are so perfectly matched."

"You are making no sense, Dimitri. We are forever squabbling with one another." She shrugged. "How could we possibly be suited?"

He hesitated, considering his words, then squaring his shoulders he peered deep in her eyes.

"The simple answer is that I love you, Emma Linley-Kirov."

Emma stumbled backward, her hand pressed to her chest in a futile effort to still her racing heart. Obviously, the heat of the desert sun had damaged Dimitri's mind.

"No," she breathed. "It is not possible."

Dimitri arched his brows, smiling wryly at her less than joyous response to his declaration of love.

"Not possible?"

"No."

He prowled forward, not halting until she was backed against the wall.

"Perhaps you should explain, since I am quite certain of my feelings," he said, the very softness of his tone conveying his sincerity.

Astonishing.

She shook her head, her mouth dry. "We have nothing in common."

"I suppose that is true enough," he readily agreed. "You are a proper lady while I am a notorious criminal and the son of a whore. I have no doubt that you are far above my touch."

She gasped. Surely he could not believe such nonsense?

"You must know that was not what I meant at all."

"Then what did you mean?"

"I am not beautiful or sophisticated or fascinating."

"Emma—"

"No." She placed her hand across his mouth. Did he know how desperately she wanted to toss aside all reason and accept his pledge of love? It was only the fear that she could never truly offer what he needed to heal his wounds that made her hesitate. "I am a simple woman who desires a quiet life. I have had quite enough adventure."

Pressing his lips to her palm, Dimitri gently tugged aside her hand, his eyes glowing with a near féverish light.

"Oddly enough, I have recently developed a taste for a quiet life, as well."

The mere thought was enough to bring a grudging smile to her lips.

"You?"

"I must admit that I am as shocked as you, *milaya,*" he teased, aimlessly rubbing his thumb over her inner wrist. "I never imagined that one day I would hand the reins of my empire to another."

"You mean—"

"As of today Josef is now the Beggar Czar," he proudly announced. "While I am a mere gentleman who is unencumbered by such vast responsibilities."

She shook her head in bemusement. It certainly seemed the day for surprises.

"Why would you do such a thing?"

He leaned down to brush a soft kiss over her lips. "Because I intend to devote myself to my wife and children."

# CHAPTER TWENTY-NINE

DIMITRI PRESSED HIS THUMB to the rapid flutter of Emma's pulse at her wrist, wryly aware that she appeared closer to swooning than leaping for joy.

How was it possible that a woman who had confronted scoundrels and kidnappers and slave traders without flinching was in a near panic at his marriage proposal?

"Dimitri," she at last managed to rasp. "What are you saying?"

"I am asking that you become my wife."

"Your...wife?"

His lips twisted. Perhaps he should have rehearsed his proposal. It was obvious he was making a botch of it.

"Am I not speaking clearly?"

She shook her head, her expression wary. "I comprehend the words, but I cannot accept that Dimitri Tipova, the scourge of St. Petersburg, could ever be satisfied spending his days seated in front of a fire in some remote estate."

"Ah, but I intend to keep myself fully occupied."

Her wariness deepened. "Occupied with what?"

His gaze lowered to the temptation of her scooped bodice. She was exquisite in the beautiful ivory gown, but she would be even more beautiful with it stripped away to reveal her own ivory glory.

He swallowed a groan as his body stirred in anticipation. "There are a few pleasant activities that come to mind."

"You cannot remain forever in bed," she muttered.

He chuckled at her ridiculous accusation. "You should never underestimate my desire for you."

"I am not jesting."

He felt her pulse leap, but she remained uneasy, as if afraid that she might shatter if she lowered her guard.

That knowledge tugged at his heart with a small pang of tenderness.

He cupped her cheek in his hand. "Neither am I, but I do have other plans."

"What plans?"

"To begin with I must learn the duties expected of a gentleman farmer." He pretended to be offended when she regarded him as if she feared he'd taken leave of his senses. "You need not smirk, I have no intention of brandishing a hoe or mucking among the pigs, but I never acquire a new business without discovering the means to make it a profitable enterprise." A determined grin curved his lips. He was astonishingly eager to begin his life on his country estate. There was nothing he loved more than a new adventure, and beginning a family with Emma would be the greatest adventure of all. "Before I am done I will know the cost of each and every seed that is planted, where to purchase the latest farming implements and which of the staff have been stealing the silver."

A grudging amusement shimmered in her eyes. "That will indeed keep you occupied."

"I shall also need to learn how to perform the typical pastimes of a gentleman of leisure."

"I am almost fearful to ask."

"I might be a master at tossing dice and picking a pocket, but I have never learned to hunt or fish or play snapdragons."

She frowned, clearly puzzled by his ramblings. "Why would you wish to play snapdragons?"

Dimitri faltered, his palms suddenly damp and his mouth dry.

He had never before been so nervous. Not even

when he had been taken hostage by a particularly nasty highwayman.

Of course, nothing before had ever been so important.

"So I can teach our children," he said, his voice thick.

Her mouth opened, but nothing came out but a tiny squeak of shock.

"Oh."

"You do want children, do you not, Emma?" he asked, gently.

"Yes." She blinked back sudden tears. "Yes, I want children very much," she husked.

He grimaced, gazing into her hazel eyes and knowing that he would never truly deserve this beautiful, courageous woman.

"I know I would not be the man that most females would choose to father their children."

Her brows snapped together, her chin tilting. She was always determined to see the best in others.

Which was no doubt one of the reasons he found her so endearing.

"You are wrong, Dimitri."

"Impossible, I am never wrong," he teased.

"I cannot imagine a more worthy man."

He shook his head. "I was raised on the streets, hating the man who raped my mother. I know nothing of how to be a decent father."

Her wariness faded, her hand lifting to cover his hand that was pressed to her cheek.

"You have been protecting and caring for others since your mother's death," she said. "Besides, there is only one thing a father truly needs to offer his children."

"And what is that?"

"Love."

With a groan he wrapped her in his arms and hauled her tight against his body.

"If I love them half so much as I love their mother, then I shall be the greatest father in all of Russia."

"Oh...Dimitri." Arching back her head, she regarded him with all the emotion she had been hiding behind her brittle composure. "I love you, too."

His heart swelled, the years of bitterness forgotten. Never had he thought to ever feel such overwhelming joy.

Certainly not with a headstrong, spirited, independent woman who refused to leave him in peace.

"I always suspected that you were a woman of intelligence," he retorted with a smug smile.

She rolled her eyes. "So modest."

"You still have not answered my question, *moya dusha.*" He paused, his smile fading. "Will you marry me?"

Breathlessly awaiting her response, Dimitri was unaware of the elegant, silver-haired gentleman who stepped in the room in a claret jacket with a black waistcoat trimmed in silver buttons.

At least he was unaware until the man had the audacity to interrupt the precious moment.

"You might wish to hear what I have to say before you give your response, Emma."

Easily recognizing the male voice, Dimitri weighed the pleasure of pulling his pistol and shooting the intruder against Vanya's annoyance at having her wedding so rudely interrupted.

At last it was the embarrassed pink that brushed Emma's cheeks that had him turning to confront the damnable man, his arm keeping her tucked protectively against him.

"Gerhardt," he growled. "This is a private conversation."

The older but still-handsome man strolled across the room, deliberately ignoring Dimitri's warning. Not surprising. Herrick Gerhardt was perhaps the second most powerful man in all of Russia.

"Am I intruding?" he murmured.

"Yes," Dimitri snapped. "Go away."

"Dimitri." Emma flashed him a chiding glance at his rudeness, reminding him that Herrick was one of the few people she could claim as family.

Herrick smiled, easily sensing Dimitri's smoldering frustration.

"I do have a reason for thrusting myself into such an obviously private moment."

"A desire for an early grave?" Dimitri muttered.

The older man's smile widened, stirring Dimitri's suspicions. What was the devil playing at?

"Actually, I have just finished a most intriguing conversation with Alexander Pavlovich," Herrick drawled.

"And why would your conversation with Czar Alexander be of interest to us?" Dimitri demanded.

"He was most delighted to learn that you have seen the error of your ways and have turned away from your life of sin."

Dimitri hissed in surprise. He would have bet his last ruble that no one beyond Josef was aware of his intent to leave his position.

"How did you discover my plans?"

Herrick adjusted the lace that peeked from the sleeve of his jacket.

"We all have our little talents."

Dimitri shuddered, amazed by the man's uncanny ability to discover even the darkest secrets. If he were not so rational, he might suspect the man of being a mystic.

"You are a frightening man, Herrick Gerhardt."

Emma stepped away from his tight grip, her expression confused.

"You came here to tell us that the czar approves of Dimitri becoming a proper gentleman?"

Again there was that worrisome smile.

"Not entirely."

Dimitri narrowed his gaze. "Perhaps we should speak in private."

"No, I suspect that Emma will be interested in the czar's decision," Herrick chuckled. "Do not glare at me, Tipova. You are not about to be hauled before the firing squad. Although in time you might prefer such a fate."

"Herrick, please." Emma reached out to place her hand on Herrick's forearm, her voice not entirely steady. "What has happened?"

Immediate regret chased the amusement from Herrick's face as he patted her hand in comfort.

"Forgive me, I did not mean to worry you, my dear. That was never my intention," he ruefully apologized. "I am an old man who must take his pleasure where he can, and I have been savoring the image of Tipova's expression when I reveal that Alexander Pavlovich has made the decision to create a new title."

Dimitri took an instinctive step backward, a sense of dread lodging in his gut.

"Title?"

"Baron Voglevich." Herrick offered a formal bow. "I hope it suits you?"

Perhaps for the first time in his life, Dimitri was struck speechless.

He was aware that Alexander Pavlovich could be unpredictable, and certainly Dimitri had performed several dangerous tasks to protect the czar from potential uprisings, not to mention the information he acquired on the streets that he provided to the Winter Palace.

Still, he had never expected to receive a title.

Hell, he never *wanted* a title.

In his mind the men of society were worthless buffoons fit for nothing more than to provide easy plucking at his gaming houses.

It was Emma who at last filled the shocked silence.

"Do you mean—"

"I mean that when you wed, you will be the Baroness Voglevich," Herrick gently completed her faltering words.

Dimitri clenched his hands, forcing himself to take a deep, calming breath.

"Why?"

"He is aware of the numerous services you have performed for the empire," Herrick explained. "This is his means of offering his gratitude."

Dimitri grimaced. "I would have preferred a large donation of rubles."

"You have all the wealth you will ever need and, to be honest, the royal coffers are notoriously bare." Herrick deliberately glanced toward the stunned woman at Dimitri's side. "And now you have a bride to consider."

Emma snatched her hand away, her eyes wide. "I have no desire for a title."

"Nonsense." Herrick regarded her with a stern expression. "You shall soon become accustomed to being a member of society. And your children, of course, will be grateful for the opportunities offered by their positions."

Dimitri heaved a rueful sigh as Emma struggled against Herrick's sly manipulation.

Clearly, they had been outmaneuvered.

Emma at last offered a reluctant laugh. "You do not fight fair."

"Never." Herrick clapped his hands together, a satisfied expression settling on his gaunt face. "We should toast your good fortune."

"I have a better notion." Dimitri pointed toward the door. "You will return to Vanya's lovely party and I shall concentrate on pleasing my wife-to-be."

Having achieved his goal, Herrick readily strolled across the floor.

"Of course. Oh, I suppose I should also mention that Czar Alexander has begun the arrangements for your wedding. He thought June would be a suitable month," he murmured, his footsteps never slowing despite Dimitri's and Emma's protests. "And, Emma, I have requested that our English relatives travel to Russia for the ceremony. I had no notion there would be so many. Let us hope they will leave once the wedding is over."

He swept from the room, leaving the two of them shaking their heads in disbelief.

"Good Lord," Emma muttered.

"It would seem you shall soon have all the family you ever desired," he said dryly. Then, noticing her pallor he pulled her into his arms, his hands running a comforting path over her back. "Emma?"

"Baroness." She blinked, her hands lifting to grasp his shoulders for support. "My head is spinning."

He brushed a soft kiss over her mouth. "Do you still love me?"

"Of course."

"Then nothing else matters."

He returned for a much more lingering kiss, his tongue dipping between her lips to taste of her sweetness.

At last pulling back to study her upturned face, he was gratified to discover the color had returned to her cheeks and a glow of excitement in her eyes.

A slow smile curved her lips. "Well, Dimitri Tipova, how does it feel to be a respectable gentleman?"

His hands curved over her hips, tugging her against the stirring muscles of his thighs.

"At the moment it feels astonishingly wonderful."

"Just so long as you do not become entirely civilized."

She lifted onto the tips of her toes, trailing a path of kisses along his jaw. "I would miss my wicked pirate."

Desire exploded through him and without giving her the opportunity to come to her senses he was across the room locking the door. Then without pause he returned to sweep her off her feet.

Headed for the nearby sofa, he glanced down at the woman who had stolen the heart of the greatest thief in all of Russia.

"Perhaps I should demonstrate how wicked I can be."

\* \* \* \* \*

# THE LARK
# AND THE
# LAUREL

Barbara Willard

LAUREL-LEAF BOOKS bring together under a single imprint outstanding works of fiction and nonfiction particularly suitable for young adult readers, both in and out of the classroom. Charles F. Reasoner, Professor Emeritus of Children's Literature and Reading, New York University, is consultant to this series.

Published by
Dell Publishing
a division of
Bantam Doubleday Dell Publishing Group, Inc.
666 Fifth Avenue
New York, New York 10103

*For Grace, with love and gratitude*

This work was first published in Great Britain by
Penguin Books Ltd.
First published in the U.S.A. by E. P. Dutton

32 lines from *Medieval Latin Lyrics* translated by Helen Waddell reproduced on pp. 119–120 by permission of Constable, London.

ISBN: 0-440-20156-X

RL: 5.6

Printed in the United States of America

May 1989

10 9 8 7 6 5 4 3 2 1

KRI

# Contents

# The Lark
# and the
# Laurel

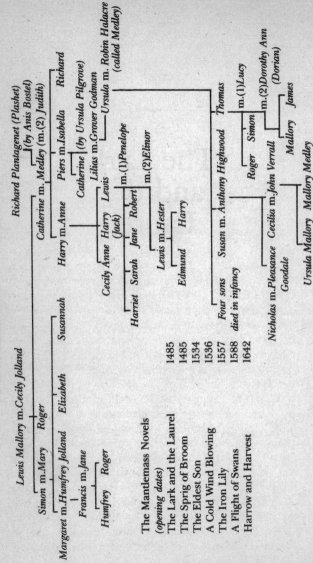

# 1

## To Mantlemass

CECILY HAD BEEN BROUGHT TO MANTLEMASS AT dusk. Already bitterly fatigued by the long ride from London, by the haste and surprise and fear of it all, she had clung to her father as if she were drowning and only he of all the world could save her. Her own misery, loud and ugly, clamored in her ears and she could not stop it in spite of the distaste and anger she saw in her father's face. She had never dared to behave to him in such a way before. She heard him say "She is distraught, sister," and he dragged her hands from their stranglehold and thrust her roughly into the arms of her aunt. Cecily struggled, but her aunt held her firmly, repeating over and over again words that were meant to soothe. Two of the maids joined in, and the old nurse they called Goody Ann, until the hall seemed full of struggling, protesting people, their shadows bobbing in the light of torches held against the growing dark by her aunt's menservants. Giles and Humfrey were there too, to increase the crowd—her father's men who would ride away with him to the coast and so across the sea to France. When they went there would be no one left with Cecily whom she had ever known.

Getting the girl to bed had been like fighting with a mad creature. She was past all reason, and it was almost a relief when her aunt struck her such a blow across the face that she was shocked into silence. She heard her aunt say in a commanding voice, "Drink, now—drink this!" She had swallowed the draught before she knew what she was doing. "Now she will sleep," someone said. And she did sleep, instantly, falling into a black pit where she was shut away even from her own misery. . . .

When Cecily woke the night was over. Without opening her eyes she called, as she always did call, "Alys! Alys! I am awake." And always when she called Alys leapt up from her bed across the doorway, though it were midnight or the smallest hour before sunrise, to ask what she needed. Only this morning, for the first time ever, there was no Alys to answer Cecily's call. For the first time ever, Cecily was in a room alone, with none to attend her, none to care whether she slept or woke.

Although the bed-curtains were closed, she could see light through a crack toward the foot of the bed. Beyond the curtains, beyond the strange house, the sun was shining. It was the last week in August, as bright with hope and promise as with sunshine, for the long war that had torn England into factions was over. A new king had been crowned on the battlefield beside the gashed and naked body of the old—a new king who would stand neither for York nor Lancaster but a union of both—a Tudor king. He would not forget his faithful followers, supporters of the Lancastrian cause. For them, a happy ending to the years of strife renewed and renewed again until this final triumph. For the others? Well, a loyal Yorkist would be recognized, no doubt, for that loyalty, even though it was to a lost cause. But there were others, mindful of their own advantage, who had changed their coats and now must expect the fate of traitors. At best, for them, the exile into which Cecily's own father had ridden after leaving her in her aunt's keeping.

All this Cecily had learned yesterday, which seemed now part of another, vanished world. She had been standing down at the waterside on the stone steps where the barge was moored. Alys was with her, as always, and they were feeding crusts to the swans that rocked gently against the river's tide. Cecily knew that, fifty paces away, her father was walking on the terrace before the house, and she knew without being told that something untoward had happened or must happen soon. She did not turn to look at him, for she was always very frightened of him, but the sensation of urgency about the place made her palms sweat and her scalp prickle.

"There is no more bread, Alys."

Alys looked about her, but there was no servant at hand.

"Fetch it yourself," said Cecily, a little sharply.

Alys hesitated, glancing from Cecily toward her father. She was a constant attendant—night or day she was at Cecily's side and seemed to exist only to serve. Or perhaps to guard. This thought had once or twice found its way into Cecily's mind. She repeated her order now, and Alys went quickly toward the house.

There was very little traffic on the river. Only one barge went by, and that was in midstream. Cecily turned away automatically, for she was alone and must not notice strangers. So she was facing the house when the visitor arrived. It was her uncle Digby, her dead mother's brother, who seldom came to the house in Blackfriars. He strode out unannounced on to the terrace where her father was pacing. His face and beard were as dusty as his boots, so it was plain that he had ridden hard through the dry summer day.

In the very instant of their meeting, the voices of the two men rose harshly, and the sensation of alarm increased a hundredfold. Cecily swung back to the swans, as though in a dutiful attempt not to hear what was being said. But the birds, ruffled by her neglect, sailed relentlessly away while the words of the two men, violent and clear, forced her attention.

"They pulled the crown out from under the bushes," the newcomer cried. "It had rolled there through the blood and the dust. They set it, dripping, on Richmond's head—I have it from a witness —and all there cried out *God save the king* and *Amen* —and they raised his standard for the soldiers to see. So died the old order, Sir Thomas. So begins the new. You will know better than I what this can mean."

"To some," replied Sir Thomas Jolland.

"To you," Cecily heard her uncle say. "And to yours. Why else am I here—at some risk to myself?"

"I thank you for it."

"I am concerned for my dead sister's child, not for her father."

Sir Thomas called, "Cecily! Come here to me." She picked up her skirts and came as fast as manners allowed. "Go indoors," he said. "Call Alys to get you ready for traveling." She stood trembling, her eyes on the ground at his feet. "At once!" he cried.

Her uncle broke in. "I will see to the girl. Leave her to me and get on your way, brother-in-law. Bet-

ter for all of us when you are gone. I would give
your girl shelter myself, in spite of everything. But
you know well that my wife is kin to the Tudors. It is
not wise. Still, on my honor I will see your daughter
safe, Sir Thomas."

"Cecily, do as I bid you—go indoors," her father
repeated. As she went she heard him say angrily,
"This is my treasure. If I may not spend it, at least I
will see it safely put away."

The sun shone on Cecily's neck as she stumbled
into the house. She was half sick with fright. What
did *safely put away* mean? Once, last spring, she had
run singing through the orchard with her head bare
and her hair streaming on her shoulders—and her
father had seen her and caught her. He had threatened as he struck her repeatedly to put her into a
convent—his younger sister was abbess of a foun-
dation near York. If Cecily could not be modest by
taste and inclination, he had told her, then the habit
of modesty must be forced upon her. *Safely put away*
sounded the same alarm in the girl's mind as she
had experienced then. . . . Or perhaps she was to
die, and that was to be her safety—then she would
pay finally for the sin of being a useless daughter
instead of a stalwart son. Her old nurse, long since
sent away, had promised her that when she died she
would see her mother again, but her mother was a
forgotten stranger, faceless and voiceless.

As she went into the house, Cecily was calling
shrilly for Alys, fear pinching her throat so cruelly
that she found breathing difficult.

Alys came running, looking excited and strange.

"I went to the kitchens for bread . . . Lord
Digby's men are there . . . Oh, lady! The tales
they tell! The terror of it all!"

"Is the world ending?"

"There is a new king. King Richard is dead on the

battlefield. His followers must surely all disperse and fly to safety! Henry Tudor is our king!''

"The Earl of Richmond. I heard my uncle say so. . . . We are to travel, Alys.''

Cecily understood her father's plight very well. A Lancastrian by birth and service, Sir Thomas Jolland had changed his allegiance when it seemed expedient to become a Yorkist and King Richard's man. Better for him if he had supported the House of York from the start of the quarrels—loyalty to the losing side was more admirable to a victor than the shift and grab of an opportunist. Cecily knew little enough of the world, but at least she knew that when men invited the name of *traitor* they must watch out for their heads. So must her father now.

Alys was wailing, "How will you do without me? Who will care for you?"

"Why—what do you mean by that?" cried Cecily.

Alys had gray eyes, and she put her hand over them as she answered. "Sir Thomas called to me as I crossed the hall. You must go one way, lady, and I am to go another."

This news stunned Cecily. She had never been alone in all her life. First there had been nurses to care for her, then Alys had been given to her for her own. How indeed was Cecily to manage without her? She had never brushed her own hair, or knotted a girdle . . . The image of her aunt, the abbess, loomed uncomfortably.

"Where am I to go?"

. "To Mantlemass, lady."

*"There?"* It was not the convent, certainly, but the household of her father's elder sister, Elizabeth FitzEdmund. Time and time again Dame Elizabeth had asked for Cecily's company—the girl motherless, Dame Elizabeth a widow, made the suggestion a very suitable one. But Sir Thomas's reply had

always been brutally to the point. Twice when her aunt had come to London and visited the house, Cecily had been locked away. She had heard a strong, unfamiliar voice ringing across the great hall: "One day, brother, I promise you I shall release your prisoner." Cecily's lip had curled at the expression, for Alys had long ago convinced her of the reason for being kept so close. It was because, Alys said, her father had in mind a high and mighty husband for her; one so noble he would demand for his bride a lily untouched by any contact with the base ways of the world.

It suited Cecily to accept this flattery, but in her heart she retained a doubt she would never have spoken aloud, even to Alys. She had known for some years that men sold their daughters to advantage themselves, though they called it *giving in marriage*. Her nurse had told her of a little cousin on her mother's side, a Digby heiress, who was contracted in her cradle to the eldest son of a powerful father. By this marriage estates would be enlarged and titles come by. The boy died of a fever in childhood, but the interest of the two fathers was not to be set aside. So the second son took his dead brother's place as the promised husband. He too died in his turn before he reached even twelve years old, and it was the third son who finally gained the bride. A daughter was an easy enough price to pay in such a bargain between parents.

This story had never been forgotten, and Cecily thought of it now, when her father so lightly consigned her to the sister he spoke of as harsh and headstrong and unwomanly.

"Where is Mantlemass, lady?" Alys was asking. "I have never heard."

"I think it is south from London . . ." began Cecily. Then she paused, *knowing* it was south from

London, and therefore well on the way to the coast where her father would find a boat to take him into France. For this reason and no other, for his own convenience, he would leave her there, shedding her as thankfully as he would some cumbersome baggage. If his younger sister's convent had stood where Mantlemass stood, then he would have left her at the convent. Realizing this, Cecily flew into a fury and stamped and struck out at Alys, catching her hard on the right ear. "Fetch my blue gown! Make me a bundle for my goods. I'll have the pearl my uncle gave me for my christening and the cross with rubies that was my mother's. Do as I bid you! Hurry, girl!"

Alys bit her lip as she clutched her burning ear, and her eyes were full of tears. An hour, half an hour ago, Cecily would have accepted the tears as grief at the parting. Now she wondered, for treachery seemed in the air.

It was a little after noon when they rode out of London, Sir Thomas in a plain, untrimmed cloak and dun-color hose, his cap low on his brow. His two men, Giles and Humfrey, were muffled too, while Cecily was veiled as closely as any princess. The day was fine, the world about its business. Part of that business gathered knots of men and women at house doors and crossways—as the subjects of a new king, they had plenty to discuss and surmise. But when London and its neighboring villages were left behind and they came to deeper country, cattle and pigs and the harvest seemed to leave little time for gossiping.

They rode steadily, since a speeding rider is more to be remembered. Once the sun began to decline a little they increased their pace. The open roads gave way to country tracks with dusty hedgerows. The horses' hoofs thudded here, giving an impression of urgency that the journey had lacked till now. Cecily awoke out of a numb misery into an active despair. She was to be abandoned among strangers. There would be no single face at Mantlemass that she had ever seen before. Tears filled her eyes and poured down her cheeks, and she tried to dry them on her veil. She rode along crying bitterly, sniffing and gulping like a child of half her age, wishing she might have been riding pillion behind her father, so that she could speak to him and try to wheedle him.

The man Giles was riding behind Cecily, and he moved up close and spoke gently to her. "Hush," he said. "Hush, my dear lady. You will make yourself ill."

"Get back to your place," she snapped, her face ugly with misery. She spurred forward in her turn till she was riding at her father's elbow. "Let me come with you, sir."

"Impossible."

"I would not be a burden."

"Yes," he said, "you would be a burden. A man in flight needs both hands free."

"Oh, please—oh, Father, I beg you . . . I shall be alone . . . I shall be alone . . ."

"You must stay till I send for you."

"When . . . ?"

"Can I tell when? Be sensible."

Hysteria made her shrill. "I shall die! I shall pine and die. . . ."

"Is it my choice?" he cried angrily. "It is God's will that we have a new king—but for me it had as well be Satan's. . . . Oh, stop your wailing! Where's your pride, girl?"

It was impossible for Cecily to check her tears. She rode at her father's side, sobbing and biting her lips. Her face was blotched and swollen.

Presently they mounted rising ground and

looked out over a vast expanse that was half forest
and half heath. The sun was setting and the atmosphere, a little hazy, seemed as flushed as the sky
itself. At a distance some light could be seen, and
Cecily thought perhaps men had lit beacons to
honor the new king. But Sir Thomas said there was
iron smelting in these parts and the glow came from
the foundries.

They were almost at Mantlemass and the parting
of their ways.

That sunset had promised a fine morning, and fine
it was. Cecily stirred in her bed at last and sat up.
Her head swam. She pushed back the covers and
pulled the curtains, looking out into the room like a
mouse from a hole, not quite able to believe that
there was no one there to watch for her waking.
Now the sun had shifted and was plunging a long
blade of light through the greenish glass of the
deep-set window. Cecily got out of bed slowly and
carefully. The wood floor was bare but rubbed to a
high polish with beeswax. There was a vast wardrobe against the far wall, a chest along the foot of
the bed, two stools, and a heavy, rough-looking
table. She looked around her with deep curiosity,
then moved to the window. She stood peering
through the windowpanes, unable to see more than
confused treetops and a sky apparently clear of
cloud. Then she found a pane that opened when
she pushed it. The clean morning air gushed in at
her, blowing full from the south and carrying still,
more than twenty miles inland, some memory of
the sea. The coolness on her forehead stopped the
ache and she stood there at the window until she
thought guiltily what Alys would say to her if she
were there. She shut the window quickly—then
opened it again at once. The gesture strangely

elated her. She was unaccustomed to opening windows but there was no one to prevent her doing so if she wished. She was alone, she was deserted—she was very much afraid—yet she knew for the first time that she existed in her own right. She was herself. She could call her soul her own. A conscious resistance to her new circumstances hardened unexpectedly as she recognized this.

Her clothes were lying tidily over the chest, and she moved toward them rather warily. The skirt of her blue gown was dusty from yesterday's ride; she brushed it with her hand, ineffectually and with great distaste. Then she shook out the gown more vigorously and looked uneasily at the fastenings. First, however, she must deal with her linen petticoat, and she struggled into it modestly under the folds of her bedgown. She fought with the folds of both garments and emerged triumphantly—she had contrived to tie the petticoat laces though they might prove more difficult to undo.

She was half into the blue gown when she heard footsteps outside her door. The key turned in the lock, and she knew for the first time that she had been held captive.

The door opened and her aunt came into the room.

Cecily was at a great disadvantage—half dressed, her hair hanging unbrushed about her shoulders, no shoes on her feet. Holding the dress up and pushing back her hair, which was straight and fine and as fair, she had been told, as her mother's, she contrived the necessary courtesy to her aunt.

"God bless you this fine morning, niece."

"And you, madam," murmured Cecily.

"I see you have slept well and are now composed." Her voice was brisk and she looked herself as though she had been nothing but composed for many years—though the effect was of strength rather than tranquility. She was tall, dark-browed under her widow's cap, straight-backed, steady-eyed. Her mouth was firmer than a woman's mouth is usually allowed to be. A dark, roughish gown without any adornment made her appear more like a farmer's wife than the widow of a gentleman. Her hands were without any ring but her marriage band, and they were brown from the summer weather. She wore leather shoes with hard, thick soles, such as Cecily had never seen before. While she eyed her aunt nervously, taking in all this, so Dame Elizabeth FitzEdmund eyed her niece, in a steady, summing-up fashion that made Cecily start to tremble.

"Now, child, you must stay calm," her aunt said. "You need not fear for your father. Sir Thomas was always a good manager." There was a sharp note in her voice that suggested a sister could feel less than love for a brother.

"He will go into France," Cecily managed.

"For sure. He has friends there from other days."

"I think he was at the French court once," Cecily said, her voice so small and faint it was barely audible.

"Come to the window and let me see what manner of girl you are," her aunt said, taking her by the wrist. "You are still trembling, Cecily Jolland. Why? It is not for you to endure your father's misfortunes." All this time she had not smiled, but now a flicker broke up the firmness of her expression. "I will tell you this at once—I too have been alone and forced to make a new life. I too had your father to thank for it. For me, there was great tribulation. For you—it shall be simpler."

"Shall it, madam?"

"Trust me—and I will see you happy. Believe me. Have faith in me. Obey me. All shall be well."

Cecily's hand moved in her aunt's grasp. She said faintly, "Yes, madam."

"Trust me, I said. And that means do not struggle." Her aunt smiled at last, though wryly, and patted Cecily's hand. "How old are you?"

"I am sixteen years old in the New Year."

"And eleven of those years without a mother. Well, you must be my daughter now. But let us understand one another. I have only this one purpose for you: to give back what has been taken away."

"Alys?" asked Cecily hopefully. Then corrected herself: "My father?"

"Not your father—and not that girl I saw at Blackfriars, that girl with the sly eyes. She's plans of her own, I'd say."

Cecily had opened her mouth to protest at *sly eyes*, but she closed it again, remembering her own sudden doubts of Alys yesterday.

"What plans?" she asked.

"How should I know? There's no need to bother with your Alys now." Dame Elizabeth put Cecily's hand from her, then, as though she had done with it for the time being. "It is almost dinnertime—you slept so late. I shall send Meg to help you today. But you must learn to look after yourself. We are not in the world of fashion here." She twitched at the bed-curtain in passing. "There's a rent in the damask; Meg shall mend it . . . And, Cecily—pray remember that God gave you a voice to speak out with, not to coddle underneath your breath."

She went out of the room, closing the door behind her. But the key did not turn.

# 2

## Her Father's Daughter

AFTER HER AUNT HAD GONE, CECILY STAYED A LONG time without moving. The strangeness of her state was almost overwhelming. Dame Elizabeth had called her a prisoner when she was at home, but what was she now? There was no escape from Mantlemass. If her father had been a jailer, what was her aunt? What, indeed, was her aunt? A woman unlike any other Cecily had heard of. At her husband's death she had instantly left his house by the river Thames at Sheen, near the royal palace, and come to this lonely place to make a new life, one unsupported by any but her own courage and determination. About this new jailer, then, if that was what she was to be called, Cecily felt deep curiosity.

She thought of her father and of how he too must make a new life. It was true that he had friends in France—once, in fact, she had been with him there herself. It was there that her mother had died of the sickness that struck them both. When the young Cecily recovered from this illness she could not even recall her mother's face. It was only in a curious, feverish dream that she believed she was able, even now, to recognize her voice. In this strange experience that came to her sometimes between sleep and waking, or when she had some chill or infection upon her, she saw first the smile of a dark-bearded man with a jewel in his ear; then a nodding, somber graybeard in a purple gown. Soon came a jumble of voices, the laughter of men and women crowding in a small chamber. Next there was a boy somewhere near her own age—she must still have been very young, since her mother was certainly there—a boy who advanced and greeted her, kissing her between the eyes as gently and quickly as some small shy animal that licks an offered hand then frisks away. . . . At this point the picture always began to fade, and as she lost it she seemed to hear her mother saying *My bird—my pretty bird* . . . Although she knew that it was she, the child Cecily, who was her mother's pretty bird, she always struggled to see clearly the device of a bird flying, carrying something in its beak. It could be a dove with a branch of olive—or a raven bearing a flower whose berries would be poison. . . .

They were ringing a bell somewhere below in the big house. That surely meant dinnertime, and Cecily began in a flustered way to pull her gown into place, dismayed by the fastenings and ready to cry at her own helplessness. Before that happened, one of the maids came running to help and then showed her the way to the hall.

Sir Thomas Jolland, it had been said, kept a state beyond his means and rank. But here at Mantlemass the whole way of life was different. The house was no more than ten or fifteen years old, a manor farm, a yeoman's dwelling of a kind increasingly to be found in the countryside. It was one of several such properties inherited by Dame Elizabeth from her husband. She held it from the Crown, and with it certain privileges—the right to keep hawk and hound for the taking of venison and game, and to collect rent from the tenantry.

"Come to table, niece," Dame Elizabeth said, turning from the knot of men she was talking to by the door. At this they bowed and left her. "Those are my fellow traders," she said. "You must understand that I am a trader now. And there is no call for any man or woman to smile at that. In fact I see you have more horror than humor in your expression."

"It pleases you to be sharp with me . . ." Cecily mumbled, at a loss to understand what her aunt was talking about.

"Well, it is all true as daylight and brings me pride, pleasure—and profit. I shall show you my trade presently. Now—come to your dinner."

Dame Elizabeth swept on into the hall, but Cecily hesitated on the threshold. The place seemed full of people and noisy with such boisterous talk as she had never heard before. When Sir Thomas entered his own hall, all fell silent and stood to do him a courtesy. But as Dame Elizabeth moved to her place, she merely added to the noise—shouting out to a man standing halfway down the table—leaning across to say something to a woman on the far side of the board, and breaking into laughter at her reply. It was only when the mistress of the house stood at the head of her own table that the household servants who would share the meal fell silent.

Cecily still hung back. The hall was a quarter of the size of her father's, with one long table and only two sideboards for serving. At one end was an enormous hearth with a canopied flue. It was not the mean size of the hall, however, or its heating arrangements that made Cecily hang back.

"Here is your place, niece," her aunt called—and

immediately twelve or fourteen heads were turned in the direction of the newcomer. "Come now, Cecily—these are my people and they shall be yours. You need not hide your face." She smiled at the girl, kindly enough, as she sat down nervously. "You will not have seen such a house as this, I daresay. I shall show you how it has many rooms, small and convenient. A great man's hall is as bustling as a marketplace. But we lesser folk are growing more private."

"So many windows," Cecily managed, in her small voice. "I have hardly seen so much glass, madam." She had hardly seen so many fellow diners, for that matter, for either she and Alys were served food upstairs or else there was none but her father at table with her.

"The glass comes from the west of this country," Dame Elizabeth said. "In summer the ways are hard and dry and I have ridden into those parts and seen the glass come liquid from the furnaces. A prettier sight than the iron worked by my own tenants hereabouts."

"Glass may be broken by intruders," Cecily offered, primly quoting what she had heard her father say.

"Perhaps—where intruders are to be found. Here we are all too busy. We depend one upon the other, as you will surely see. This is thought to be a wild part of the countryside and many outlaws seek refuge here. Yet we all serve and respect one another. The forest binds us, one to the other." She turned to Cecily and took the girl's hand in her own, holding it palm uppermost. "This is the hand of a cosseted gentlewoman. What skills has it?"

"It can embroider with silks."

"And—?"

"I have—I had—my lute."

"And—?"

Cecily was silent. She could think of nothing more a gentle hand need do.

"Now take my hand," said Dame Elizabeth. "This hand also is the hand of a gentlewoman. But it has taught itself to grow strong. It has learned many skills. This hand will bake, will brew, will write accounts fairly, will strike in anger, soothe in sickness, be silk or iron on a rein. It will cull herbs, bind up sores, carve meat, shear a fleece, or gut a coney. Yes, indeed—you will tell me it has grown hard with all this service. But I shall answer that it has grown proud."

"Yes, madam," said Cecily, wondering if her aunt was at least halfway to madness.

"And so, dear niece, shall yours."

Cecily clasped her threatened hand with its fellow. They were smooth hands, the fingers frail and pliable, graceful and useless. Yet honesty told her they could strike in anger as much as her aunt's hands might; and even her father had praised her for the way she could control her horse.

The rest of the company had all this time remained standing down either side of the table. Now there came hurrying to Dame Elizabeth's side a small, thin man in a shabby brown habit. Dame Elizabeth rose, and Cecily with her, and the newcomer said a somewhat breathless grace. After the amens, the maids began at once to serve the dinner.

Cecily was hungry by now, but distress at her aunt's talk, resentment at eating in this public fashion, closed up her throat and the good food would not go down. Was she to spend the rest of her life, then, in bondage to this unwomanly woman with her plain clothes and her downright way of speech? Was it for this that her father had kept her so carefully? *I have only one purpose,* her aunt had told her, *to give back what has been taken away.* She must have spoken whimsically—she could only have meant these simple employments that any woman might call her right but that a lady carefully nurtured would thankfully relinquish.

"She has come to be a daughter to me," Dame Elizabeth was saying to the friar. "Cecily, Friar Paul is here from time to time on his wanderings. He will hear our confessions and say a mass for us. . . . The child is sad at losing her father," she explained, "but I shall see that she is happy here as never in her life before." She smiled slightly. "As you will see, she doubts this."

"You are fortunate in a good guardian, my child," said Friar Paul. He was short of his front teeth and having some trouble with his dinner. "Give this good lady your daughterly duty and God will bless you both."

Cecily made some murmured reply, and then the conversation went on without her. Her aunt and the friar spoke of country things, of harvest and next year's sowing, of pannage for hogs and the grazing of sheep. There were complaints of a neighbor who had felled a copse five years too young, and that led on to the urgent problem of wood being cut for charcoal to keep the iron workings of that neighborhood going summer and winter.

"We suffer too much from this," Dame Elizabeth said. "The roads are broken into bog by the carting of the iron. We shall soon be living in a quagmire. We shall have no timber soon to mend the barn roof or keep our fences against the deer."

"But if men are given these materials in the earth and the skill to work them—there's a divine purpose that must be bowed to," the friar answered.

"There's little divinity in the muck and the row of the forges," Dame Elizabeth said coarsely. "And if men stopped their quarrels there'd be no need of weapons."

"So they would beat their swords into plow-shares," replied Friar Paul, unexpectedly chuckling, "and the noise would be just the same."

"Well, it is a song I find hard on my ears, Friar Paul. I am concerned with quieter ways of trade. Unless they are clumsily killed, my coneys are as silent as shadows."

None of this talk made the least sense to Cecily. Farther down the table, the conversation was even less intelligible, for it was full of strange words. Across the table from the maids sat two or three men whose employment Cecily tried to guess. One looked very quiet and clerkly, though he wore secular dress, and another, broad-shouldered and brusque in manner, with a fine red beard, seemed to be laying down the law to any prepared to listen —or unable to avoid hearing. He might be her aunt's bailiff, Cecily thought, while the thin dark man listening with a half smile was probably the manor reeve; he looked kindly, a good go-between for tenants and workers and dame of the manor alike.

"I come my way by Salehurst yesterd'y," Redbeard was saying, "and I doddled by a bit where they make a goodish warren on stoachy ground— pilrag, maybe. That'll be priory doing. Two of the monks come by Mantlemass last spring and saw our warrens, and took the notion."

"There's a slocksey way to talk of the brothers, Master Henty," said the dark man, with a warning glance toward Friar Paul. "What if the lady of the house hear what you say?"

"She does hear," said Dame Elizabeth, snapping into the conversation so roughly that Cecily flinched. "Mind your manners, Henty."

"No offense, madam," said Henty, but without humility.

"Then keep your opinions locked behind that fine great beard of yours—or there'll be offense in plenty and penalties to meet it." She called to one of the maids. "Serve me the salad now, Bet. And a dish here for Friar Paul." She glanced at Cecily. "Drink your ale, niece. It will nourish you."

Cecily drank obediently. The ale was strong and spicy and caught the back of her nose so sharply that she sneezed.

"God keep you," said her aunt. Those who heard her, and had heard the sneeze, crossed themselves quickly, for all the world as though they thought the newcomer might have brought the plague from London.

"It was the ale tickled me. I am used to wine," said Cecily sullenly. Talk broke out again and she sat silent, no longer even trying to make sense of what she heard. The voices had a roll to them, and this allied with the outlandish words left her bewildered and bitterly lonely. Even her aunt spoke differently—there was little trace in her speech of the London English Cecily knew, and still less of the pinched accents in which Alys had so often mocked fashionable ladies she had heard and that Cecily had often tried to imitate. These country people were worse than strangers—they were foreigners.

At last the meal ended, grace was said. Dame Elizabeth led the way from the table. Now, Cecily thought, she could be alone—she could run to her own room—she could bring the key to the other side of the lock and turn it firmly . . .

Perhaps her aunt knew this, for she instantly cut off all retreat.

"Now, my child, I shall show you Mantlemass. If this is to be your home, then you must know it, walls

and windows, barns and byres. Show me your feet.
. . . You shall be better shod once this dry spell is
past, but today you can manage well enough. Pick
up your skirts, or the hem will soon be soiled. We
must get you more sensible wear than this fine stuff.
Mary Butterwick and Meg shall set about it—Goody
Ann's sight is not strong enough these days." She
looked rather sharply at Cecily, who had made no
reply. "What did I say about your voice? I cannot
live with a silent niece."

The change in her circumstances seemed brutally
presented. Yet looking resentfully into her aunt's
face, Cecily could find no cruelty in Dame Elizabeth's expression. She might have seen courage,
boldness, honesty—and even loneliness, though
certainly she could not have named it. Groping for
reassurance, Cecily knew positively that though her
aunt might have a high anger, though she might
prove an opponent, she could not frighten. With
this conviction there came a quick faint lifting of
Cecily's spirit, so slight it was barely perceptible—
yet like a crumb to a starving man suggesting most
certainly that there was still bread in the
world. . . .

Dame Elizabeth was proud of her new-fashioned
manor house—she led the way to the winter parlor,
quite apart from the hall, where she said they would
dine in winter away from the drafts. Soon they came
to the kitchen, where a woman was scouring pots
with a girl and two kitchen boys to help her.
Kitchen, bakehouse, and brewery formed three
sides of an inner court, and in its center was the
well. The cellars ran alongside and below the hall,
well stocked with vats and butts. It was cold down
there. In the corners the floor ran with water that
trickled greenly in the rushlight Dame Elizabeth
carried. It seemed like a place to hide away an en-

emy from the light of day, to hide him till he was
forgotten, all but his bones. Cecily was glad to go
up the stairs again, and then up once more to the
bed chambers. Over these was a great loft reaching
into the roof rafters.

"This is where the maids sleep," Dame Elizabeth
explained. "Look how the chimney comes up from
below. Put your hand on the wall here—it is warm.
They are pampered, I can tell you."

The high roof of the hall divided the house into
two parts, and they had to descend and cross the
hall, then mount another stairway to the sun room.
Here the furnishings were very handsome indeed.
There were tapestries on the walls, and on the floor
too, in place of rushes. There was a fine carved
hope chest, two enormous high-backed chairs, and
many sconces to hold lights once dusk came down.
And propped on a carved stand was an open book
with letters picked out in gold, and designs of fruit
and flowers, birds, and animals in the wide margins.

"All these things were in my husband's house by
the river. It was too prodigal to leave them—though
I would have done so if it made any sense." Dame
Elizabeth's voice was noncommittal, but the words
painted a comfortless picture of a widow who could
have done without any reminder of the husband she
was rid of. She fingered the book, turning the magnificent pages. "You shall read to me, Cecily."

"I cannot read, madam."

Her aunt frowned. "Nor write?"

"Oh, yes—yes. My name. I can write Cecily Jolland."

"My brother does nothing by halves. I could read
and write when I was nine years old. And so could
he—our father would not have it otherwise. . . .
Well, Cecily Jolland, I shall teach you this as I shall
teach you many other things you need to know."

They went down the narrow stair and out of the house. The afternoon was so full of light that Cecily put up her hand to shield her eyes as she looked out over the wide countryside.

Mantlemass stood on a ridge of ground that stretched east and west almost in a straight line. The house faced defiantly south, while northward a stand of fine beech trees broke the coldest winds. Ahead of the main courtyard, which here was nothing grander than a wide stretch of beaten earth, the ground dropped away in increasingly shallow terraces that looked almost man-made. At last the land flattened into a narrow valley, and there the river ran. On the far side the ground rose again, but only to the west, and a quarter as high. Beyond, the view extended interminably over rolling countryside, half heath, half sprawling woodland that hung like a thick cloak on the shoulders of the hills. On the open ground were great spreads of heather, and among the trees there was already gold enough to prove that summer was passing. On the farthest horizon, barer hills stood against the sky.

"The ocean is beyond," Dame Elizabeth said. "It is something over twenty miles. Not too long a ride in good weather. Your mother's daughter should know how to sit a horse—your uncle, Lord Digby, could tell you something of that. Now come this way toward the farm. I shall show you my trade."

About the farm there was great activity, a number of men coming and going. Each of them Dame Elizabeth called by name, asking after wives and children, receiving replies that were free and friendly, open and without humility. They were her tenants and bound to serve her, but they seemed to regard her with a frankness that Cecily found a little shocking.

The farm had many buildings, the tithe barn biggest of all, but almost matched by its neighbors. All were built of stone, the color of honey streaked with treacle. It was the local stone, quarried for building in all these parts, but smelted too in the nearby furnaces for its iron ore. All these necessary buildings were thatched with fine reeds similar to those used for the floor of the hall.

Dame Elizabeth led the way toward a group of three buildings standing a little apart from the rest. She pushed open a heavy door and went inside. Cecily hesitated to follow, checked by the stench that was so strong she had to clap a hand over her nose and mouth. Her aunt called to her to close the door behind her, and she went in reluctantly. The building was stacked with piles of small dried pelts.

"You see," Dame Elizabeth said, taking up a pair and shaking them, "this is my trade, Cecily. I am a skinner, no less. These are coney skins. We breed the coneys in warrens on our own ground—you will see them presently. Rabbits are fine breeders, but they must be contained and kept from the crops. I have a growing trade in these skins. They sell to London for the trimming of mantles and caps. I sell also to France, and to the Low Countries, and to Italy—the fashion is on my side. This is how I prosper. This is why my hands have hardened, niece—in a manner I see you do not approve. In the next building I shall show you the skins stretched for drying. We pin them and leave them long in the sun before bringing the racks indoors." She looked at Cecily's wrinkling nose and laughed. "Yes—the smell is unfortunate. But no more odious than the smell of any other dead animal—including man. . . . Ah, you think me sadly coarsened. But you and I will eat and grow fat because I have hardened my hands and my heart and set about my own salvation. It is true I have this manor held from the

Crown. One day I may gain the freehold for myself and for my heirs, but meanwhile I depend for my living on myself—and am grateful that I do so."

As they came into the air again, the redbeard, Henty, was crossing the yard, bringing a small dark man who snatched off his cap the instant he saw Dame Elizabeth and bowed half a dozen times as he approached her.

"This is the Frenchman who sells my skins across the water," her aunt told Cecily. "Where are you going?" For the girl had turned away, pulling at her veil as if she would hide her face. "And what are you doing? I see I have quite forgotten fashionable ways. We live an honest, open life here. None of us is so bad that he may not look at his neighbor's face —and none too good to be looked at."

"My father—" began Cecily.

"You must learn to obey me now. But move apart, if you wish. I have business matters to attend to." She called out to the little dark man. "Good day to you. What bills have you brought me?"

Cecily looked about her. Privacy was not easily come by. Wherever she turned she saw people watching her curiously—a boy carrying an armful of skins, a herdsman with a dog at his heels, two dairy-maids with pails slung on yokes, an old man chopping wood, and a small, dirty-faced child, who came close, staring. Each of these people looked at her, smiling or solemn, shy or bold, and their interest was almost frightening.

She walked slowly away from the yard. She came over a little ridge and there she seemed shut off from prying eyes. A clump of bushes, brambles and gorse, sprawled down the slope, and she stepped a few yards that way, feeling at once curious and un-naturally bold. Here there was a spread of grass, cropped close, but clean. She sank down, curling

her feet up under her skirts, recalling as she did so
how her aunt's skirts swung above her instep like
those of any peasant woman, and how freely she
walked because of it—yet somehow lost no dignity.
Cecily sat frowning in the sunshine, plucking curious and unfamiliar thoughts from a mind that
whirled with resentment, with emotion and change.

Although the bustle of the farm continued out of
sight, utter stillness held all that she looked out
upon from her shelter. Beyond the river the young
trees stepped gracefully up the gentle slope, the
ground beneath them cleared and trampled into a
firm floor by pigs rooting for acorns. There was no
movement now among the trees, but over the little
river a heron flapped low and lazy, then dropped to
fish. She had watched such birds often from the
riverside in her father's London home, and their
distance as they settled in the far verges had seemed
infinite. The meadows beyond were a world she
would never enter, and she had seen no reason why
she should. Now, on the slopes of the forest, that
first day at Mantlemass, the almost unwelcome
thought came to Cecily that she might cross the
narrow water here and walk among the trees, if
indeed she chose.

A horse came picking its way over the hillside as
she watched, slithering every now and again on the
narrow track, reins slack on its neck as the rider let
the animal find its own way. The rider was a lad in a
torn shirt. Cecily could hear him whistling. He had
a brown dog with him, nosing and snuffling as it
came. The simple picture made by the boy, the dog,
and the horse filled Cecily with a feeling of warmth
and promise—as though there was an ease and contentment in life that she too might somehow share.

Her aunt's loud voice behind her made Cecily
spring to her feet. Dame Elizabeth was waving her

arms, fists clenched, and shouting across the valley at the boy on his horse.

"Lewis! Lewis Mallory! Get that dog off my land! It'll be the worse otherwise! Do you hear me, boy?" Her anger was only mocking, Cecily thought—she sounded as though she would as easily laugh as shout. "Heed what I say, Lewis Mallory! Off! Be off!"

The boy looked up. He pulled off his red cap and swept it in a low bow that threatened to tip him from the saddle. It was impossible to see his face, but he could only have been grinning. He twitched the horse's head and moved off among the trees, unhurried. Soon the woods had swallowed him.

"Must he not ride here, madam?" Cecily asked, gazing after him.

"The land is mine—though his people claim a right of passage over it. I cannot have dogs there— the mouth of one warren is above the river. Besides, he'll be in trouble if he runs his dog so freely. The verderers and those who should keep the forest for the Crown have grown slack enough, but a new king may stir them up. There are strict laws about the keeping of dogs and hawks—horses too, though we have a dispensation."

"Then why does he ride there?"

"I have told you his people claim they have right of way. It is a shortcut from the high road to Ghylls Hatch. That's the Orlebars' farm, where the boy belongs."

"You called him by another name," said Cecily.

"Mallory. Orlebars are cousins to Mallorys, though in a humble kind."

The boy had looked humble enough himself, Cecily thought, with his tattered shirt; she pictured the Orlebars as crude peasants scratching a living from barren ground; though both names, Orlebar and

Mallory, had a good Norman ring to them. The boy's gesture, his mocking bow and refusal to make any haste, went better with his name than with his clothes.

"Have you heard the name spoken?" her aunt was asking.

"Orlebar, madam?"

"Mallory . . . No—I see it means nothing to you. Yet when I chose my new home—and I could have had one of five manors about England—I chose Mantlemass because my neighbor's name was known to me."

Cecily smiled rather loftily—so much concern for such people . . . "You make it sound a mystery."

"Perhaps it is; though not of my making. . . . Come indoors now."

"But pray—unravel the mystery first."

"I may not have the means."

"Then tell me the parts of the riddle," Cecily urged, frowning and impatient.

"Not now. But keep your heart up. It is almost certain we shall both see the solution one of these days."

# 3

## Mallory and Orlebar

As soon as he was out of sight of Mantlemass, Lewis whistled up his dog and got on his way. He was still grinning to himself at Dame Elizabeth's furious shouts, for he had known her a long time—her bark was ferocious but her bite was practically unknown. He had been only ten years old when she came to Mantlemass and he to Ghylls Hatch. They had met for the first time when she found him crying in the forest because he had decided to run away from his cousin's house, and he had lost himself almost immediately. First she had scoffed at his tears, then she had called him a coward; and then she had told him to run back quickly to Ghylls Hatch on the path she would show him, for she would like to know that she was to have him for her neighbor. That was something he had never forgotten—people seldom spoke so reasonably and kindly to a mere child. There were many miserable moments during that first year in his cousin's household, but he did not think of running away again. Dame Elizabeth never came to Ghylls Hatch without asking for him, and they had fallen into a teasing way together—so that when she bellowed at him he knew her shouts could easily turn to laughter, and when he defied her and flouted her orders they both knew that he would never do anything to distress or harm her. . . . It was said that Dame Elizabeth's niece had come to Mantlemass now, and that might have been the girl he had noticed standing beside her as she shouted to him about the dog. A girl in a rich gown that looked strange, if not ridiculous, next to Dame Elizabeth's homespun.

He rode on along the familiar track, Mantlemass and Mantlemass land away behind him and the open pastures that surrounded Ghylls Hatch opening up to the north. There were six colts in the bottom enclosure, tearing in wide and wider circles, their manes and tails flying. It would be his job and his pleasure to take a hand in breaking them when the time came. Skittish as they were now, they showed already some sign of the deep-chested weight carriers they would become. Lewis Mallory's cousin Orlebar bred horses for battle and for jousting, a profession he had inherited from his father. For his own pleasure, he also bred swifter animals for the chase. If a lad was obliged to leave his own home, his parents and his brother, and come to a new way of life, then none was better than this one; Lewis was quite certain of that by now. And because to recall the past baffled and disturbed him, it often seemed as if his life had begun somewhere about his tenth birthday.

"But why must I come here? Why must I stay?" he had cried in despair in those early days.

"You are to be my heir," his cousin had replied.

And the boy had looked around Ghylls Hatch and seen only a meager inheritance, thinking of how much would have been his if he had not been inexplicably passed over by his father in favor of his younger brother. . . . Nowadays he looked at the horses, at the broad acres won over the years from the forest, and his fortune seemed fair enough.

"Pick up your feet, you sloven!" he told Diamante as she pecked at the hillside. He put her into a canter, calling again to the dog, and the three of them made quick work of the last mile home.

When Lewis rode into the yard, Master Orlebar was in the stables with a lame mare. He emerged with a long face, saying the animal would be good for nothing after this and might as well have her throat cut, for the tendon was hopelessly damaged.

"She'll make a good brood," Lewis said.

"She was bred for the chase."

"Even so. We can put her to Ebony or Duke and she'll more than make her keep."

"She was bred for the chase, boy."

"And so shall her progeny be," insisted Lewis, every bit as stubborn as his cousin.

At this Roger Orlebar laughed a little, for he and Lewis had come to understand one another very well.

"How if I give her to you?"

"Give her to me? Give me Iris?" Lewis sounded incredulous. "If you truly mean that, cousin—"

"I do. I do. It is time you had your own responsibilities. Not that I mean you to neglect mine in consequence."

"When I sell my first foal I'll pay you back her keep," Lewis promised. "And then the line shall be mine forever after."

Now Orlebar was laughing deeply from his big throat. He was a short square man, black-with-gray about the hair and beard, with surprising blue eyes that looked too mild for his disposition, and a certain modesty, or shyness, in his manner. He had proved a good substitute for a father, though he had no sons of his own. His father having been a gentleman who willfully chose country ways, Roger Orlebar had been brought up here in the forest and had never been sent out into the world for his education, as a gentleman's son should be. He was an unsuitable husband for any bride his father had considered worthy, and too proud himself to marry a country girl. His sister Jenufer kept his house, at least nominally. But she was so simple as to be spoken of as half-witted.

She was coming from the kitchen as Lewis went indoors. Ghylls Hatch consisted of a straggle of buildings, and the family lived in the largest, a small yeoman's dwelling that had been put in order by Roger Orlebar's father. The place was ill cared for, but since there was no true lady of the house, nobody noticed this. The same rushes lay on the floor from year's end to year's end.

Jenufer, a tiny wispy woman older than her brother but girlish, often distressingly so, in her manner, was in her good mood today—a pleasant alternative to those days when she wandered about the house weeping, tears pouring, but making no sound. She ran to Lewis and seized his hands and shook them up and down.

"Where have you been, my lovely boy?"

"Past Mantlemass." He stooped and kissed her cheek. "Dame Elizabeth shouted at me. She had a stranger at her side."

"My brother says her niece has come to stay. And she screamed and fought and bit because she had no wish to remain there. Anis Bostel came from Mantlemass with a cheese, and she said it was so."

"She did not look as though she would bite, Cousin Jenufer. I think you have been nabbling, you and the Mantlemass reeve's wife."

"Well, I shall never speak with the girl," said Jenufer, sticking up her chin and pursing her lips, "for her family and ours have disagreements."

"Her family? Her father can only be Dame Elizabeth's brother. We have no disagreements with her."

"Well, this girl—this girl's father . . ." Jenufer began to look troubled and her voice trailed off into a murmur. "I cannot recall his name. He is—who? I cannot tell at all. It has quite gone from my mind . . . Oh, how shall I remember?"

"There," Lewis said, "what does it matter?" He hated to see her worried. "It is nothing to the point," he assured her. "Not near so much as brushing your hair like a lady, cousin. And where is your cap? What a slattern you look, to be sure."

"I'll do it," she said. "Now." And she ran away quickly, as light as a girl.

Roger Orlebar had come into the house, and he watched his sister run away.

"She should have a new gown for winter," he said. "Poor blessed soul, I am a sad brother to her, always forgetting her needs. I'll see about some yarn and you shall ride with it to the weaver. One of the maids can cut and stitch the cloth when it's done —Susan is neatest and cleanest. Ah, poor Jenufer— poor Jenufer. What a burden!"

When they had done with supper, Roger Orlebar sat at the cleared table, peering by rushlight at his bills of accounting that he read with difficulty and calculated with much reckoning on his fingers. Lewis escaped before he could be called upon to help.

The night was clear with a moon moving into the second quarter. Lewis took the track that ran south and west from Ghylls Hatch. He felt elated by the business of the mare and he came very quickly to the priest's house by the old, half-ruined palace. Though it was called a palace, it was in fact a hunting lodge; but kings had come there to hunt and so made the place royal. The chapel, however, was maintained in good shape, thanks largely to the chaplain. It was a curious benefice. Day by day the priest, Sir James, said mass in the chapel and performed every office of the holy calendar. Sometimes his congregation was two or three; sometimes there was none but himself to pray. If he was free of work at the right hour, Lewis would serve mass for him. This was a man he respected and loved quite beyond his priestly importance. The priest was long past middle life but carried his years buoyantly. He had thick white hair and a skin browned by all weathers. He lived off his own bit of land, tithes from his few parishioners—these were contested by the parish priest of the church in the village four miles or so away—and the venison that was a perquisite of his office; he could take two bucks a year for himself, and he would enjoy the meat fresh until he sickened of it, cure what he could by smoking it in his own chimney, and give the rest to the needy.

Sir James had taken upon himself to give Lewis some sort of learning. He had taught him to read, to write, to calculate; to name the stars; to watch the life of the forest, bird and plant and animal, and to interpret the science of heraldry. He had also taught him to forgive injustice, to accept a humble place in life without rancor, to play the lute and recorder, and to sing.

"You are my choir, my deacon, and my pupil," the priest often told Lewis. "I should have had a poor time of it, these years, if you had not been sent to me."

So this evening he was glad to see Lewis, and drew him to sit by the fire immediately.

"And what have you done through the length of this fine day, my son?"

"Worked before noon, worked afternoon, rode in late afternoon, and ate my supper like a grateful Christian. . . . The best news is, my cousin has given me the chestnut mare, Iris—that went so lame —and I am to breed from her for my own profit. So this day is important, Father. I have become a man of affairs."

"And does that mean you will stay the rest of your days at Ghylls Hatch as your cousin Orlebar has done? And see nothing of the world?"

"It might be so."

"You are the son of a noble and prosperous gentleman, Lewis. Is it enough for you to stay a forester?"

"You will recall that the noble and prosperous gentleman disowned me and preferred my brother. I am content with what I have. I have forgotten ten years. Yes, Father, it is enough to stay a forester. Though I'll not stay a bachelor, like my cousin. A country girl can make me a good enough wife, I daresay. I am past seventeen and should be thinking where to seek her."

"There is no hurry," Sir James said.

Lewis laughed. He did not see many girls and was wary of those he did see—at farms and cottages about the forest, and in church on Sundays, not at the palace chapel, but in the village. Some of these were so lumpish he could not tolerate the thought of them. But some had charm. Master Urry, who smelted iron over in the southeast corner of the forest, had three shy flaxen-haired daughters, and he had kissed the youngest last Christmas, in the dark, as they left the church after the first mass of the day. And there was a girl at the mill he had admired—though his cousin Jenufer assured him she was no better than she should be.

"When I have chosen a wife," Lewis said, "none but you shall marry us."

"There is no hurry," the priest said again, frowning slightly. And he began to speak of other things, of forest matters, of the determination of that same Master Urry to use a great hammer driven by water to beat out his iron; and how he had been laughed at by those who went to work less ambitiously. "The skills they're happy with have barely changed since the days of the Romans," Sir James said. "Master Urry looks to the future and newer ways."

"Will it work—the big hammer?" Lewis wondered.

"Not there, where he is trying. The water is too little, and the ground too flat. But I wish him well of his ambitions. Though it will make a devilish enough noise when he succeeds."

"That'll enrage Dame Elizabeth," Lewis said. "Already she complains of the noise—and that's beating by hand." He grinned as he spoke of her. "We all say the same, Father—do you notice? How will this seem to Dame Elizabeth? What will Dame Elizabeth do? Beware of Dame Elizabeth! She rules the forest, it seems to me."

"A fine woman who might well be a bitter one. A hard life, my son—she has had a hard life. Her tongue may be sharp but she is a good friend when a friend is needed."

"I know it," Lewis said. "How was her life hard?" He often tried to trip the priest into confidences and rarely succeeded, but tonight Sir James spoke out because he wished to defend Dame Elizabeth. He said she had suffered a sad marriage.

"You mean she has no children—and that has caused her sadness?"

"Women can seldom choose how their lives shall be lived. She was wed to a man of some standing . . . Lewis Mallory, this is tittle-tattle—I'm being a nabbler, as these people say."

"A man of some standing—but . . . ?"

"Well, there is no secret in it. FitzEdmund. The name speaks for itself. He was royally connected—but not in wedlock. He had his own misfortunes—a crooked back besides a crooked birth, and no doubt these things worked on him. We must not judge him —but he was a cruel man."

"Was it her father made her wed?" the boy asked.

"Her ambitious brother . . . Lewis, that is all I may say. It will be forgiven me, for it excuses some harshness in her."

"They say her niece has come to Mantlemass. Is she the daughter of that same ambitious brother? Then what may he have in store for her?"

He remembered the girl standing on the edge of the farmyard in her fine clothes. He had little occasion to think fondly of his own father—but at least he seemed free to choose whom he would marry.

"Take the lute," said Sir James, putting an end to the conversation, "and I will have the recorder. We'll have some music to send you home tranquil— and it must be soon, or you'll find the door barred against you."

It was some time before Roger Orlebar obtained yarn for his sister's gown. Lewis would take it to the weaver, who was to dye it, for there was none more skilled than he in this particular.

"And let it be a fine purplish mulberry," Jenufer decided. "Now tell him my wishes, cousin—a fine mulberry I must have."

"Then mulberry it shall be," Lewis said. "But

when it comes home you must promise not to expect saffron, or scarlet, or blue."

"I never change my mind," she said positively,
"and that you should know as well as I do."

There had been rain at night in the past weeks
and this had advanced the season. Soon the colored
leaves would fall to the first frost; the bracken, already gold, would flame before it died. The preparation for winter, proceeding steadily from the harvest, would speed to a frenzy against the first
snowfall that so often came before Christmas, gripping the forest for a week or more before releasing
it until the severe and lasting falls of January. The
weaver's cottage was a few miles from Ghylls Hatch,
set halfway up a shallow bank and approached
across a ford. The stream was only four feet wide
and very gentle. Lower down it was dammed and
slid over a gushing weir into a pool. Here the
weaver, Halacre—or Halfacre, according to some—
bleached, shrank, and tented his stuff on pegged
frames.

Halfway between Ghylls Hatch and the weaver's
cottage there was a track that ran double, the one
part three or four feet higher than the other, with a
screen of trees between. Lewis rode on the higher
track, idling because the day was fine. It was some
time before he caught a glimpse of riders on the
lower path. He heard a woman's voice—indisput-
ably that of Dame Elizabeth FitzEdmund. Occasionally a lighter, softer voice replied—lighter and
softer, but a little sullen. Lewis was too curious to
forgo the privilege of eavesdropping.

It was soon apparent that he was not the only one
taking yarn to the weaver.

"It shall be a russet red," Dame Elizabeth was
saying, "for this is a color at which he excels. A
warm color for winter too. That reminds me, niece,

that the cloak you rode in when you came from London is not heavy enough for our winter."

"I shall stay indoors," said the girl.

"I could spare skins enough to line the hood and shoulders," Dame Elizabeth said, ignoring the reply. "Perhaps even a little more. Second-quality fur, but very well for such a purpose." Then she paused and waited, but the girl said nothing. "At least," said her aunt very dryly, "I will do it if you will thank me."

"I do thank you, madam," murmured the girl.

"But today is a black day with you, and so you wish to punish me for being thoughtful!"

"No, madam."

"*Yes,* madam," said Dame Elizabeth.

Lewis nearly laughed aloud. He rode very carefully and Diamante seemed to sense his caution, for she trod so lightly no twig snapped to betray them. The two women remained unaware that they were overlooked, though sometimes Lewis was quite close, peering down at them through the trees whose leaves had conveniently thinned. The girl was riding a rough little chestnut mare that had gone to Mantlemass from Ghylls Hatch a year or two previously—Cressyd was her name. The girl rode gracefully, straight-backed and light-handed. Country women rode like bundles, Lewis always complained, or else they never stirred except pillion behind their husbands or their fathers or their sons. Cressyd was quite a pretty little creature, though she was poorly groomed at present, but the boy decided that her rider deserved a better mount. The idea pleased him. He would see if he could persuade Dame Elizabeth to let her niece try the beautiful gray Zephyr, the finest of them all.

Lewis kept his distance, and when the weaver's cottage came into view, he hung back behind the screening trees to watch. Dame Elizabeth moved swiftly on a track long familiar, but the girl followed more warily until her aunt looked back and called. Then she hurried—but Lewis could tell from the set of her shoulders that she was in a bad humor. Poor thing—she was a stranger here, and he could remember what that meant, though for him it was long past. He watched her pick her way across the ford, then speed Cressyd up the hillside. Though she was in a bad humor she showed none of it in her treatment of the little chestnut, and Lewis warmed to her. Dame Elizabeth was already calling to the weaver and he came hurrying to greet her. It was noticeable that he did so without any humility. He laid his hand on her bridle and looked up smiling and confident. These forest people, Lewis knew, had no fear of the lady of Mantlemass, whether or not they were her tenants. Her brusque manner, her loud commanding voice that was nonetheless without arrogance, was acceptable to them—they respected her firmness because it went hand in hand with fairness.

"We have brought you an autumn task," she was saying to the weaver. "Your best weaving for the best sort of yarn. Let me see what dyes you have at present."

"Come to the vats, lady," he said. "You know the way as I do."

She dismounted while he held the horse's head, then, instead of tethering the creature, she tossed the rein to her niece, who had now reached her side. The girl's astonishment was obvious—she might as well have spoken aloud: *Does she think I am her groom?* But she said nothing, and sat like a statue, holding big Farden as she had been bidden. At this short distance Lewis could see that her fine gown had become very draggled about the hem. Her veil showed signs of having been roughly fingered by branches and briars, but it would have filled any local maid with envy. She still looked too grand for any country lad to speak to without fawning. On a leather thong around his neck, hidden in his shirt, Lewis wore a ring engraved with his family crest. He had stolen it from his father's closet on the day he was sent from home—and he wished he might display it to prove his quality.

He prodded Diamante and in his turn rode over the little river. He knew the girl was watching and he made his approach up the hillside a showy affair, bringing Diamante prettily on to her haunches before leaping from the saddle. He stood for a fraction of a second, wondering whether to conclude the gesture by asking her to hold his horse, since she was holding one already; but he had not quite the impertinence to do it. He contented himself with snatching off his red cap, bowing extravagantly, and calling "God save you, lady." He tied up Diamante and went striding on and into the cottage after Dame Elizabeth. He had to stoop at the door, not because he was unusually tall, but because it was a mean entry. As he turned his back on the girl he was conscious that his leather jerkin was slit across the shoulders where he had broadened over the last six months or so.

Dame Elizabeth and the weaver had passed through the cottage to where six or eight vats of dye stood under a thatched lean-to shelter, or cove.

"The russet," Dame Elizabeth was saying, and she handed her yarn to the weaver, nodding to Lewis.

"The russet, then, it shall be," he said. "And what for you, Lewis Mallory?"

"A mulberry. It is for my cousin Jenufer."

"How does that poor soul fare?" Dame Elizabeth asked.

"I think as usual, madam. Neither sad nor gay for long."

"I shall come visiting shortly. I have business to discuss with Master Orlebar. I need marl for my fields from the Ghylls Hatch pits, and I think he will spare it to me."

"I know he will," Lewis answered. "Shall it be your men to dig it, or ours?"

"It shall be mine," said Dame Elizabeth firmly, far too good a businesswoman, as he very well knew, to add to the price by employing another man's labor. "And tell your cousin that my man, Nicholas Forge, has been about my accounts in London, and the talk there is all of the new king and the new ways. Riding home, he met with the forest reeve—by spring or summer there's to be a survey of all royal parks and chases, of freeholds and copyholds and cattle. So tell your cousin we must all look to our boundaries and stand firm for our rights."

"I'll tell him, madam," Lewis promised. Then he handed the weaver his hanks of yarn for Jenufer's new gown.

"No more than a quarter as fine as what our good lady has brought me," Halacre grumbled, fingering the yarn and pulling a long face. "There'll be nubbles in the cloth, most likely. Bad spinning—though the texture of the wool's fairly suent."

"Do your best, then."

"Surely. A bit of good sewing after I've done my part, and the lady shall look gimsy enough."

"As gimsy as the maid at your door, weaver," said Lewis, since Dame Elizabeth by now was moving on her way and should be out of earshot.

"That's a poor pretty thing and no mistake," the

weaver replied. "Too delicate for these parts and I can only pray she'll settle."

"How long will she stay?"

"That none knows. They say her father's gone into France. He was the last king's man, they say."

"Who told you so?"

"I do forget that, percizely," the weaver said.

He stood at Lewis's side and they looked out through the cottage to the sunshine on the far side. In the frame of the small doorway they saw Dame Elizabeth mounting and riding away, and the girl following. She glanced back once over her shoulder, then moved out of sight.

"She see you," said the weaver. He looked up into Lewis's face and laughed gently.

# 4

## Her Aunt's Niece

WEEKS AGO CECILY HAD GROWN SICK OF HER LONDON gown, with its dirty hem. Fine-lady clothes seemed increasingly out of place as she watched her aunt so free among her tenants and her house servants. The forest was not such an unpeopled desert after all—only it was dwelt in by such as she would not have supposed worth any notice. She listened to Dame Elizabeth talking to Anis Bostel, the reeve's wife, about her children; discussing the horses with Simon Carter, to whom they were his family; inquiring of Nicholas Forge on his return from London if he had met with his sister while he was away, and how was her marriage going? It was not only coneys and coney skins and orders for distant places that Dame Elizabeth talked over with red-haired Henty —she was concerned for his only son, born blind and for his daughter, who cared for the boy, since their mother was dead, and who had been asked in marriage but would not leave her father and brother to be looked after by strangers. Janet in the dairy would never go home to visit her mother because she boxed her ears; Meg cried because nobody seemed eager to marry her; Goody Ann had lost her last tooth and must be especially cared for . . . a need to become a part of all this stirred and grew in Cecily, and it was her unsuitable dress that seemed to isolate her. It must be weeks before the cloth could be fetched from the weaver. . . .

"Perhaps, madam," she said at last awkwardly to her aunt, "there is some old gown of your own that could be made to fit me . . ." She looked quickly at Dame Elizabeth, who, however, showed no sign of finding the suggestion unusual. She did not raise her eyebrows nor smile in a manner that would seem to say: *So you have come to your senses.*

"There's a blue wool that might serve," she said. "Somewhere about the color of your own. I'll see how it is."

Cecily had asked for the gown, but when it was cut down to her size the rather faded blue disgusted her. She plucked at the neck, finding it harsh against her skin. She thought of Alys, of the silks and the velvets that had come to her father's house, bales and bales brought by merchants because Sir Thomas Jolland had a name for loving fine things. These men would be waiting somewhere in the outer quarters while Alys looped and draped the stuff, sweeping and strutting across the floor to show off the folds . . . Cecily put her hands to her face, hungry for the memory of Alys, who—sly-eyed or no—had made her feel she could do no wrong. . . .

"Be still a moment," said Mary Butterwick, who was measuring the hem of the blue dress. "Else I'll get it curly as a shepherd's crook."

Cecily looked down and saw her feet and ankles uncovered for all the world to stare at.

"Too short! It's too short!"

"Longer, it'll trail in the gubber," Mary said.

"Lord, girl, talk Christian talk or be silent! *Gubber* makes no sense to me."

"Gubber's stoach," explained Mary patiently.

"I can't tell a word you speak!" Yet *stoach* did seem to explain itself. "If you mean mud, why can't you say so?"

"That'll be spilt with a long hem," said Mary, beginning to flush and stammer as she strove to make herself clear.

*"Spilt?"*

"Stoach—I mean mud, lady—mud'll spoil it," Mary managed.

Cecily again considered the hemline and her own feet. The feet looked distressingly sturdy. The display of ankle was appalling. If her father saw her now he would surely beat her for immodesty . . . But he could not see her. He would not be back to see her yet, that was sure. There was a great deal he must do before he could send for her to join him— wherever he might be. Why—it could be a year, two years. Perhaps he would never come, finding more important things to do, glad to be rid of her. . . . She could not cast off years of closely ordered up-bringing to say she was glad to be rid of him—that would be a dreadful thing for any daughter. But she was glad to be rid of the fear that he caused her—to be without that was almost to be reborn.

The feel of the hem swishing against her ankles gave Cecily a sudden sensation of daring, of free-dom, and as she pictured herself in her imagination —striding slightly, in imitation of her aunt—all thoughts of Alys and of her father's return became unimportant.

"Very well," she said. "Stitch it, then. I am in the country now and I must forget courtly ways."

This grand expression and the manner in which

she made it, sighing gracefully, letting her hands hang limply away from her body, caused Mary Butterwick to look awed and respectful.

"And did you see the court, then, lady?"

"Of course. Often," said Cecily, not quite truthfully, for she had been once only. Something at the time had angered her father—Alys said it was that too many gallants admired her—and after that he had kept her closer than ever before. "The ladies at court wear tall headdresses like butterflies' wings, Mary. Gold thread is stitched into their veils. Their foreheads are high and smooth—except when the hair grows again that they have carefully plucked out."

"Never so!" cried Mary, sitting back on her heels. "Plucked out? I'd bawl with the pain! Oh, you quite frit me, you do indeed! You never did so heathen a thing yourself, that I trust?"

"Maybe—and maybe not," said Cecily. She remembered the time she had set Alys to plucking out the hair. The tears streamed from her eyes at every tweak, till she was sobbing with pain and Alys refused to go on. "And how am I to wear my hair now, Mary Butterwick?" she demanded. "Will you stitch me a cap like yours?"

"This evening, I will—if the mistress allow me a light."

The dress and the cap were ready by next morning. Now grown accustomed to looking after herself, Cecily was soon into the dress. Then she tried the white linen cap. Mary's covered all her hair but a few reddish curls that hung out on the nape of her neck. Cecily's fit very snugly, fastening under the chin, but her long fair hair hung free down her back, for there was too much of it to conceal. It made her nervous to leave it uncovered but there was nothing else to be done. She wished she could see how she looked. At home in her father's house she had had a looking glass of her own, but she had seen none at Mantlemass; no doubt her aunt despised such vanity. She looked down at the woolen dress, at the hem swinging above such shoes as she had never worn before. The cobbler in the village had made them skillfully enough, but they felt heavy as lead after the deerskin slippers she was accustomed to.

It was time to go down to prayers. Goody Ann was already ringing the paternoster bell that hung by the big studded door. The door would be standing open and there would be entering a whole crowd of people Cecily now knew by name—the Bostels and their children; Henty and his daughter; the secretary, Nicholas Forge, with his old mother; and all the maids and indoor servants. But those who worked outside, the herdsmen and Sim Carter and the dairymaids and all the rest—always slipped in by the small side door and stood against the wall. There it was to be hoped that the blessings asked for would still fall on them.

Cecily stood some time at her door, listening. She had by now become accustomed to moving about among a number of people, but this morning she had a new face, a new Cecily Jolland to present to them all. An angry shyness overwhelmed her and she had to force herself down the stairs. She went as quickly as possible to take her place beside her aunt.

"God bless you, my child," said Dame Elizabeth, quite gently. Her glance flicked over the blue gown, the white cap, the long fair hair. She turned her attention to conducting her household's devotions. After the last amen she gave them her orders for the day. "Now come with me, niece," she said.

They went out of the hall and across the yard in

the bright early morning. Dame Elizabeth made for the dairy. The maids were ahead of her and there was a fine noise and argument going on, for there was a shortage of salt. Each girl furiously blamed the other, but silence fell when the mistress of the house walked in.

"You must use the salt set aside for herrings. Go to the kitchen and ask Moll Thomsett for the crock —and say I sent you if you want to save yourself from her sharp tongue. You, Agnes Bunce—you're the strongest to carry the crock." Agnes rushed away, and then Dame Elizabeth said to Cecily, "To-day Janet shall teach you how to churn butter."

Cecily had been ready, so she thought, to please her aunt if possible. But at this indignity she was filled with black rage.

"Maybe I am your countrified niece, madam; but I am no dairymaid."

"Nor I. Yet I can do as I command others, I thank heaven."

"You have put me into country clothes," cried Cecily, "and now I see why. I am to be your servant!"

"You asked for the plain gown. And I have plenty of servants."

"Then let them churn, for I will not."

"Bread can always be eaten dry," said Dame Elizabeth, quitting the dairy.

Cecily saw Janet looking at her open-mouthed. "Don't stare, girl!" she snapped. She ran out of the dairy and hid inside the nearest barn while she fought with tears of fury. Yet these, if indeed they fell, would be less painful tears than any she had shed since babyhood. Like a scared animal that is rigid in despair, then turns on those who have caged it, Cecily's spirit was rising. Not only her appearance had changed, but her thoughts and her impulses—how had she dared speak to her aunt as she had just done? She knew she had to ask forgiveness, and she ran out of the barn and almost went ankle-deep into a puddle spreading where the churns had been swilled out with spring water. The sun turned the puddle into the mirror she lacked and, looking down, Cecily saw herself reflected, head to toe. She saw a stranger. She stood there looking and looking, not at her father's daughter— but at her aunt's niece. It was all too clear, as she watched the scowl gradually easing from her reflected face, how her apology should be offered.

She struggled against the necessity, beating her clenched fists together painfully. But there was no escape from her conscience. She went slowly but firmly back to the dairy, slamming open the door with her last flare of resentment.

At last it was time to go to the weaver to inquire after the russet cloth. Cecily should go herself, Dame Elizabeth said.

"Who shall go with me?"

"You know the way."

"I cannot—" began Cecily; then paused. They were in the barn where the skins were sorted. Cecily looked sideways at her aunt, who was weighing a batch of skins, one against the other, for pricing. There was a rhythm to the work as the skins were tossed into two heaps, the good and the indifferent. "Do you mean I should ride alone, madam?"

"What do you fear?" With a piece of chalkstone Dame Elizabeth marked each pelt before throwing it on to its appropriate heap.

"It is not that I *fear* . . ." murmured Cecily.

"But you think a gentlewoman should not ride abroad unattended. What have I told you? We live differently here. Treat the forest as your own parkland. Be a woman, Cecily," she said—much as a father might say to his son: *Be a man*.

Cecily said no more. Part of her hesitation was less a matter of convention than of sheer incredulity. It seemed impossible that such things should happen to her. Sometime after noon she herself asked Simon Carter to saddle up Cressyd. It was the first time she had ever given an order in her own behalf.

"I am to ride to Halacre, the weaver," she said, waiting to see if Simon frowned or looked astonished, as any servant of her father's would have done.

"And a good day for it," he replied. "Cressyd know her way. Not like old Farden, now. He's a sworly beggar and a proper scambler."

Cecily had no idea what that meant, but she smiled and the man smiled back. He brought the mare around himself and helped her to mount. She moved off at once toward the forest track that led two miles or so to the weaver's cottage.

The scene was changing. There had been several sharp frosts and today there was a keen wind blowing from the southeast. At the head of the track Cecily pulled in her horse. She was moving into a different world where she would no longer be protected but must rely upon herself. If she lost her way, then she must find it again. If the horse stumbled and threw her, then she must pick herself up and remount—and no one would cry out that the horse had been at fault. Ever since she had changed her gown and learned to walk in hard shoes, and had handled a churn in the dairy, Cecily had become each day bolder. But this journey alone was the culmination of her new experiences. As she hesitated, looking down the track, she knew that once having ridden out by herself, she would have en-

joyed something it would be almost impossible to
forgo. As she accepted this thought she accepted
another—that in the house by London's river she
had lived like a painted, tottering image of a girl,
while here she might one day become herself. *She
shall be happy here as never in her life before*—that was
what her aunt had said to Friar Paul. And it could be
true. But for how long?

She twitched the bridle, twitching away her
doubts as she did so. Cressyd moved off at once.
The track immediately descended and curved a little toward the south. The house, the farm, and all
that lived and moved about them were snatched
from view. Ahead the heath opened up briefly, then
melted into true forest. More than half the leaves
were down now, and beneath the beeches the
ground was as bright as the trees' highest tops. The
bracken by the side of the track looked as if it had
caught sparks from that blaze and broken into
flame. Briefly, as the horse descended toward the
trees, there was the sound of metal on metal, ugly
and powerful. Then that receded and was finally
carried away. Robins sang piercingly among the
scrub.

In the stillness and silence of the hollow in which
she found herself, Cecily heard this song and the
small sounds of birds calling in alarm at her passing, shifting among the branches, flying like arrows
above her head. Cressyd pricked her ears as a rabbit
bolted out of the bracken and away with a strong
*pad pad* of hard-clawed feet on dry ground. Horse
and rider, content together, moved along the narrow bottom, then jogged gently up the next incline,
coming out above a second valley. They were still
sheltered from the wind and the sounds it carried,
but here the river gushed noisily, dropping loudly
and lustily over sharp edges of rock, then spreading

into pools. Riding down the bank side, Cecily could see the water winking among the shifting branches of small trees, almost leafless now.

Then she heard a new sound. Down by the pool someone was whistling quietly. She paused. Curiosity was still new to her. She gave it its head as she gave Cressyd hers.

She was almost certain who she would find.

Alongside the pool Lewis had paused to see if his old friend and enemy, a fine brown trout, had got through the summer and was facing the winter in good health. He was on his way to the forge in the village, to find the smith and beg a day of his time for Ghylls Hatch. Their own man was sick, coughing so badly that he seemed unlikely to recover. The fine afternoon was too good to waste on nothing but a working-day errand, and to spin it out Lewis had chosen to walk. This pool in its clearing, with the young surrounding trees to make it private, had always been one of his delights. It was near enough home to take away any feeling of truancy, and far enough away for no one to know where he was. It was his place, his own, where seldom another soul passed by. So he broke off whistling and leapt up in a rage when he heard a horse on the track. Then he recognized Cressyd and after that her rider.

Lewis pulled off his red cap and stood waiting. He was silent but smiling now. He stood easily, and Cecily would have said he looked more like one of the young squires she had watched serving their masters at her father's table than like the countryman he seemed to be. He watched Cressyd picking her way down the track. Then he saw how the girl was changed, her fine clothes gone, her hair down her back, her veils exchanged for a plain linen cap.

Yet she retained some difference, and in a way they both looked strangers to this place. He accepted that she was a stranger, but she did not know yet, he presumed, that he had not been born and spent all his years on the forest.

"A good day to you," he said as she came near. "You're bringing the mare to drink, I see."

"Yes," she said. He was not to know that this was the first time she had ever spoken to a stranger, and the first time she had found herself unattended in the presence of man or boy. Or that she was finding it a good deal less alarming than she had been led to expect.

"There's shallow water this end of the pool," he said. "Take care—the brambles. If you dismount I'll lead the mare to a good place."

He came to her side, took the bridle, and held out his hand. When she dismounted he led Cressyd away, slipping the bridle over a jut of stone so that the mare had ample freedom to drink if she chose.

"Are you going to the weaver's?" he asked.

"Do you know everything?" She sounded amused and condescending.

"As much as the next man—we all know one another's business. There's not much Dame Elizabeth FitzEdmund can do that's not talked of about the forest in a matter of hours. That's country living for you."

She had sat down on a boulder when he spread his jerkin for her. She seemed to listen to him intently. He liked her gray eyes and dark lashes, but he was irritated by her clipped and finicky way of speaking—it was as though she held her voice and her tongue like little dogs on tight leashes. As for him, he knew he might seem uncouth to her. He had the same roll in his speech as anyone else in these parts, though he seldom used their outlandish words.

"It's a full two months since I came to Mantlemass," she said—and he almost jumped at the change, for she had dropped her voice several tones. He gave her a sharp glance, looking for mockery; but there was none in her expression now. "That's a long while," she said.

"Why did you come?" he asked.

"To visit my aunt—why else?"

"They say your father left you because of matters he must attend to in foreign parts."

"And so he did," she agreed, now looking down at her hands. And she added, but he thought with little longing in her voice, "And shall return to fetch me."

Lewis narrowed his eyes. "Is your father a king's man?"

"It's King Henry now."

"Then is he King Henry's man?"

She fidgeted under this and seemed to seek about for some way of escape. "When my father was at court, it was King Richard."

"Well, some had to be for York or there'd have been nothing to fight about," he said reasonably. He wanted to help her. He remembered his cousin Jenufer had spoken slightingly of her father, and mad or not she sometimes knew more than would have been expected. "I daresay you would not have him change. Fidelity is what matters. He is best abroad, therefore, and you must bear it."

"I do bear it." She was blushing slightly now. "Fetch the mare," she said.

He smiled and said he would see her on her journey. "You have come a little out of your way, so I'll set you right."

"Where's your horse?"

"I'll walk at your stirrup, lady," he said courteously.

"If you wish it," she said, sounding a little haughty; but she still spoke in the new, easy voice and seemed pleased by his offer.

He helped her to mount and kept his hand on the bridle. They moved off along the narrow track. Lewis walked politely /bare-headed, his red cap tucked into his belt.

"Men hereabouts always favor the House of Lancaster," he said, still eager to put her at her ease. "It is natural enough. You know what all this forest is called? It is the free chase of Lancaster Great Park." He laughed. "That means that the only people free to hunt the game are kings and princes and nobles —by law, that is. But it's a long time since any king rode this way, and the reeve and the rangers are foresters by birth—better friends to other foresters than to their masters, I'd say. All these acres were given to a one-time Duke of Lancaster. He was the king's son. It was King Edward then. The third of the name."

"You know a great deal."

"Your aunt will have spoken of Sir James—he is priest at the palace chapel. And my tutor. He knows everything that is past. It was that Duke of Lancaster named Gaunt. John Gaunt, I think. But we mostly call the place by its other name—older or newer, that I can't say: Ashdown."

"What palace?" She frowned. "Can there be a palace here?"

"Up on the high ridge. The roof's in. Now there's a new king and the wars are over, maybe they'll mend it and come hunting again."

He had led her back on to the main track and now they were rising up out of the valley. When they came to the summit of the next bank he would be able to point out the weaver's place and continue on his own errand. As they mounted to the skyline the wind caught them, and the noise of the iron workings suddenly clamored at their ears. It was an ugly sound, yet robust and powerful.

"That'll be the big hammer at Master Urry's," Lewis told his companion. "It's only half successful, I'm told. The Romans worked iron there once."

"Who?" she asked, looking very puzzled.

"Did you never hear how the Romans came and took this country and ruled it?"

"I know nothing of that," she said.

"Well, so it was; and that is history. But it matters very little," he assured her, for she was looking very vexed by all this knowledge coming from a country-man. "I would not know it if Sir James had not told me." He suddenly jerked on the bridle, checking the mare so sharply that her rider swayed in the saddle and cried out in surprise. "I thought an adder crossed. But it's already too cold for such creatures. Strangers must beware of them in warmer weather. And in rainy weather they should beware of the bogs—they fill up and become treacherous. But that is chiefly a winter danger, and winter is not yet arrived."

"What else?" she asked.

"What other dangers? None that I can think of. The deer run in a fair-sized herd and you must keep away from the bucks at this season, when they are mating."

"What more?" she insisted.

"You need not fear man or boy, woman or child besides, that I do know. No forester will harm another forester. We depend upon one another. Of course there's many an outlaw in hiding, if we did but know precisely where. But they'll mostly keep themselves to themselves. And there's Goody Luke in the great birch wood—she gets called a witch by some. I'd say she's a wisewoman, rather . . . Your horse has sense to carry you through boggy places in winter; but on foot watch always for the adder in sunshine."

He was walking barefoot, his hose cut off above the ankle, and he saw her look down and shudder. Then a bird cried, so shrill and harsh and close at hand that she gripped her saddle and hunched her shoulders in fright.

"What's that? What's that?"

Lewis pointed. "There he goes, look. That's the yaffle. See him? See his green and gold?"

The bird was flying ahead of them, its swooping convulsive flight drawing scallops in the air. Then it came to a tree and clung to the bark, tapping fast and furiously.

"And his red cap," cried the girl, childishly pleased with her own observation. "What did you call him?"

"He's the yaffle. The galleybird. The wood-pecker. Take your choice of his names."

"I'll choose yaffle." She was smiling now. "You've a red cap too," she said.

He laughed. "A friend gave me a red cap, long past. I wear its grandchild! You're smiling at last. What's your name? I know you're niece to Dame Elizabeth FitzEdmund—but what's your name?"

"I'm Cecily Jolland." Again she smiled. "And you're Lewis Mallory. My aunt told me."

Now they had climbed the steep bank and the weaver's cottage was close at hand. There was no longer any reason or excuse for continuing that way, so Lewis released the bridle and stepped back.

"That's your way, look. I'm going on to the forge. Good day, then, Cecily Jolland; God keep you."

"And you," she said, a little patronizing. "And I thank you for your company—Master Yaffle!"

She broke into laughter at that, and pulled at Cressyd's rein; to get quickly away, no doubt, from the dangers of making a joke with a stranger. Lewis watched Cressyd carry her rider briskly over the stream and up to the cottage. The weaver was already at his door, the folded cloth on his arm. Lewis watched for a second or two more, then went on his way. As soon as he got home, he would try to interest his cousin in the idea of selling Zephyr to Dame Elizabeth as a more suitable mount for her niece.

# 5

---

# The Taste of Freedom

THERE WAS A GREAT DEAL TO DO BEFORE WINTER SET in. At Ghylls Hatch this meant men's work, but at Mantlemass orders came from the mistress, and in the shortening days Dame Elizabeth's household, indoors and out, was occupied for every hour and every minute. The corn off the two fields had been taken to the miller long ago and now the sacks of flour stood against the granary walls, with oats and grains to feed both man and beast in the months ahead. The pigs, which could usually fend for themselves, had still to be catered for in case of snow. The harvest of acorns was immense, but this was made as far afield as possible, that the hogs might root near home in fine weather. It had been a good harvest. There was plenty of hay, plenty of straw, and vast loads of the cheap litter harvested off the forest itself, the bracken that sprang up in June and covered the shallow slopes below the house. They cut heather too, for bedding, and refilled mattresses with straw, for last year's was broken down to little more than chaff. The old rushes were

cleared and burned and the floor of the hall freshly
strewn. Under the canopy of the big fireplace there
and in the kitchen hams hung to smoke, and the
haunches of venison that were the perquisites of the
manor. There was not the shortage of meat in winter in this household that troubled many. The pi-
geon loft was full too, and there would be variety
and plenty in the Mantlemass winter fare. Only the
stew pond was giving trouble. It had been newly
made a year before but in the early autumn the fish
had suddenly died and none would live now in the
dull water. Nicholas Forge, who was a knowledge-
able man, said the pond was badly placed. They
must dig another, well away from this one. The
sewage from the house, he said, was dispersed care-
lessly, and had run into the pond and poisoned the
water. But no one else could make any sense of this.
Didn't they put farmyard muck on the fields to the
advantage of the crop? Then why should a crop of
fish be harmed by human waste?

Cecily had now learned to churn butter, to strip
dried herbs and pound them, to preserve eggs by
dipping them into a solution of beaten whites with
gum arabic—a precious recipe Dame Elizabeth had
had years ago from an old servant in the early days
of her marriage. They would grow a little stale, she
admitted, but almost all would be edible. Dame
Elizabeth also spent much time making a paste of
rabbit meat, well spiced and sealed into jars under a
thick layer of lard. Besides all this, there was the
year's brewing standing in the cellar—ale from
hops grown over by the church, much stronger stuff
than the small beer of everyday; wine made from
elderberry and cowslip in their season; and nettle
beer. There was honey enough this year for a brewing of mead, though this was not always the case,
Dame Elizabeth told her niece.

There was a great coney-catch in November. Every Mantlemass tenant came to that, for as the animals were skinned their carcasses were given away for meat. Henty sent ferrets into the warrens, and half a dozen dogs were employed. The rabbits poured from the warrens, which had nets covering their openings. Cecily had gone to watch because her aunt was there and had taken for granted that she would go too. But she was unprepared for what took place. The rabbits tumbled and struggled in the nets and the men set about clubbing them. It had to be skillfully done, for the pelts must not be torn by broken bones. With the dogs barking and snarling, the men shouting, many rabbits screaming as they died, the noise was horrible and Cecily had to run away.

Her aunt was pleased with the day's work.

"We build up our stocks during winter, and then the buyers come in spring to collect the skins. I shall show you how to stitch the pelts, Cecily, and between us we might make a cover for your bed."

"I had fur for my bed in London," Cecily said. "I never thought how it was got."

She had hardly thought at all, it seemed to her by now.

The russet wool gown had been cut and sewn, and Cecily was happy to wear it in the increasingly chilly weather. The change in her life was so great that the immediate past began to mist over like last week's dream—though it did not merge with that other dream, older, darker, and lying always a little below her consciousness, waiting to catch her in feverish or half-waking moments.

That riddle remained unsolved, but there were other riddles that surely could be answered. When she sat with her aunt in the winter parlor and they stitched the fur coverlet together, each questioned the other. Dame Elizabeth sought her answers sometimes boldly, sometimes subtly; and Cecily learned from her in this as in other matters.

There was no word of Sir Thomas, no message came, no rider thundered to the door in pursuit; her father might as well have died. Sometimes for days Cecily could hardly remember what he looked like. Nor did she miss Alys any longer, for she had all too clear a notion of how Alys might behave in these countrified surroundings.

"Why did you say that Alys had sly eyes?" she asked her aunt as they both sat stitching.

"Sly eyes—sly heart—either will do. She loved you to your face, but she loved your father more. She was set to spy upon you and tell your father all you did."

"I did nothing . . ." Cecily frowned. "She loved my father more?"

"And has followed him, if I know women," Dame Elizabeth said, stitching fast and angrily. "And I will tell you this, niece, now I have told you one thing— though I am his sister, I am not his loving sister. Once I was dutiful enough—as a sister is bound to be toward her brother when their father has died. He made use of me for his own advancement. When that happened—then I became his enemy. Do you understand?"

Cecily understood nothing, she was completely bewildered. Only her suspicions of her father's plans and purposes seemed suddenly to overwhelm her. "Would he use me too in such a way?" she asked in a low voice. Trying to vindicate him and comfort herself she added, "I heard him call me his treasure. . . ."

"And so, indeed, you are. And he will spend his treasure in his own good time. You have a fortune, Cecily, from your mother, which your uncle Digby must give up to you when you have your own household."

"Then," cried Cecily, for she was still his daughter and he could still command her, "then if he were so vile as you suggest, he would have seen me wed long before now."

"Matters are not always as simple as they seem, my child. But you need not fear. I have only one purpose in my life—and I have told you of it already. I shall see you happy. Not only for your sake, but for your mother's. The dearest friend any girl could ask for—and I was a girl then. For the sake of three women, Cecily—for your mother, for you, for myself—I shall save you from your father."

She was bending over her work, her fingers taut, her needle stabbing at the coney skin, and her voice was so low and intense in tone that Cecily began to tremble.

"He will come for me one day, madam."

"And is that what you wish?"

The girl hesitated, blinking at sudden tears. "I have already learned to live differently. Mantlemass is an easier home than my father's . . . Oh," she cried, bursting out with it. "I was a poor thing when I lived in London with my father and with Alys!" She remembered the frail hands, the tiny steps, the covered face, the small sighing voice—and she made a sound of complete revulsion. "Oh, what a doll—what a puppet! I was a dead thing—a bundle of sticks tied with gold thread—I was nothing, nothing!"

This outburst completely transformed Dame Elizabeth. She laid down her work, flung back her head, and laughed. It was the first time, Cecily realized, that she had heard her aunt laugh quite so loud and free, and it was a good sound—robust and rather coarse, as honest as the farmyard.

"For that truth, my dear niece Cecily, I am ready to bar my door against twenty fathers and all their might!" At last she was obliged to wipe her eyes, so furiously had the laughter taken her. "There now," she said, recovering her breath, "you have told me everything I needed to know. Truly all daughters, all sisters, are pawns in the game played by their menfolk. Only, Cecily, there was once a move made in this particular game that has not been revoked. . . . Now put away the fur and we'll stitch at the tapestry for a change."

The tapestry was a set of bed hangings, enormous—could it ever reach completion? The design was of a great tree, and in every branch there perched birds and butterflies and insects of every kind and color. Aunt and niece sat together at the big frame, stitching almost in unison, brought together now in a new and stirring companionship.

"How many of the birds can you name for me, Cecily?"

"The thrush, madam. And the ousel. The redbreast—the owl—the swallow. And here's a swan. And a merlin. Oh—and I see one I have only lately learned. A forest bird—clinging to the tree trunk, you see, as true as life. That is the yaffle," Cecily said with pride.

"So it is. You are learning. Was it Henty who instructed you? He has a wide knowledge of such things."

"No," said Cecily. "It was the boy with the red cap. We—passed—on the way to the weaver's." Since her aunt made no exclamation of surprise or disapproval but bent over the tapestry, Cecily let her own pleasure in that meeting carry her to further confidence. "You told me his name was Lewis Mallory. But because of his red cap I call him Master Yaffle!"

"You have reminded me of something I must do," Dame Elizabeth said, rethreading her needle. "I need a load of Master Orlebar's good stone for mending the byre wall. Tomorrow would be as good a day as any other to ride over to Ghylls Hatch. You shall go with me for company."

The next day was cold, dry, and still. Round about noon, Simon the carter brought the horses to the door, Dame Elizabeth's big bay, Farden, and little Cressyd. Cressyd was skittish, and without any thought for meekness or manners Cecily rode her hard up the long slow track to its summit, then turned and walked her back.

"You suit one another well enough," Dame Elizabeth said as Cecily settled in at her side. "But I think you have some of your mother's skill with a horse. Her brothers treated her as one of them and took pride in her. She rode like a boy."

"My father did say once that I sat my horse well."

"And for that reason it may be you deserve better than Cressyd. She came from Ghylls Hatch—and so might another."

"He said—that boy—Lewis Mallory—he said they had a full stable."

"Horses are Master Orlebar's trade as coneys are mine."

"Is he an orphan, madam, that he lives here with his cousins?"

"Lewis? Not so. His father is a man of wealth and influence whose eldest son was promised in marriage to a king's daughter, but he died at ten years old. So Lewis should be his father's heir. But he was passed over in favor of the youngest son, and sent away to grow up into a country bumpkin."

"I thought only daughters were hardly treated. . . ."

"The world is ruled by ambition. . . . Do you know that your father married me to a royal bastard? It was a step up the ladder—and why should he care that his sister must suffer a husband with a deformed mind, let alone a warped body. Well, I thank God no child was born alive. . . . Look— they're digging a minepit in the wood there," she said, with no change of tone. "What a load of trees they've cleared. There won't be a hearth on the forest burning wood this winter, if so much goes for charcoal. I must tell Bostel to see we stack more peat."

The men at work looked up as the two riders passed. Dame Elizabeth called out a greeting to them, and they returned it easily. Perhaps it was the hard metal in which they worked that taught them to be proud, or the knowledge that they traded in life and death—in plowshares and pitchforks, in swords and arrowheads, in nails and horseshoes. . . . Without iron men would be helpless.

When they came to Ghylls Hatch the jumble of buildings, many of them rather mean, surprised and disappointed Cecily. She had expected another house as graceful as Mantlemass, but here it was as though the stables took precedence. Over the acres of grassland the horses moved all the time.

"He's grazing his animals late," Dame Elizabeth said. "There's Lewis Mallory on the black stallion— riding along by the yard wall. And that's his cousin Orlebar who's watching." She made an approving noise. "The boy's a handsome rider. There's not much to be taught to either of them, I daresay, when it comes to horses and their ways."

It was Lewis who saw the two women approaching. He wheeled his horse and rode fast toward them, then pulled up short, so that the horse reared showily.

"We have admired your horsemanship from a distance, Lewis Mallory," Dame Elizabeth said dryly. "Take me to your cousin. I've business to discuss." When she had greeted Roger Orlebar she said at once, "I'll go into the house with you. There are two matters to speak about—stone for a wall, for one." She touched Cecily's arm briefly, saying that this was her niece, who had come to be a daughter to her. "While we talk, Master Orlebar, let the boy show her some of your horses."

This was easy manners. For a second, the gentleman's daughter Cecily increasingly forgot to be stiffened her spine and jerked up her chin. Then pleasure defeated vanity. She said eagerly, "Yes, pray do that if you will. I should delight in seeing the horses."

"They are a fairish lot," Lewis said, dismounting. "It'd take a week of Sundays to show you all. But I'll show you the best. That's gray Zephyr. She's half sister to your Cressyd—their dam was a skewbald, chestnut on white. She's a pretty thing, swift and light. A mount for a lady."

He began walking off as he spoke, and she had to run to keep up with him and hear the rest of Zephyr's praises sung. The mare was grazing within a stockade fenced with sturdy posts and rails of chestnut. Lewis whistled softly and the creature pricked her ears and looked over her shoulder. Again he whistled, but on a sharper note, and she pawed the ground and tossed her head, then wheeled toward him, long mane and fine tail flying with her easy canter.

"She is an angel of gentleness," Lewis boasted when he held her head between his hands. "Now put your palm against her mouth and feel the softness of it. Have no fear of her, for she will only nuzzle."

Cecily did as she was bid, and the mare pressed against her palm, blowing with her lips, warmly and gently.

"Oh, she is pretty—pretty!" Cecily cried. "Oh, if she were mine! I love Cressyd, but Zephyr is as beautiful as a dream. How far and fast I might ride on her! Where might I ride to?"

"As far as the sea."

"I never saw it in my life. How should I know the way?"

"Why, I should ride with you," he replied. "It would not do to have you lost."

"And do you know the way?"

"I know all the ways about here," he boasted.

"Then—when?" she asked, as bold as she was breathless, intoxicated by the freedoms opening up before her, widening and promising. "When will you show me the sea? When shall we ride—and may it truly be on Zephyr?"

"I have watched you on Cressyd. I know you can handle a spirited horse."

"I have not ridden so many horses. But sometimes I rode for exercise with my father, and we went over the hills above London. But at the most I have ridden three or four different animals." She frowned. "Will you trust me with Zephyr?"

"As I trust Zephyr with you." He looked up at the sky. "It should be fine for another day or two. To-morrow?"

"As far as the sea?"

"Perhaps not to the water's edge—but to the top of the downs, where we may see it all spread before us. . . . I will bring out Zephyr and you bring Cressyd, and where we meet we will change saddles."

"Where will that be?"

"By the water where we talked?" he suggested.

"Where the pool is." He grinned. "Where you called me Yaffle. As good a place as any, since you know it well."

"Oh, yes, I know it very well," she cried, "for I have been there since—" She had gone there looking for him, and the realization made her blush. "I hoped I might see the yaffle again," she said quickly; but that only made matters worse. "Of course I must ask my aunt if she will allow me to go with you," she said, finding a haughty tone of voice.

"Of course, lady," he said. But he was laughing. They were both laughing, underneath the play of recollected manners. "When will you be there— supposing Dame Elizabeth consents? It must be early, for the days are short. We shall need to ride hard. You must miss your dinner: Are you ready to ride on an empty belly?"

"You talk like a farm boy!"

"Well—how else?" He slapped Zephyr's neck and sent her racing away. "Country living means country ways. Before you came to look a country girl I hardly would've dared speak in your ladyship's presence. Or wanted to," he added rudely. "Look— your aunt has come from the house and my cousin with her. They are looking for us."

The sight of Dame Elizabeth alarmed Cecily, for she seemed far more solid and likely to be obstructive than had seemed possible while Lewis was talking of riding hard to the sea. Life had changed, truly, but could it have changed as much as this?

Sir James had come to Ghylls Hatch just as Dame Elizabeth and her niece were leaving.

"Your pupil is bolder than he should be," Roger Orlebar said to the priest. "He is set to sell Zephyr to Dame Elizabeth for her niece—and the dame, God save us, has consented to their riding out together tomorrow. And all she will say to my frowning is that she will send Nicholas Forge with them—if she does not need his services herself." He shook his head at Lewis. "This girl is no milkmaid, cousin. You should offer her more respect than to race harum-scarum about the countryside with her."

"It's great respect to let her ride Zephyr," Lewis said. "What a fuss you're in, Cousin Orlebar. I'll see she comes to no harm."

He had rarely heard such firm talk from his guardian, and he looked hopefully at the priest for support. But Sir James too, who was a most tolerant man for all his calling, looked unexpectedly solemn. Lewis remembered what Jenufer Orlebar had suggested—that there was some disagreement between the families. But if any such disagreement stemmed from his father, he felt little obligation to take on the quarrel as his own.

"Well, it is for Dame Elizabeth to decide the matter," the priest said at last. "Perhaps by tomorrow she will have had second thoughts."

# 6

## Her Mother's Daughter

THE THOUGHT THAT DAME ELIZABETH MIGHT INDEED change her mind disturbed the rest of both Lewis and Cecily. Each, waking in the night, experienced the doubts that can come with darkness. The prospect was altogether too easy to seem probable. For Cecily it was the absolute reverse of all she had known, and though so many changes had taken place within her and in her outward circumstances, she could not quite believe that any guardian of any girl of her age would be so free of convention. For she had actually said, as they rode home, "I must deprive you of Nicholas Forge, my child—I have a document I want him to draw for me." Lewis knew nothing of that, and by morning had gloomily concluded that the secretary would ride with them, even if they were finally permitted to go at all.

But when he reached the meeting place, riding beneath the dawn sky, Cecily was ahead of him.

"Well," he said. And then said no more, for he had to laugh with pleasure at the sight of her. She was wearing a dark hood that tied under the chin, and the bloodless look that he had noticed when he first saw her standing beside her aunt had given way to a subtle glow of health and good humor.

"Change saddles," she said. "I cannot wait to be mounted on Zephyr." She added primly, "My aunt regrets, but Nicholas Forge is busy today."

"Unfortunate," he murmured. "For him. But the lady knows me well and knows I am to be trusted. And I take her confidence very kindly."

"Shall we see the palace?" she asked as she settled into her saddle and watched him mount a rather surprised Cressyd.

"Not today. It is behind us. We must ride hard if we are to return before dark." He was fiddling with his girths and did not look at her as he said, "Did you speak to Dame Elizabeth of where we were to ride? How long we might be?"

"I could not say how long if I did not know," said Cecily. She flushed slightly. She had hurried from the house at the last, terrified that her aunt would call her back, that the whole thing had been a silly joke. . . . But Dame Elizabeth said nothing and Cecily had fled unchecked.

"Have you brought food?"

"I have four honey cakes and two apples."

"You'll starve on that. Just as well I took meat and bread enough for two."

"How far till we see the sea?"

"Sixteen—seventeen miles, some such." He straightened in the saddle at last, caressing Cressyd, who was restive at the change of weight. "Are you ready to go? We have a very fair day for the ride."

"Yes. Yes, I am ready."

As she followed after him she was half sick with excitement. How long since she had pursed up her mouth at riding without an attendant? How long since she had covered her face before strangers, lowered her eyes before her father, trembled at the thought of taking a step alone? She recalled what Dame Elizabeth had told her of her mother. For her, freedom had come first, then bondage. But Cecily had been bound and was now free. It was as though everything in her sight had been shrouded and small and gray—and now gushed big and full of color. There was a threat in all this, but she would not think of it today: to return to bondage would surely be to die. . . . She would think only that her aunt had promised happiness.

They cantered up the long track from the river below Mantlemass and the forest opened out in heathland bared to the wind. Ahead of them rolled more wooded slopes, but already the thoughts of both strained onward to those farther hills from which they would see the sea.

Lewis touched Cressyd with his heel and she flew into a gallop. Without any urging, Zephyr followed. The wind was keen on this upland and the speed of their passing increased it a hundredfold, so that Cecily's hair streamed out behind her as bravely as Zephyr's splendid tail, and her hood began to slip back and back until her head was bare. The chill air bit at her temples and made her gasp. Lewis, glancing back at her, saw that she was smiling widely. Then the woods were ahead, and he pulled in Cressyd gently and easily. Zephyr fretted a bit and tossed her head, but Cecily held her without difficulty until she had dropped to a walk.

Lewis shouted over his shoulder, "You have her well in hand. She is a bird on the wing! Have you ever flown so fast and far before?"

"Never! Never!" *My pretty bird,* her mother had said. . . .

The track here was narrow. They walked singly

through the trees that were at last bare of leaf. Out of the wind the pale sun was warm, the sky so high and open it was almost colorless.

"Look there," said Lewis, checking his horse and pointing down into the valley. "That's where John Urry made his big hammer."

"It's quiet."

"There's been no rain for weeks. There's not enough water to drive it—nor ever will be just there, so Sir James says. He must get himself a better flow or give up. He's a man too sensible to be clever, as they say in these parts. His neighbors are laughing. Old people never want to change," Lewis said angrily. "They'll go on and on in the same ways —what was good enough for their fathers is sure to be good enough for them. But that's no way to live. I pray Master Urry will take his plans to a better site and show them all he's got more sense than they have."

"Will he make swords and lances?"

"He'd like that—but he's the smelter, not the smith. Still, such things are important. When the king last went to war with France it made a goodly trade for this countryside. Sir James told me this. Arrowheads and bolts for crossbows. Do you know about the old battles—Agincourt? Crécy? There's pounds of Sussex iron in France by now. Do you know about this?"

"From ballads," she said, ashamed of her ignorance but proud of him now for knowing so much.

"Sir James could tell you the whole of history. Oh, he is full of tales—I could not have a better teacher. . . . Now we turn due south. We must drop down to flat ground before we work up again to the downs. Is all well with you, lady?"

"Yes, sir," said Cecily. She pulled her hood on and settled it firmly, smiling because he was smiling. And she felt the strangeness in the lives of both of them—both newcomers to their surroundings yet becoming native by the very effort of learning new ways and almost a new tongue. Now Lewis was moving off again, and she followed after. They set off briskly through a scattering of trees, then out of them again on to heathland. The village was on their right hand, with the market town ahead, but they cut off behind it and came to flat ground where they picked up a broad road. Lewis shouted over his shoulder that it had been made by the Romans. It stretched ahead as far as Cecily could see, and the horses broke into a canter that did not flag for miles.

Now they came suddenly in sight of the downs, which had crept near without any warning foothills. They reared up out of the plain unlike anything Cecily had seen or imagined. Coming from London to Mantlemass it had been necessary to cross a ridge of hills, but not like these, whose sides seemed shaven to the neatness of moss, whose tree-less horizons swooped and scooped against the sky.

The broad road turned a little west, then south, and from the head of a gentle incline it was possible to see a fair town with a castle set above it like a crown. The road ended where the town began.

"Now we must take a marshy way by the river for a while," Lewis said. "You can look across the valley and see St. Pancras Priory below the town. It is all of four hundred years old. At least—"

"—that is what Sir James says," Cecily finished for him.

"Mock, if you must," he said airily. "I'd be an ignorant clod without him."

It was noon as they rode a slippery chalk track up the side of the downs.

"Are we almost there?" Cecily called.

"Almost. Give me the bridle and I shall lead Zephyr. And you, Cecily Jolland, close your eyes till I command you to open them."

She laughed, winding her hands in Zephyr's mane when the reins were taken from her, and closing her eyes tightly. She swayed giddily and cried out as the horse was led onward, and clutched wildly at the saddle.

"You dare not open your eyes!" he cried. "Do so —and I swear to see you never ride Zephyr again!" He seemed to be leading her on and upward interminably, but at last he reined in and the horses stood still, their sides heaving. "Now," he said. "Open your eyes."

They were higher than she had expected. Ahead, the cropped turf dropped away, and beyond and above the wintery green the great expanse of the ocean stretched forever against the sky. Sprinkled with the glitter of the winter sunshine, the sea, which Cecily had only imagined or seen pictured, was less silver than pewter, and on the metal there winked and shimmered and shifted and slithered what looked like innumerable coins, or the scales of uncountable thousands of leaping fish.

"Oh, God save us all!" she cried. "What a wonder!"

"It is France on the far side," he told her. "You cannot see it, but it is there. Do you know why this is so?" He looked over his shoulder, as though there might be someone lurking in that quiet place—the shepherd, say, who must be somewhere near, for his flock was moving over the ridge. "Sir James believes it to be because the world is as round as an orange. But never breathe it to anyone. It could be called blasphemy." .

She had never heard such nonsense and she burst

out laughing. "If I am standing here on an orange," she cried, "you had better hold me lest I fall off!"

"Look around you, lady," he said, fierce and despising her foolishness. "What do you see but a clean line of the sky that does not end? It is a circle around us. As though we stand on a platter." He added, with some pride, "Sir James thought of the orange, but the platter is my idea."

"And when we come to the edge of the platter— we tumble over into France?" She was helpless with laughter.

"I should have known better than to tell you. Women have not the wit to understand such matters."

He was looking very stern, his eyebrows drawn darkly together. He had fine eyes, full of fire and purpose, and his nostrils were drawn back scornfully. She found herself, checked in her laughter, studying his face with eyes that had not until now been properly opened. He was handsome, proud, noble, brave . . . The words streamed through her head and she was startled by their vehemence. She had looked at him with pleasure from the start, but now she truly saw him. What she saw seemed the best that life had ever shown her. In this keen intelligent face, the mouth already firm but kind, she knew without any doubt at all she was seeing all the future that she would ever desire. Tears rushed to her eyes, tears of promise, of hope, of anxiety and dread of loss . . . He was too busy with his platter and his orange to notice her silence.

"Sir James himself shall instruct you," he declared.

"Yaffle! Yaffle!" she mocked, her voice high and excited. "That's a true name for you—for there you go, boring away into mysteries as though they were tree trunks! Mind what you say and who you say it to, Master Yaffle. Any one of us may be charged with blasphemy!"

"Then it must be you who testify against me," he retorted, "for none else has been given the chance."

"Is this a quarrel?" she asked, not minding, for she knew it would be made up.

"No, it is *not* a quarrel!" His frown eased out. He began to grin. "It's hours past dinnertime. Shall we eat here, before we turn back?"

"Let us wait until we reach the sea."

"That's another league, I'd say. The dark will catch us long before we're home."

"I want to see how it looks where it meets the earth. Are there great waves? Take me to see, Lewis. I'll ride as hard as a messenger all the way home."

"Your aunt will be angry—"

Cecily prodded Zephyr and shot past Cressyd, making for the long shallow track that ran along the side of the hill and at last flattened out into the valley that became the river's mouth. She heard Cressyd thundering behind her—if Cressyd with her light swift gait could ever be said to thunder. Lewis was edging up to overtake Zephyr, but the track was not wide enough and he was obliged to drop back again. Cecily looked over her shoulder. She was breathless with laughing as she had never laughed before, with riding as she had never ridden before. Lewis defeated her by stepping his horse off the track, taking a lower scoop and coming up a hundred yards ahead of her. Zephyr was the swifter horse, but Cressyd's rider was the more experienced horseman. They checked, as winded as the horses. Here the track steepened and they had to pick their way. Suddenly they were at the foot of the hills, riding sedately by a hamlet with a church that stared along the river's back to the sea.

This was marshy land, and they crossed it along an ancient causeway. Reeds on either side rattled their winter bones, and on a smaller, lighter note the seeds of sea poppy chattered in brittle pods. Close by the shore that stretched on either hand to chalky cliffs, a mill stood whose great wheels were turned by the ebb and flow of the tide. Where the fields met the shingle Lewis dismounted and gave his hand to Cecily. They led the horses along the high bank, watched by the miller, his blank-faced wife, and half a dozen tousled children.

"Look there!" Cecily cried as Lewis tied the horses to a willow stump. "There it is! The great ocean and the waves breaking!" She darted forward, but the shingle shifting under her feet threw her to the ground. Lewis pulled her up and they struggled over the beach together. The waves were small in the quiet winter sunshine, breaking in pearly bubbles along the edge of the stones. "Oh— if I had never seen such a thing!" she cried. "That I might have died without knowing! Should we let the horses drink?"

He gave a shout of laughter. "You are the most ignorant creature I ever did see, Cecily Jolland. It's salt! It's salt as tears! Did no one ever tell you?"

"Why should they?" she demanded. "And why would I care—until I saw it?" She crouched down and dipped her fingers in the cold water and tasted them—then sprang back shrieking as the sea ran trickling over her shoes.

Presently they came to a place where shingle had mounded on three sides of a hollow. Lewis shook out the cloak he had carried rolled on his saddle and spread it on the fine stones. He bowed Cecily to a seat and then crouched down and began to unwrap the cloth that held meat and bread and a wedge of goatsmilk cheese. Cecily in her turn took from her pocket the honey cakes and the apples. The cakes were sadly flattened.

"Those make a poor show," Lewis complained. "You could have done better than that. Anyone knows that Dame Elizabeth keeps a good larder. My cousin Orlebar has only his sister Jenufer to care for his household. And she's a sad sort of manager. A bit *dunch* as they say. The servants mock her and the place is dirty often as not."

"Why do you live there?" asked Cecily.

For a second he did not reply. The bold question had taken him by surprise.

"Why should I not?" he said at last.

"That's another question. The first deserves a better answer."

"I am there by my father's wish," he said, busy with the food, dividing it neatly—but deciding that he needed more than she did because he was bigger, older, stronger, and a man.

"As I am at Mantlemass."

"Partly so."

"Why—how is it different for you?"

He sat back on his heels and said very calmly and coldly, "Your father has not disowned you, I think."

"I was a hindrance to him. He left me with my aunt because it suited him, though he despises her." She was trembling as she said this, and she added boldly and bitterly, "He did it for his own safety. Nothing else would have persuaded him to leave me at Mantlemass."

"You are in good hands."

"I never wish to live with my father again," she cried, excited beyond sense by the confidence she felt in Lewis Mallory, and in herself. "My aunt will not make me return."

"But he can make you, if he wants," said Lewis somberly. "Fathers do as they wish with their children. They break their hearts if it suits them, as easily as they would wring a chicken's neck to make a meal!"

Cecily was silent. She would not be shaken. For her it was to be different. There was a mystery and the mystery would save her. Her aunt had said: *There was a move made in this particular game that has not been revoked.* Though the words were without any sense, yet they were a reassurance. They suggested a locked door whose key had been thrown away; before the door could be opened, the key must be recovered. . . .

"My father had three sons," said Lewis, handing Cecily bread and meat. "It is like a ballad. But I am only the second son. It is always the youngest who is the hero."

"Now the next verse . . . ?"

"I know that I was once dearly loved. I cannot recall anything I did to lose that love. But I think of it as little as possible. It is over now and I am settled. It is far better to forget." But because she was waiting and listening he was obliged to continue. "When I was seven years old the king went into France, all of us and my father with him. The eldest son, my brother Geoffrey, rode into battle as his page. He was ten years old and he died with an arrow in his throat."

Cecily bit her lip and was silent.

"So then I was my father's heir, and made much of. I turned eight that year, and I remember being taken to court and to many other fine places. To France, and once even farther—perhaps to Rome, but I cannot remember. One thing I do recall—it is that King Edward gave me a sword that was three times the length of my own arm!" He frowned,

tossing a handful of pebbles up and down, so that
they scraped and scratched together monoto-
nously. "I wonder who has it now. It was taken away
with all the rest."

"What could you have done to deserve it?"

"If I knew that . . . Well, what does it signify
now? I have my own life and I know it is a good
one."

"Was it long ago that you came to Ghylls Hatch?"
Cecily asked, for he had told her too little and she
had to prod him on to further confidence. "How
old were you then?"

"Near ten—as Geoffrey was when he died. Perhaps my father could not bear to see me in his place.
. . . All I know now is that my father one day was in
a high rage. How it started—that I can't remember.
I only have a memory of his roaring fury and the
noise in the great hall, and my mother weeping and
shrieking and my old nurse with her. . . . And I
remember riding on a rainy day to my cousins—not
Orlebar, but some others I forget now, in a country
place north of London. But I was only there a short
while—some months, perhaps—and just growing
used to the change, when my father came roaring
after me yet again, and brought me in a day's journey to Ghylls Hatch. And I have never seen nor
heard of him since. He would not know me, I daresay, nor I him. For he will have grown old and I have
become a country lad."

"Fathers are indeed beyond comprehension,"
Cecily said.

"So you see," Lewis said, smiling at her rather
wanly, "the youngest son was the hero, for he became my father's heir in my place." He moved restlessly. "You must eat. Surely you are hungry? I am."

They sat for a while in silence, then Cecily asked
the question she needed to ask, whose answer she

dreaded. "What shall you do, now that you are grown?"

He stopped munching and looked at her, his face bulging and comical. When he had swallowed he said, "What would you have me do?"

"You must answer."

"I am man enough to fight and die. Shall I go to be a soldier? There are always battles."

"But you are only the second son," she reminded him. "The first son is the warrior; the second may be a scholar."

"A scholar . . . a cleric? You mean I should enter the church?" he asked, frowning.

"I cannot see you a cardinal, Master Yaffle—and none else in the church wears a red cap!"

"Finish your meat," he said, trying not to laugh. "What shall I do now? No doubt I shall stay as I am. For it is not so bad to be a countryman, Cecily Jolland. The priest will teach me all he knows of scholarship, and if I remember one quarter of it I shall be a learned fellow. Horses and books are as good company as any man could wish. Though they say ladies prefer a hero."

"A dead hero—or a live scholar . . . I know which I would choose," cried Cecily. And then corrected herself: "I know which I would choose to be."

It was warm in the hollow out of the wind, where the sun shone unclouded. The waves pulled on the shingle in a rhythm Cecily had never heard before. Then the miller's children came to stand and stare, very close and gazing piercingly at the food the two were eating.

"Shall I give them the cakes, Lewis?"

"I am still hungry!"

"They are hungrier. What little scarecrows—and thin as last year's bolster! Here!" She held out the cakes and the children shifted nearer; but like birds afraid to venture the last yard for a crumb, they kept darting back and hiding one behind the other.

"It is more than time we turned for home," Lewis said. "Leave the cakes on the stones. Lord—what a stench!" he added, pinching his nose. "The farmyard's like lavender and roses to this collection of young animals."

It was a steep pull up out of the hollow, the shingle shifting and falling around their feet. Lewis gave Cecily his hand and pulled her up to the ridge, and kept her hand in his until they reached the horses. Behind them the children pounced on the four cakes that must be divided among six, and their cries of fury were far harsher than the cries of the gulls that swooped above them.

"At least you and I have never starved," said Lewis soberly. "You asked what I should do with my life, but what will you do, Cecily Jolland, if your father does not send for you?"

"I shall live at Mantlemass."

"Yet you hated it when you came."

"I was another person. I was a dead thing—I was nothing—nothing!" cried Cecily, clinging now to his hand with both her own and speaking so wildly and fiercely that he was dismayed.

"Well, you are not a dead thing anymore," he said, in the gentle voice he would use to a frightened horse.

"But now I know—I know it quite clearly and suddenly—I know I should die if I had to go back."

"You have told me your aunt would not let you go."

"What if something should happen to her—if she should take sick and die—?"

"All this death and despair . . . Your eyes are full of tears!"

"But what should I do without her?"

"You have other friends. You have Orlebar and Mallory." He urged her to her horse. "We must ride home. We have stayed far too long. And we have come too far as well. We have only two hours of good daylight."

"It was my fault. I will tell my aunt so."

"You are not to weep for what may never happen," he said seriously as he helped her to mount.

"I am better. Forgive me."

"Follow me closely then. We must not waste any time."

He led off and she followed obediently. Already the sun was leaning well down the sky and they had a long way to go. They rode at an easy canter, and in silence. Sometimes Lewis looked around to see that all was well with Zephyr and her rider, but he did not pause until they were breasting the downs. The forest lay ahead of them, the dusk already gathered to its steeper slopes. In these last hours the sky had subtly changed. The wind had dropped, the cold had increased. There was a hint of saffron in the sky, and along the horizon clouds curled like heavy plumes of gray and purple.

Lewis dropped to a trot and they rode side by side until they came to the road. "There's snow to come," Lewis said. "This side of January it need not be severe. It is after Christmas that the trouble comes. Then, if there are drifts, it is all but impossible to move about the forest. We are mewed up under our own roofs until the thaw." He looked at Cecily through the growing dark. "Is all well with you again? Are you ready to ride hard the rest of the way?"

"Yes. I am ready." She looked pale and tired but she was bound to obey him. It was her fault they were late, she insisted, but he knew he should not have given in to her desire to reach the shore.

There was still some light in the sky when they came near Mantlemass and the spot where they had met that morning. But Lewis would not consider parting here at this time of the evening. Nonetheless, he did halt and wait for her, for he thought he had found a means to reassure her. It was true enough that some ill might befall her aunt, and then indeed she might need friends to help her.

"Before we part, let me say what is in my mind." He moved up close. He put his hand to his throat and pulled out the ring he wore hidden under his shirt. "This is my talisman," he told her. "Give me your hand."

Cecily expected to feel some holy medallion in her hand, but what he gave her was a heavy ring. When she had grasped it he closed his hand over hers.

"This is to pledge my friendship and my duty," he said solemnly. "What I vow on this ring, which is all I have to prove I am my father's son, I must in honor perform. So I vow to you, Cecily Jolland, that I shall strive to see you content and safe in that way of life you shall choose. And if any disaster should come to your aunt, then I will take up her task, and I will stand between you and whatever you detest. Even your own father and even in the face of death. . . . Amen. And you—you also say amen."

"Amen," said Cecily, her voice light and breathless.

"Hurry, now," he said.

But she still held the ring, and in doing so she held the wearer tethered. "Let me see it," she said.

"There's not light enough. I'll show it another day. It is not known that I wear it," he told her warningly. "So do not speak of it."

She opened her hand then, releasing him, and they moved off at once. They reached the door of Mantlemass just as lights were being carried to the hall. Dame Elizabeth, wearing a cloak against the cold evening, was crossing the courtyard from the farm. Cecily shrank a little when she saw her, as if she could not hope for anything but anger. But there was no anger to come.

"How far did you take her, Lewis? I looked for you two hours ago."

"Madam, we did ride far indeed. I should have known better. To the seashore, no less."

"God save us," she said, laughing, "it was not a lazy day you chose. You have never seen the ocean, niece?"

"No, madam. And how strange it is, and how beautiful." Her mind was filled with the pledge Lewis had made to her and her voice sounded far-away in her own ears. "And Zephyr," she managed, "is like a creature from a dream."

"Then we will ask Master Orlebar if he will part with her."

"He will part with her to this rider, madam," Lewis said, "but to none other!"

"We'll speak of it very shortly—tell your cousin. . . . I have come from the byre. One of the cows is sick and may very well die. That's a poor start to the winter. Come in now, Cecily. Good night to you, Lewis Mallory."

"Good night, madam," Lewis said, bowing. He bowed also to Cecily. "And to you, lady. God rest you both."

Indoors, out of the biting cold and standing by the bright burning logs in the winter parlor, Cecily was so struck with fatigue that she sank down by the hearth and felt she would never move again.

"You rode too far," Dame Elizabeth said. "But I

see you are your mother's daughter after all, and
that pleases me."

"I was afraid you would be angry."

"Angry? Why should I be? I have known young
Mallory long enough to trust him—even with you,
my dearest Cecily."

Fatigued as she was, Cecily still felt vaguely puzzled by her aunt's easy ways.

"He told me about his father," she said, fighting a
yawn, "and how he is disowned."

"Did he? What did he say? Did he tell you why his
father treated him in this fashion?"

"He cannot tell at all. Do you know, madam?"

"How should I?"

"You know so much . . ." This time the words
almost smothered themselves as the yawn defeated
her. "What is the Mallory crest, madam?"

"A lark within a wreath of laurel, and a laurel leaf
in its mouth."

The heat from the fire was suddenly so great that
Cecily was dizzy and almost fainting. She tried to
recover herself, hearing her aunt's voice echoing
and repeating endlessly: *A lark within a wreath of
laurel and a laurel leaf in its mouth* . . . She struggled
against the words for already they were leading her
into that strange half-conscious dreaming that both
lured and frightened her. She sank into the confusion of familiar images—she saw the winking jewel
in the ear of the dark-bearded man, the purple of
his gray-bearded elder, the shy boy. *My bird—my
poor bird* . . . came the voice she knew to be her
mother's.

As she struggled back she saw the emblem of the
bird carrying something in its beak, and she named
it triumphantly. It was the lark and the laurel of the
Mallory crest. She was sure of it, even though she
had not seen the ring that hung hidden round Lewis

Mallory's neck. Everything seemed quite clear to her then. Her dream, if dream it was to be called, was not as she had all this time supposed a memory of the past, but a prediction of the future. As Cecily opened her eyes on this conviction, it was as though she and Lewis were already promised to one another.

# 7

## Snowfall to Christmas

DURING THE NIGHT, THE SNOW BEGAN. LEWIS WOKE and slid under the bed covers, the room was so cold. If this had happened yesterday there could have been no ride to the coast, no confidences, no solemn promise. He had assured Cecily that early snow never stayed long. He remembered now that in one winter soon after he came to Ghylls Hatch the snow began on the twentieth day of November, and that same snow was still there, buried under many feet more, when March brought a thaw. If that should happen this year it could mean that Ghylls Hatch and Mantlemass would be quite cut off from one another. The thought made Lewis groan. But if the snow was severe enough to keep him from seeing Cecily, it would also keep her father away. That at least was a more comfortable thought. He was glad when morning came. He went out with a lantern to see what was happening. The forest was only thinly covered, but the snow was still falling. Lewis went at once to the stables. There would be a heavy day's work to get through, for there was not a full winter's stock of litter and feed in the lofts. He called as he went for the boys, Peter and Timothy, who worked with the horses.

Peter came running from Zephyr's stall. He had just tumbled down the ladder from the loft where he slept, and his hair was full of straw.

"Sir, there's no Timothy. He never come to his bed. I woke up dunnamany times and looked across for him."

"What's he about, then?"

"Gone, I reckon. Gone." Peter looked at Lewis as though he was too scared to say any more, but then the words burst from him. "He's taken Zephyr with him!"

As the snow continued, the animals grazing free in the forest had begun to move in toward home for shelter. At Mantlemass there was a scurrying of men and maids about last-minute tasks. The sick cow had died in the night and had to be buried in hard ground. Henty brought more coney pelts to be stacked within the house, to be worked during the winter. Wood and peat were carted indoors.

Before dinnertime, Cecily found a small boy crying in the hall. She knew him vaguely. He was the son of a girl who worked in the kitchen.

"Why are you here, Davy?" she asked him. "And what are you crying for? Where's your mother? Where's Joan?"

At this he broke out into terrible bawling, sobbing and shaking and smearing his dirty face with his filthy hands. He could not speak a word—not indeed that he ever managed more than two at a time, though he was easily four years old.

"Come with me to the kitchen," Cecily said. "We'll find your mother."

She was chary of the mission, for she had twice

tried to speak to the boy's mother and been shame-
fully intimidated by Joan's bitter, mocking manner
and the harshness with which she treated the child.
Moll Thomsett, who had charge of the household
cooking, in her turn shouted and struck at Joan; so
that the Mantlemass kitchen could not be said to
invite visitors. Agnes Bunce from the dairy was
working with Moll when Cecily appeared, with Davy
close behind her skirt.

"Where's Joan, Moll?" asked Cecily, trying to imitate her aunt's commanding manner.

"Well may you ask it! Gone from here and left her
brat behind her. Gone with that Timothy that works
with the horses at Ghylls Hatch—that's what Agnes
say."

"He come last night," said Agnes, "and Joan was
off pillion. He stole the horse, most like."

"Be hanged if they catch him," shouted Moll
Thomsett. "The slummocky villain!"

"Is it really true?" cried Cecily, horrified. "You
mean she has left the boy?"

"What would you suppose? The sooner he goes
after her, the better for all. There's no place under
any decent roof for his kind. Let him get on his
ways."

"He's a baby, Moll. Where would he go?"

"Back to the swank where his mother bore him.
Where else?"

"I don't know what *swank* means . . ."

"Means boggy," murmured Agnes. "They do say
she had him down the hollow—it's rare swanky
thereabouts."

"You are abominable! Both of you! My aunt shall
hear of your talk." Cecily swung around to leave the
kitchen. If need be, she would look after the child
herself. "Where is he?" she cried. "Where's he
gone?"

Moll Thomsett laughed, turning back to the fire, but Agnes, younger and kinder, said quickly, "He'll not be far, lady. I'll find him."

"Stay where you are and mind your work!" snapped Cecily.

She ran from the kitchen and across the hall, calling the child's name. There was no sign of him; but when she went to the door she saw his tracks in the snow, rapidly filling as the fall continued. Without stopping for thought, she ran out into the lightly falling flakes. The snow spun aimlessly, spiraling through the quiet air that seemed quite warm, for there was no breath of wind. Almost at once the boy's footprints were covered and she lost the track. She stood calling and calling, so that the carter, hearing the distress in her voice, paused in his work and asked what was wrong.

"Sim—have you see Joan's Davy? Did he run this way?"

"A minute past. Going home, I thought. But Joan's not there—"

"I know that!"

Cecily turned and ran. The snow was in her hair and on her shoulders, but she could not stop. She picked her way to the hovel where Joan had lived with her boy—one room and a chimney, a beaten earth floor, and a bed of rags and sacking. The place was empty, but she picked up his track again and followed it down the slippery hillside below the farm. The rapidly filling prints ended at a tangle of gorse and bramble that made a shelter against the weather; the child had crept inside. He was crouching there with his knees drawn up to his chin, his eyes black and enormous in a face smeared with tears and dirt, his teeth chattering where they met—for he had lost the bottom two.

"Davy, Davy," wheedled Cecily. "You must come

home out of the snow. Give me your hand and I will help you." The snow was becoming troublesome, dragging at her skirt and piling and clinging in her hair. She tried to pull the boy out of his hiding place, but he fought her, hard and silently, until she lost her temper out of sheer annoyance and discomfort. "Do as I bid you!" she said.

It was what he was used to, and he crawled out at once, looking terrified. Before she came to Mantlemass she would have thought such a child far removed from her interest. But now she clasped him against her skirt, brushing off the snow and pulling a fold of the stuff around him. She began to struggle up the track with him, slipping and slithering and almost falling. She had not gone more than a few paces when she heard a shout behind her. A black horse appeared from behind the thickening veil of falling white. It was Ebony, with Lewis Mallory in the saddle.

"Are you out of your wits?" he called. "The snow's all over you. You have white hair, Cecily Jolland."

"I had to find this child. His mother's left him. Joan from the kitchen's his mother."

"Joan?" cried Lewis. "I know all about her. And I know who's gone with her." He swung out of the saddle and began to beat the snow from Cecily's shoulders and hair. He took off his cloak and wrapped it around her. "If you want to keep the boy warm you must take him before you. And that means you must ride astride as your great-grand-dam would have done." Without asking any permission, he took her around the waist and hoisted her into the saddle, then swung Davy up in front of her, tucking the cloak around him. "It's my stable boy, Timothy, that's gone with her," Lewis said. "And it's Zephyr they've ridden away on."

"Oh, not Zephyr!" she cried. "Not my Zephyr!"

"Farewell to your lovely mount, my lady."

As he led Ebony toward the house the snow fell on his red cap and almost covered it. Cecily was abashed by her situation, for it did seem the height of barbarity and immodesty to find herself with a foot in either stirrup and her skirts rucked up to her calves. Yet for all that she felt safe and sturdy, and the warmth that had glowed in her from the moment she heard Lewis's voice must surely be enough to thaw a mountain of snow and ice. The loss of Zephyr was almost nothing to her now. She had more important matters to dream about.

"Let me down here," she called as they came near the house. "I'll swear my aunt has ridden like a man in her day, but I won't have the servants jeering. Let me down, Master Yaffle."

Lewis lifted her down, but then held her by the elbows for a second. "This is a fierce snow. Maybe the winter will be a hard one." He looked down at her, smiling slightly. "If we are all mewed up, remember me till spring."

He released her and turned at once to remount.

"Your cloak!"

"Keep it till you are in shelter. I'll come for it when the weather clears."

The moment he was in the saddle he wheeled Ebony and spurred off, and the snow swallowed him on the instant, as if it were fog. . . .

Dame Elizabeth was angry with Joan and full of grumbles about Davy. He would have to go to his grandmother, who lived somewhere about the forest.

"I will care for him," Cecily said. "He shall make no trouble for another living soul."

"You will tire of that, niece. . . . And do you mean to keep him in the house?" demanded Dame

Elizabeth, as if Cecily had begged to introduce a piglet or a lamb. "For if so, he must be cleaned."

"Yes, I will clean him," Cecily agreed, eyeing Davy's matted hair and feeling her fingers curl slightly. "In a year or two, madam, he will make a splendid little page."

Her aunt laughed at that, saying her niece was growing shrewd; but no more was said about sending the child away.

"Now you have me to care for you," Cecily told him, as he sat looking over the folds of Lewis's cloak like a black-eyed goblin. But she was not too sure that he understood, or, if he did, whether he fancied the arrangement.

Cecily called Mary Butterwick and Meg. Mary was too fastidious to touch the child, but Meg, a compassionate girl, entered readily into the business of cleaning him up. She soon filled a tub with warm water. Davy, rigid and screaming, bore it only because there was no escape. Meg held him firmly and Cecily scrubbed, her sleeves rolled up, her face red with exertion. Once Moll Thomsett came from the kitchen and stood in the doorway to watch; but she said nothing, and presently went away.

"We must guard him from Moll," Cecily told Meg.

"She's got a swingeing tongue, truly. I seen her swork and I hear her sworle—"

"*Swork*, Meg? *Sworle?*"

"Well, that's plain enough, surely," Meg protested. "It mean she get angered and snarly like a dog."

"We must cut his hair off and burn it."

"Sweal it, shall we?"

"Oh, *Meg*—how am I to know what you mean? Fetch me a shears!"

"Sweal's what you do with a taper to clean a pig's hide," Meg explained. "Still—the pig's dead."

By now Davy had stopped screaming and merely sobbed. Cecily clipped his hair short as a monk's, then ducked him back into the water and washed his head with such vigor that Meg put in a word for him.

"Mind he don't fall faint and swimey, the way you were taken last evening, lady!" She was laughing and Cecily laughed too.

Cecily was happy. She was learning companionship. She and Meg were at this moment far indeed from the mistress and servant relationship that Cecily had known with Alys. They were merely two girls of an age, employed on a task that was bound to make them laugh. Now Davy was clean, and the effort and the grief of it all had made him drowsy. He leaned more and more against Cecily, and at last his eyes closed altogether. She sat by the hearth and he slept against her knee. She would be kinder to him than his mother had been, she told herself; but which of them would seem the better to him?

Meg was kneeling near Cecily, and now she sat back on her heels and looked at the pair.

"When shall you and I be wed, lady, and have our own?" she said in a small soft voice.

"What talk!" cried Cecily, but softly too, for fear of waking Davy. "Is there some lad you fancy, Meg?"

"There's Sim Carter's son, John. But he's a bit faddy and looks above him. Still, if all fays well—it might be he'd think of it." She looked under her lashes at Cecily. "And you, lady?"

"The country grows many things, but not suitors," Cecily replied. "How hot the fire is—I'm quite burning my cheek."

"But there's none of us needs more than one," Meg murmured.

"Where shall Davy sleep?" Cecily asked, deciding, though in a friendly way, that Meg was going altogether too far. "It had best be with me. He shall be my bodyguard and sleep by the door."

The wind blew from the north for ten days on end, and almost all that time the snow was falling, now fast, now sparely. Each day at Mantlemass the men worked to dig paths between the house and the farm, where the animals steamed and stamped. Muck and snow piled up in the byres. Thin, scummy ice covered the pond where the fish would not breed. Now the long preparations, the storing and the brewing and the preserving, kept the household at Mantlemass in good heart. There was provision made, her aunt told Cecily, for every day to be snowy from now until the spring. When the wind dropped the sun came out and all day long the sky was blue. The snow melted on the branches, then froze again at night, so that next day in a small breeze branches and twigs tinkled together. Deer came out of the forest and stood in a cluster at the edge of the trees. Henty would gladly have taken a buck for fresh meat, but all were thin and poorly-looking and not worth the effort. Dame Elizabeth thought they should be fed some litter and grain and so fattened for another day. At this Henty, who was no respecter of persons, gave a guffaw out of his big red beard that echoed over the farmland and sent the deer bolting back among the trees.

"Now we have lost them, skin and bone and all," said Dame Elizabeth. But she sounded indulgent. She never contrived to outface Henty, and perhaps she liked him all the better for it. "If I had my way," she insisted, "we might dine off fresh fat meat at Christmas, housebound or no."

"There'll be a thaw before then," he promised her. "Give it three more frosts and then we'll see."

"We're a long way from freedom yet." Dame Elizabeth looked at her niece, who was sitting by the table making six-inch bags out of fine linen to be filled from a great bowl of lavender and rose leaves. "What do you say, niece? Should you enjoy a feast at your own board this year, if the weather is kind? There shall be Master Henty, with his daughter and his poor son. And Tom Bostel and Anis, and perhaps their eldest girl. And Nicholas Forge—but not, save us, his old mother. And all the rest shall come who serve me about the house. For it is a feast for man and master alike. Besides, though we have not so many neighbors, we have some. What do you say then, Cecily?"

"What neighbors?" Cecily asked, stitching the linen so fine she had to bend her head and hide her face to see what she was up to.

"What neighbors would you choose to see?"

"Master Orlebar seems a good-hearted man," Cecily murmured. "Should he come?"

"Indeed he should come. Likewise his poor sister. And shall we ask also his cousin?"

"Why, yes—if it pleases you, madam."

"There's my good, sweet, submissive girl! See how obedient and long-suffering your father's harshness has made you. For my sake you will endure Master Orlebar's cousin. Bless your sweet temper!"

"But," said Cecily, crimson in the face, partly at her aunt's teasing and partly with the effort of checking her laughter, "we are in God's hand. For first the snow must melt—and on the right day."

"We will all pray for a thaw. And we will ask Sir

James too to take a seat at our table. Which should be pleasing to heaven as well as to us. For he is a fine, good man, with a very pleasant humor."

They must have prayed well, for the thaw began on the last Sunday of Advent, three days before Christmas Eve. The still forest gushed and streamed. Whatever had been dry became wet, and now there was more chance of drowning, so Meg said, than of sliding and falling and breaking bones. Davy ran down to the water's edge and poked about with sticks. It was strange to see how he never went near the place where he had lived with his mother, but ran in and out of Mantlemass as though it had always been his home.

Dame Elizabeth sent Nicholas Forge riding to Ghylls Hatch to ask the Orlebars for their company at noon on Christmas Day, and from there he was to go in search of Sir James. Although Cecily was sure in her heart that they must come, she waited on pins till her aunt's secretary returned with the answer.

"Sir James was already at Ghylls Hatch," he told Dame Elizabeth, "so my journey was halved. And all thank you for your courtesy and will be glad to come to Mantlemass on Christmas Day."

"There now, Cecily," said her aunt. "You and I must set about ordering the feast."

While she waited for Nicholas Forge to return from Ghylls Hatch, Cecily had been adding to the pile of lavender bags, at which she stitched for some time every day—Dame Elizabeth had said she needed one hundred. She counted them—and there were fifty. Her fingers were sore with stitching. Her hands by now were greatly changed; what had been so white and tender had hardened and darkened. What would Alys say if she could see them? And what, in heaven's name, would her father think of the coming feast, the freedom and the assorted company with whom she would happily sit down? Since the moment when she had seemed to see her own future, when the lark and the laurel swam out of dream into reality, Cecily had banished all thought of her father. Now she experienced a sharp spasm of fear, and if Lewis had been there she would have cried out to him for help as she had done as they walked together by the shore. She still had a father. Unless he died, she was bound to see him again. Where was he? And was Alys with him? And what plans were they making, far away in France, that even now might come between her and what she most desired?

In the flurry of preparing the feast, even Moll Thomsett grew a shade more mellow, though she had chilblains and the worst was on her nose. But the planning and the counting, the baking and boiling and roasting pleased her sense of self-importance. The feast would not happen save for Moll being there, and the knowledge gave her great pleasure and puffed up her pride.

The weather stayed warmish and damp. At night the stars shone mistily, the moon floated through a cloud. Early on Christmas morning they rode through the dark to the church three miles away. They made a fine cavalcade—Dame Elizabeth and Cecily, Henty and the Bostels and Nicholas Forge. Henty's daughter rode pillion, Nicholas Forge took Mary Butterwick, and since Anis Bostel had her own mount, her husband Tom took Meg behind him. The rest of the household had to make do with whatever devotions they could manage for themselves.

The church was cold and in poor repair, damp peeling the colored paint from the walls and tarnishing the gold ornamentation. The priest too was

very old and tired, and Cecily wished they could
have gone to the palace chapel, where Sir James
would officiate—and where most certainly Mallory
and Orlebar would be kneeling with their own people. Here in the village church the congregation
was of a fair size, for men and women alike had
ridden or tramped in from the forest and the ham-
lets to hear mass on this good day of the year.
Afterward, as neighbor greeted neighbor, Cecily
stood at her aunt's side in her coney-lined cloak
feeling happy and secure. The day was ahead of her,
she had forgotten all her fears. She felt warm in
body and comfortable in spirit and full of love for
God and man. She could hardly wait until they rode
home to Mantlemass and set about the next part of
the day. The wind had gone back to the north and
they rode into it. Henty looked at the sky, only just
growing light, and said that winter would soon be
back. . . .

The guests rode in precisely at noon. Cecily was
still struggling to change her dress. Last night her
aunt had suddenly thrown open the lid of her biggest chest, and inside was a purple gown she
planned to wear for the feast and a white damask,
embroidered with red flowers over the high bodice
and along the hem, that Cecily might wear if it fit.
Dear Meg had seen to that, and now she was struggling to get it fastened while Cecily fidgeted with
impatience to run down to the hall. She saw the
visitors from her window—Lewis in the lead, wearing two pheasant's feathers in what was most certainly a new red cap, and with a lute slung on his
shoulder. Then came the priest, Sir James, whom
Cecily had not yet spoken to, and Master Orlebar
with his sister riding pillion.

"Hurry! Hurry, Meg!" cried Cecily.

"There—that's the last. Wait, now, till I brush

your hair. Lord, how it shine!" Meg said, admiring as always. "What I'd give for such a head!"

There was a little embroidered hat to match the dress—such, indeed, as her own mother might have worn, set back off the forehead and tied under the chin. It should have had a floating veil, but when they took it from the chest the veil fell into wisps and had to be thrown away. Meg frisked Cecily's long fair hair back behind her ears and pulled the hat snug, then brushed and brushed till Cecily thought she would never be done.

"Let him wait, lady," said Meg in a whisper, close by Cecily's ear. "Be still a moment more."

Cecily stood still then, her mind brimming with mysteries—not least how she had put her rigorous upbringing away from her with such speed and ease that when Meg at last said "There!" Cecily turned and embraced her. She kissed her on the cheek, warmly and confidently. "Dear Meg, dear Meg—a happy, happy Christmas!"

Then she whisked up her skirts and ran from the room, flying as fast as she could to the hall, where the company was gathered.

The place seemed packed with people, and the talk and the laughter was rising every minute. Bet and Janet, Mary Butterwick and Agnes Bunce, were carrying around jugs of steaming wassail. Tom and Anis Bostel stood on the outskirts of the crowd, modestly smiling, but red-bearded Henty counted no man his better, and his was the loudest laugh.

Cecily saw Lewis at once, standing out of the crowd as though painted in colors sharper, bolder, stronger, than anyone present. And he saw her, but waited in a mannerly fashion as she moved to her aunt's side.

Dame Elizabeth in her purple gown was a different woman from the one Cecily knew. She had exchanged her plain cap for a tallish headdress with a turned-back front. Around her neck she wore a fine jewel on a thick gold chain, and there were rings on her fingers. She looked handsome as Cecily would never have believed possible, and her gracious manner with her guests was full of courtesy and hospitality.

"And here is my good niece, Sir James," Dame Elizabeth said to the priest standing at her side. She took Cecily's hand and drew her forward. "I have turned her into a country girl and I dare to claim that she is ten times more content than when she first came. Is it so, Cecily?"

"Yes, dear madam—oh, yes, indeed! But twenty times, not ten!" And just as in the warmth that filled her when she had embraced Meg, so now she pressed her cheek to her aunt's hand, not only in gratitude, but with an affection she would never have believed it possible to feel for so forthright a lady. Then quickly she made her courtesy to the chaplain.

"Bless you, my dear child," he said, in a good easy voice that reminded her of the London days. "Bless you at this Yuletide and at all other times. My pupil has spoken of you."

"And he has spoken of you, Father," she said. She looked with interest at his keen dark eyes, at the creases in his cheeks that proved he laughed often. Here, she saw at once, was another friend should she need one.

Then there was Roger Orlebar to be greeted, and Jenufer, whose manner today was inclined unfortunately toward the wistful. Cecily felt uneasy with her, but Davy, who was running among the guests with the freedom of a lap dog, hung on her hand and leaned against her skirts and seemed ready to stay with her all day.

Now she had done her duty and greeted everyone, and nothing need keep her any longer from giving Lewis his due. She held out her hand and he took the tips of her fingers and bowed extravagantly, till his hair fell into his eyes and he seemed on the point of overbalancing.

"What a fine lady you are today, Cecily Jolland!"

"And how fine a gentleman you have grown, Lewis Mallory!"

He was wearing a short padded jerkin that was as out of fashion as her own dress, but he had on new hose of a matching green, and the points of his shoes were well stuffed with straw—he would fall over them, he said, unless he walked all day on his heels.

"If Dame Elizabeth allows," he said, "we might have some music. I have brought my lute, and we have three recorders—two for my cousins and one for Sir James. Or you may play instead of Cousin Jenufer—she's in a doubtful frame of mind today. But I think you should dance in that gown."

"Oh, I will play—I will play!" she cried. "But let it be your lute, Master Yaffle, if you please. I have missed mine." Made even bolder by his smile she added, "And I will sing."

"The woodpecker and the lark in concert," he said. His eyebrows shot up. "You look so startled— why?"

"For no reason that I know." The lark—the lark . . . "They are going to table," she said.

Sir James spoke a brief and friendly grace that all might understand, not the Latin gabble that Friar Paul would have given them. Then they sat down, all manner of them comfortably settled, and the feast began.

From this moment the day began to race toward its end, its delights so many, its warmth so manifest that there was not time enough to hold it. Dame Elizabeth sat at the head of her table with Sir James on her right and Master Orlebar on her left. Next to the priest sat silent Jenufer, and next to Roger Orlebar came Cecily. Then Nicholas Forge beside Jenufer, with Anis Bostel on his right. And best of all, on Cecily's left sat Lewis Mallory, waved to his seat by Dame Elizabeth in a most friendly fashion. Under the table was Davy, shuttling from side to side, from Cecily to Jenufer, who fed him tidbits when he tugged their skirts. On down the table on either side sat Henty and Henty's son and daughter, Tom Bostel, Forge's old mother, who would not stay at home, with Goody Ann, the Bostels' older children, and the maids who served and then sat down, then leapt up again to carry other dishes—till Cecily wondered if they had a chance to eat at all.

It was a day like no other Cecily Jolland had ever known, a day free and friendly, bound only by kindliness and good manners. When the meal was over at last, the board cleared and taken away, they had their music, changing the instruments about. So first it was Sir James who played the third recorder and Nicholas Forge who took the lute, while Cecily and Lewis, Meg and Henty, Tom and Anis, danced. Then Lewis played his lute, the recorders went to Henty, to Tom, and to Jenufer, while Roger Orlebar led out Dame Elizabeth. At first she had refused, saying she was too old for dancing; but the sight of the first round added to the pleasures of good food, good wine, and good company changed her mind. The grand lady in the purple gown began to lose her great dignity and to laugh and stamp with the rest. She and Roger Orlebar danced alone, an unexpectedly fine pair of performers, while all the company but the musicians clapped out the rhythm, singing la-la-la because there were no other words.

"Now take the lute, Cecily," Lewis said; he had called her by her name before, but not in company. "Sing, as you promised you would."

"Maybe none of the others wants to hear. . . ."

"Yes, sing—sing!" cried Dame Elizabeth, fallen back in her chair and fanning herself fast. "I have heard you about the house. I know you have a voice."

Only the pleasure she had in fingering the lute again and feeling the music plucked from its belly gave Cecily the courage that she needed. Lewis placed a stool for her in the middle of the hall, and there she sat, with the rest waiting to hear her. Moll Thomsett and those who had been helping in the kitchen came to stand at the door. Silence fell. In the silence the lute answered Cecily's fingers. Whether they knew it there or not, she sang for sheer joy of the occasion. First she sang for Christmas, then she sang for winter—songs that she and Alys had learned together long ago. Then she sang of returning spring and all things green, of birds singing and the renewing year:

> Gay comes the singer
>     With a song,
> Sing we all together,
>     All things young;
> Field and wood and fallow,
>     Lark at dawn,
> Young rooks cawing, cawing,
>     Philomel
> Still complaining of the ancient wrong.
>
> Twitters now the swallow,
>     Swans are shrill
>     Still remembering sorrow,

*Cuckoo, cuckoo, goes the cuckoo calling*
  *On the wooded hill.*

*The birds sing fair,*
  *Shining earth,*
  *Gracious after travail,*
  *Of new birth,*
*Lies in radiant light,*
  *Fragrant air.*

*Broad spreads the lime,*
  *Bough and leaf,*
*Underfoot the thyme,*
  *Green the turf.*

*Here come the dances,*
  *In the grass*
*Running water glances,*
  *Murmurs past.*

*Happy is the place,*
  *Whispering*
*Through the open weather*
*Blow the winds of spring.*

One song led to another, until they were singing all together, a carol for the season. All joined hands and danced in a slow circle, singing as they went.

Then suddenly the day was long over, dark at the door, and the guests far from home. While they feasted the wind had increased. It blew now strongly across the forest, fiercely north, and already it carried some snow.

"Now comes the true winter," said Roger Orlebar. "Who knows when we shall be together again?"

"If only the snow were fierce already," cried Cecily, "the whole company must stay at Mantlemass!"

"Then we could play and sing away the winter,"
Orlebar replied, laughing his deep-chested laugh.

"Well, we shall have music some time in the
spring," Sir James said, looking from one to the
other as Lewis and Cecily stood together, spinning
out words of good-bye. "You, my dear daughter
Cecily, shall come with my pupil to the palace
chapel. There I have my viol, and a rebec. Between
us we might do very well."

"Master Yaffle shall show me the way, Father."

"Jesu have you in his keeping, child," said the
priest. "And may he bring us an early spring."

"Amen," said Lewis and Cecily both together,
and very devoutly.

Though it was time to part, the company
lingered, for all by now were flushed and gay. The
maids scurried about the hall, Forge and Bostel and
Henty pursuing them for Christmas forfeits. So too
the rest embraced as they parted, laughing. Dame
Elizabeth offered her cheek to Master Orlebar, and
Jenufer was kissed smackingly by Henty, once he
had dealt with Meg and Mary, Agnes and Janet and
Bet.

"I brought you a Christmas token," Lewis said to
Cecily, "and I have forgotten to give it to you. It is
here safe in my pouch." He brought out a small flat
object wrapped in a piece of cloth, and handed it to
her with a bow.

She unwrapped the little pack and found inside
five small bright feathers, two greeny-yellow, two
speckled brown and white, one red—and all clipped
together with a pin to make an ornament.

"The smith made the pin. It is true steel. You
know the feathers?"

"The woodpecker. The yaffle . . . Thank you,"

said Cecily, so quietly she hardly heard herself speak, "thank you for your care and kindness."

Lewis took her by the hand. Bending forward and smiling, he kissed her quickly on the brow.

# 8

---

## Snowfall to Spring

IN THE WINTER DAYS, WITH THE SNOW PILED HIGH against the walls, the windows fretted with icy patterns, Dame Elizabeth set herself to teach Cecily to read. She was too high-tempered and sharp-tongued to make a good teacher; while Cecily, an unaccustomed pupil, was frightened out of her wits by the immensity of the task. Dame Elizabeth banged with her fists in sheer frustration, Cecily wept at her own stupidity. Quite awestruck, Meg and Mary Butterwick sat in the background stitching at coney skins. Meg was all sympathy for Cecily; but Mary felt that Dame Elizabeth was poorly rewarded for taking such pains.

Each morning Cecily opened her bed-curtains and called to Davy as she had once called to Alys. The little boy ran on bare feet over the cold floor to the window. He blew on the obscuring frost until there was a hole big enough to peer through. Each morning Cecily hoped to hear a cry of excitement that would tell her the snow was melting; but the winter went on and on with no sign of respite.

There were bright and brittle days when the house and the surrounding forest looked like some splendid table decoration—one of those delicate inventions of spun sugar that the master cooks called subtleties, which sparkled and glittered in intricate designs. But the sun made no impression on the depth and hardness of the snow. What dropped from the trees was replaced overnight, and the drifts grew constantly higher and more treacherous.

Mantlemass was a place under siege—a world cut off from every other world and subsisting on itself. It was so for every household about the forest—Ghylls Hatch, the weaver's place, the forges with their stone dwelling houses close at hand, the small huddled cottages of the charcoal burners and the iron workers—all kept their own counsel and existed on what stores had been gathered in. Mantlemass was well provided and those who lived and worked there might count themselves fortunate. For the rest, with little with which to supply themselves and less space for keeping, the outlook as the winter lengthened became bleak. The deer languished and the birds died on the branches, hares and rabbits fell to the foxes prowling and crying in the bitter nights. There could hardly have been less food for the taking. Cecily thought of the coney warrens, where the Mantlemass animals were nourished for the profit of their pelts; it must be bitter for half-starving foresters to know of all that pampered meat. But for the depth of the drifts, the warrens would surely have been raided.

Sometimes Cecily walked out fifty yards or so with Davy, on the few hard paths that had been dug again and again and trampled by the men about the place. The snow on all sides was scored and pitted by innumerable prints—not of men, who could not venture there, but of birds and small animals. Mice made tracks so delicate they were like the frost patterns on the inside of the windows. Birds of all sorts and sizes scrabbled for dropped berries, or rested their exhausted breasts against the snow, leaving an imprint light and despairing. The owls flurried a yard or more of the surface when they swooped after mice and birds; once Cecily found the strangest mark of all, made by the stiff short tail feathers of the woodpecker, as he rocked back off his claws that had not been made for the ground but for the bark of trees.

The feathered pin that Lewis had given Cecily at Christmas she wore always as a talisman, and it was like some magic key to these small signs scratched on the surface of the winter. It was she who showed Davy where the fox had loped his almost single track, where rabbits had sprung from their strong hindquarters to their modest forepaws. This was a language in itself, a reading that needed no learning and that gave her greater pleasure than what she must learn from books and Dame Elizabeth. It made the winter bearable, and because she could teach Davy what she knew, she recovered from the humiliation of finding it difficult to be taught herself.

At Ghylls Hatch the winter was a more uncomfortable experience than at Mantlemass. The house was older, draftier, the winter provisions were not even half so well ordered. Jenufer huddled by the fire and cried because her bones ached with the cold, the servants complained of short commons, and Lewis groaned with boredom. He could neither get to his lessons with the priest, nor find excuses to visit Mantlemass, or do half the work he needed to with the horses. With enormous effort the yard was cleared of snow each morning, and that was the only place where the animals could be exercised. One heavy fall and then nights of frost would have been easier to deal with than each night's snow soft-piled on yesterday's. To make matters worse, a young stallion had broken out of his stall and careered into a snow drift, breaking both forelegs; a great loss, for Lewis had planned to use him for the lame mare, Iris, who would be ready to breed in the spring. This, added to the loss of Zephyr, caused great gloom at Ghylls Hatch.

It was the deepest winter Lewis could remember, and the only comfort he got from it was the knowledge that the most determined father could not carry his daughter away at such a time. As for how the world was going, and whether indeed Sir Thomas Jolland might safely venture back to his own country, there was no means of knowing. In the first days of the snow, before it deepened and drifted, Friar Paul had asked for shelter at Ghylls Hatch and slept the night there. He had been about the countryside as far as the outskirts of London, and his story was that the land was quiet—though he had been told of trials and executions actually in the city. None could confirm if this was fact or legend, and it was little enough to go on. Nonetheless, the friar had been convinced that civil strife had reached its end, and its only legacy among the people was a fear of disbanded soldiery. Even at this date, nearly five months after that final battle on Bosworth Field, there were still soldiers without employment wandering at large. After the proclamation of the new king many of his soldiers had been absorbed into the work of the harvest and so slipped back into everyday life. But some remained, of the kind that were vagrant by nature; and these might be feared, for they would plunder or kill as the occasion suggested.

"But winter will cool them," Friar Paul had said, "and by spring they will be dispersed or dead—who knows which?"

Such wandering bands sought places like the forest for shelter and hiding; but the foresters were far too jealous of their own rights in the place to stomach poachers—though they would harbor a fugitive whatever his crime.

For Lewis the short days were too long, the long nights full of uneasy dreams. Now separated from Cecily, he had time to understand what had befallen him, and he was torn with doubt and distrust, with jealousy of those who saw her daily, with anxiety that she might not think of him as he thought of her; with a bitter fear that even if she did think so, they would be kept apart. And yet how freely Dame Elizabeth had seemed to encourage their friendship. This, in itself, made Lewis uneasy. Why had she done so? Was it because she found him so far below her niece that there could be no thought or fear of any union? But she knew him to be of good stock—better, in the world's eyes, than her own. Then was it because she schemed to see Cecily out of harm's way—out of her father's way, that was—by settling her before Sir Thomas came or sent to claim her? Well that would please all but her father—so long as it would please Cecily; for Lewis would not have her at all unless she willed it as much as he. . . . But at the back of his mind there moved a more subtle fear. He could not quite forget Jenufer's garbled hints about some enmity between the families. He knew from Sir James that Dame Elizabeth had reason to hate her brother, and even an innocent in the ways of the world would recognize her as a woman to whom revenge could be very sweet. Could she, in fact, use Cecily to further that purpose, by encouraging her in pursuits bound to enrage him? He himself had cause to respect Dame Elizabeth, but now he was ready to be suspicious of heaven itself.

There was so much in all this that was mysterious and unexplained that his doubts grew upon Lewis as he fretted out the winter. In the cold and lonely days, and in the snow-lit nights, his nightmare was that he must lose his happiness almost before it had begun. He could bear his own heartbreak, as any man must—but how, if indeed she loved him, would he also bear Cecily's?

With all this turning and churning in his heart and mind, Lewis woke one night after an hour in his bed, and knew that the wind had changed. It was blowing from the southwest and the thaw had begun.

Cecily too, when she woke in the darkness, heard the almost forgotten sound of water dripping from the roof.

"In two days," said Dame Elizabeth next morning, "it will be spring."

It was true. The thaw was fast and complete. The snow was like an army in retreat, fleeing before a strong enemy. The sun shone brilliantly, everything changed. It was a brown sad earth that first appeared, shriveled by the months of cold and darkness. But within a week the pussywillow catkins showed silver along the gushing rivers, and in a little less than a week more Davy came running with a primrose squashed in his fist.

A week and almost a week was a long time; long because although they brought callers they did not bring the one Cecily looked for. Fourteen days and no sign of Lewis. Perhaps in the long winter he had fallen sick and died, and she would never see him again. She was crushed by her feeling of desolation when he did not appear. It had all been a game and now he was busy with some other . . . How would she live if either thing were true?

"Now that the winter is over," her aunt said one evening, "we must consider how the world goes. It is six months since your father left England." She grimaced as she named him. "We cannot hope that he will fail to get some word soon to Mantlemass."

Cecily had begun to tremble and she clasped her hands together to hide their shaking. "What word will it be, madam?"

"What indeed? Either he will have settled himself as only he knows how, or he will be deeper in trouble than before. And as I am not able to wish him well," Dame Elizabeth said with a rough laugh, "I wish him with trouble enough to keep him far away."

This bold way of talking never failed to make Cecily pray to heaven not to take her aunt too seriously. If death or betrayal came to her father, her conscience would have a hard time with the fact that she had listened to her aunt's ill-wishing.

"At this time of year," Dame Elizabeth said, "I send Nicholas Forge about my business to London. He is likely to be two or three weeks away from home. He will bring us news of how the new king is ruling and what changes there are, or likely to be. And if he has no other means, then he shall go to your uncle Digby to inquire for news of Sir Thomas."

"I think my uncle has cast us off altogether," Cecily said.

"Well, he may be appealed to if all else fails. . . . And so tomorrow, Cecily, you will oblige me by riding an errand. I always send to Master Orlebar to know if he has any commissions for Nicholas. They go to London from Ghylls Hatch later in the year, with the horses. At this time the preparation there is so great there's neither man nor beast about the place that can call his soul or his time his own." She looked at Cecily and smiled slightly. "I am sorry to send you, child. But there is a great deal to do at Mantlemass also, and I cannot spare any of the men."

Cecily murmured, "Yes, madam," her heart leaping into her throat with pleasure and with dread.

She set off next morning after prayers. Her aunt was busy with Nicholas Forge, discussing who he must see when he went to London. Cecily had thought she would take Davy with her to Ghylls Hatch, but she could not find him. Since the snow ended he had taken to disappearing for hours on end, and nothing would wring from him where he had been.

The morning was so beautiful that all Cecily's fears seemed foolish. In the sunshine that had come after a night of rain, she knew there would be some easy reason for Lewis's neglect. As she rode away from Mantlemass she was singing to herself and Cressyd the same song of spring she had sung so hopefully at Christmastime. She went up through the woods where she had first seen Lewis riding, and then took the short way to the main track leading to Ghylls Hatch. The little path would take her near the pool where she had talked to him on the day she went to the weaver's cottage, the first time she ever rode alone. For sheer pleasure of the memory, she turned out of her course to pass that way. . . .

He was there. She saw his red cap. And then as she tried not to smile with pleasure at the sight, she saw him look up. Himself unsmiling and almost unnaturally pale, he pulled off his cap and stepped forward. As she shifted Cressyd down toward the pool, he put out his hand and laid it on the bridle.

"Where have you been?" he demanded.

"Where . . . ?" Cecily almost gaped in her bewilderment and outrage. "Where have *you* been, Lewis Mallory?"

"I have waited for you," he said sternly, "day after day."

"Here?"

"Where else?"

"But this is not precisely where I live. And my aunt's house is not hard to find."

"I needed to see you here," he insisted, "not among your people. I was sure you would come. It has not been easy, I can tell you, escaping day by day. We are all off our feet with work."

"Well," she said, defeated, laughing at him for being so absurd, for relieving all her doubts and fears, for being here at all, alive and well and needing to see her. "Well, I am here. I have come. I have done as you expected me to. And better late than not at all—so my aunt says."

He lifted her from the saddle. "I have much to say to you, Cecily Jolland. The winter has been like eternity. I might well have gone out of my mind."

"I have learned to read," she boasted.

"Then your mind has been well occupied."

"I ought to say, my aunt has been trying to teach me!" She was ready to tease him out of his somber expression, but she felt unable to mock him at all. "Look—I am wearing your Christmas token. The feathers are as fine as ever."

"I said I have much to say to you. You must stop chattering and listen. And you must answer truly what I ask you. I have been thinking what I must say to you almost since Christmas day. But swear you will answer honestly and steadfastly, not sparing my feelings."

"Well—I will swear if you wish me to. But I am to be trusted."

"It came to me suddenly," he said. "I knew without warning—or so I thought . . . But then I wondered . . . I could not be certain—not without seeing you and speaking to you. . . . I came here —well, I could not have spoken quietly to you anywhere else. . . . You must understand that."

"Oh, Lewis—please! Who's chattering now?"

"If indeed we love one another," he said flatly, "then certainly we should be made man and wife." He frowned deeply. "This is what I have thought. And you? Now it is in answering that you must be steadfast."

She delayed a moment, but only for the delight of hearing his words repeating in her head. . . .

"Cecily . . . ?"

"I have thought too. And now I know I have thought the same as you."

"And that is the truth? Be very sure of it."

"I said I would swear. Yes. That is the truth."

"To be together always." He was gazing at her, but still not smiling. "You know they will try to prevent it," he said harshly. "You do understand that? They will do all they can to keep us apart. I have thought how your aunt has seemed to draw us together. But it makes no sense to me. It can only be baseless cruelty—would she be cruel? I think she would. Would she let us take hands and then tear us apart?"

"Hush," she said, amazed by his quiet fury. "Take hands, then, and swear not to be torn apart. Take hands and swear to hold fast. Forget the rest— and say what you said before."

"To be together always . . . ?"

"Besides that, you said—"

"That we love each other . . . ?"

"Yes! That. That is the true part. Let it be enough. We need not fear yet—need we? This is a wonderful thing!" she cried, excitement catching her. "To love at all is most extraordinary. But to love rightly—surely that's a miracle? Only think— that we should have met at all—out of all the world of men and women that we should be here in this place, both at one time! And that we should feel the same—each for the other. Oh, Lewis—how has it happened?"

"You are right. It is truly a miracle."

"We must make a vow that nothing can separate us. As you vowed to stand between me and trouble —on your father's ring. Do you remember?"

"I remember the smallest thing that has happened since I first saw you. I remember nothing else. The rest has all gone from me—my father's treatment of me, and the loss of my mother and my brothers—such things mean nothing to me now. I forgot my childhood when I came to Ghylls Hatch, and now I have forgotten all the rest." He fumbled for the thong around his neck and pulled out the ring. "Take it in your hand."

She did as he told her and as before he closed her fingers on the ring and then enclosed her hand in his own.

"We must call this our betrothal," he said. "I vow to Cecily Jolland—my dear love—that I will die rather than be parted from her. . . . But I should not have said that."

"Because I must vow the same?" She shrugged. "What else should I vow? I would die anyway, now —without you. Lord, how the winter dragged!"

He smiled for the first time, and she made the same vow as he had made. They kissed, solemnly.

She was still holding the ring. She opened her hand
and it lay on her palm. At last she saw the emblem
she seemed to have been seeking, dreaming and
waking, through all the days of her life.

"My pretty bird," she heard herself say, in her
mother's sighing, just-remembered tones. . . .

There was still Cecily's errand to Master Orlebar,
and they rode to Ghylls Hatch together, the horses
stepping close enough for their riders to take
hands. Just within sight of Ghylls Hatch they moved
apart. They had decided that no one should know
of their betrothal, for the secret seemed too good to
share.

No spring had ever seemed so fine. If there were
days when the sun did not shine, then neither was
aware of them. There were days, many of them,
when they did not meet, but it seemed enough that
they breathed the same air. Cecily went daily to the
meeting place by the pool, and mostly Lewis contrived to get there too, though their visits did not
always coincide. Whoever was there first left a token
—a mark scratched in the bark of the sturdiest tree.
Whichever of them found a fresh mark then cancelled it with a second.

There was a lot of work for Lewis at this time of
the year. The clearing up and mucking out after the
winter was a colossal task, and there were the mares
in foal needing extra care. In May twenty or so
horses would be taken to London for sale—perhaps
to the royal stable, where they were needed whatever the name of the king, or else to be disposed of
in the open market. Lewis had never accompanied
his cousin on these annual expeditions, but this
year he was determined he would go. With Cecily to
strengthen him he felt twice himself. Because his
mind was full of plans—even plans to carry her off,

if need be, and go to some far place where no one could find them—his manner began to change, becoming within a few days twice as assertive. To the youthful spring of his long-legged stride was added the aggressiveness of a boy moving suddenly and positively into manhood. Now his life had found its purpose and his self-doubts fell from him like an old coat.

It was not long before he realized that his cousin was watching him curiously. He said nothing until Lewis asked if he might go to London with the horses.

"Far better not," said Roger Orlebar. "There's little there to interest you." The loud laugh that interrupted him made him frown. "There's neither sense nor manners in that, boy. It's not my task to take you to the world, but rather to keep you out of it."

"That's blunt, at least." Lewis's laughter died and he began to feel something of the helpless anger that had plagued him as a child in his early years at Ghylls Hatch. "I have put up with my father's roughness—*why* he disowned me seemed no matter. But I'll ask you now—now that I'm grown and got some sense—why? Why?"

"You may ask. It'll do little good if you do. I was never told."

"You took me in—and never knew why you had to do so?"

"Your father was my kinsman." Orlebar's dark, weathered skin began to redden. "Well—if it must be said . . . I was poor and struggling to make a living here. I was proud of his trust perhaps—a man of his standing in the world. . . . Also he rewarded me handsomely. And before you accuse me, Lewis —I was unwilling and I was bribed—but it is not by your father's wealth that I have been repaid. I think you know you have become as dear as a son to me."

Lewis looked briefly into his cousin's troubled face, and as briefly smiled. He fumbled after the right words. "And I . . . And you. . . ."

"Then," said Roger Orlebar, smiling in his turn, "I shall speak to you as a father must. You are too much concerned with Dame Elizabeth's young niece."

"Dame Elizabeth has not said so."

"Dame Elizabeth FitzEdmund is a law unto herself. We both know that. What her purposes are no man rightly knows. But there are things I do know —that you and the girl meet about the forest—that you have been seen riding together—"

"Where's the harm in that?"

"Lewis, you must attend to me. One thing I know, for all my ignorance—between your father and Sir Thomas Jolland there is something deep and dangerous."

"What thing? And how do you know?"

"From words dropped. From one certain happening. I know this—that at one time these men were brothers in arms, that they fought under the same standard—both were for Lancaster, both were close to the king. But then, when things were going badly, Sir Thomas turned his coat and fawned on the Duke of York. When York became king of England, Sir Thomas was very well placed."

"Less well when that king died at Bosworth!"

"The girl's the daughter of a traitor. It is preposterous for your father's son to think of her. Mallorys have been pillars of the Lancastrian cause. You know that at least about your own people?"

"They are not my people anymore. . . . From words dropped, you said, and from *one certain happening*. What was that?"

"Before he brought you here, your father took you to connections of your mother's—and afterward he moved you here."

"I remember that much," said Lewis, bitterly recalling his misery.

"That was in Buckinghamshire—and there was a manor two miles or so from where you were left. It was one of several granted by the crown to Dame Elizabeth's husband—you know he was the son of a royal duke, though born on the wrong side of the blanket, as they say. Then your father learned that Dame Elizabeth might go to live there—for nearby there was a manor of her husband's—so he fetched you away. There's the measure of what Mallory owes Jolland in the way of love."

"And brought me here?" Lewis said incredulously. "Where also Dame Elizabeth has a manor?"

"Mantlemass had stood empty since it was built. There wasn't one of us about here knew who the owner was. Over a year before he brought you to me, your father questioned me about my neighbors —and how he did question me!—I told him freely everything I knew. It was six months and more after that before Mantlemass was lived in, and its dame proved to be Elizabeth FitzEdmund."

"And if you had told my father then, you would have lost what he had given you."

"Not a material loss only. Believe that."

"I do believe it. But if you are my father now, then I am Orlebar, not Mallory. And what reason has Orlebar to frown on an alliance with Jolland?"

"No, Lewis, no!" his cousin cried. "This is bold beyond words! Alliance, indeed! I gave a solemn undertaking to your father. . . ." He threw up his hands and turned away impatiently. "Let that suffice, boy! Let that suffice."

Bitterly troubled, Lewis watched him stride off

toward the stables. He had always shown himself good, kind, and honest. Today he had stopped short of final candor. Lewis had no doubt in mind that there was something more his cousin could have told him.

Just as Lewis was much occupied with his work in the spring weather, so Cecily had her hands full of jobs about the house. The linen must be looked to and repaired and the bed-curtains taken down to be beaten and hung in the sun. Outside, the warrens were undisturbed at this time for the creatures were lustily breeding. The cattle were turned out by day and the muck raked from the byres until the midden grew as high as the neighboring barns. There were already two new calves and the lambing pens were full. Davy ran from place to place as the days increased the young stock; but he still vanished for hours together and Cecily had given up trying to discover where he went.

Now between Cecily and her aunt there existed a curious quiet. No confidences were given, nor were they sought. Cecily knew that her aunt watched her, but with a distant contemplation that seemed to suggest a standing back from events. She did not speak again of her brother's possible return, but when Nicholas Forge had not returned from London at the end of three weeks, she grew restless.

"He should be back. He must have taken some sickness and been delayed."

"You said he had much to do for you."

"Yes, so he has. I am impatient. He has taken a petition for me too. Now that we have a new king I need to confirm my rights in Mantlemass. Then I may be certain it will go to my appointed heir."

"Then he is sitting day by day in some anteroom," decided Cecily. "For I do remember my father saying it took time to get the king's ear."

As she spoke she wondered briefly if she might be her aunt's heir, as she now knew she was her mother's. And because she was in a state to dream, she dreamed of living there at Mantlemass with Lewis and seeing their children grow in the place. She longed to confide in her aunt then. She would look for Lewis tomorrow, she decided; she would look all day until she found him, and tell him they must no longer keep her aunt in ignorance of how things stood between them.

The next day was warm and misty, the sun held behind a haze of thin cloud. The forest steamed. The ground was now thick with flower, anemones and primroses lingering as the first bluebells shot above them. Cecily went on foot to the meeting place. He was not there and he had left no sign since yesterday, when he had carved a crescent in the tree trunk and she had later carved it into two against his next visit.

If he had not been yet, then he would almost certainly come later, and she sat down to wait. In the complete stillness of the misty day she heard every sound with a startling and beautiful clarity. Birds fidgeted and sang. A stoat ran by and paused, rearing up rigid as a stick till her quiet soothed him and he went on his way. And for the first time since she had come to the forest, she saw a snake slide by. She watched it carefully, ready to leap up and fly from the place; but it was a green grass snake, mild as milk, moving harmlessly across the path.

It was long past noon when she heard the sound she was waiting for. Lewis came riding down the track on Diamante, and the moment she looked at him she knew that something was wrong.

\* \* \*

"Nothing is changed," Cecily said positively when Lewis had told his tale. She was frightened by his gloom. "Why did you tell your cousin what we had sworn to keep secret? I longed to tell my aunt, but I did not."

"There was no need to tell him. He knew. It was in my face, no doubt. I daresay I have never looked like this before."

"But nothing—nothing—is changed," she insisted. "Your father has left you all these years— why should he care that I am my father's daughter? What can it matter to us if they are enemies?"

"We are bound to suffer for their pride and ambitions; for their revenge. In law we are still children, and they will part us for their own purposes. Yes— even your aunt."

"Oh, no, Lewis—no. She promised me happiness. Now that I know her, I believe in her deeply. If we confide in her, who knows, she may help us."

"It is too dangerous. Your father still has more power over you than she has."

"Why should he not abandon me, as yours has abandoned you?"

Lewis shook his head. "I am thinking what could happen to you if he learned what we intend—"

"What could happen?" she asked, holding his hands tightly. But she knew, she had known since that afternoon in the orchard, in that other life. "My aunt in York . . . the abbess. . . ."

"He would do it, wouldn't he?"

"If it suited him. . . . You mean we had best be married and forestall him? We must do that. They cannot part us then. They dare not."

"You have twice my courage. I'm ashamed. My cousin has still not told me all he knows—I am sure of that. But let it go. That's another world—the

world of great men. We can turn our backs on them
and keep our roots and our roof here in the forest."

"Then go to Sir James, Lewis. Ask him to help us.
He is the one who can save us."

"I'll go to him this evening. You go home now,
Cecily. And if you must tell your aunt, then do so.
You will know what is best, though I would sooner
keep the secret."

Cecily did not go directly to Mantlemass. She
watched Lewis ride away and then sat a long time by
the water. She held her head between her clenched
fists, trying desperately to think what was best, wondering whether to ask her aunt for help, wondering
what Sir James would say to Lewis—for after all he
had a duty too, to her guardian and to Lewis's. She
sat with closed eyes, praying desperately that she
need not lose her happiness. When at last she could
neither think nor pray anymore, she got up stiffly
and started for home. Halfway there, Davy ran out
of the bushes and threw himself against her skirt.
She took his hand and they went home together.

The mist had thickened as the day declined, and
it was many hours now since Cecily had gone in
search of Lewis. As she reached the house she saw
Sim Carter leading away a bay horse. That meant
that Nicholas Forge had returned. Bringing with
him—what news? There was a second horse that
she did not recognize, tethered near the door. She
went into the hall, with Davy still hanging on to her
hand. Her aunt was there, and two men with her.
One was Nicholas Forge.

The other, who turned as she entered, was her
father's servant, Giles, who had ridden with him
into exile last September.

# 9

## The Marriage

CECILY SAW AT ONCE THAT GILES HAD BETTERED HIM-self. He no longer wore the livery of a serving man but a sober respectable suit that suggested a gentleman's steward or secretary. She remembered that he had spoken to her kindly on the ride from London to Mantlemass, and that she had answered shrewishly. His face had changed since then, as well as his clothes. He was lean, upright, bold, and his eyes were those of a self-seeker. No doubt he had learned from his master.

Of all this Dame Elizabeth too would be well aware. Her shrewd, ironic dignity dominated the hall.

"Your father has sent this man with a message, niece. We had best hear what it is."

"His secretary, madam," said Giles, looking around for his master's daughter. He had glanced at Cecily without any recognition as she came indoors, a girl in a plain gown with a small boy hanging on to her hand. He looked so shocked at the change in her that she almost laughed in his face.

"Good day to you, Giles," she said. From this moment she was calm. She had everything to gain or to lose and she needed all her wits about her.

"Lady," said Giles in a mourning tone, dropping on his knee and taking her hand as if to kiss it. "You have been sorely treated! Alas, that your father's daughter should be so humbled!"

"Alas, that my father's servant should be so bold!" she retorted, snatching away her hand. For a second it looked as if she might lay it about his cheek and he ducked his head involuntarily, so that she laughed. "What's your message?" she demanded.

"Madam—I am to say to you that Sir Thomas is well settled in France and shall remain there. That he has two good tidings for you and awaits your return under his roof."

"I am my aunt's ward and must abide by her wishes."

"You are your father's daughter, lady," he repeated virtuously. "I have told you his wishes."

"Doubtless you have some written instruction from your master?" Dame Elizabeth said.

"Why—no, madam. But I have my own years of service to Sir Thomas—the lady Cecily knows me well and can vouch for me."

"You speak very prettily, I must say, considering your earlier place with my brother—were you not one of his grooms? No doubt Sir Thomas would gladly be reunited with his daughter. But are you to be her escort?"

"Sir Thomas expects that her maid will attend her, naturally—"

"Oh, we are quite differently placed here, Master Giles. My girls are far too simple to travel from home, and in any event I cannot spare a single one of them."

"Pray tell your master," said Cecily, "that I am very content where he placed me." She gave her aunt a rather sly look as she spoke, and Dame Elizabeth returned her glance, straight-faced and straight-backed. After all the dread of how such a summons as this might come, the uneasy presence of one man seemed almost frivolous.

Giles was looking at Cecily with his eyebrows drawn together and his mouth down at the corners. He had never heard her speak so much before, and her voice must seem to belong to another. What a tale to take back to his master! The delicate girl turned to a sturdy wench ready to stamp on his toes if he did not keep them out of the way. . . .

"You spoke of two good tidings—were those your words?" she said. "What tidings?"

"Sir Thomas is to give you a new mother, lady."

This time he made the sensation he wished. He heard with obvious satisfaction Dame Elizabeth's abrupt, derisive exclamation.

"And has she great estates?" she demanded. "And titles? Sir Thomas has lacked titles. His last attempt to gain some went astray."

"The lady is a widow of a French nobleman, and has indeed her own titles. Of her three brothers, one has the ear of the French king, the second is a cardinal, and the third is as fair as the day—"

"Indeed!" Dame Elizabeth's voice was icy sharp. "Then this time Sir Thomas is well settled. What do you think of this, Cecily?"

"I wish him every joy," said Cecily, her eyes on her folded hands. "Though I thought he was true to my mother's memory. He always told me so."

"A good way of saving himself for better times, no doubt," said her aunt. "Memory is a sad companion. Be generous, Cecily. Relieve the lady of a stepdaughter—women seldom love such a relation."

"Sir Thomas has made his plans, madam," Giles said. "I have not told you the rest. Two good tidings, I said. So here is the second." He looked at Cecily and smiled. "You may rejoice, lady. Your father has chosen you a fine husband."

Cecily did not remember leaving the hall and going to her own room. But she was there now, lying in her bed, with Meg and Mary crowding round, and Davy sitting near her feet with his black eyes starting out of his head.

"Ah, no wonder she took swimey, poor soul," Mary was saying, "the way he talk. . . . Why don't she wake? Oh, she look very particular, Meg!"

*Particular* meant unwell, and Cecily, trying vainly to force her eyes open, murmured protestingly, "I am neither swimey nor particular, so hold your tongues, the pair of you."

"Run down quick, Mary, and tell the mistress our young lady's come to her senses."

Cecily did not protest this time. She was in her nightgown, so the girls must have undressed her and put her to bed, and that would have taken time. Perhaps she had fainted, but she could not remember it. She had wanted so desperately to escape from Giles and his hateful smiling words that her senses seemed simply to have released her and wafted her from the room. But the words had indeed been spoken, and there was no true escape from them.

"Meg . . ."

"Yes, my dear sweet lady?" answered Meg, taking Cecily's hand and stroking it.

"Has he gone?"

"Yes, he has. He made a fine belver, but she sent

him off. Oh, her voice—you should've heard! Chizzly as old grit, it sounded."

Now Cecily could close her eyes no longer. She sat up in bed. "He'll come again, Meg. What shall we do?" Sick of discretion, she cried out, "You know the only one I'll ever marry!"

"I see that—oh, long ago I see that, as I think you know. And night and morning, ever since, I pray for your happiness."

"I will be happy!" cried Cecily, clenching her teeth and gripping Meg's hand so hard that she had to pull it away. "I will be! I will be!"

"Hush—that's a slattern face. Look—you frit poor Davy."

"The uglier I look, the better. That fellow thought me sadly changed, thank God. Noblemen do not marry with country girls, and they cannot remake me twice. What if I stained my face and hands and sheared off my hair? That should frit *him*, Meg."

"That's wild talk, I'd say."

"But did you hear? My father is to marry—and I am to have the lady's brother for my husband! It cannot even be decent. Perhaps it will not be allowed. . . ."

"He'll save you," Meg said softly. "Your lovely lad—him, Lewis Mallory. And all here shall help him. True enough, you do have a bit of a foresty look these last months. Now here's where your home is. You'll see how the forest won't care to give you up."

"My father's a powerful man. . . . Oh, God help me!"

"Here's your good aunt come to you," Meg said, moving respectfully away from the bedside.

"Leave the room now, Meg," Dame Elizabeth

said. "And take that boy with you. And when the door closes, keep your ear from the keyhole."

"I never do anything but that!"

"And your eye too, Meg, if you please."

Meg called to Davy and flounced away. Cecily lay back and watched her aunt walking the room, her head bent, her hands clasped tightly together. Cecily had grown very accustomed to what had shocked her—Dame Elizabeth's dominating manner, her loud firm voice and its mockery, her ease with the men about the place, her quick coarse humor. It was a surprise to see her, as she seemed now, at a loss for words.

"Tell me what I must do," Cecily said, to break the silence.

Dame Elizabeth came to the bed and sat down. "Nicholas Forge has told me that Sir Thomas is thought to be in England. Your uncle Digby parted with this news after much soliciting. He could not say where, but it probably would be safer for him not to know. There's no welcome for Sir Thomas in his own country for the present, that's sure."

"Where might he be?" asked Cecily faintly, half glancing over her shoulder as though she expected him to be already at the door.

"No nearer than the coast, I daresay. He'll be in harbor, waiting to take the first tide after Giles brings you to him."

"But I am not to go with him, madam? You would never send me . . . ?"

"No, no—my dear child, you must learn to trust me. But he'll come again, Cecily. And a second time he will not come alone."

"Then—who will come with him?"

"Your father could venture as far as this, no doubt. Once he reaches the forest he's almost certainly secure. But you are not to fear him. I have promised you—have I not promised you time and time again that you are to be happy?"

"But have you mocked me, madam?" Cecily's voice rose dangerously as despair touched her. "I have thought and thought of all your riddles and your mysteries that you would not explain. I know you hate my father and I know why. But I can see you might be revenged on him through me. I have tried not to see it. But it is too plain."

"Why, yes, I might do so. But can you think I would? Is this all you have learned of me?"

Cecily burst into loud and bitter tears. "Why— why have you let me make Lewis Mallory my dearest friend? I know now that his father and mine are enemies. And you know it. Is this indeed your purpose—to plague Sir Thomas through me and my misery?"

Dame Elizabeth caught Cecily by the wrists and shook her.

"What would he care for your misery? It is through your happiness I shall pay my account. . . . Cecily—answer me truly. Is he—young Mallory—is he indeed your dearest friend, as you call him?"

"As I am his! And always will be! And if we are parted we cannot live! This is the only truth I know and if you take it from me—I must die."

"Hush, now! You will make yourself ill. I need you calm and sensible."

"How can I be? I understand nothing. I don't know whom I may trust. I am afraid of everyone, except Lewis. Of everyone—everyone!"

"Oh, be quiet and listen to me!" Now Dame Elizabeth had Cecily by the shoulders, alternately soothing and shouting, but with no effect. "Be calm! Even now I could fail in what I have planned all these years—yes, years, Cecily. We must know what we are doing. Are you listening to me?"

Cecily was now past reason. She could not have stopped sobbing if she had wished to, and she was so far gone in misery that she did not care. Her aunt released her, and she fell back, her eyes closed, but the tears pouring under her lashes and soaking the pillow.

Dame Elizabeth was at the door, calling "Meg! Where are you? Come here to me, girl."

Meg's voice came faintly up the stairs. "You did say I should take my eyes and ears away. . . ."

"That'll do. Bring me a cup of the wine posset. The herb recipe—you will know the one. And get about it sharply—there's no time to waste." She returned to the bedside and tried again to quiet Cecily. "You will make yourself ill, I tell you!"

Meg came scuttling with a covered cup, and Dame Elizabeth took it and sniffed at it.

"This is strong, Meg. But maybe that is best. I must speak to her and then she can sleep, and to-morrow we must act as best we can." She was talking to herself more than to Meg, whose sympathetic face was pink and tearful at the sight of Cecily. "Hold it for her, Meg. Come now, niece. Drink it down."

The first mouthful made Cecily gasp, it was so strong. She remembered the drink. Her aunt had given it to her the night she arrived at Mantlemass, then as now beside herself with misery. It had made her sleep and dream the old dream. She drank obediently enough, her tears checked. The soothing herbs acted quickly, and she sighed and lay back drained and exhausted.

"Now listen carefully," Dame Elizabeth said, bending over Cecily after Meg had gone away reluctantly. "I will tell you now why your father kept you so close, and then we will thank God together that you were left here because it was convenient to a threatened man. You are sleepy already. Then take this comfort with you for the night: Before you can be married to this nobleman of France—this husband of your father's cunning choice—vows must be cancelled and contracts set aside. Do you hear what I am saying?"

Cecily murmured something. The draft was so strong it was like a blow between the eyes. The bitter taste of it was still in her mouth but she was already drowsy. She had difficulty in keeping her eyes open and her aunt's face swam and blurred before her.

"Your father has been very patient. He has waited years for what even he can hardly have hoped for— a cardinal! A cardinal for a brother-in-law! Are you listening?"

"A cardinal . . ."

"He needs such a man—he needs a sympathetic churchman who will speak for him in the only possible quarter. You cannot marry without a papal dispensation. Do you understand? *Do you understand?* That fool, Meg—however much of the foxglove did she use? It could be poison! Cecily!" Again she had her by the shoulders, shaking her, gently at first then much harder. "You must listen to me. The Pope will be petitioned to release you from your first marriage. *Your marriage*, Cecily! Oh, do wake up a little!"

Cecily opened her eyes, then, her head swaying. "I am awake. . . ."

"Your father gave you a husband, my dear, when you were only five years old—a solemn ceremony. Your fortune from your mother was to buy him a useful alliance. But he sought to better himself sooner by political means—and then the marriage

was useless to him, obnoxious to the other parties.
. . . Such ceremonies, you know well, are binding.
They cannot be set aside unless the church consents. And so you are bound to your husband, Cecily. . . . Do you hear me? He cannot marry you to
any other without a solemn annulment from His
Holiness the Pope. . . . Cecily?"

Cecily's eyes were now half closed. She could just
see her aunt's face, and by its expression Dame
Elizabeth was shouting out in rage and frustration.
Cecily could not reply. She was already slipping
giddily into the crowded darkness she knew so well,
where the dark-bearded man was smiling as always,
and she was a child seated on his knee. The light
from a high colored window was caught by the jewel
in his ear. She had put out her hand to touch his
doublet. The padding in the folds was soft and fat,
but the gold thread worked into a design of lines
and lozenges felt harsh under her fingers, and she
drew them away, curling her hand into a fist. She
looked up into the face of the graybeard in his purple gown who stood close by, and watched him
nodding his head. There was music and the room
seemed full of people she could not see.

A woman whose face she did not at first distin-
guish swept her up from the lap of the dark-bearded
man and held her, crooning "My bird! My pretty
bird! My poor bird! Your wings are to be clipped
already!" This was her mother, in a tawny gown
with jewels like a collar around her throat. A fine
light veil floated from her tall headdress and the
hem of her gown was deeply braided with rich em-
broidery.

"Set her down," a man's voice said. "She is not a
baby now." And that was her father.

Even now, lying in her bed, chasing the images
through her memory, in and out of a half sleep,

Cecily drew herself together at the tone—the voice lighter than she knew it, but the command the same, and the coldness. This was her wedding day, which none had told her of since; which she was too young to understand at the time; whose image had remained to her in the vague shape of an unresolved dream.

Her mother set the child on her feet and she stood in the center of the watching circle, the focus of all eyes, not knowing why—but pleased to be so and smiling prettily if uncertainly to make them smile and nod in return. There could not be any apprehension in so young a creature—the fear was the experience of the grown Cecily, for whom the pictures unfolded as they had never done before, full of sound and detail and as brightly colored as the margins of her aunt's great books from which she had tried to read.

The crowded room was hot. The women fanned themselves and there was sweat on the men's faces. Only two were bearded. Some wore long gowns and some short, and their shoes with toes upcurling, some chained to the knee, made the small Cecily shrill with laughter.

"Hush!" someone said. "Little wives are to be quiet and gentle."

Then there was a sudden jostling and shifting, for outside a voice had cried that the archbishop was riding into the courtyard. . . .

When they were in the chapel there seemed fewer people and it was easier to breathe. Now her father held Cecily by the hand—and she saw it was he who wore a dark beard and an ear jewel, which was why she had failed in the past to recognize him—she remembered him always clean-shaven. Had he shaved off his beard, perhaps, with his Lancastrian loyalties?

The archbishop, a tall broad man, spoke to her quite long and earnestly, and only the prettiness of his purple cap kept her attention fixed. Perhaps he was telling her not to be afraid, that after the ceremony she should go home with her mother and her father, and remain with them until she was old enough to be sent as a wife to her husband's home. . . . Now the gay music had changed and was solemn, the voices of young boys soared to the chapel roof. There was linen and lace and the archbishop wore a magnificent cope gold-embroidered on every inch. The little girl looked at the ground and feared to raise her eyes, for she was growing tired and everyone seemed far away from her, busy about affairs that depended on her but did not concern her. Her gaze at ground level ran about the feet of the gathering as dartingly and uncertainly as a mouse; then rested on the shoes of the boy on the archbishop's other hand.

Impatience seized the grown Cecily, wrestling half conscious with pictures that came so fast and changed so ruthlessly that she seemed to hear herself cry out. She struggled to wake, yet knew that she might wake too soon. With his shoes of tan doeskin the boy wore saffron hose. Over a white shirt he wore a short doublet of gold damask, trimmed with narrow fur and gold-belted, and a gold chain around his neck.

Her father stirred behind her, answering some word from the archbishop. She moved forward as he told her. The boy moved forward too. The two grown men, the fathers, each took his child's hand and laid it in the hand of the other. Both hands were warm and a little sticky, and both children seemed uncertain about this hand-taking and tried to sheer away. But first the fathers held them, and then the archbishop put his hand over all and held them firmly together. Under this pile of hands the smallest wriggled and winced against the pressure of bones and muscles and the hard fierce edges of rings. At last, pinched beyond endurance, the girl shrieked and began to cry.

Although this caused a discreet tumult, it was not of disapproval. The men murmured together and smothered laughs, while the women sighed and exclaimed. It was right and seemly that a bride should weep. . . . Bless the little creature, she was a woman already in her submissive sadness! The archbishop released the hands just in time or the bride would have struck out in pain and fright.

They were leaving the chapel. Talk burst out among the adults, and the two children seemed forgotten as congratulations passed from father to father, as the mothers embraced, as the contracts drawn by lawyers were duly signed and sealed. The boy and the girl were recollected then, for they had each to make their mark on the parchments.

"Salute your bride, boy," his father ordered, to the loud laughter of the company. "Kiss her now, for you must wait many a long year before you may see her again."

His father holding him by the shoulders, thrusting him forward, the boy approached. As he advanced he stretched his thin neck nervously, kissed her quickly between the eyes, and flinched back. Even though she would not look at him, Cecily felt that wincing away. The patter of amusement from the crowded room made her flush violently and clench her hands together. . . .

As always at this moment in the dream she began to struggle—either to wake, and know herself safe—or to dream on and see more. Her struggles woke her for an instant and she cried out wildly, for all she was aware of was her father's face, which seemed stooped above her. Immediately she began to sink back again. This time her sleep was absolute, so still, so deep that she seemed hardly to breathe.

Toward morning, Cecily stirred. After opening her eyes with difficulty, she saw that the bed-curtains had been pulled back. Her aunt had no doubt come in the night to see how she was. The room was empty now, and Meg must have taken Davy to another bed, for his own in the corner by the door had not been slept in.

"Lewis must know," murmured Cecily. But it was impossible to recall what it was she needed to tell him. She was so fuddled she could not order her thoughts at all. Was it that Giles had come? She did remember that. Or something that her aunt had said to her—she had talked a lot, but what had it been about? Or perhaps there had been something in her dream that she needed to confide . . . if she could recall at the moment what the dream had been about. Yet Lewis must know, Lewis must be found—she would surely know when she saw him what it was she had to say.

She fumbled her way out of bed, her head swimming so that she had to catch hold of the curtains. Once, between the bed and the chest from which she had picked up her clothes, she fell; but the bundle she carried muffled the sound of the fall.

One thing her muddled brain did tell her—that soon the household would be stirring. Her aunt would surely come again to see if she were waking. It was growing light very fast, and Goody Ann would be jangling the bell to bring them all tumbling and yawning down the narrow stair from the big room under the rafters. If she was to go, she must go now.

In the first light then, the birds now stirring, Cecily left Mantlemass. The bolts on the big studded door might have troubled her, but in spite of her groping, half-numbed fingers they slid as though buttered, and there was no creaking of the heavy hinges as she slipped outside.

The air was sharp, there was frost on the ground as well as a cuckoo calling in the distance. The forest was utterly still, waiting to take breath and begin the day, and she paused, looking out over wood and heathland, afraid of the mystery of the place yet longing to find shelter there. Then she picked up her skirt and went stumbling away from the house, down the narrow path toward the river. She slipped on the stepping-stones and her shoes filled with water. With great difficulty she pulled herself up the far bank, but the effort exhausted her, and she fell to her knees, then toppled forward and lay with her cheek against the ground, longing to sleep again. But she was much too near home. She dragged herself up and continued on her way, and now she was seeking a hiding place. Ahead of her there was an expanse of scrub, gorse and bramble and holly matted into an inviting shelter. She crawled in, rather as Davy had done that first day of the snow, and this time the intense drowsiness won and she slept again.

When Cecily next woke her head was entirely, almost frighteningly clear. She remembered Giles, her father's plans, the dream of the marriage, and why she must find Lewis. She knew that because the drink, which should have been soothing, had been like a blow on the head, Dame Elizabeth had been unable to finish her tale. There was more. Everything that had happened since she came to Mantlemass began to fall into place. Her aunt's sympathy, the promises she had made of happiness, of giving back what had been taken away. Once she had said *There was a move made in this game that was never revoked,* and had claimed to have come to Mantlemass because she knew who her neighbors were; with something like triumph she had cried out, "Answer me truly. Is he—young Mallory—is he indeed your dearest friend?" Through Cecily's happiness, she had claimed, she would be able to square her account with her brother; but she had added, truly, that she might still fail. . . .

Cecily left her shelter. Now her feet were firm under her, her heart thudding, her thoughts racing. She knew she had seen the emblem sharp and clear in the last moments of her dream, not, as it had seemed on a previous occasion, as a promise for the future—but as a promise continuing from the past.

Now indeed she knew what it was she had to say to Lewis Mallory.

It was *Can you remember?*

# 10

## Forest

LEWIS THAT NIGHT HAD HAD NO FEVERED DREAMS AS Cecily had done. Instead, he had not slept at all, but had sat on his bed or walked the floor, trying to persuade himself that she would understand why, after all, he had not sought the help of Sir James. The suggestion that the priest should solve their problems by marrying them had been easily made. While they were together anything seemed possible. But reason had to prevail. Cecily would surely see as he did how hard a choice this would offer Sir James. His affections, his sympathies were with them—the young—but his responsibility could only be to their elders. He could not in conscience do as he was asked. In the darkness and quiet of midnight this was overwhelmingly clear to Lewis and he was quite bowed down by the difficulties of the situation. Cecily's conviction that her aunt would help them appeared to him too fantastic for belief. This was not necessarily because he had come to mistrust her motives, but because he could not easily imagine how any woman, even one as bold as Dame

Elizabeth, would be able to overcome the authority of a father. He knew because his cousin had told him how his own mother had tried to prevail and keep her son—but what good had that done him? Women were simply not able to overrule such circumstances.

It seemed to Lewis, increasingly despairing as the night plodded over, that their only hope lay in flight. If they were to hope for any happiness together, then they must leave the forest and go very far away, and struggle to make their own way in the world. This would demand great courage. If he was to ask it of her, then he must make sure she was aware what the consequences would be if they were overtaken. She would be bound to suffer for her disgrace, while him they would certainly kill.

The morning did not bring Lewis any great comfort. When they next met, which would surely be today, he would have to tell Cecily the conclusions he had come to, such as they were, and how, if they were to be secretly married, it could not be by Sir James. He greatly feared her distress. He set about his work that morning with a dogged kind of energy, for the sooner he was finished with it, the sooner he would be free to seek her. He was grooming his own Iris, whom no one else must handle, when Nicholas Forge rode into the yard.

Lewis left Iris and took the visitor's horse. "When did you return from London?" he asked.

"Last evening before dusk. I have your cousin's business to discuss."

"He's indoors. His sister is in a tantrum and only he can calm her. Go to him—I'll see to the bay."

"I will tell you this before I go," Nicholas said. "I was not the only man to ride to Mantlemass last night. The other was a servant of Sir Thomas Jolland."

He might almost as well have said at once that all plans were in vain. The shock of the news was so great that for a second Lewis could not reply. "What did he want?" he said at last. "Where is Sir Thomas, then?"

"I heard in London he had quit France on a journey. He's not so many miles from here, I'd say—he sent his man to fetch the young lady to him."

"To fetch her . . . ?"

"Well, this I judged to be his purpose. I could not eavesdrop the whole conversation. But it seemed Dame Elizabeth would not discuss the matter. The fellow was sent away. But he will come again, she says." Nicholas looked at Lewis in a questioning way, as though uncertain how much he should say. "Next time, she says, he will not come alone."

"Thank you for your confidence," Lewis said, and turned away, because he was ashamed of what must be in his face for all to see. He went to the stable and, abandoning Iris, began to saddle up Ebony. As he led the stallion out, his cousin Orlebar came into the yard from the house and greeted Nicholas Forge, still dallying and looking uneasily after Lewis.

"Where are you going?" Roger Orlebar asked, seeing the horse saddled.

"To Mantlemass."

"Not now. I need you. Master Forge and I have matters to discuss and you shall hear them."

"I have had bad news. I must go."

"Bad news? And you must go to Mantlemass?" He looked at Nicholas. "What now?"

"Before I left the house last night a servant of Sir Thomas Jolland was there."

"And what of that?" Roger Orlebar cried. "I would be happier if I had never heard the name Jolland!"

"I mean to change it," Lewis said, growing paler and prouder and more foolishly bold with every minute.

"You mean *what*? Now God be my witness, Lewis —you cannot have her! I have tried to tell you this, but I see I should have been a sight more direct. I have only had one confidence ever from Dame Elizabeth. But it was this: that the girl was contracted in marriage by her father when she was barely out of the cradle. If it weren't for political troubles she'd have had her own household by now. There. Now you have it."

Lewis laughed.

"Are you determined not to believe me? You know well that Sir Thomas lost your father's friendship and respect when he turned traitor to Lancaster. The same act, so Dame Elizabeth says, lost him his son-in-law. But the marriage was made and has not been undone. No doubt it will be, fast enough, when he finds another husband who'll be useful to him . . . Well now you will see why I have been amazed at her frivolity in letting you two have so much freedom."

"I think you must be lying, sir," Lewis said. He spoke with difficulty for his teeth seemed to be chattering and he could not get his tongue around the words. "She never spoke of it. . . ."

"How should she, poor child? She was a babe, I tell you—she would not even remember. How much do you remember of your time before you came here—but you were older than she must have been at that time."

"I forgot through necessity, cousin." He turned and put his foot in the stirrup.

"Lewis! You are to stay here with me!"

"I must speak with her!" shouted Lewis, throwing himself into the saddle and moving off fast before he had even found his second stirrup.

"You poor young fool!" Roger Orlebar bellowed after him, deeply distressed. "Why—why could you not be warned in time?"

Cecily pushed her way through the scrub and ran down the slope toward the wider track that led one way to Ghylls Hatch, the other toward the weaver's cottage. Then she heard a sound and slid behind a tree to watch.

There were two riders, mounted on a roan and a chestnut, making their way in her direction. They moved uncertainly, pausing and pointing one way or another, consulting together, perhaps quarreling, for she could hear a rise in their voices. They were strangers to the forest, a man and a woman.

Neither was a stranger to Cecily, however. The man was Giles. The woman was Alys.

Cecily shrank in her hiding place, then, stepping back a pace or two, let the neighboring bushes swallow her. She watched the pair as they picked their way with distaste and obvious unease along a boggy edge and reached the open track. They halted no more than ten yards from her.

"I came to the place the other way last night," Giles was saying. "There was a fellow ahead of me —I followed his lead. How was I to know I should be forced to ride the same way again?"

"You might have known it. Men! Did you think— you and sir Thomas—that such a woman as Dame Elizabeth would hand the girl over with no fuss?"

"There was no reason to think otherwise."

"What fools!" Alys cried impatiently. "I should have been with you."

"Which way now then?" Giles asked. "Since you

know all that should be done, which way do we turn?"

"I know nothing of the way," snapped Alys. "I only know he bade us make great haste. If we don't fetch her to him soon, he'll come after her himself."

"I pray he may like her when he gets her. Your pretty creature looks as rough as a milkmaid. She's found her tongue too, and it's a sharp one."

"So you say—so you say. But I know her well. She's soft and easy and her tempers are only childish. I have always been able to show her what's best for her own good. I shall do so again."

Cecily's fingers curled and uncurled. So Alys had been sent to persuade her she should return to her loving father—to paint pretty pictures, no doubt, of the joys of marriage and the glories of a high situation among the French nobility. She might even, Cecily thought, willing to believe in any treachery now, tell her that this was the very suitor they two had so often spoken of, the peerless knight for whom she had been saved, whose perfection demanded equal perfection in his bride . . . Had Alys known all along, Cecily wondered, that before any marriage could take place that earlier ceremony must be declared officially null and void?

"The sun's to our left, Alys. I think we should turn north."

"Does no one live in these outlandish parts, to tell us the way?"

"See for yourself," said Giles, then changed his tone. "No, wait—there's a child coming this way. See him? If he can talk at all, and God knows only savages could exist here, he may at least know the name Mantlemass."

Cecily peered anxiously through the bushes. Davy was coming along the track. He had not yet seen the riders. He was jogging along and she could hear him mumbling to himself. Was he looking for her—or making off about his secret affairs?

"You there—boy!" called Giles.

Davy stopped in his tracks and turned tail. But when Giles bellowed after him he paused, as usual responding to harshness as he never did to kindness.

"Come here and answer me civilly," Giles ordered.

Davy stood shuffling his feet and ready to bolt. Giles nudged his horse up and the boy took a pace backward, but Alys also moved her mount swiftly and headed him off. He stood between the two of them, staring up in panic at the strange faces. He was not accustomed to seeing anyone but those he knew, and Cecily was hard pressed not to go to his rescue.

"Which way for Mantlemass?" asked Alys.

Davy was very small, standing there by the horses, both of which by chance were tall and rather raking beasts. He looked around him as if judging the best way to escape. As he did so, he glanced under the belly of the roan toward the inviting scrub. He looked directly into Cecily's face.

His expression was always guarded, but it lightened so pleasingly that at any other moment she would have rejoiced at this proof of his concern. She slid her hand toward her face, terrified of making any sharp movement, and laid her finger on her lips, slightly shaking her head. It was not much of a sign to give a child of doubtful intelligence. If he failed her there would be nothing for it but instant flight. Although by now she knew her way about the tracks, she would have to plunge into the undergrowth if she was to escape pursuers on horseback, and there was no doubt at all that she would very soon be lost. She stared at Davy, willing him to understand, and he stared back, while Giles and Alys bullied and wheedled above his head.

"Which is the track for Mantlemass? Are you dumb, you young lout?"

"We are friends of the pretty lady, child. Can you tell us where she lives?"

Davy frowned. It was painful to watch him thinking. It was as though his brain began to stir for the very first time—and as though the sensation was too strange to be enjoyable.

At last, very slowly, he withdrew his glance in a sliding manner from Cecily, turning his shoulder to her. He raised his arm and pointed down a side path that led nowhere of the least interest to the riders, but through much delaying mud and roughness eventually to the iron workings of Master Urry.

"There! Good child!" cried Alys. "Toss him half a farthing, Giles."

"I've no time to fumble for rewards. And half a farthing's a fortune to an idiot's child. Besides— how do I know to trust him?" He cracked his whip, and then sent the leash curling around Davy's ankles. "You shall show us the way. On with you now, or I'll whip you to a better pace!"

With no cry of protest, with no glance for help, Davy ran ahead of the horses, leading them firmly in the direction he had chosen. Soon they were out of sight. Cecily stayed where she was, uncertain where to move next and worried about Davy, lest he should suffer for his deception. Yet she felt fairly confident that whatever his inability to express himself, he had a native sense that would take care of him.

She moved cautiously from the shelter of the bushes. Now her course was not so easy. If she went by the obvious route to Ghylls Hatch, she must follow a part of the way behind the riders. This thought made her uneasy, for what if they suddenly turned back the way they had come? If they found her alone they would not ask her aunt's leave to take her, that was sure. She was sturdier than she used to be, but she was still small and light and could easily be carried away against her will. This threat filled her with a wild panic, for the thought that she might still lose what she had almost gained was not to be endured. She took to her heels and ran on the path that linked with the one leading near the weaver's cottage, and so in a broad loop back at last to Ghylls Hatch.

The sun was now shining strongly, the sky was clear, and nothing remained of the early morning's chill. The forest burgeoned as she looked at it, the trees increasingly green, the bluebells deepening in color, the pale wood sorrel rioting with violets both white and blue—and all seeming to grow around and over her, threatening almost to imprison her. The ground that sloped away to the river running in its valley below the weaver's cottage seemed to carry her with it, helping her along. Outside his cottage she saw the weaver seated and milking a black-and-white goat. At the same moment she felt a drumming in the soles of her feet and knew that within seconds she would be overtaken by a galloping horse. There was no scrub here to shelter her, and the trees were tall. She threw herself down to the river and scrambled through the water and up the far bank. The weaver looked up but did not speak, and without any more than a glance she ran straight on into his cottage. She stood inside the doorway and peered out.

It was red-bearded Henty who shot into view below. He pulled up short when he saw the weaver and shouted up to him.

"Has anyone passed? Dame Elizabeth is seeking

her niece. Has she been by here, weaver? Would you have seen her if she had?"

"I should've seen her, surely," replied the weaver. "Get off with you now, mus' Henty—you're fritting poor Nanny."

"Oh, be hanged to poor Nanny! The girl's vanished herself and must be found."

"Justly so," agreed the weaver. "And good day to you."

He watched Henty out of sight, then stripped the last drops of milk into the pail and slapped Nanny off to her grazing. He came into the cottage, pail in one hand, stool in the other. "Are you there, my maid?" he asked softly.

She was leaning against the wall and answered him faintly, out of breath from leaping up the bank.

"You look fairly jawled out," he said. "Wait till I find a dipper and I'll hand you some milk."

Even then, Cecily smiled at the words. She accepted the warm, cheesy milk and was glad of it. She had eaten no supper last night and the drink her aunt had given her was poor preparation for a day's running through the forest.

"Mus' Henty goes seeking you," the weaver said. "Will you get home to Mantlemass?"

"No," said Cecily. "For it is not only he who seeks me, and I will go nowhere and speak to no one till I have found Lewis Mallory. So if he should come this way, weaver, tell him I am gone through the forest to his home and will wait for him there. And tell him there has never been anything in his life or mine so necessary as that we should speak together at once. Tell him."

"What has come to you?" he asked.

"The best," she said. "Or the worst. When I have asked a question—then I shall know. But I have my wits still," she added, seeing his startled look and knowing that she did indeed sound a little mad. "I am bitterly hungry, weaver. Have you some bread?" His hesitation was so fine she was not sure she had seen it. It was only when she had eaten the bread that she realized it might have been his own dinner. "You have helped me," she said quickly. "I shall help you when I can."

When she had left him she retraced her steps, facing again toward Ghylls Hatch. If Henty was out looking for her there could be others—Nicholas Forge, Tom Bostel, Sim—half a dozen more, and none of them would she trust, lest her father had bought them. She began to run. Above all else in life she needed Lewis. The best or the worst, she had said to Halacre, the weaver. If it was the worst, then she would remember what they had vowed together. She would die, if need be, but she would not live without him.

The forest was increasingly trampled by riding men. Had her father sent an army to seek her? Once she saw Tom Bostel, and once Roger Orlebar—she almost called to him. But there were many strangers, and it was some time before she remembered that the ordinary business of the forest remained, and not all these riders sought her, but went, rather, about their concerns—with the iron workings, or the mill, or the weaver, or with the business of ordering charcoal, inspecting timber, or even poaching game.

This realization did little for Cecily. She was deathly tired and this caused her increasing panic. Now she felt as her aunt's coneys must feel when, driven by barking and snapping from the warrens, they found themselves tangling in the wicked nets, and turned and twisted and screamed in vain. She began to run wildly, to mistake the tracks. She slid out of sight in clumps of seedling birch and flung herself down in concealing hollows, though sometimes she was running from nothing but her own imagination and strained eyes. She was forever coming full circle. Her hair was in her eyes, her shoes sopping from scrambling through the many little rivers. The hem of her dress, soaked and heavy, slapped against her ankles—she had lost all sense of direction, and even the sun, being directly overhead, could not help her. She stopped to think, hunching her shoulders in fear, clenching her muscles and trembling. Meg had said the forest would not let her go, and perhaps she had been right. Perhaps there was nothing more than to drop down and die here in the tangle of undergrowth, taking with her her hopes and her love, and never knowing what Lewis would have answered to the question she had had no chance to ask him.

She lay still where fatigue had dropped her, thinking of all this, and the sun declined and the trees made some sort of dial for her to read if she could. But all she learned was that Mantlemass, Ghylls Hatch, the weaver's cottage, the meeting place by the pool, were all somewhere behind her— no finger pointed the way she should take now. She pulled herself to her feet, trying to feel angry with her own stupidity in getting so completely lost, rather than helpless and afraid. She pushed on through a copse of young birch tangled with newly sprouting brambles. Some sort of clearing was ahead of her, with a tumbledown hovel huddled into the curve of the trees. It looked like many charcoal burners' cottages she had seen, and because she feared the darkness and the roughness of the burners, she faltered. The place was shabby with stamped-out fires, a dilapidated faggot stack, a broken well-head from which hung a battered wooden bucket. The windows of the hovel were stuffed with rags and the stench of poverty defeated even the clean forest air. It was the meanest place Cecily had ever seen, and instinctively she turned from it. But there was a woman in a tattered brown dress standing by the door looking at her. Peering around her skirt was a very small boy, and cropping the grass close at hand was a fine gray mare with flowing mane and tail.

The woman was Joan; the boy was her son Davy; the mare was Zephyr. . . .

Davy ran to Cecily, then paused. For a second, torn and weary as she was, he must have wondered if she was another stranger.

"Davy, Davy . . ." she said, her voice faint with fatigue. She looked at his mother. "Joan—is it you?"

"And is it you, I might wonder! What a sight to be sure! I got turned off by that fellow Timothy from Orlebars. But I left him shy of a mount. Yon's your Zephyr."

"I see it is."

"You're looked for," Joan said, her manner as ugly and defiant as ever. "But if they saw you they might not want you. Where's my lady now? There's Mantlemass men and strangers—there's a fine straight man, as bold as a nobleman—all looking for you. Why's that?"

"Bold as a nobleman . . . My father's here, then. He sent for me. But I will not go. . . . May I drink from the well?"

"You've need of more than well water, by the looks of you. . . . Come indoors. Here's where my mam lives, and I come back to her, and Davy come back to me. Did you hear of Goody Luke? A wise woman, she is. That's my mam. She'll help you."

Cecily hesitated. Though she was too tired to be troubled by the squalor of the place, she was uncer-

tain if Joan was to be trusted any more than the next
one. Perhaps she had spoken with the fine straight
man, as bold as a nobleman. . . .

"Take her hand, Davy," Joan said.

"I wondered where he went for so long . . ."
Cecily murmured. Her head swam and she caught
at Davy as though he were big enough to support
her.

"Do I have to say it loud?" cried Joan angrily.
"You done well for my boy. What could I do but
well for you? Choose, then, and sharp about it. Stay
or go?"

"I'll stay," Cecily said, and let Davy pull her indoors.

Goody Luke was nothing like the crone Cecily
had expected. She was twice as handsome as her
sullen daughter, with black silky hair and a white
skin that made her look like some beautiful wicked
fairy. She took Cecily's chin in her hand and tilted
up her face, and then pulled down her lower eye-
lids, making sounds of increasing disapproval.

"Black as sloes," she said. "That's over-much of
foxglove. Who give you the drink, lady dear?"

"Meg made it as she was told to—too strong, my
aunt said. It made me dream and it made me sleep
—and I think my head's still swimming with it."

"Bring a mug of poad-milk, Joan. The best for
cleansing and lucky we got it for her. . . . Drink it
slow," she said, when the mug was in her hands.
"That's the first from the heifer just calved, lady."
She looked Cecily up and down and shook her
head. "There's a dissight! And my Joan tell me
you'm so picksome and dainty."

"How far to Ghylls Hatch?" Cecily asked.

"Too far, I'd say."

"Then I'll take Zephyr."

"You'll be out of the saddle and break your

neck," Joan said. "Rest here. Didn't they tell you anyone running is safe with foresters? Davy boy— go find Lewis Mallory and bring him this way. Run fast, there's a good boy. Run fast! And Davy—" He paused, looking so small it did not seem possible he had the legs to run for miles through the forest. "Keep hid from strangers, Davy."

Halfway to Mantlemass, stupefied by what his cousin had told him, Lewis met Meg running wildly. He pulled up Ebony at once, calling to her, shouting to know what was the matter—for it seemed to him that no disaster was too great to fall upon him.

"Oh, quickly, quickly!" Meg cried. "Gone from Mantlemass, she has, and none knows where, and last night there come her father's man to fetch her away—"

"I know that. What are you saying—she's gone from Mantlemass? Have they taken her?"

"If they did, then it was right from her bed—it's not likely. She run out, Lord knows how early— early as dawn and frost on the ground. And soon after Sir Thomas himself, her own father, come roaring and sworling after her. All through the house he went, with Dame Elizabeth watching—for she knew my young lady was gone. He pulled the very curtains from the beds and flung the covers on the floor. He cursed and roared, and she—the mistress—she cursed back, till Mary and me must cover our ears."

"Go on—go on!"

"At last he were done with Mantlemass, and he rid off, and he was swearing still and blaspheming. Then my mistress sent every man about the place to get horses and seek through the forest. And I'm sent to Master Orlebar to ask his help, for there's not a man or a lad left at home. Nothing I ever saw were so bad as the mistress crying and sobbing, as none ever thought to see her. Oh, Jesu, she say, over and over, find her—find her 'fore he do and carry her away!"

"Go quickly to Ghylls Hatch, Meg. I'll ride on. And Meg—if you have any breath left in your body by then, take word to Sir James."

"It might be my last living act—but I'll do it," Meg promised. "And do you ride fast and strong, for it's you she needs."

Yes, she does need me, Lewis thought, but not as I am now—cast down and a coward. . . . He straightened himself in the saddle. The forest displayed itself before him as he paused a second on the summit west of Mantlemass, uncertain which way to choose. Not yet in full leaf, the fast-thickening trees seemed to be as dense as high green walls. The scrub too was filling out in the first strong growth of the year. The open heathland stretched to the south, so pitted and dipping into deep ghylls and twisting combes that it seemed to Lewis then as impenetrable as any other part. Somewhere in that wide wild place Cecily was running or hiding or lying injured and afraid, and the only advantage her friends had over her enemies was their knowledge of the ground. But there were places she might hide where not even the deer ran, and fugitives had been found too late before now.

As Lewis chose his direction, ready to cover every foot of ground if need be, his thoughts were so bleak and cold it might well have been deep winter still. For if her father or her father's people found her, then he must never hope to see her again, even to say good-bye; and if Dame Elizabeth's people found her, since she was already promised and signed away in marriage, the good-bye must still be spoken. And half his anguish was what she must feel when she learned the truth, for unless she had been told as recently as he had, then he knew she was ignorant of what had taken place so far in her childhood. *She was a babe,* his cousin had said. . . . There was no end to the pain of Lewis's thoughts as he rode searching. As the day went on the possibility nagged at him that, lost and stumbling, she might have made her way into fatal bogland; that she might have fallen into one of the many disused mine pits and broken her neck, or if it was flooded, drowned. Or that, drowsy from snakebite, she was lying hidden and helpless, dying and alone. Often he tethered Ebony and beat about in the undergrowth.

At noon he saw Henty and Bostel, consulting together, weary with riding and with worry. And once he saw a stranger. He too was perplexed, pausing baffled at the mouth of a long ride. The man was Sir Thomas Jolland, and Lewis knew him, strangely, because of his daughter's likeness. He was half surprised by the fine proud looks, expecting rather that any man who had been called traitor must of necessity look sly and slinking. For the first time ever in his life, the desire to strike and kill an enemy moved hotly in Lewis; he put his hand on his knife and loosened it in its sheath, and waited. But Sir Thomas saved him his decision by moving off impatiently, and soon he had disappeared among the trees.

From then on, getting deeper and deeper into the forest, Lewis saw none but charcoal burners and the like who, when he asked, knew nothing. It was their nature to know nothing, to hide the fugitive. But he knew they would have told him what they could; he was a forester as they were, and many of them must have seen him about the forest with Cecily, riding side by side and hand in hand.

At last, in the very early evening, he rode once more to their meeting place by the pool. She was not there. But Davy came running to meet him.

# 11

## The Lark and the Laurel

IT WAS DUSKY ENOUGH IN GOODY LUKE'S COTTAGE even when the sun was bright. Now that evening had almost come the place was full of shadows, and with only a rushlight to help him Lewis had thought at first that he would not be able to read Cecily's face. He was uncertain what he expected to find there. There must be fear at her father's return, but he had no means of knowing whether it was he who must break to her the bitter news his cousin had given him that morning. He dreaded what it might do to her. Lesser disasters had made both men and women lose their wits. He had told himself that he must renounce her in the first instant of their meeting—must resist the impulse to hold and comfort her and must never embrace her again. For even if he was ready to sacrifice his own hope of heaven, he would not sacrifice hers . . . All this he had thought as he rode as fast as he could, with a sleepy Davy perched on the saddle in front of him and likely to roll off unless he were securely held. He had thought far and deep into the future, learning minute by minute how much he must lose—not least the pleasant image of holding his own son before him as he now held Davy.

But the instant Lewis came through the door of that dim, rank hovel, Cecily sprang up and threw herself into his arms, kissing and caressing him and even laughing with relief and delight to see him. He was powerless then. His resolves fled utterly and they clung together in comfort and warmth—so that immediately it had seemed impossible that they could ever be parted.

"You were about seven or eight years old," Cecily was murmuring as he kissed her cheek where the brambles had torn it. "Lewis—listen to me. Do you remember the archbishop?"

For a second he thought all his fears had been justified—the shock of this business had sent her out of her mind. "What archbishop, love?"

"Think back. Please, please—think back, think hard. You told me once you were with your father in France. . . ."

"I thought it was so—my cousin told me it was so. But I have forgotten."

"Oh, Lewis—pray think, think. Was there not some day when you dressed in your best?"

"Well—I would suppose so. The king was there. They must have kept some state. But you know I have forgotten those times. I never think of my parents or my home—you know that. I will not do so. There is a great wall raised up between then and now—I have told you this."

"Dearest Lewis," she said, "for both our sakes, tear down the wall. For when I was in France there was just such a day for me. I was dressed in a stiff white gown—my wedding gown, Lewis—it was my marriage day. No—don't move away from me but hold me hard. I was five years old. . . ."

"My cousin told me. This morning he told me. I thought I felt my heart break. But you—you seem hardly to care."

"Oh, Lewis—remember! You must remember! Were you not there too? In a gold doublet and saffron hose and shoes well pointed? You think I am mad but I am truly sane—perhaps as never before. Now my father comes with news that he has chosen me a new husband, one with a high connection in the church who will set about the annulment of that older contract. But it must be confirmed, not broken. Remember—oh, please, remember! Think of all that has been said and done—think of my aunt and her mysteries—of your father casting you away. Was it not because a useful marriage had become a dangerous one—because my father had forsworn his allegiance and found himself betterment another way?"

She was steady as a rock now, her voice low and full of a passionate excitement. It was he who shivered and sweated.

"If I could remember," he said, "what should it be?"

"You are afraid to say it!" she cried. "Oh, you coward, Lewis Mallory! You would remember that the day I was wed, when the ceremony was done, your father pushed you toward me and told you to kiss your bride. . . . Yes, Lewis—yes! You were the bridegroom! His hands were on your shoulders and I saw the ring. I saw it—the lark and the laurel engraved there in a red-brown stone."

His hand moved to his throat and he pulled out his ring on its leather thong. "How do you remember so much?"

"I have never forgotten—I have never quite forgotten. It has always been a half dream—"

"Ah," he said, "but a dream nonetheless. And a

sweet dream, Cecily. But too good, too easy. . . .
Oh, God, if I could remember! You seem so sure. If
you are right—then are we married? Safe?"

"When my father knows we have found one another—then, yes, surely we are safe."

"We must be certain."

"Let my aunt tell us. Last night she would have
told me, but I slept too soon. . . . That's another
story. . . . If I had known what I was doing I might
not have left Mantlemass this morning. When I
came to my senses I had to see you before anything
else in the world. I am sorry I have troubled you
so."

"Your father was at Mantlemass. As well you
left. . . ."

"We'll go to my aunt now. I am certain what she
will tell us. I am sure and certain. I have seen it all."

"But a dream, Cecily—you said it was a dream."

"I call it a dream. Remember, Lewis—remember!
Dreams are not shared—only realities."

All this time Joan and her mother and Davy had
remained outside, but now Joan came quickly indoors to say that Sir James was crossing the clearing
to the cottage door.

"I'll send him packing, if that's what you tell me
to. The priest's no friend of mine."

Lewis was at the door before she had finished. Sir
James wore his cassock tucked into his belt and his
bare legs showed how far and how deep he had
ranged about the forest that day.

"You must leave here," he said at once, not pausing for a greeting. "Your father, my child—surely a
most fierce determined man. He's going from cottage to cottage, threatening to burn the thatches
about their heads. There's two foresters in the river
already and another with a broken head. Come now
—you must come with me. If need be we'll get you

into sanctuary in the palace chapel. He dare not touch you there."

Lewis took Cecily's hand and led her quickly outside. He put her up on Ebony and mounted behind her. "Go with your mother and the boy into the forest, Joan," he said. "Let him find the place empty. Father, take the gray. She and Ebony are well matched. The saddle, Joan!"

It was slung over the branch of a tree, and between them Joan and the priest dragged it down and he was mounted almost as soon as Lewis had settled Cecily in comfort.

"We'll need to go by the causeway," Lewis said. "We've two good horses and they'll carry us with no panic. But that way we must go, for sure."

"You know best, my son." The priest paused, looking down at Joan. "My good girl—" he began, and she laughed, for it was not the way she was usually addressed, least of all by a churchman. "I pray you," he said, flushing, "go to Dame Elizabeth and tell her where her niece will be."

"I'll do it for her," Joan said, jerking her head at Cecily, "and that means I'll be doing it for Davy."

"God bless you," he said firmly, defying her to reject the words. Turning Zephyr's head then, he followed at once after Lewis.

Between the high ground that swept strongly east and west, where Mantlemass and Ghylls Hatch stood at several miles distance, the forest swooped down toward a broad bottom. The river running there crossed many miles before sinking down and finding its own level, exchanging as it did so its clear running breadth with many falls for a wide area of bog and marshland. Here at one point it broadened into a lake, the surface so weed-covered that it looked from above to be part of the valley floor. Local lore declared this lake to be bottomless, and Lewis could remember when Jenufer had frightened him with tales of a great serpent living in its depths. He had never quite outgrown a supersti-tious fear of the place, and he would go a long way around at any time to avoid picking a path along the sagging causeway, built so long ago that time had almost worn it away. To reach the palace chapel on the far ridge, however, in the quickest possible time, the obvious route ran here. Lewis had known horses refuse the causeway, but he was sure of Eb-ony and Zephyr—Ebony would carry him any-where, and Zephyr would follow.

The urgency and speed of their departure from Joan's cottage had put an end to words. Lewis rode silently, his mind whirling. Cecily, in her torn and dirty dress, her face scratched, her hair tangled with bits of briar, leaned warmly against him, clutching the horse's mane. He could scarcely see her face and had indeed little opportunity to look at her, for his eyes were on the road ahead, and on the hori-zon, north and south, where an enemy might ap-pear. Yet he knew without seeing it that danger had not taken the strange contentment from her fea-tures. For him, in spite of all she had said, the doubt and the puzzlement and the fear of bitter sorrow remained. She had spoken of a dream. It was a fatal word. Dreams could be no better than wishes, he knew that.

They rode warily, even before they left the copses and the coverts, not crashing a way through, but steadily avoiding those places where fallen branches could crack and splinter, or where over-hanging greenery thrust aside would swish and sigh and sway after they had gone, marking their pas-sage. At last they emerged from shelter and faced down the south side of the wide ghyll. The dusk was

flushed with the end of a fine and promising sunset,
so that the slopes with their heather cover just making new dark leafage were plum-purple, broken
with black peat scars and the livid green of coarse
tufty marsh grasses. There were still some lingering
patches of dead bracken, which in this light glowed
iron-red. Since it was still spring, the weeds that
covered the bottomless lake were not entirely
grown, and the exposed stretches of water gave
back the curiously tinted sky. Wisps of mist were
combed over the bog.

It was only now that Cecily stirred and asked how
far—how far to safety?

"Three or four miles. But on the causeway we
must be patient. It is not a ride to make at speed."

"I see where it runs—along the water's edge. Is
that the way?"

"Yes."

"It is very narrow."

"So is a horse's tread," said Lewis, unwilling to
admit that for almost three hundred paces the
causeway ran with fathomless water on one side and
deep bog on the other. He had once asked the
priest how the causeway came there at all, and he
had said that perhaps men even more ancient than
the Romans had tried to drain the marsh and culti-
vate the rich soil. So to the strangeness of the place
there seemed to be added the ghosts of men long
gone—their bodies, perhaps, lying quiet still in the
bog.

Cecily looked back across Lewis's shoulder. Sir
James was riding some four lengths behind. In the
increasing dark she could not see his face clearly,
but his presence gave her reassurance. She wondered if Joan would truly go to Mantlemass, and
believed that she would. Perhaps already Dame
Elizabeth was calling for Farden and setting out

toward the palace. Cecily looked up the valley toward the swoop of the skyline. Almost unconsciously she looked for her aunt—and immediately seemed to see her. There was a horse, small in the distance yet so sharp against the skyline that it was possible to see a woman's skirt blowing against its flank.

"My aunt is coming, Lewis."

"Your aunt? No—she will not come this way." Lewis looked back in his turn, and then so did the priest.

"There are two," he shouted. "A man and a woman."

"Giles and Alys," said Cecily, tightening her hold. "We must go faster!"

They were still far away, but they would see as clearly as they were seen in this curious light. The final upflushing of the sunset seemed to sharpen all the forest contours, and the two distant riders poured themselves over the horizon and came fast on the sloping track toward the bottom of the ghyll. Their flight was aided and speeded by the lay of the land, but those ahead had slowed to a delicate walk as they took the head of the causeway. The distance between the two parties was like a snake swallowing its tail.

"They are bound to check," Lewis said. "They cannot take you here, be sure of that."

"But they might drown us all!"

"Yes. They might do that!"

"Take care!" she cried, pressing against him.

He laughed. "Leave me some breath, then." He laid his cheek briefly against her hair. "No parting without meeting," he said, so quietly that he could not tell if she heard. "At least we have that comfort."

By now Ebony was halfway across, Zephyr well up

behind. The pursuers seemed to fly down the last incline. Now they in their turn had reached the causeway. But the first horse refused. It reared, squealing, and both Lewis and the priest looked back and simultaneously laid a hand each on the neck of his own horse. For Ebony and Zephyr had flattened their ears at the noise behind them. Zephyr tossed her head and snorted, her nostrils widening.

Between quieting Ebony, unused in any case to a double load, and glancing back constantly to see how the pursuit went, Lewis was much occupied. He was concerned too for Zephyr. The priest was a robust rider, but the gray was such a sensitive creature she might in emergency resent a stranger's hands and kick up her heels. Now both the pursuing horses had been forced by their riders onto the causeway. Ebony needed only twenty or so paces to reach firm ground, but Lewis dared not hurry him.

Sir James called, "They're moving up! They are riding it too fast—they'll kill the lot of us!"

At the same moment there was a flurry behind. The leading horse, ridden by Giles, had picked up a defiant speed and could not be held. He struggled to check the creature, whose hindquarters dipped perilously as one hoof struck on the moss-grown stone on which the causeway was founded. There was a great sound of striking, struggling hoofs. Giles shouted, and behind him Alys gave a thin, high scream that made Cecily bury her head against Lewis's shoulder.

"Don't look around," he said. He felt Zephyr pressing up behind him and heard her blowing. He heeled Ebony and the horse rose nobly in a great leap over the last stretch and went tearing up the bank over the blessed hard earth.

Lewis reined in then. He looked back and down.

Giles and his mount were in the water, the horse strongly swimming, the man grabbing at its tail. Then, as though the legendary serpent had seized him and dragged him down, the man sank like a stone and did not reappear. Alys screamed and screamed, her horse on its hind legs and threatening to slay her too. But somehow it turned, half plunged and recovered, then went fast, fast back up the hillside and far out of sight.

Zephyr, riderless, came at a gallop up the hill, checked at the sight of Ebony, and shuddered to a standstill. As he snatched at the rein, Lewis was trembling for his tutor. Then he saw that Sir James was kneeling on the causeway and knew that he was sending a hopeful prayer after the drowned man. The horse had reached dry land and stood for a second, water pouring from its back, reins dangling, stirrups flying, before following after its fellow up the hill.

By the time Sir James had plodded up the hillside, Zephyr was quiet and he remounted easily enough. No one spoke. They rode on, the priest now leading, and, cantering easily over a grassy track, they came within minutes to the roofless palace sprawling on its ridge, with the chapel and the priest's lodging as quiet and untroubled as if this evening were an evening like any other.

"Now come safe inside, my dearest children," the priest said. And he shot the bolts of the great door behind them.

The chapel was very fine. Even in her present state of mind, even in the pale light of the oil lamps Sir James had kindled for them, Cecily saw the color and the gold, the high roof, the painted glass. She held Lewis's hand tightly, determined that he should not escape her, and it was she who led him after the priest to the altar.

"Father," said Cecily, making Lewis kneel beside her, but still holding his hand, "when I was a child I was given in marriage. For all the years of my life I had a dream about this, but only last night my aunt made it clear for me. It is my true conviction that the husband I was promised to then is kneeling beside me now. Pray, Father James, let us be married again, knowing what we do."

"What do you say to this, Lewis?" Sir James asked his pupil gently. "Am I to marry you because your Cecily has had a dream?" He was half smiling, half frowning. "I cannot break the early contract, you know that. If she is wed, then she is wed and there is nothing we can do."

"I saw the ring," Cecily insisted, beginning to falter. "The lark and the laurel that is the Mallory emblem. I saw it, on his father's hand. And I should not have called it a dream, but a memory that has been there always, waiting for me to understand. Give me the ring, Lewis. Put it on my finger and put your hand on mine. And even if he will not bless us, I will swear to be faithful only to you."

She had begun to cry, and the tears fell on Lewis's hands as he did as she asked. The ring was huge on her finger, but he held it in place.

"I implore you, Father." Cecily wept. "I know this is the truth."

"Poor children," he muttered. He put his hand on theirs, unable to resist her tears and wanting only to comfort both of them. And because this was a moment of great concern for him, his grip was hard and painful, the large ring bit into Cecily's finger and she cried out, her fingers fighting under Lewis's. . . .

"Oh, God in heaven," Lewis said very quietly, "it was the archbishop, just as you said—in a gold-

embroidered cope. . . . Your hand was hurt—and
you cried. . . ."

Sir James had bolted the big door of the chapel but
no one had remembered the side door, and it was
that way that Dame Elizabeth came. They were still
on their knees, but Cecily sprang up at once and ran
to her.

"Your father is with me, child. Do you know yet
what I was trying to tell you last night?"

"Yes," said Cecily.

"Then all is well with you both; and with me.
Good evening, Father. Shall we sing *Nunc Dimittis*?"
She laughed a little. "Sir Thomas and I have tired
one another out with cursing and hatred. I think
you need not fear him, Cecily."

It was strange for Cecily to see her father there.
Lewis had her hand again, but for all that she trembled when Sir Thomas entered. "Sir," she said, her
voice shaking, "I think you know this is Lewis Mallory, my husband."

He stood in the half light by the altar steps and
looked her over slowly, head to toe and back again.
He was tired from the unending day, the pursuit
and the fury, the frustration of his plans and the
triumph of his sister, whom he could not love. He
had grown his beard again and perhaps there was
some gray in it. It was possible to see that he was no
longer a man in the prime of life but one whose
disappointments, largely of his own making, had
taken their toll.

"This is my father, Lewis," Cecily said in the
same shaken tones.

"And shall I say: This is my daughter?"

"Indeed, sir—it is your daughter." Looking at his
baffled, exhausted face, she felt her heart turn in
her breast with sorrow. For he had not always been

harsh with her. Her mother, it was said, had loved him at the start. And between them there existed, whatever the circumstances, the strange pull of shared blood.

"I could still take you back," he said. "You know that. I could find a dozen ways of shaping you to my own will. You know that—you know it still. It is not you who have defied me but my sister who has connived and plotted to strike at me. Well, be comforted. She has succeeded. If I took you back with me tonight, I swear I do not know at all what I could do with you. Your aunt has made you into a scarecrow."

"They use the word mawkin hereabouts," his sister said.

"And hereabouts is all she's fit for," he said bitterly. Again he looked at the torn and dirty gown, at her tousled hair and roughened hands. Then his eye went slowly and dismissively over Lewis. "As he is." He laughed then, but without any enjoyment. "Well, my treasure, as I once called you—you are well and truly spent. Your fortune lies with your mother's brother, but you'll get a thin dowry from Lord Digby now. Ask your husband what he thinks of that."

"Nothing, sir," said Lewis. "I know how to live, and that's what we need."

"And besides," said Dame Elizabeth, "my rights in Mantlemass are confirmed in perpetuity. The one condition—I may not leave it in the female line. See that Lewis shares it with you, Cecily."

"Shall we live there?" Cecily said. "Is it possible? You have made Lewis your heir?"

"The will is drawn up, sealed by my sovereign— and so in every respect ratified."

"God save my future from scheming women," Sir Thomas said. Again he looked at his daughter.

"What a pretty thing you were that day—a rich relation to the wench you've become." He heaved a great sigh. "No blessings from me, child. But I am too tired for curses."

He turned away and went slowly to the door and out of the chapel. They heard his horse stamp as he unhitched the bridle.

Cecily broke from Lewis and ran to the door. But he was already riding away. She called out, certain she would never see him again: "Father!"

She could just see through the darkness that he turned in the saddle briefly and raised his hand. How terrifying he had been in his power—how sad and lonely he seemed now in defeat. She still stood there, the last of her old life swallowed in the darkness. Then Lewis came out to her, putting his hand over the lark and the laurel slipping hugely on her finger.

"The smith could make it smaller," he suggested. "I cannot hope to hold it on your hand forever!" He smiled. It was too dark for her to see, but she knew that he smiled. "Come, wife," he said. "It's time we said our farewells and went home."

# The Mantlemass Chronicles

## The Sprig of Broom

"You must believe what I have done for you is better a thousand times than what the world might do."

With this strange assurance from his father, Medley Plashet faces a life full of riddles. His father is a humble forest guide, so how was it that he had such a friend as fine Kit Crespin? Why did Crespin ride from London, where Tudor reigned now instead of Plantagenet, to speak of a "warning"? And why, on leaving, did he smilingly hand Medley a flowering sprig of broom, as if it were some symbol?

Then tragedy strikes. Roger Plashet flees, hiding from his mysterious past. Medley, in his loneliness, finds himself drawn to the aristocratic Mallory family, and falls in love with young Catherine Mallory.

Now the question of his parentage is crucial. Medley sets off to search for his father and the answers to his many questions. Will what he finds be a noble secret, or will it bar him forever from marrying Catherine Mallory?

## A Cold Wind Blowing

When Henry VIII set about destroying the monasteries, the life of young Piers, the second son of Master Medley of Ghylls Hatch, was much changed. On the day that the prior of St. Pancras gave up his authority to the king's commissioners, Piers finds himself sworn to support and cherish a mysterious girl named Isabella.

The Medleys welcome Isabella into their family, and Piers is irritated yet fascinated by her mysteriousness. She could not, or would not, say who she was or where she was from. Then suddenly Isabella's past comes raging down on them, sweeping through the village and threatening to destroy their happiness. Can Isabella's secret be kept from the king's men?

## The Eldest Son

Of Master Medley's three sons it is Harry, the eldest, who inherits the past. A dark, dominating strain in his nature sets him apart, and he is forever in conflict with his father. At Ghylls Hatch, where the family breeds horses, only Harry prefers a different way of life. He would cast his lot with progress, and build an iron foundry. He longs to master an element that can never be tamed, whereas horseflesh is tamed to obedience and docility.

The one softness in Harry's nature is his love for his wife, Anne, and their children. But even that is threatened when one day a foreigner brings a beautiful tiny horse to Ghylls Hatch and Harry buys it for his young daughter. From this intruder, disaster springs. It destroys life as they have known it and spills over to nearby Mantlemass. From that devastation, there emerges for Harry a triumph both exalting and terribly bitter.

## The Iron Lily

When her mother dies suddenly, Lilias learns that she has no true place in the household in which she was brought up. So she marries a rough ironworker, who sets up his foundry in the wealden forest of the southeast. After his death Lilias takes over his work and becomes the only woman iron master in the forest. The foundry prospers. It is a time when guns and gunstones can make fortunes, for England is threatened by the Spanish Armada.

Long before she has achieved her deepest ambition, finding her true family, Lilias has survived in a tough world, and forged her own identity. She will leave her daughter, Ursula, heiress to far more than riches—the amazing secret of Mantlemass which is already generations old.

## A Flight of Swans

As the Spanish Armada sails to England, Humfrey and Roger Jolland are the guests of their kinsmen, the Medleys of Mantlemass. Humfrey, bold and thoughtless, rides off secretly, hoping to see a great battle. He does not return, but Roger—a strange boy, not strong but possessing a "seeing eye"—is convinced that his brother is not dead. Roger is left at Mantlemass to be lovingly cared for by his cousin, Ursula Medley. Growing up, he becomes absorbed in the affairs of Mantlemass and the ironworking at Plashets.

As war threatens England, the greed of traitors taints the wealden forest. Horses vanish from their stables, plans for weapons turn up missing from the forges, and smoke curls from the chimney of a cottage long empty. Treason is lurking within the wood of Mantlemass. Ursula wonders who might betray England and turn against her?

## Harrow and Harvest

Dissent between King and Parliament and open warfare between neighbors could only mean bitter conflict within families too. In the southeast corner of England sympathy runs mostly for Parliament. But the manor of Mantlemass was given to the Medley family generations ago as a freehold by the Crown. If the master of Mantlemass declares himself a king's man, chaos and violence will erupt in the forest. Where do his loyalties lie?

Nicholas Highwood and his sister Cecilia, are Medleys on their mother's side, and Nicholas is master of Mantlemass in default of a direct heir. He struggles to keep Mantlemass and the forge at Plashets safe from the armies that are moving closer and the treachery lurking within his own family. Only Cecilia knows how the family divided years ago. A secret well-kept for generations and the appearance of her orphaned cousin Edmund could change their lives irrevocably. Does Cecilia have the courage to speak of what she has found?

Praise for the Mantlemass Chronicles

"Superior historical fiction, flawless in cohesive ambiance and smooth and assured in the telling." —*Kirkus Reviews*

"These are true historical novels rather than novels which happen to be set in a given period. They are seriously concerned with events of public importance: the overthrow of Richard III and the plottings against his successors; the dissolution of the monasteries, the religious swings of the mid-sixteenth century, the troubles with Spain, the Armada, and finally the Cicil War."
—*London Times Educational Supplement*

"Willard creates realistic country people and vividly shows how changes in England's economy effects them . . ."
—*Library Journal*